SONG OF
THE SELKIES

BOOKS BY SARAH PENNINGTON

Bastian Dennel, PI

The Midnight Show
Gilded in Ice
Mask of Scarlet

Daughters of Atîrse

Song of the Selkies

Other Fairy Tale Retellings

Blood in the Snow
Mechanical Heart
Through a Shattered Glass

SONG
of the
SELKIES

Sarah Pennington

This is a work of fiction. All characters, locations, and events are the product of the author's imagination. Any resemblance to actual persons, living or dead, places, or events, is entirely coincidental.

Song of the Selkies

© 2023 Sarah Pennington

Cover design by Sarah Pennington.

All rights reserved. No part of this book may be scanned, uploaded, distributed, or transmitted in any form or by any means whatsoever without written permission from the author, except in the case of brief quotations used in articles and reviews. Please do not participate in or encourage electronic piracy of copyrighted materials. Thank you for supporting the author's rights and not being a pirate.

Published 2023

Printed in the United States of America

ISBN: 9798851679148

This book is dedicated to Wyn Estelle Owens.
She knows why.
(And I apologize for none of it.)

CONTENTS

Chapter 1: Sister's Celebration 1
Chapter 2: An Unexpected Future 11
Chapter 3: A New Plan. 23
Chapter 4: The King of the Selkies 29
Chapter 5: Consequences. 39
Chapter 6: A Grandmother's Wisdom. 45
Chapter 7: Into the Sea 55
Chapter 8: Transformation 61
Chapter 9: King and Stranger 69
Chapter 10: Journey to Emain Ablach. 77
Chapter 11: Arrival 87
Chapter 12: The Sisters. 97
Chapter 13: Settling In 107
Chapter 14: Finding a Voice. 119
Chapter 15: Exploring Emain Ablach 127
Chapter 16: Stories of the Seal-Folk 141
Chapter 17: Blood Ties. 155
Chapter 18: At the Court of King Fionntan 163
Chapter 19: Questions and Answers 177
Chapter 20: Revelations 193
Chapter 21: A King's Comfort 203
Chapter 22: Sisterly Interference. 213
Chapter 23: Plans Made 223

Chapter 24: Wishes 235
Chapter 25: At the Dawnwood Spring 249
Chapter 26: Calling Home 261
Chapter 27: Growing Comfortable 273
Chapter 28: Spectacle and Wonder 285
Chapter 29: The Faery Market 299
Chapter 30: Seeking What's Lost 313
Chapter 31: Making the Most of Time 325
Chapter 32: Return to the Halls 333
Chapter 33: Singing to the Lost 345
Chapter 34: A Heart Torn 355
Chapter 35: Leaving Emain Ablach 371
Chapter 36: Intentions Unmasked 383
Chapter 37: Imprisoned 393
Chapter 38: Battle at Emain Ablach 405
Chapter 39: Awakened 423
Chapter 40: Alliance 435
Epilogue: Vows to Keep 453
Acknowledgements 461
About the Author 463
Other Stolen Songs Stories 465

SONG *of the* SELKIES

Chapter 1
SISTER'S CELEBRATION

As betrothal ceremonies went, Ceana couldn't help but feel that this one was rather lackluster. She should know—she'd attended five before this just for her own sisters.

True, all the elements for such a ceremony were present. The seats of the castle chapel were filled with the most notable Atìrsen nobles, along with many of the lesser lords and ladies who lived within a week's travel and ambassadors from most of Atìrse's nearer neighbors. The chapel, while not as grand as the one at the royal seat, looked lovely. The afternoon sun streamed through the many tall, narrow windows, setting the enameled murals on the walls aglow, gleaming on the pale stars beneath the Maker's Hand, the scarlet footsteps of the Shepherd's Path, and the vibrant flames of the Gèadh Naomh. Banners hung on either side of the murals, displaying the colors of both Atìrse and Glassraghey.

And Mirren herself, standing at the front of the chapel with King Seòras and Queen Isla, her and Ceana's parents, and Lord Pherick, the Glassraghean ambassador, looked so lovely that she might have been ready for her wedding, not just her betrothal: serene and solemn, her honey-brown hair falling past her shoulders beneath a web of thin braids held in place with gold pins tipped with tiny jewels that matched the sunset hues of her kirtle and gown. The skirt, sleeves, and neckline of the gown were nearly covered in embroidery, all done by Mirren's own hand, the tiny stitches forming designs intricate enough to be the envy of any woman. It was, Ceana knew, Mirren's favorite gown, and she added to its embellishment any time she came up with a new idea. Beside her, everyone else practically faded into obscurity. Still, something seemed to be lacking.

With effort, Ceana tried to focus her attention on the ceremony itself and on King Seòras's speech. "We are honored by the chance to join our family to that of Glassraghey and to solidify the bond of peace between our peoples. Dèanadair has truly laid His blessing upon Atìrse, allowing us to seek friendship with our neighbors and lay aside suspicion, and we seek to honor Him in maintaining that peace ..."

Perhaps that was part of the problem. King Seòras had given nearly the same speech a year and a half ago, when Rhona, the third-youngest of the sisters, had been betrothed to Prince Gwynfor of Addewedig. He'd changed some of the details for today, removed some small parts and added others, but much of the flow and wording remained the same. Of course, after having given similar speeches five times before, he was probably running low on new things to say. All the same, Ceana couldn't help wondering how many others had noticed.

King Seòras finished his speech, and Lord Pherick began his. "On behalf of Prince Martyn and their majesties, King Austeyn and Queen Mureal, allow me to express the royal family's joy at this coming union, and their great sorrow that they could not be personally present ..."

Ah. That was another part of the problem—the greatest part, even. The whole ceremony would have been far better if Mirren's intended were actually *here*, rather than represented by Lord Pherick. True, Prince Martyn and his family had good reason for their absence. Just the week before, they'd sent a mirror-message to say that several members of the royal household, Prince Martyn included, had fallen gravely ill, and so it would be best if Pherick stood in their stead. Even so, it wasn't the same, and Mirren really did deserve better.

A sharp nudge in Ceana's side warned her that her thoughts were beginning to show—or, at least, that they were visible to

Onora, the crown princess and Ceana's eldest sister, who stood beside her. Ceana hastily recomposed herself. If she couldn't give Mirren better, she could at least keep from spoiling things further by letting her thoughts show.

At the front of the chapel, Lord Pherick went on with his speech. "The greatest gift Dèanadair grants any of His people, after the gift of the Path, is the opportunity for each of us to serve our neighbor. And with this union and the greater peace it brings between our lands, so may our two nations more freely partake of this gift ..."

Well, that much was true! And that—the betrothal, not the betrothal ceremony—was the important part. Every betrothal and marriage between Atìrse and her neighbors was another step towards ensuring a friendship between the nations that would, Dèanadair willing, last for generations. Ceana and Mirren, like their sisters, had grown up knowing it would be part of their duty to contribute to this peace—duty and honor both! For what greater service could there be than ensuring peace for one's people, both in the land of one's birth and the land of one's marriage?

And, technically, they needed none of this pomp to make a betrothal official. Atìrsen law only required that any royal betrothal be finalized in the presence of a certain number of noble witnesses. Making it into a grand affair just provided an opportunity for the nobility who wouldn't be able to travel for a foreign wedding to show their support for the union. In that respect, today's ceremony was more than sufficient.

Lord Pherick finished his speech, and now came Mirren's turn to speak. She flushed slightly as she began: "I am truly honored to have been accepted as Prince Martyn's future wife. Though I do not yet know the prince, I know of him, and I look forward to building a life with him that will benefit both Atìrse and Glassraghey and will honor the name of Dèanadair. May His blessings be upon us both and upon our countries."

Even with the blush, she delivered her statement well—as she ought, given that she'd practiced it nearly a hundred times last night and made Ceana and Onora listen to most of those repetitions. Onora had privately commented afterwards that she'd felt less nervous about her own wedding than Mirren evidently did about this ceremony—but that was Mirren for you!

With the speeches now ended, King Seòras, Queen Isla, Lord Pherick, and Mirren all bent and signed the betrothal contract, one after another. Then King Seòras and Lord Pherick shook hands, and Lord Pherick bowed to Mirren. Had Prince Martyn been here, he would have kissed her hand—but he wasn't, so he couldn't. With that, the ceremony ended, and King Seòras offered his newly-betrothed daughter his arm to depart the castle chapel for the banquet in the great hall.

Lord Pherick followed just behind, escorting Queen Isla. Next came the Dowager Queen Moireach, Ceana's grandmother, leaning on an elegantly carved ivory cane. Then came Onora, escorted by her husband, Prince Alasdair. Ceana brought up the rear of the procession, escortless—for now. Not for long, if she knew her father and mother.

She stepped outside just in time to see King Seòras give Mirren a quick squeeze of the shoulders, then leave her with Onora and Alasdair as he, the queens, and Lord Pherick moved off to speak together. Now that the ceremony was over, Ceana dropped her formal pace and hurried over to hug Mirren. "Congratulations! How does it feel to be properly betrothed?"

"A lot like being not-betrothed, so far." Mirren wrinkled her nose, but returned the hug. "And Glassraghey can still back out."

"But they *won't*. They want an alliance as much as we do." Ceana released Mirren, though she kept her arm looped through Mirren's. "Isn't that right, Onora?"

"If Glassraghey changes their mind at this point, it means something has gone very wrong indeed." Onora raised herself on tiptoe to give her husband a kiss on the cheek, then pushed him in the direction of the main keep. "Go distract anyone who tries to enter the Great Hall, won't you? That ceremony finished faster than I thought, and I don't think the servants have had enough time to set up."

"Bossy," Alasdair teased, returning the kiss. "And who's lord of this castle, I'd like to know?" Nonetheless, he set off towards the keep, walking as if it had been his idea in the first place.

Onora took Mirren's other arm. "See what you have to look forward to?" Still, she laughed. "Don't you worry. Everything will be fine. By all accounts, Prince Martyn is quite taken with what he's heard of you."

Ceana grinned around Mirren. "Oh, your *agents* afield are keeping track of our allies' love lives now, are they?"

"Well, naturally," Onora replied, raising an eyebrow. "Part of their job—" She paused as a stub-tailed cat darted over to rub himself against her legs. "Oh, bother. Càirdeil, what are you doing out here?" She let go of Mirren's arm, bent, and scooped up her cat. "As I was saying, part of their job *is* to find out who would be best suited and most amenable to an alliance so I can advise Athair and Màthair. Should Prince Martyn be infatuated by some local lass, we'd not about send one of you off to marry him."

"I'd go anyway," Mirren murmured, though she didn't sound entirely certain of her statement. "If I needed to. I'd have every cat in the palace to keep me company if the prince didn't care to."

Càirdeil chose this moment to let out a rumbling meow, as if to say he approved. Onora gave a little shake of her head. "Maybe, but a marriage with nothing between husband and wife is a dishonor to Dèanadair and a disservice to both countries it binds." She set off towards the keep, and Ceana and Mirren followed her. "I don't know why we're fussing over this anyway. I already told you that Prince Martyn fancies you, as much as he can without having met you."

"True, you did." Mirren's lips quirked upwards. "So if you're helping Athair and Màthair find marriages for the rest of us, who do you have in mind for Ceana? It's her turn now."

Was it Ceana's imagination, or did a hint of worry cross Onora's face? But Onora just shook her head. "What Athair and Màthair have planned is for them to say in their own time. I'll not spoil the anticipation—not before Mirren's feast is over!"

"As if they won't tell her anyway in a few days!" Mirren protested. "Surely you can tell us."

"'Tis theirs to tell, not mine." As they neared the keep, Onora turned towards the great doors. "I'd best see how the servants are faring. I'm sure Alasdair can only hold the crowd so long. Go mingle, and I'll see you at the feast."

She hurried away, her full skirts swishing around her legs. Ceana and Mirren called farewells after her, then made for the crowd gathering in front of the main doors.

As soon as they reached its edge, guests started coming forward to offer Mirren their congratulations. Ceana stood politely by her sister, smiling and occasionally nodding or responding to comments made in her direction. But her thoughts were already flown past the feast towards her own future. Tomorrow, she knew, the king and queen would come to her or call her to meet with them so they could tell her who they had in mind for her to marry, just as they'd done for all her sisters.

But who would it be? That was the thrilling question. Someone from Addewedig to the south or from the Talaschean Kingdoms to the west would be most likely—and that would put her close to either Rhona or Mey. Joining Mey in Talascheal would make sense; they had five royal families there, plus a high king, and that meant plenty of potential matches—and more opportunity for Ceana's marriage to really *mean* something. Addewedig had been a strong ally to Atìrse for generations upon generations, but the Talaschean Kingdoms had only recently made a proper alliance. And surely it would be worthwhile to create ties to all five kingdoms?

With effort, Ceana pulled herself back to the present. Today they celebrated Mirren's betrothal; she ought to focus on that. She'd have plenty of time to dream later.

Thankfully, the doors to the Great Hall of the keep opened not long after, signaling the beginning of the feast. The crowd streamed in to find their seats: Mirren in the place of honor between King Seòras and Queen Isla; the rest of the royal family, various

Glassraghean representatives, and other particularly important guests arranged around the high table; and the remaining attendees at lower tables according to their rank and where they could find space. King Seòras blessed the meal, thanking Dèanadair for Mirren's good match and the bonds of friendship forming between Atìrse and Glassraghey.

And then the servers brought forth the food! The dinner began with thick, savory vegetable and barley stew. Next to the table came every manner of fish, perfectly roasted, some in cream and some in sauce, some on beds of wilted greens and flecked with spices, and some served over crisp-edged potatoes and brushed with parsley sauce. Along with the fish came a splendid venison roast, so tender the meat practically fell off the bone at the first touch of a knife.

Ceana could have happily finished with the venison and fish—but the servants next brought forth roasted poultry: peacock for the high table and those nearest it, and duck and goose for the rest. One servant slipped Ceana a plate of duck without having to be told, and Ceana gave him a quiet thank-you in return, making a mental note to tell Onora the same later. An occasion like this demanded the fancier peacock meat, which Ceana had never much cared for, but duck prepared by Onora's cooks was a delight, common fare or not. With the fowl were roasted vegetables and fluffy rolls still warm from the oven, their tops glistening with butter.

At last, however, only bones remained of the birds, and the servants cleared away the platters, replacing them with trays containing tarts laden with creamy custard and spiced stewed pears. Ceana could only manage one, she felt so full from the rest of the feast, and she couldn't even touch the accompanying bowls of honeyed plums and candied nuts.

Yet when the court musicians struck up a tune and King Seòras escorted Mirren down to the floor to open the dancing, Ceana sprang to her feet and hurried down after them. She allowed Onora's brother-in-law, Evander, to claim her hand for the first dance and set to the steps with as much energy and enthusiasm as she could muster. Failing to dance, after all, would be an insult to her family and to Glassraghey—and it would be bad luck for both her and Mirren, besides.

She stepped and spun through seven dances before her stomach and legs' mutual protests convinced her that she had better rest a moment. So, she made her way back to the high table. King Seòras had returned to his seat as well, she noticed, and Lord Arran, along with his wife, had moved up to sit across from him.

Onora still danced, so Ceana slid into her seat beside the king without hesitation. King Seòras gave her a side-smile as she did, but Lord Arran only nodded and went on with the conversation with barely a break. "Your majesty, with all due respect, I urge you to push for better terms when the treaty with the selkies is renewed. That they should maintain such harsh sanctions over an offense that was old and half-forgotten when our great-grandparents were children is, frankly, ridiculous."

"That we refrain from hunting seals is no great hardship, Arran, nor is paying the little they ask." King Seòras spoke with a tone of weary patience. "We have paid more for safe use of ports in some other lands, and had less good of it."

"Your majesty looks far too kindly on such extortion." Lord Arran's face was all thin, disapproving lines. "The sea belongs to no one, human or selkie, and it is madness that these seal-folk think they can claim it as their own."

"Yet the selkies travel the same routes we use, and they have done so longer than we have. If we can claim the land as ours, I am willing to let them have the sea." King Seòras shook his head, leaning forward with his arms resting on the table's edge. "And I have no desire to anger them such that they start attacking our ships again."

Lord Arran just scoffed. "Your majesty should have more confidence in your people. The selkies would find us far harder to sink than they have in the past, and I think they would soon learn to leave our ships alone."

Ceana stifled a sigh and instead exchanged a sympathetic look with Lord Arran's wife. Lady Eilidh's expression suggested that she'd heard this rant too many times before. True, she almost always looked like she were trying and failing to remember what a smile felt like, and her eyes—huge and dark as the storm-tossed sea—frequently held the kind of bone-deep weariness that Ceana mostly associated with grieving mothers. But today, she seemed especially defeated.

Another day, Ceana might have invited Lady Eilidh to walk and talk with her. Though the lady spoke little, and she struggled when she did speak, she always seemed to appreciate the escape from her husband's presence. However, today, Ceana needed to sit, so she remained where she was, listening to King Seòras and Lord Arran debate policy and treaties until she'd recovered enough to leave them again and rejoin the dancing.

The next time she looked towards the high table, Lord Arran had gone, and Queen Isla sat beside King Seòras, leaning into him, her head on his shoulder and his arm around her as if they were still young newlyweds who could be excused such things. Ceana smiled as she saw them and mentally whispered a prayer to Dèanadair asking for that same blessing for Mirren and herself. She knew her parents had met the first time only a few days before they wed, but they had been as determined then as they were now to do right for their countries, and love had sprung from that shared determination like snowdrops after the first spring thaw.

Someday, that would be her fate. Someday soon, she hoped. Now that only she among all her sisters remained unattached, it was only a matter of time.

Chapter 2
AN UNEXPECTED FUTURE

The celebration continued until long after the summer sun had set and the moon had climbed high in the sky. But at last, the guests dispersed, and Ceana and Mirren climbed the stairs together to their chambers, which were connected by a door. Once, all seven sisters had shared these two rooms—the keep here was smaller than the royal family's main residence, and even princesses had to squeeze to make room for guests. But that number had dwindled rapidly after Onora took up permanent residence here and other sisters had wed and moved away one after another. Now only Mirren and Ceana remained, and the chambers that had once been crowded with giggling and squabbling girls echoed with nostalgic emptiness.

Ceana allowed her maid and lady-in-waiting to help her out of gown, kirtle, and shift and into a soft linen nightgown. Then, as was her tradition, she sent both of them to their own beds and slipped through the door into Mirren's room. As expected, Mirren, now also in her nightgown, sat in a low chair by the window, her hair loose and tumbled around her shoulders.

Ceana fetched a brush from the nightstand and joined her sister. She separated out a portion of Mirren's locks, frizzed and tangled from the ocean air and from the night's energetic dancing, and began working out the knots. "How are you doing?"

"Well enough." Mirren gave a short laugh. "Everything feels very nicely settled just now. I think the nerves will set in later, when I have more time to think. How much embroidery do you think I can manage in six months?"

"Miles of it, probably, if you don't do anything too elaborate and don't overwork your hands. You've always been so fast at needlework." Ceana finished one section of hair and moved on to the next, being careful not to pull too hard. "Are you already planning your wedding gown?"

Mirren gave no answer but a sheepish smile, but Ceana needed nothing more. She shook her head, pausing to pull free a hairpin that the maids had missed. "Of course, you are. You were probably planning it three months ago. Green, blue, or red? Or another color entirely?"

"Green, I think, with white and gold trim and embroidery." Mirren stared off at some faraway point, no doubt seeing the gown in her mind's eye.

"Green for prosperity. Or green because you're hoping to match Linnhe for how many children you have?" Ceana saw Mirren flush and laughed to let her know she'd been teasing. "Màthair will be pleased. That was her color." She caught the tip of her tongue between her teeth as the brush hit a particularly stubborn knot.

"I know—*ow*." Mirren made a face, but didn't comment further until Ceana had worked the tangle loose and continued on. "I hope she'll let me take some pieces from her dress, since she can't wear it anymore. You know, for luck."

"She let Linnhe and Rhona, so I don't see why she wouldn't let you." Ceana finished brushing and gathered the hair back, splitting it into three sections for a braid. "Is that the real reason you picked green?"

"No. I like green, and everyone says it suits me. Besides, the way things are going, I may not see Prince Martyn at all until we're both before the altar, and I'd like his first sight of me to be a good impression."

"You never give anyone anything *but* a good impression, no matter what you're wearing." Ceana shook her head. "If you're truly worried, ask Athair and Lord Pherick to have a set of message-mirrors made for you and Prince Martyn, and then you can start getting to know him before the wedding."

"I'd rather write letters." Mirren paused. "I think I *will* write a letter, actually. I'll ask Lord Pherick to send it with his next packet. I know you don't mind the idea of marrying first, then getting to know your husband, but I think I'd like to understand him a little better beforehand."

"There's nothing wrong with that." Ceana paused in her braiding. "Ribbon, please."

Mirren handed back the ribbon. "I'll miss this, you know. After I leave. I miss when we had all of us together. I wish Glassraghey had another eligible match or two so I wouldn't be the only one there."

Ceana folded the ribbon in half around the middle section of the braid, matching each half with one of the other strands, and continued braiding. "I know. We're all so spread out now. Onora and Linnhe here, Sorcha in Gormthall, Mey in Talascheal, Rhona in Addewedig, and now you going off to Glassraghey. And even Linnhe's on the other side of Atìrse from us." True, it was less a distance than most of the others, who would have to cross either the Rhwyster Mountains or the sea to get here, but it was still no easy journey—especially not when Linnhe seemed to be pregnant again every time you turned around, as if she were determined to make up for Onora's lack of heirs by ensuring she had several to spare. "There's the mirror-messages, at least."

"It's not the same, and you know it." Mirren sighed in a puff of air. "Oh well." One corner of her mouth quirked up in a weary smile. "Maybe Athair and Màthair will send you off to marry one of the faery folk like Thrice-Great Uncle Diarmad. Then they can bargain for regular guides on and use of the Paths."

"If they do, I'm going to make sure that letting me regularly visit the rest of you is included in the conditions. All Uncle Diarmad ever does is send letters—not even mirror-messages, and *he's* the reason the rest of us have them." Ceana looped the ends of the ribbon around the end of the braid several times and then tied them in a secure bow. "Done."

"Your turn, then." Mirren stood, and the two traded places, Ceana sitting down and Mirren taking up the brush. "Who do you hope Athair and Màthair have you marry?"

"I don't know." She'd been careful not to think about it, though she wouldn't say so. She didn't want to fantasize a future with someone she might not wed. She knew her parents would allow for her preferences if they could—they'd done so for some of her other sisters—but she didn't want a foolish desire to keep them or her from serving Atìrse's needs.

"Don't you?" Mirren tugged the brush through Ceana's hair, working swiftly through the dark blonde waves. "You've always been more eager to get married than any of us. Don't tell me you haven't even thought about who."

"As long as I'm marrying a good man and I'm doing good by the marriage, I'm happy." Ceana glanced up as much as she could without interfering with Mirren's work. "Really. I'm not just saying so."

"I know you aren't. The rest of us wish we were as good as you." Mirren sighed in loving resignation. "And you'll find a way to be happy, no matter where you find yourself."

"I will," Ceana agreed. "*And* I'll find a way to see the rest of you as often as I can, wherever I end up." And tomorrow, she'd learn where that would be.

The next day came, and Ceana spent every moment waiting for her parents to call her aside so they could tell her who they were considering for her betrothal. She did her best to stay focused on her duties: on the morning service at the Tùr-Faire just outside the castle walls, on discussions of the upcoming renewal of Atìrse's treaty with the selkies and reports from the nobility of Atìrse on the states of their holdings, on helping Mirren compose a letter to Prince Martyn, and on her needlework. Still, she couldn't shake her anticipation, nor did she want to.

Yet day and evening passed, and night fell, and neither King

Seòras nor Queen Isla made any mention of any potential betrothal. Ceana went to bed that night in poor spirits, wondering what could have caused the delay. Perhaps, she told herself, they were still figuring out details—but, then, they had never waited until all the details were settled before telling any of her sisters their intentions. They made sure they had a feasible plan, then proposed it to the appropriate daughter to make sure she didn't object and allow her a say in the rest of the negotiations. Usually, they did so within days of the previous daughter's betrothal.

So, then, why the wait now?

Ceana endured another day and a half before she could take it no more. That afternoon, she made her way to the solar, where King Seòras and Queen Isla were discussing something with Onora and Alasdair. She'd asked after the day's schedule and confirmed that the king and queen had nothing planned after this meeting, so it should be the perfect time to ask them.

A part of her whispered that they must have a reason for waiting; that she should be patient until they brought it up. But it was *her* future, for all that she would gladly spend it in whatever way would best benefit her family and country. She had a right to ask after it.

Much of the afternoon had come and gone before the door opened and Onora and Alasdair stepped out, King Seòras and Queen Isla just behind them. Ceana hastily stood, tucking the sash she'd been embroidering in her pocket. "Athair, Màthair, may I speak with you?"

She couldn't miss the look that passed between her parents and Onora—a look of decided concern and even resignation. For a moment, she wondered if she should retract her request. But then King Seòras nodded. "Of course. Onora, will you see to it that what we discussed is put in place?"

"I'll give the orders at once." Onora patted Ceana's shoulder as she passed. "I'll be upstairs with Mirren if you need me after you finish your conversation."

"All right?" This was decidedly *not* promising. But she could do nothing else but follow the king and queen back into the room. Windows in the far wall looked out on the open sea and let in the salty air and the cries of seagulls and seals.

King Seòras sat in the largest of the wooden chairs arranged around the room, and Queen Isla took her place next to him. "Well, Ceana," he began, "what is it you wish to speak with us about?"

Ceana didn't sit, not yet. Instead, she clasped her hands in front of her and replied, "Mirren's betrothal is finalized now, I believe. All is in order?"

"As Dèanadair wills, yes." King Seòras nodded. "Lord Pherick sent the official documents yesterday afternoon, but there should be no complaints with those."

"I'm glad to know it." A part of her had feared that some unknown issue with Mirren's betrothal to Prince Martyn had caused the delay. She'd prayed it wasn't so, that such hardship wouldn't fall on Mirren. "'Tis only…when Onora's betrothal was finalized, you waited only three days before telling Sorcha that the prince of Gormthall wished to marry one of us. When Sorcha's betrothal was decided, you told Mey the next day that you wished to seek an alliance with Talascheal and asked if you might offer her hand to one of their princes. Each time one of us is settled, you waste no time in telling the next what to expect. Now Mirren's future is decided, but I am still wondering what you have in mind for me. Who am I to wed?"

King Seòras and Queen Isla exchanged a look, one Ceana had seen before and knew meant roughly "Which of us is doing this?" The look ended in a raised eyebrow from Queen Isla, which Ceana also could interpret—usually, it meant either "This was your idea" or "This is your mess," and either way, she certainly wasn't responsible to explain or solve it for the person on the receiving end of the expression.

King Seòras stood. "Well, my daughter, who do you wish to wed?"

"I—" Ceana's thoughts, which had been sailing along quite swiftly despite the choppy, uncertain waters around them, came to an abrupt, jarring stop as they struck the hidden rock of the king's question. "Whoever you wish me to wed, of course. Whoever Atìrse needs me to wed."

"And if Atìrse's need and my wish is merely that you are safe, happy, and cared for?" King Seòras asked.

His tone was kind, but the words nonetheless rent a gash in Ceana's thought-boat so it began to rapidly sink. Ceana fumbled for words. "I—I don't understand. Is something amiss? Have I done something wrong to displease you?"

"Have you done—no! Certainly not!" King Seòras stepped forward and clasped Ceana's shoulders. The gesture usually comforted her, but today it did little to ease Ceana's heart. "You are and ever have been the best of daughters. You and your sisters have done all that your mother and I have asked, all that Atìrse has asked, and you have done it willingly. I could not be more pleased."

"Then what did you mean before?" Ceana asked, trying and failing to keep her voice level. "It sounds as if you have no plans for me to wed."

"I certainly plan for you to wed, unless you object," King Seòras replied. "But as you know well, Ceana, Atìrse is blessed and at peace. Our people are fed; our treasuries are full. We are bound in both friendship and marriage to every one of our neighbors who will have us, some multiple times over."

Queen Isla seemed to take pity on her husband and spoke up now. "It is a rare gift for a princess to have her marriage be based on her own choice and not on the needs of her country and family. Your father and I would have liked to give that gift to more of your sisters, but since we can give it to you, we chose to do so. If you have a man in mind whose company you enjoy and you think would be a good husband, your father and I will seek to make the match. Or if you have no one yet in mind, we will gladly help you choose—but the choice is to be yours."

King Seòras nodded, clearly grateful to no longer be alone in explaining this fresh horror. "As your mother has said, it is a rare gift. And so, I ask, have you a man in mind who you wish to wed?"

"I..." This could *not* be happening. Ceana shook her head, unable to do more than tread water in the chaotic waves of her mind. "I expected to marry whoever you asked me to marry, so I didn't—I never—I didn't wish to become attached to a future that couldn't be." And yet, somehow, she had anyway. This was so *unfair*. "Are you sure there is no purpose my marriage needs to fulfill? Talascheal has five kingdoms ..."

But King Seòras was shaking his head. "Talascheal has five kingdoms, yes, but only three have eligible princes, and if we are too aggressive in proposing unions between children of our two lands, they will begin to wonder if we intend to take them over. Of course, should you truly care for a man of Talascheal, and should he care for you in return, we would gladly try to facilitate the match. But do not think that it is needful."

"I see." Ceana had always thought that ladies who claimed to feel faint at shocking news were silly—but now, she found she knew just how they felt. "It is to be entirely my choice, then?"

"Within reason, yes." Queen Isla nodded. "So long as he honors Dèanadair and is noble in both name and character. Once we return home, we will see what can be done to allow you to meet such men more frequently, now that you know you need not wait upon our pleasure. We are sorry for not telling you sooner, but we wished to wait until Mirren's betrothal had been finalized."

"I understand." She didn't. She didn't understand *at all*. She didn't *want* to understand. She wanted this to be a joke. But instead, she forced herself to smile and say, "Thank you, I suppose. I...I need some time to think on this."

"Of course." King Seoras squeezed her shoulders in a way that suggested he'd like to hug her, but wasn't sure how well it would be received. "I'm sure this is a bit of a surprise."

A bit of a surprise! That was putting it lightly! But Ceana just nodded and backed out of the room. And as soon as she stepped outside and made sure no one was nearby, she picked up her skirts and ran to find the one person who might still be able to help: Onora.

She found Onora and Mirren exactly where she expected them: in the sitting room off Onora's chambers, busy at their needlework, with Càirdeil purring in Onora's lap. By that time, sheer shock had worn away into a sick feeling in Ceana's stomach and the sting of threatening tears in her eyes.

She burst into the room, gasping a little for breath after her run up several stairs. Both sisters looked up as she entered, and Onora set down her work with a little sigh. "Oh dear." She picked up her cat and set him aside too, then beckoned to Ceana. "Come here, then."

Ceana needed no more invitation, running to her oldest sister and falling to her knees by the chair so she could bury her face in Onora's skirts like she had when she was only a little girl. Now the tears broke free, along with sobs that shook her whole body.

Onora let her cry, stroking her hair gently and humming until Ceana's tears slowed and her breathing steadied. Then, she said, "So, do you want to talk about it?"

Ceana pulled back and settled herself so she sat instead of kneeling, still leaning against Onora. "Yes. I'm sorry for getting your skirts all wet."

"They'll dry." Onora picked her needlework back up. "Tell me what happened. Do you want Mirren to leave?"

"She can stay, unless she wants to go." Ceana pulled her knees up under her skirt and wrapped her arms around them. "I asked Athair and Màthair about who I'm to marry."

"I thought so," Onora replied, sadness tinging her voice. "And you didn't like what they said."

"They said they didn't need me to marry anyone in particular, and that it was mine to choose. I don't *want* to choose!" Ceana knew her words sounded more fit for a petulant child than a princess of marrying age, but she couldn't help herself. "I was happy to have them pick someone, and now...and now ..."

"Mm." Onora reached down to rub Ceana's shoulder again. "Some people would say that being able to marry based on love and not necessity is a blessing."

"I don't *want* to marry for love!" Ceana's voice pitched upwards into a near-wail. "I don't! Aunt Gaie married for love, and now look where *she* is."

Ceana felt, rather than saw, her sisters wince. Everyone in the family knew well the ongoing drama of their father's sister and her life and marriage. Instead of wedding the man chosen for her, she'd insisted on marrying a minor noble from Deàrrsadh County, claiming she loved him more than life itself. Thirty-some years later, she and her husband didn't seem to be able to look at each other without starting a fight, and their three children had fled their home as soon as they were old enough to find appointments as squires or ladies-in-waiting elsewhere.

But then Onora's hand shifted to rub a slightly different location. "Plenty of people marry for love and turn out just fine, Ceana. And you're nothing like Aunt Gaie."

"That's true," Mirren said and, without a hint of sarcasm, added, "You have more sense than she ever did or will."

"Mirren!" But Onora's tone made it clear that the scolding was only for form's sake, and she quickly returned her attention to Ceana. "You know Athair and Màthair wouldn't give you this responsibility if they didn't believe you could handle it well."

"That's what they said. They tried to make it sound as if it were a gift." Ceana sniffled. "I should be grateful, probably. I know you all probably would've been. I wish it could've been one of you instead! I would've been happy to go to Glassraghey or Talascheal or anywhere if someone else didn't want to."

"Not me!" Mirren shuddered. "I may not be as happy to marry a stranger as you are, but I shouldn't want to worry about meeting people and picking a good match."

"We were all willing to do what Athair and Màthair needed us to do." Onora took her hand away and started stitching again. "But I think they wished sometimes that they could ask less of us."

"But—" Ceana's mind snagged on something in Onora's words. "Wait. You knew about this, didn't you?"

"Athair and Màthair mentioned it to me." Onora sighed. "I told them that you probably wouldn't take it well, but they insisted." She paused, working out a tangle in her thread, and then added, "Perhaps it'll be easier to bear if you think of it as them giving you the responsibility of finding the man who'll best serve the needs of the family and Atìrse."

"Maybe." Ceana sighed, slumping forward to rest her head on her knees. "I just wanted my marriage to *mean* something, like the rest of yours do."

"All marriages mean something," Onora replied, in the wise-older-sister voice she'd perfected by now. "Yours will just mean something different, is all."

"That's not what I meant, and you know it," Ceana grumbled. But she didn't say anything more, and eventually she lifted her head, pulled her embroidery from her pocket, and started working on it once again.

Ceana's poor spirits persisted the rest of that day and into the next as the reality of her suddenly-uncertain future continued to hang over her. She did her best not to let her parents see just how upset she was—they'd be terribly disappointed if they knew—or to let her feelings keep her from her responsibilities. Nonetheless, she couldn't shake her sense of gloom, and she kept more and more to solitary pursuits.

One golden afternoon found her walking the paths along the cliffs that overlooked the sea. A pair of men-at-arms and her lady-in-waiting accompanied her, but they kept well back out of deference to her ill mood. So, Ceana trekked over the packed earth and stone, willing the sunshine and summer air to chase away the dark clouds in her spirit.

She stopped by a great-standing stone and turned to look out to the ocean. She could just make out a pair of seals frolicking in the water some ways out from the shoreline, popping their heads above the waves and sporting with each other. Were they only seals, or were they selkies in their seal-shapes? Everyone said the two were indistinguishable until they came ashore, at which point the selkies would take on the form of humans garbed in sealskin cloaks.

Most likely, the seals she could see were only ordinary animals. For the most part, selkies kept well clear of Atìrse, even with the treaty. And yet...

In two days, the king of the selkies would come to renew the treaty between the seal-folk and Atìrse. Perhaps these *were* selkies, then. Perhaps they'd arrived early and were waiting in the waters until the time came for the treaty signing.

This would be the tenth selkie king to sign the treaty, Ceana knew. Each time the rulership of one of the peoples changed, the treaty had to be either renewed or rescinded. While Ceana knew little of this latest selkie king, she had heard that he was fairly young, still unmarried, and had ascended the throne just a year ago, after his father passed on. Even Onora's agents could learn no more than that.

Lord Arran wanted to end the treaty. Ceana frowned at the thought. The thought of going back on the treaty was nonsense, after her family had worked so hard to make peace with everyone else. And yet...it was strange that, after so many years, the selkies remained as distant as they always had been.

A sudden thought flickered in Ceana's mind, sending sparks of hope upwards. Perhaps, now that they'd made allies of all their other neighbors, even Tryggestrend in the north, the time had come that they should seek a better relationship with the seal-folk. Perhaps they could be proper friends, not wary neighbors.

Perhaps her marriage could mean something after all.

Chapter 3
A NEW PLAN

Ceana felt quite proud of how well she restrained herself from telling her parents about her idea the moment she returned to the castle. It was a good idea, she was sure—but she would need to present it properly so they would see it as such, and that meant she'd need to do some research.

She began in the castle archives. The archive here was smaller than the one in the royal seat, but the treaty with the selkie had been established here, back in the days when *this* had been the royal family's main residence. Even after the royal family moved further inland, the treaty signing remained here, on the coast. And so, Ceana had no trouble finding the records she needed.

Reading through them took several dusty hours, at the end of which Ceana's face ached from holding in sneezes. But by the end of that time, she felt satisfied with what she'd learned, and she went down to dinner with a lighter heart than she'd had since the day of Mirren's betrothal.

Cornering Onora after dinner proved more of a challenge than finding the records had been. She never would have managed it had Càirdeil not decided to demand attention from his mistress at an opportune moment, catching Ceana's ear and keeping Onora in one place long enough for Ceana to pull her aside and pour out her plan.

Upon hearing it, Onora pursed her lips pensively, still stroking her cat's fur. "It could work. If it does, it would certainly be a blessing. But are you certain this is what you want?"

Ceana nodded. "As long as it'll help Atìrse, yes."

"Very well." Onora scooped up her cat so she could stand while petting him instead of crouching. "I imagine you want to know what I know, then. Here's what I can tell you ..."

Armed with what she'd learned from the records and from Onora, Ceana set about preparing her proposal. Alone in her room, she detailed exactly what she wanted to suggest and listed the benefits of her idea. She mulled over possible objections to the plan until she'd come up with counterarguments to every one of them, and she rehearsed over and over how she would phrase her main points and primary defenses.

By the time she finally went to bed, she felt confident that she would have no trouble making her case. She dreamed that night of blue waters and of selkies beneath them, swimming sleek and swift towards the castle. In her dream, she floated above the waters, reaching down towards the selkies—but every time one seemed to notice her, some unseen force pulled her away from the waves.

The next morning, the castle was all abustle with preparations for the treaty renewal the following day. Ceana slipped through it all to the solar where she'd met with her parents the other day, where they'd broken that *horrible* news to her.

She found the door open and her father inside. Good. If she could convince him, she'd have a much easier time convincing her mother as well. Ceana knocked on the open door. "Athair?"

King Seòras looked up and beckoned her in. "Good morning, Ceana. What is it?"

Ceana stepped inside and shut the door. She took a deep breath, straightened her shoulders, clasped her hands in front of her, and began, "Athair, the other day, you and Màthair said that we are friends with every one of our neighbors. However, I fear you have overlooked one neighbor in your reckoning."

King Seòras raised an eyebrow. "Is that so? Do tell me what your mother and sister and I have failed to see, daughter of mine. Who have we left out?"

"They aren't precisely *left out*, and that is why you've failed to see them," Ceana replied. "On the night of Mirren's betrothal, I listened to some of your conversation with Lord Arran." Seeing King Seòras's expression darken, she hastily went on, "I think his position that we could break the treaty with the selkies a foolish one, and I know you think the same. But he is right that the treaty has been in place for many years, and it is strange that we should remain at spear's-length with our neighbors for so long."

King Seòras shook his head slowly. "By all accounts, they are the ones holding the spears. They mistrust us still."

"Perhaps." Though his words might have *sounded* like an objection, Ceana knew better. She could recognize his tone and the look in his eyes well enough to know he was mulling the idea over. So, she continued without hesitation. "But we have not sought to bridge that mistrust in generations! I looked in the records. The first few times we renewed the treaty, kings and queens of Atìrse offered a better alliance, and the selkie kings refused. After that, both our people and theirs merely maintained the status quo. But it has been long since then, and Onora says that this new king is young. Perhaps he would be more open to friendship. In any case, it can do no harm to ask, and if he refuses, the treaty we have remains."

"Perhaps so," King Seòras replied. "But what would either side gain from this alliance? Thus far, all anyone has asked for is safety from the other and tribute for old offenses—and the tribute is no great sum, whatever Lord Arran might believe."

Now he was simply testing her. Seeing how well she'd thought this through, giving her the opportunity to prove her idea was sound. "As in any of our alliances, both sides would receive the promise of aid in times of trouble and defense should one be attacked, as well as trade relations. The tribute would end, as I am certain that the offenses that prompted it have long since been paid for, though we would still refrain from hunting or harming seals. The selkie-folk, rather than just not attacking our ships, would be invited to serve as guides and guardians—in exchange, of course, for fair pay. In exchange, we could provide the selkies with resources from inland that they might not be able to access otherwise."

"Hmm. Your proposal seems weighted towards benefit for Atìrse rather than equal gain for both, but no doubt the selkie king would have some ideas of what would best serve his people." King Seòras straightened up. "Allow me a guess at another benefit you would offer the seal-folk: a marriage between royal families to solidify the bond."

Despite her best intentions, Ceana found herself blushing. "Well, it is only fair. We offered as much to all our other allies, even the Daoine Math."

King Seòras snorted in a most unkingly fashion. "As I understand it, they asked for the marriage first and then we tacked the alliance on as a condition."

"Well, yes." By all accounts, the alliance had come about when a faery princess decided she could have no other husband than Thrice-Great Uncle Diarmad. While the rest of the family rapidly made plans to protect Diarmad from being spirited away by their magical neighbors, Diarmad had gone out to bargain his future for that of Atìrse. "It was, nonetheless, an alliance with marriage as a condition, as we have with other nations. The selkies need not accept the offer, but if they wish it, I would be willing."

"Are you certain?" King Seòras asked, voice full of gentle concern. "You know as well as I that the seal-folk cannot spend more than a day on land at a time. If the dawn finds them ashore, they perish. It seems that would be a lonely life for you, and I would see you happy even if it means a friendship with the selkies must wait."

That had been one of Ceana's own greatest concerns with her idea. But she had prepared a sound enough argument to convince herself, and now the words tumbled from her mouth. "They cannot spend more than a day on *our* shore, perhaps. But in every picture I've seen and every record I've found, the selkies carry metal weapons and wear worked garments. Nothing I've heard suggests that they are on better terms with other human kingdoms than they are with us, so they must make these things themselves. They must have a settlement of some kind somewhere, in a land like what Tìr Soilleir is for the Daoine Math. But from our records of the treaties, I think time passes for them the same as it does for us."

She took a breath, forced herself to slow down. "If that is the case, I need have no fear of loneliness. But if I am wrong, I'll find ways to cope. We have other castles like this one that stand by the sea, even if they're less grand. Make one part of my dowry, and I'll dwell there, where my husband can easily come to me and return to the sea in time to be safe. Or—we know nothing about whether or not *aboard ship* counts as above shore." She managed a little laugh. "I can dwell upon the sea like Queen Dagrún the Explorer, follow my husband where he and his folk will, and visit with my sisters in between."

"Well, let none say you failed to think this through." King Seòras stood. "If this is what you want, Ceana, I'll not forbid you. I suppose this is my own fault for teaching you to think so much of duty. Come, then. Let us see what your mother has to say about this, and if she agrees, we will decide what to do when the selkies come tomorrow."

"Yes, Athair." Ceana followed as King Seòras made for the door, dancing inwardly with as much joy as she had at Mirren's betrothal. Queen Isla rarely gainsaid her husband once he'd made up his mind. Then all that would remain would be to propose the alliance to the selkies—but surely, after all this time, they would be ready for friendship as well. After all, at this point, what remained for them to hold against Atìrse?

Chapter 4

THE KING OF THE SELKIES

The next day dawned bright and golden. It was, Ceana thought, the kind of day on which good things happened. And, therefore, it boded very well indeed for that day's events and the results of her plan.

As usual, she and Mirren ate their breakfast together: scones with honey and porridge with berries and cream. As they ate, Mirren waggled one of her scones at Ceana. "Are you sure you really want to go run off to live with the selkies? They probably don't even know what scones *are*. I bet they catch their own breakfasts in the sea, even the king, and you'll have to eat fish for every meal."

"Don't be silly. They're not *uncivilized*." Ceana rolled her eyes. "And if they truly don't know about scones and baked things, I'll have Onora's cook teach them. Then they'll truly see the benefits of properly allying with us."

"Mmmm, the knowledge of scones would be a compelling reason if *I* were them." Mirren paused, her expression sobering. "You don't have to do this, Ceana, really. None of us will hold it against you if you marry for love instead of duty. And you *could* wait and come to Glassraghey with me when I get married and see if there are any nobles there you like. Then I won't be all on my own."

"If this doesn't work, I'll consider that, but I want to *try*." Ceana set down her spoon. "I know you don't think I need to do this, but it really is what I want."

"You're impossible." Mirren sighed affectionately. "Well, if you're sure, we'd better hurry up and finish so you can get ready. It wouldn't do to meet your potential future husband in your nightgown."

Ceana couldn't help laughing at that. "No, certainly not!" And with that, she focused her attention back on her food.

After breakfast, Mirren hurried back to her own room, and Ceana, with the aid of her maid and lady-in-waiting, set about preparing for the day. Her best gown and kirtle, thankfully, remained clean, and she put these on over her linen shift. The kirtle was of a brilliant blue-green color like the sea at sunset, which everyone said brought out her eyes and set off the reddish undertones in her hair. The gown was of a lighter green, the color of seafoam, with short, wide sleeves and a split skirt. Embroidered knotwork and flowers decorated the edges of both garments, stitched by Ceana's own hands over the course of many a winter night and summer afternoon.

Once Ceana had dressed, Sìne, her maid, turned her attention to Ceana's hair. She brushed faery-made potions into it to nudge the natural waves towards proper curls and to make sure every lock would stay in its proper place. She braided the front part of the hair into multiple smaller braids, pulled them back, and secured them in a twist with forked copper pins. The rest she left loose. She topped everything with a slim circlet of gold set with tiny pearls and then stepped back to survey the effect with a pleased nod.

Last of all, she produced more jars of faery potions and lotions, reserved for the most special of occasions, and set to work on Ceana's face, applying each with an expert hand. One she dabbed around Ceana's eyes to bring out the color and make them look larger; another she rubbed into cheeks and nose and forehead to hide blemishes and even out the color; another she brushed along Ceana's lips to enhance their color and shape; and so on. Ceana endured it all impatiently, trying to focus on the day ahead as a distraction from her current situation, until at last Sìne set down the last jar and smiled in satisfaction. "There. If his majesty of the selkies doesn't fancy you the moment he sets eyes on you, it's not by any fault on your part."

"Or yours. Thank you." Ceana stood and offered Sìne a smile. "You've done very well."

"I do my best, your highness." Sìne dipped into a partial curtsey. "Is there anything else you need?"

"No, that will be all. I'd better go down and be ready when the delegation arrives." Ceana swept up her skirts in one hand and hurried from her room, down the stairs, and outside. The gates of the castle stood open, as did the doors to the keep. Tradition demanded that, until the treaty had been renewed and the selkies had departed, no doors would be shut save the one to the room in which the negotiations took place, and even there, the window had to remain open.

The rest of her family was already assembled in the courtyard, as were many of the other nobles. Not Lord Arran, Ceana noted with relief, nor any of those who were of his circle. Even if they were only planning to maintain the treaty with no change, Lord Arran's influence would make things no easier.

Ceana made her way to her father's side. "Any sign of them yet?"

"None. But we have watchers on the cliffs who'll sound their horns when the king and his delegation surface." King Seòras glanced down at her. "You look very nice."

"Thank you!" Ceana beamed. "It is a special occasion, after all."

"A special occasion on which you have plans to catch someone's eye." King Seòras raised an eyebrow. "Make sure you don't go too far to make your catch, daughter of mine."

"I would never!" Ceana wrinkled her nose playfully at him. "I'll behave myself, Athair, just like I always do."

"I know," King Seòras replied. "When you hear the trumpets, you and your sisters are to come stand by your mother and me. We'll formally greet the selkies as a family."

"I'll be ready." Recognizing the dismissal for what it was, Ceana slipped away to go speak with her sisters and some of the younger noblewomen of her own age while she waited. But she found herself glancing frequently towards the gates and the sea just visible beyond them as the sun rose higher and higher in the sky.

At last came the sound of the watchmen's horns, ringing off the hills and castle walls. Ceana perked up, hastily ended her conversation with Mirren's friend, Lady Eisia, and hurried to her parents' side. King Seòras indicated a spot next to him. "Here. Onora, by your mother, with Alasdair beside you. Mirren, by Alasdair."

Ceana stood where she'd been told. She smoothed her skirts and plucked at the sleeves of her gown, trying to make sure they fell in the most flattering way possible. A second horn-blast stilled her hands, however, as the selkie king's party appeared through the gateway, striding up the path from the sea. She clasped her hands in front of her, straightened her shoulders, and lifted her head high, sending up a quiet prayer to Dèanadair: *Please, please, let this go well. Let the selkie king be amenable; let him find me pleasing, and let me find him the same.*

The heralds blew a third horn blast as the selkies crossed the keep threshold. One of the party passed a herald a paper, and he read it swiftly, then declared, "King Fionntan of the Daoine Ròin!"

The selkies did not slow their pace, nor did they pay any further heed to the heralds. There could be no doubt which among them was King Fionntan. He walked at the head of the party, tall and proud, with a thick circlet of bright gold resting on his dark, wavy hair, which was still damp from the sea. The face beneath was grave and noble, fierce and strong as the sea from which he came, with keen, dark eyes and a well-trimmed beard along his chin. A sealskin cloak hung round his broad shoulders, and beneath it he wore a white tunic, only sparsely decorated, and sturdy hose of deep green, with wrapped leather guards around forearms and legs. Though his cloak bore no brooch or decoration, there was gold on the clasp of his tunic at his neck, and on the buckle of his belt, and edging the leather of his armor, and a golden chain round his neck held an emblem of worked metal and green jewels. A long sword hung from his belt, and Ceana had no doubt from his build and the way in which he walked and held himself that he could use it well.

As the selkies approached, Ceana saw, out of the corner of her eye, Mirren leaning over to whisper something to Onora, and she silently gave thanks that neither of her sisters were standing next to her. She had difficulty enough controlling her thoughts enough to keep a blush from her face on her own—with a sister to nudge and whisper to her, it would be entirely impossible. There was, of course, more to a man than his looks—but if she found herself looking at Fionntan for the rest of her life, she *certainly* wouldn't object.

Behind and beside the king came his escort. Two, one man and one woman, looked to be nobles. The man was dressed much like King Fionntan, but he stood half a head shorter, with grey speckling his dark hair and a more rounded shape. The woman also wore a cloak of sealskin, along with a gown the color of spring leaves that ended some inches above her ankles. Rather than an overdress, she wore a surcoat of pale blue with a scalloped hem.

The other four were clearly guards, though, strangely, one of them appeared to be a woman. All four carried spears with gleaming points in their left hands and bore a short sword on one hip and a long knife on the other. Each wore a dark blue tunic, dark hose, and leather armor, though the woman's tunic was longer than those of the men. Like the king and the nobles, they wore undecorated sealskin cloaks. But while the other seal-folk wore their hair loose, the guards' hair was pulled into multiple oiled braids, after the manner of the Tryggestrenders.

As King Fionntan and his party neared, King Seòras stepped forward. "King Fionntan, my family and I welcome you on behalf of all Atìrse. I am Seòras, king of this land, and this is my wife, Isla."

He offered his hand to Fionntan, who warily extended his own hand. "And on behalf of the Daoine Ròin, King Seòras, I thank you for your welcome."

The two men clasped wrists and shook. Then, King Seòras waved his daughters forward. "May I introduce the rest of my present kin? This is my eldest daughter and heir, Onora, who, with her husband, Alasdair, holds this castle."

Onora bent in a slight curtsey. "Your majesty, it is an honor to make the acquaintance at last of our neighbors."

King Fionntan inclined his head in return. "An honor indeed, your highness."

King Seòras went on, "Most of my middle daughters are wed and dwelling with their husbands, but the youngest two yet remain with me. This is Mirren, who was just this week betrothed to Martyn of Glassraghey. And this is Ceana, my youngest."

Ceana dipped into the most elegant curtsey she knew. "Your majesty, I am pleased to meet you."

"Indeed." King Fionntan bowed his head as he had for Onora, though perhaps a bit more quickly. "As for my own party, these are Lord Muir and Lady Mairearad, two of my closest advisors."

The two nobles both bowed, murmuring greetings, which King Seòras returned with a dip of his own head. "An honor. They are welcome as you are, King Fionntan." He straightened again, and raised a hand to indicate the courtyard. "It is long since we welcomed any of your folk here, and I am sure you are wearied by your journey here. Will you take rest and refreshment with my court before we turn to business?"

Again, a guarded look crossed King Fionntan's face, but he replied politely, "With due respect, King Seòras, it is not our custom to linger on land, especially not when the treaty has lapsed. Let us do what we came to do before we turn our thoughts elsewhere."

"As you wish." King Seòras gestured towards the open keep doors. "Perhaps after all is in order, you will be more at ease. It is our custom to celebrate any successful treaty, whether old or new, with festivity, and we would be glad to have your company as we do so."

"We will see," was all King Fionntan replied. He spoke a few words to his companions in a language Ceana didn't understand, and then all seven of them followed King Seòras into the keep. Queen Isla, Onora, and Alasdair came after, accompanied by a pair of guards.

Ceana carefully hid her disappointment as she watched them leave, keeping her shoulders straight and her chin high. That the selkies refused to mingle boded ill if they were to make a true alliance—but, then again, they had come expecting a routine renewal of the treaty, nothing more. They didn't know to look for friendship in Atìrse's court.

Mirren slipped over to Ceana's side and caught Ceana's hand in her own. "Well! Did you *see* his majesty?"

"I don't know how I could have missed him." Ceana shook her worried thoughts away and focused her attention on her sister. "I don't think he's even Onora's age."

"Certainly not!" Mirren exclaimed. "He's only a few years older than I am, I'd say. *And* handsome!"

"I noticed." Ceana ducked her head. "But it's not as if that really matters. What matters is his character and whether or not he agrees to the alliance."

"It may not matter, but it doesn't hurt." Mirren glanced towards the keep. "I'm surprised you didn't go up with them."

"Athair and I discussed it, but he thought it would be better if I remained outside." Of course, when they made that plan, they'd expected King Fionntan and his people to accept the invitation so she'd have a bit of time to talk to him and make an impression—or ask King Seòras to pull back on the marriage part of the alliance, if she had concerns. But that hadn't happened, and King Fionntan had barely looked at her when they met. "Though—I know which room they're meeting in, and I know there's a bench quite close to the window."

"And you thought you'd listen in?" Mirren didn't wait for an answer before releasing Ceana's hand and giving her a little push. "Go on, then! I'll cover for you here."

"Thanks!" Ceana shot Mirren a grateful smile and hurried off around the castle.

The window in question looked out on the courtyard garden, and there was indeed a stone bench just beneath and to the side of it. Ceana dusted it off, then sat down and pulled her embroidery from her pocket to keep her hands busy while she listened.

From her seat, she could hear voices from above, though most of what they said was too indistinct to understand clearly. Even listening as hard as she could, Ceana could only pick up phrases here and there: King Fionntan saying "We have kept our side of the treaty," and King Seòras replying, "As have we with ours." She caught something about the terms remaining the same—but then all voices dropped too low for her to make out more than a murmur.

Some minutes later, more words fell to her ear: King Fionntan, asking "And what manner of change do you propose?"

Ceana strained to hear, but her father's voice was too quiet for her to understand more than a word or two here and there: something about "closest neighbors" and something else that sounded like "seek friendship."

An unfamiliar voice, but with the same accent as Fionntan—Ceana thought it was the older selkie noble—spoke next. "Your majesty, allow me—King Seòras, the treaty has served both our peoples well. What do we gain by entering a full alliance with you, and what would you expect of us in return?"

King Seòras replied. Ceana caught several phrases that sounded very like what she'd told him the other day, as well as mention of other things that must have been suggested by Onora or Queen Isla. He ended, as far as Ceana could tell, by saying, "Of course, if there is aught else you would ask of us as part of this friendship, say so and we will gladly consider it. As I have said, we have made friends of the rest of our neighbors and are willing to do what we can to make friends of you as well."

The old noble spoke again, surprisingly quickly, as if cutting someone else off. "We have noticed your campaign to build alliances with all who will have you, and of sealing such friendships by marrying away your daughters."

His tone was just a touch too diplomatic, a touch too cool. Ceana's hands stilled, and she strained her ears to catch every word of the conversation above.

King Seòras replied, "I do my best for both my people and my family, and if I may display and solidify our alliances while also seeing my daughters wed to good men, I will do so. Should you desire to pursue an alliance, of course, I would extend the same offer to you, King Fionntan. My youngest, Ceana, is not yet betrothed, but she is of an age for men to seek her hand."

"Oh, would you!" King Fionntan spoke loudly enough that Ceana could've heard it without even trying; it sounded as though he'd been holding the words in until they burst out, all storm and fury. "Would you buy our forgetfulness with your daughter's life? Would you see to it that your descendants can lay claim to the dearly-defended throne of my fathers?"

King Seòras's voice started to rise in protest, but King Fionntan went on before he could get more than a word or two out: "King Seòras, we have no need of friendship with kidnappers and slavers. Had I not already set my oath to the treaty our forefathers established, I would refuse even that for the insult you do me."

Ceana didn't wait to hear more. She stuffed her embroidery back in her pocket, picked up her skirts, and hurried back towards the main gathering in the front of the courtyard. How had that gone so *wrong*? She'd known the selkie king might refuse, but to take it as an *insult* —!

She slowed once she was out of sight and earshot of the window, mentally offering up a quiet prayer. *Dèanadair, let this turn out no worse than it already has. Don't let King Fionntan turn away from the treaty.* If the selkies started attacking ships again...well, the Atìrse merchants and navy might be better-armed than they were long ago, but it would still result in loss of life on both sides.

All this from a simple proposal. How had everything gone so wrong?

Chapter 5
CONSEQUENCES

Ceana reached the courtyard just in time to see the selkies departing, cutting swiftly through the crowd of assembled nobles. She caught a glimpse of King Fionntan's face, a raging storm barely concealed behind a mask of cold diplomacy, and wondered again what about the suggestion had so offended him. They *had* kept the treaty, so far as they were able to. They paid the tributes; they kept away from seals and selkies both. They and the selkies had coexisted for generations without trouble.

And now...this. And it was, in part, her fault.

Her family arrived a moment later, walking slower than the selkies had—though the redness in some of their faces suggested they'd been hurrying a moment ago and had only just stopped to keep from alarming anyone. Neither the king nor the queen looked in Ceana's direction—but Onora caught Ceana's eye, and a knowing look flickered in her gaze.

King Seòras raised a hand to call for attention and signal the heralds, who blew an only slightly delayed blast on their horns. Gazes turned towards the royal family from the departing selkie king, and King Seòras lowered his hand again. "All is well. The treaty is renewed, and peace remains."

A cheer went up—but it had an uncertain edge, as if the crowd still wasn't sure if they would need to panic in a moment. King Seòras waited until it began to die away, then added, "As planned, a feast will be held this afternoon to celebrate another generation of coming peace. Unfortunately, King Fionntan and his party will be unable to join us, but we will toast their health nonetheless."

Another cheer, this one more confident. Ceana could guess

the thoughts of most of the crowd: if there were trouble, the feast would have been cancelled—but as the feast would go on, so too would life as normal. Ceana clapped along with the rest, doing her best to hide the fact that she knew just how bad a turn things could have taken.

When it became clear that no more announcements were forthcoming, the crowd's attention returned to chatting with their neighbors or drifting off to go about their plans for the rest of the day. King Seòras and Queen Isla turned and made their way towards Ceana, and Ceana hastily assumed what she hoped would come off as a hopeful look. "Well?"

"Not here," King Seòras replied, quietly. He put a hand on her shoulder and guided her away from the main courtyard, back towards the garden where Ceana had been a moment ago. Once they were out of easy earshot from the crowd, he spoke again. "King Fionntan refused the alliance. I'm sorry."

Ceana allowed her face to fall again. "He looked rather upset when he was leaving."

"He took less well to the suggestion than any of us expected, to be sure," Queen Isla said, her tone diplomatic even now. "I imagine it caught him off-guard."

"But ..." Ceana hesitated. "Will there be problems between us and his people now?"

"Dèanadair willing, no," King Seòras replied. "We both put our oaths to the treaty, so it will stand. Fionntan's advisors insisted that we do so before we discussed any changes, in fact. Should they try to start trouble, we have a promise to fall back upon, and we will seek to make up for whatever insult we unknowingly made."

"But we're further from friendship than we were before." Ceana couldn't keep the glumness from her voice. "I'm sorry. I ought to have left well enough alone."

King Seòras shifted to give her a one-armed hug. "Don't hold this against yourself, daughter of mine. You may have suggested the alliance, but your mother, sister, and I made the decision to act upon it. And make no mistake, it was a worthy idea, whatever your inspiration. It's easy to lean upon the way things have always been, and sometimes there can be blessing in challenging that."

Her father was right, Ceana knew. But that didn't change what had happened. "Still—I shouldn't have rushed you into it. Had we taken more time to learn about them ..."

"We could only have done so much, even if we had all the time in the world," Queen Isla pointed out. "They send no ambassadors and refuse any emissary we might send—for good reason on both parts. Our knowledge of their culture is bounded by the little that was recorded in the days before we were at odds. And Onora, for all her resources, is still limited in where she can place people. We offered them as fair an alliance as we could and the opportunity to suggest what could be better. They chose not to take it."

"Indeed," King Seòras agreed. "And you cannot hold yourself responsible for the choices of another." He gave her shoulders another little squeeze and then released her. "I know you hoped for a marriage out of it as well, but I fear you'll have to content yourself with a land-dwelling man."

He said the words with a smile in his voice, if not on his face, but Ceana couldn't bring herself to smile back. "I'd...I'd rather not talk about that just now."

"I understand." King Seòras nodded gravely. "We have things to attend to, so we'll let you be. But if you wish to speak further, come and find us."

"I will," Ceana replied. "I'll be fine. Don't worry about me." After all, her parents had more pressing things to think upon.

For that matter, so did she. Whatever they said, this mess had been partially her doing. And somehow, she needed to find a way to make it right.

She managed to endure the rest of the day without letting her distress become too obvious. She could tell from the looks Onora and Mirren kept giving her that they knew something was wrong—no doubt they also knew what. Mirren would have been told of King Fionntan's reaction to the alliance proposal, and of course Onora had been there for it. Mirren knew, too, that Ceana would have been listening at the time—and if Onora didn't *know*, she'd probably guessed. Still, no one else seemed to catch on.

That night, Ceana lay awake in her bed, listening to the sound of the waves and the wind. Amid them, she could just make out the sound of several people singing: sweet, strong voices rising in a melody that flowed like the tides and a language at once foreign and familiar—foreign because she still did not know what it meant, but familiar because she had heard it many a time whenever she and her family stayed by the sea.

The selkies were singing, she knew, in their secret language that they shared with no man or faery. She and her sisters had often speculated about the reason for the selkies' songs and why they performed them so close to human lands. Rhona suggested that the selkies sang to praise Dèanadair, for no music *but* praise could be so beautiful. Sorcha had rolled her eyes and said that the selkies sang because they wanted to sing and they couldn't do so when they were underwater in seal shape, and that it was mere coincidence that they sometimes did so by the shore. Mey wondered if there were something about the cliffs that made the sound resonate particularly well, while Mirren and Linnhe theorized about selkie magic. Practical Onora, for her part, typically settled the debates by saying that everyone was probably right to some degree.

Whatever the reason, it had always tugged at something deep inside Ceana, and she'd liked to think even then that it meant some selkies wanted to be friends with humankind, and that the songs were the only way they had to show it. Now that seemed a foolish hope. More than likely, all the selkies were like King Fionntan—they had all certainly seemed upset when they left.

But, as she listened to the music in the wind, she found herself praying anyway that it meant the selkies weren't *too* angry. Surely if they were going to hold a grudge, they wouldn't continue to sing, not here, not so close to human lands. Not where they could be heard.

Ceana sighed, rolled over, and thought back to what she'd heard and what had transpired. Something bothered her about King Fionntan's words. *"Kidnappers and slavers,"* he'd called Ceana's family and the people of Atìrse as a whole. But the treaty had been put in place, as far as Ceana knew, because the selkies were angry that their people were being mistaken for ordinary seals and hurt or sometimes even killed by hunters. And who would kidnap a selkie anyway? Everyone knew that you couldn't keep a selkie from the sea too long without killing them—and if you let them back in the sea, you had a full-grown, *angry* seal on your hands.

If he'd said *murderers*, she could have understood some of his position—not why he'd held onto his people's anger so long when seal hunting had been outlawed for years and years, but at least the reasoning behind the anger. Yet, he hadn't said *murderers*. He'd said *kidnappers*. He'd said *slavers*. It didn't make sense.

She should've tried to learn more. She should *still* try to learn more. If she understood why he'd said what he had, maybe she could find a way to set everything right. Maybe she could, even now, make things better than they had been before she'd ruined it all. She wouldn't hang her hopes of marriage on it this time. King Fionntan had seemed almost as upset about the idea of marrying her as he had about whatever past Atìrsens had done. But maybe figuring out how to marry for choice would be easier if she'd done something else that mattered all on her own.

But how? If there were records elsewhere than this castle, Ceana wasn't sure how or where to find them, and they would only tell what long-ago selkies had thought anyway. They might not even include what had happened to create the rift. She needed to talk to the selkies themselves in order to understand—but they only came on land for the treaty and to collect their tribute. She couldn't go to them either; they wouldn't accept a human into their midst. And even if they did, how would she or someone else keep up with them when they dove beneath the depths?

Unless...

Ceana turned back onto her back, staring at the ceiling. What if she could find a way to disguise herself as a selkie? There were faery-made spells for breathing underwater, she knew. And there were other spells for transformations and hiding one's identity. Maybe they could be combined somehow. It would be difficult, she knew, to fool the selkies when she had so little background knowledge to work with, but perhaps she could pretend to be from another part of the sea or something.

Of course, if the selkies found her out, it could make things worse—*far* worse. But even then...her parents had taught her diplomacy since she learned to talk. She could try to convince them of the truth, that she meant no harm and only wished to learn their true grievance. Or, if the very worst came to pass, she could tell them that she came of her own doing, not by her family's wishes, and beg that whatever consequences they chose would fall upon her own head and none other. It might mean her death, but at least it wouldn't damage things further.

In order to do that, though, she'd need the right magic. And for that, she'd need her grandmother, which meant she could do nothing until the morning. But at least she had a plan now. With that thought in mind, Ceana snuggled into her pillow, shut her eyes, and waited for sleep to come.

Chapter 6
A Grandmother's Wisdom

The next morning, Ceana rushed through her breakfast and then made a beeline for her grandmother's rooms near the very top of the keep. Now that the treaty was signed, she had only a day or two before her family would leave to return to the royal seat. She could probably find an excuse to stay—but she needed to know first if staying would be worth it. If her latest idea had no hope of success, remaining by the sea and hearing the selkies sing would be nothing less than torment. But if she could do something, anything at all, she would.

And if anyone would know what could be done, it would be the old queen. Queen Moireach was the mother of Ceana's father and had reigned with her husband for many years, but she had spent most of those years dwelling at various castles along the coast, rather than remaining at the royal seat inland. And when she had stepped down from ruling life after her husband's death, she had retired here.

More importantly, she had been a particular favorite of Thrice-Great Uncle Diarmad and his wife. They'd written hundreds upon hundreds of letters to her, answering all her questions about magic and Tìr Soilleir, the kingdom of the Atìrsen faery folk. When she was Ceana's age and younger, they'd even allowed her to come visit them for a brief time in the summers, being careful to ensure it *would* be brief. Humans, of course, couldn't do magic—but no one on this side of Tìr Soilleir knew more about it or came closer to being able to use it than Queen Moireach.

Ceana reached her grandmother's door and knocked twice. Queen Moireach's voice replied, "Come in," a moment later.

Ceana pushed the door open and stepped into her grandmother's sitting room. She found her still sitting at her breakfast table, sipping a cup of tea. The remains of breakfast—oatcakes, fresh berry jam, soft cheese, and soft-boiled eggs—were evident only as crumbs and smudges upon plates.

Queen Moireach set her cup down and beckoned Ceana over. "Ah, good morning. And what brings thee to my chambers on this fine morning? I would think thou wouldst be with thy sisters." As always, she spoke in the old-fashioned style, like the Daoine Math did, with its distinction between informal and formal address—the informal *thee* and *thou* for family and the closest of friends; the formal *you* for everyone else.

"I wanted to see you." Ceana crossed to the table and sat down across from her grandmother. "To talk with you." She glanced around at the maid standing in the corner. "In private, please."

"Ah, I see how it is." The old queen nodded knowingly, then made a sign at the maid. "Tessa, you may clear the table and then be dismissed. Leave the tea things; I fancy my granddaughter may need a cup, and if she does not, then I shall take a second."

"Yes, your majesty." Tessa obeyed swiftly, loading dirty dishes onto a tray and whisking them and herself away and out the door, which she somehow managed to shut even with full hands.

Queen Moireach indicated the teapot and the spare cup. "Tea, Ceana?"

"Yes, please." She'd already had tea today, but visiting with her grandmother had a certain ritual, and she *would* keep to it, even if the circumstances were extraordinary. She waited as Queen Moireach poured the tea, scooped a dollop of honey from the pot, placed the spoon in the cup, and passed it over to her. Only then did she speak. "I need to ask you about magic."

The old queen's eyebrows rose slightly. "Oh?"

Ceana nodded, holding the teacup without drinking from it. "You heard about what happened with the treaty, didn't you?

Athair or Màthair told you?"

"Onora did, actually. But yes, I heard of thine idea and the trouble it caused. It is lucky for us that King Fionntan's advisors insisted that the original treaty be signed before any changes were discussed. Dèanadair be praised for that blessing." Queen Moireach took a long sip of her own tea. "And now thou art faced with the prospect of choosing thine own husband, yet thou comest to me about magic?"

"They're not connected," Ceana hastily explained, catching the unspoken question and the implied caution. "I'm not looking for any sort of love magic. I've heard all your stories; I know better."

"I did wonder if I should have to reeducate thee. I am glad to hear I shall not." Queen Moireach studied her granddaughter intently, her blue eyes sharp and keen. "What art thou after, then?"

Ceana took a deep breath. "I want to learn about the selkies. That's where my idea went wrong—we didn't know enough to avoid offending them. And what they said about us doesn't fit with what we *do* know."

Queen Moireach made a thoughtful hum. "There are records in the archives here and in thy main residence."

"I checked the ones here before I started all this, and they'd be more likely to have information about selkies. I didn't find what I need." Ceana glanced out the window towards the sea. "The only way to find out what I need is to talk to them. But they don't talk to humans—so I have to find a way to make them think I'm one of them. You know more about magic than anyone; do you have any idea if that's possible?"

"That would be considered espionage, Ceana." Queen Moireach set her teacup down and fixed Ceana with a look. "Thou art undoubtedly aware of the consequences of such an action?"

"I know. But if it comes to it, if I get caught, I'll make sure they know it was my doing and mine alone—not anyone else's." Ceana managed to keep her voice steady, which seemed like quite an accomplishment on her part, though she couldn't quite manage to hold her grandmother's gaze. She focused on her teacup instead.

"And...I know this started because of what I wanted in a marriage. But I *do* think it's a shame that the selkies are the only people we're still keeping at a spear's length when they're closer neighbors than any other save Addewedig, and I want to see that changed. I'll not seek out state secrets or weaknesses—I only want to talk to normal people to find out what our people did to theirs and how we can set it right. I'll be sure of that."

"Hmm," Queen Moireach said again, thoughtfully. "Hast thou prayed over this choice?"

She should've expected that question. Ceana took a hasty drink of tea to cover her expression, then replied, "A bit." Mostly of the *let this work* variety, though.

The look on her grandmother's face let her know that her caginess hadn't succeeded. Queen Moireach stood, using her chair for leverage. She took hold of her carved ivory cane, which had been leaning against the back of the chair, and said, "Finish thy tea and come with me. We will go to the Tùr-Faire to sit in the presence of Dèanadair and ask His guidance. And then, if thou art still set on this course, we will see what may be done."

"Yes, Maimeó." Ceana gulped down the remainder of her tea and then stood, moving to Queen Moireach's other side in case she needed extra support. Queen Moireach put a hand on Ceana's arm, and then the two started for the door and down the stairs.

Ceana had expected Queen Moireach to go to the small chapel within the keep's walls, where Mirren's betrothal ceremony had been held. But instead, they—with their ladies-in-waiting trailing after—made their way outside the keep to the larger Tùr-Faire set on one of the cliffs nearby. In the bright daylight, the light at the tower's top was barely visible. Long ago, Ceana knew, before Atìrse's alliance with the Daoine Math, it would have been a great bonfire kept ever-burning, shining a light and a path to Dèanadair. These days, most Tùr-Faire used magical lights instead, which were brighter and more reliable and required far less tending.

But if the light at the top was modern, the rest of the tower was not. Some people liked to say this was one of the oldest Tùr-

Faire still standing, and it certainly had been built in the old style: a three-story stone tower with a shelter on the top for the light, set with many large windows and a pair of great doors that wouldn't have looked out of place on the royal keep.

The doors stood open just now, so Queen Moireach simply swept in with Ceana at her side. The large, open first floor was still set with rows of benches and chairs for worship and a broad altar at the far wall, under the largest window. Had this been winter, the chairs would have been pushed to the side or into smaller sections to make space for poor folk and travelers to shelter from the cold, with fires burning in the hearths on either side of the chamber. But now, in summer, the only indications of life were the faint voices from the next floor up, where the priests dwelt.

Queen Moireach made her way to one of the chairs near the front of the space, the same one she sat in during worship. "I will stay here to pray. Thou mayst stay with me, or go elsewhere. But for a matter as serious as thine, I suggest going to the altar. I would do so as well, but I do not think my bones will allow me to kneel for so long."

"I'll go for you, then." Ceana waited until she was sure her grandmother was comfortable and then made her way to the altar. She knelt beside it, resting her hands in her lap, and bowed her head.

At first, she could only think to pray the same thing she'd been praying already: *Dèanadair, let this work. Let Maimeó agree and let her have something that will help. Let Onora be willing to help as well. Let the selkies believe me when I seek them out, and let me be able to learn what I need to know. Open the path for me to set things right. Surely, You didn't intend for our peoples to be at odds forever.*

She finished the prayer and snuck a glance back towards Queen Moireach. The old queen still sat with her head bowed, lips forming silent words, with no sign that she intended to move soon. So, Ceana turned to face forward again and repeated her prayer over a second time, and then a third.

After the third repetition, she stopped, letting her thoughts drift as she studied the carvings that decorated the sides of the altar in ribbons of repeating patterns, interspersed with painted knotwork borders. The topmost ribbon showed the Maker's Hand shaping sky and sea, land and growing things, stars and sun and moons, and at last living beings. Above and below it was inscribed the phrase: *Let us not forget the One who made all things; let us honor Him in life until we return to Him in death.*

Dèanadair had made all things at the beginning of time, the priests said. He had crafted the faeries and the selkies and the humans all from the same mold and blessed them each with different gifts and different realms in which to walk. But, the priests said, though He created different realms, He did not intend for His creations to be at war with one another, but to each use their gifts for mutual aid.

Dèanadair, why have you allowed human and selkie-kind to be at odds for so long? Both our peoples honor You, and when we return to You, we shall both come to the same place. There is no reason why we should be against each other now. Let me be able to communicate that to the selkies. Let me be able to reach them somehow.

The second carved ribbon showed a winding path with tiny footsteps along its length and, every so often, an image of a crumbling wall through which the path passed or of a mountain guide with staff and pack. Tiny chips of ruby marked out a trail of footsteps and the bottoms of the guide's feet, indicating the blood that had been spilled to open the way. A second phrase was engraved on either side of the ribbon: *Let us not stray from the shepherd's path; let us walk in the way that leads to life.*

Just as the Daoine Math dwelt in a realm apart from humans, the priests said, so Dèanadair had His realm to which none could come without a guide. Humans and faeries and selkies had waited in hope for one who could show them the path—and at last Cìobair, the promised guide, came, and through His blood the barriers were broken and a path to Dèanadair's realm established.

You did not wish us to be separated, Dèanadair. Not from You, and not from one another. I seek to open the path between humans and selkies. The way was not meant to be shut, but it has been made so. Am I not walking in Cìobair's footsteps in doing this?

The third carved ribbon had many figures, but the one that showed up most often was a goose. Sometimes it had its wings wide and its neck extended to ward off indistinct and ominous figures shaded in black. Sometimes it poked at human figures or pointed into the distance to indicate where they ought to go. Sometimes it was wreathed in flames that encircled it without consuming it. Above and below the images ran a third phrase: *Let us not ignore the guidance given us; let us listen when the guardian speaks.*

Cìobair was the guide to Dèanadair's realm, the priests said, but the Gèadh Naomh was the guide for all, mortal or magical, in this life. Not one of Dèanadair's people could step off His path without the Gèadh Naomh relentlessly worrying them back onto it. When that path was unclear, the Gèadh Naomh pointed the way. When people were tempted towards the old, pagan ways, the Gèadh Naomh cried out in warning and did battle with the temptations.

Ceana sat staring at the last ribbon for a long time, listening and wondering. *Dèanadair, if what I am doing is not part of Your path for me, not part of Your path for Atìrse or the selkies, make it known to me. Show me where I am going wrong. I know that I came up with this plan out of fear. I had my own plans in mind for my future that I didn't want to let go of. I believe You may use them as well, but if You do not desire it, make it clear to me, and give me peace for wherever You guide me.*

She stayed there for quite a while longer, other thoughts replaced by a single prayer: *Show me the path You have for me, and give me peace with whatever it may be. Let my plans be in Your hands, not mine.* She repeated that again and again in her thoughts until she found she could believe it and say it with sincerity.

And then she sat, listening and waiting.

At last, she glanced back and saw that Queen Moireach seemed to be finished with her own prayers. So, Ceana climbed to her feet, wincing at the ache in her legs, and returned to her grandmother's side. "Are you ready?"

"I am." Queen Moireach took her cane in one hand and Ceana's arm in the other and levered herself into a standing position. "Art thou still set on the plan thou told to me?"

Ceana nodded. For all her listening, she had sensed no forbiddance in her spirit, no sense of warning. "If it can be done."

"We shall see." Queen Moireach started for the door. "Come with me."

They made their way back to the castle and the keep and Queen Moireach's chambers. There, the old queen dismissed maids and handmaidens alike, then guided Ceana into the bedroom. "What thou dost ask—to go among the selkies in the guise of one of them—can be accomplished by no mixture of magics that I know."

Ceana's heart fell. A spiteful voice in a crushed corner muttered, *why didn't she say that sooner?* But Ceana stamped it down and asked, "Then my plan is impossible?"

"I did not say that." Queen Moireach produced a key from her pocket and unlocked the old cedar chest that stood beneath the window. Ceana peered over her grandmother's shoulders at the contents: strange devices, shimmering fabrics, engraved boxes with small, rune-marked locks, and many leather-bound books.

The old queen sorted through all of this until she reached the bottom and produced a bundle wrapped in faded blue cloth. "Here it is. If thy plan is to be accomplished, it will be through this or not at all."

She unwrapped the cloth and held up the contents. As she did, silvery-grey material speckled with black fell in folds from a seamless neck and hood. Ceana recognized it at once, for she'd seen its like just yesterday. "Is that a seal-cloak?"

As Queen Moireach shook out the material, the smell of salt and cedar filled the room. "After a fashion. This is a treasure passed down to me by my mother, as it was passed down by her mother and her mother's mother and so on. I do not know when it originated, save that it must have been in the days before the treaty. Nor do I know who made it, but I have been told that the one who wears it will take the form of a selkie and be able to walk and swim among them undetected, though they are not themselves born as one of the seal-folk."

Ceana gasped, reaching out with one hand to brush the silky-smooth material and run her fingers along its wavy, irregular edges. "Truly?"

"So I have been told. I have not tested it, for I was also told that the magic is limited. It will last only so long before it begins to fade. When I received it, I was instructed to keep it secret and safe and to use it only at need." Queen Moireach paused. "But I have prayed on this, and I believe that now is the time for which it has been preserved." She folded the cloak again, wrapped it once more in its cover, and placed it in Ceana's hands. "Use it well, Ceana. Be careful, be clever, and be kind, and trust to Dèanadair's path whatever comes."

"I will." Ceana hugged the bundled cloak tight against her, keenly aware of the treasure which she had been granted. "I won't disappoint you, Maimeó."

"I know thou wilt not." Queen Moireach smiled fondly—and, Ceana thought, a little sadly. "Now, I am sure thou hast other parts of thy plan to lay. Give me a hug and then go see to them."

"Of course." Ceana set the bundle aside and embraced her grandmother tightly. "Thank you for your help."

"Of course, my girl." Queen Moireach held Ceana tight, stroking her hair with one hand, and then released her with a little push. "Now, be off with thee. Thy time is short, and I'll see thee waste not a minute of it. And may Dèanadair bless every step of thy path."

Chapter 7
INTO THE SEA

Ceana had little trouble convincing her parents to let her stay at Onora's castle for the rest of the summer rather than returning to the royal seat with them. A polite but plaintive request and a comment that it had been a long time since she'd had much time to spend with her eldest sister and grandmother put them in a mood to agree, and Ceana sealed it by pointing out that Onora frequently entertained noble and royal guests who traveled by sea or who simply came to visit her and her husband. Meeting and getting to know potential matches would be just as easy here as it would at home, perhaps even more so since the setting was far more relaxed than at the royal castle. She felt only the smallest twinge of guilt when she saw how relieved that comment made them.

Only Mirren protested her decision to stay. When Ceana broke the news to her, she made a face and complained, "See, you're leaving me already! I thought we should have months together yet before I have to go off to Glassraghey." But then she shook her head. "Oh well. I'll manage. I *will* miss you, though."

Ceana just laughed and gave her sister a swift hug. "I know. I'm sorry. But we'll still have some time together before you leave. And I'd rather stay with Onora just now."

"You're up to something, aren't you?" Mirren sighed. "I won't ask what. I don't want to know. But *do* stay out of trouble!"

"I will." And with that, Ceana kissed Mirren on the cheek and went to seek her oldest sister.

She found Onora in the study, writing letters, her cat purring on her lap. The door stood ajar, so Ceana let herself in without knocking. "Onora? Can I talk to you?"

"In a moment." Onora scribed a few more words, dotted the end of the sentence, and placed the quill back in the inkwell. She slid the letter to the side and straightened up. "What do you need?"

Ceana shut the door and went to stand in front of the desk. "Might I stay with you over the rest of the summer, after a fashion? Athair and Màthair have given their permission."

"You're always welcome to stay, but what do you mean by 'after a fashion'?" Onora's face took on a familiar look of sisterly suspicion. "I thought you were going to help Mirren with preparations for her wedding; you wouldn't give up on that if you didn't have some other idea in mind."

It was a good thing, Ceana reflected, that her plan relied on Onora knowing what she was up to; otherwise, she wouldn't have a hope of success. She could hide things from her parents when she needed to. She could hide less from Mirren, but Mirren could be trusted to leave well enough alone, especially when she had other things on her mind. But Onora had a way of seeing right through her, and she wouldn't let it go if she thought one of her siblings likely to get herself into trouble without her approval.

Ceana rapidly explained her idea and the help she'd already received from Queen Moireach. Onora listened to the whole thing with brows knitted. Then she shut her eyes for several long moments, lips moving slightly with either unspoken prayers, inaudible exasperation regarding impulsive sisters, or both. Finally, however, she opened her eyes and sighed. "Did Maimeó give you anything to let you contact home if you get into trouble?"

Ceana shook her head. "No. Does that mean you'll help, then?"

"If Maimeó already agreed to your plan, I certainly won't stand in your way." Onora gave a little laugh. "After all, if anyone's going to find a way to talk the selkies into forgiving us after all these years, you probably have as good a chance as any and a better chance than most." She bent and fiddled with something on her side of the desk. Ceana heard a click, and a moment later, Onora straightened, holding a silvery torc. However, rather than the braided or twisted styles Ceana was most familiar with, this one was made of a single piece of metal, flattened and shaped into a partial circle and then wrapped with a filigree lattice of silver wire.

She passed the necklace to Ceana. "Take care of that. It may not be as precious as the cloak, but I only have so many of them, and they take quite a while to replace. It functions like a message mirror, but with no visual on your end, and it links to one of my mirrors."

Ceana held the necklace gingerly. "Mirrors activate by touch—will this one always be active, then?"

"No; you have to touch a particular spot on this one—there's a bit of etching on the main band; press your finger to the left side of that. Right here." Onora indicated the spot. Now that Ceana knew where to look, she could indeed see the swirling pattern etched into the metal and beginning where Onora pointed. "The wire hides it and ensures you're less likely to activate it by accident."

"Thank you." A thought occurred to Ceana, and she frowned. "But won't this implicate you if something goes wrong? Or raise suspicion, at least?"

"Only if you're exceptionally foolish about using it." Onora bent again, and Ceana heard another click before she sat back up. "The enchantment is worked in such a way that it's nearly indetectable, even when it's in use—it won't trigger most of the methods used to search for active magic, and my responses should be only audible to you as long as you're wearing the necklace. The only way it will be discovered is if someone catches you talking on it. Which, to be clear, you should *not* allow to happen."

"I won't." Ceana tightened her grip on the necklace. "I'll be very careful."

"Good." Onora gestured towards one of the other chairs in the room. "Now that I've made sure you won't be running off into the open sea with no way whatsoever to call for help, sit down and let's discuss your cover story. If you're going to do this, you're going to do it right."

The next few days were a slow trickle of departures. First to go were the nobles who had visited for Mirren's betrothal ceremony and the treaty renewal. Lord Arran left last out of all of these, and Ceana couldn't miss the look of suspicion on Onora's face as they watched him and his party go, no more than she could help noticing that, after he departed, Onora shut herself in her study for quite some time. Ceana wasn't sure what she was doing, but she heard a muffled murmur of voices each time she passed the door.

On the second day, King Seòras, Queen Isla, Mirren, and their attendants set out for the royal seat. Ceana hugged her family goodbye, cheerfully assuring them that she'd be fine staying with Onora and that if she changed her mind, she'd let them know at once. She couldn't help a sigh of relief once they were gone; at last, she'd not need to hide her plans from them!

The third day was the day for worship. Ceana attended the service at the Tur-Faire with Onora, Alasdair, and Queen Moireach, savoring every minute of it in the knowledge that it might be some time before she could return. She spent the rest of the day in final preparations for her own departure: rehearsing the cover story she'd use among the selkies, reviewing how to use the message torc with Onora, and making sure she had everything she would need for her venture—not that she could take more with her than what would fit in her pockets. She'd procured a plain, comfortable, lightweight dress of dark blue cotton to wear on the venture, as all the clothes she had with her were far too fine for her to pass incognito or to wear while adventuring.

She and Onora also put the final touches on how Onora, aided by Queen Moireach and a trusted inner circle of servants, would hide Ceana's absence from the castle. Anyone who asked after her might, at various times, hear that Ceana was closeted with Queen Moireach in her private chambers, ill and staying in her own room, spending a week in solitary contemplation and prayer as she considered her future, or on an excursion to visit one of the lesser nobles who lived within a few days' ride. Taken in full, the itinerary of excuses would last all the way until Mirren's wedding, though

Ceana hoped to be back long before then.

Ceana made sure to nap much of that afternoon, even though she felt too excited to rest. She would need her energy, she knew, and sleep might be in short supply for however long it took her to locate the selkies. So, she forced herself to lay still and keep her eyes shut as she drifted in and out of a doze.

At last, evening came. Onora embraced her privately after dinner, bidding her farewell and reminding her to use the message torc if she needed help or learned anything particularly interesting. Ceana returned the embrace and the farewell and nodded at the instruction. Then the two parted ways, Ceana to her room and Onora to her chambers.

The final few hours were interminable. Ceana watched from her window as the sky slowly darkened, slipping from blue to pink to red to purple and at last to midnight blue-black. She waited as the moons rose and the stars came out one by one. And then, once full night had come, she changed into her plain gown, put Onora's torc around her neck, picked up the bundled selkie cloak, and crept from the castle and down to the shore.

The sand crunched under the soles of her shoes as she made her way along the beach, walking lightly and periodically sweeping a branch behind her to hide her tracks. Onora might be covering for her absence, but she'd also warned that it would be better not to leave a trail that led only into the sea without other footsteps leading out at some point.

So, Ceana walked carefully, only relaxing once she reached the damp sand left behind when the tide receded. She tossed the branch she'd used out to sea, then unwrapped the seal cloak and shook it out. Then, she slipped it over her head. She'd been worried about how it would fit, with no seam and a cut meant, almost certainly, for someone else—but it settled over her shoulders comfortably, if a little loosely, and the ends of the cloak only just brushed the sands. The neckline, Ceana noted, hid the mirror-torc nicely.

Satisfied, Ceana folded the fabric that had wrapped the cloak in half diagonally and tied around her waist so she wouldn't lose it. She started to walk forward, then paused. She glanced back up at the castle one last time, dark against the night sky, then towards the light of the Tùr-Faire on a nearby cliff, shining brightly over the ocean. Without speaking, she sent up a prayer: *Dèanadair, protect me and guide me on a true path.* Then, she drew the hood of the cloak over her head and stepped into the sea.

Nothing happened immediately, so Ceana took another step, and then another. The wet sand sucked at her feet, and her dress clung to her legs. Still, she continued moving forward, even as her mind raced. What if the cloak didn't work? What if its magic was spent? What if there was some word or phrase, now lost to time, that she needed to speak to trigger the enchantment?

Yet she kept taking one step after another as the water climbed from her knees to her waist to her chest. Then her foot missed the ground, instead plunging into nothing but water. She had just enough presence of mind to gulp down a breath of air before she stumbled and fell beneath the waves.

Chapter 8
TRANSFORMATION

There came no sudden transformation. But as Ceana plunged downwards, she felt something wrap around her, soft and warm. The more it enveloped her, the more the barrier between herself and that *something* faded until it wasn't there at all.

Then, rather than sinking, she found herself shooting forward, propelled by flippers instead of feet. Her vision cleared until it was sharper than it had been on land, though she could see only in shades of grey and black. Every little ripple and current in the water were suddenly known to her, and she navigated them without a thought.

Instinct led her to swim some distance further before she surfaced, poking only her head out of the water. Above the sea's surface, her sight blurred strangely, and she found herself grateful that there was no light save for that of the stars and moons. Even the shining beam of the Tùr-Faire seemed too bright now.

She blinked, breathing deep. Then she plunged beneath the waves once again, swimming swiftly away from shore and towards the open ocean. She had expected to be afraid at this point. She'd wondered if she'd be able to figure out how to navigate the world in seal-shape. But the magic of the cloak seemed to adjust her instincts as long as she didn't question it. When she *did* think too much about what she was doing, she found herself floundering, thrashing with unfamiliar limbs as her mind panicked over how long she'd been underwater without taking a breath. But if she just let herself focus on her surroundings and the wonder of the experience, she found herself swimming, diving, and surfacing as if she'd been born to it.

Ceana spent several hours doing just that, giving herself time to get used to her new shape and senses. Besides her sharpened eyesight under the water, she found that her sense of smell had also improved, as had her hearing—she'd never realized how much sound there was beneath the waves, nor how much noise fish could make. But the sense of the vibrations rippling through the water amazed her the most. It seemed almost like a sort of second sight, though not the type that allowed some people to see through faery illusions, and she marveled at it over and over again, every time she sensed a nearby creature or dodged an obstacle that she hadn't even seen before she moved to avoid it.

And, with surprising swiftness, she ceased panicking every time she realized how long she'd been underwater. Instead, she exulted over every minute past what she could have endured as a human. She dove deeper and deeper, just to see how far down she could go—though she was still careful not to push herself too far.

Eventually, however, her amazement settled into a sort of background buzz in her mind, and she set to the business of finding the other selkies. Onora had been able to provide little information about where the selkies dwelt, only that they were spotted or heard more commonly towards the north. So, Ceana turned northwards, setting herself a steady pace. If she kept to the right direction and area, she supposed, she'd have to run into some selkies eventually—and if worst came to worst, she could go ashore near a fishing town and ask if there'd been any recent sightings.

She traveled in that manner for several days, going in zig-zags so as to cover more ground. Occasionally, she spotted ships or fishing boats, but she gave these a wide berth, aware that accidents could happen even with the treaty. In any case, she couldn't speak to them without transforming, and she wasn't sure how to do that without leaving the water entirely.

The first few nights she spent at sea, she hauled herself half out of the water to sleep on convenient rocks or beaches without leaving seal-shape. But on the third night she did so, she woke in the predawn to hear men's voices speaking nearby. "Look there," one said, in a low, eager tone that suggested he'd come across a rare stroke of luck. "Seal on the rock, all on its own. You don't often see that these days."

"Seal or seal-folk?" another voice replied, an edge to his tone that made Ceana's skin prickle. "From the looks, it could be either."

"We'll find out once we get it the rest of the way out of the water, won't we?" the first speaker said. "Come on—quick, before it wakes!"

Ceana didn't wait to hear more. She scooted off her rock and dove as deep as she dared, then swam swift and straight until she could no longer see the men's boat or hear their voices. Only then did fear boil away to anger. She'd thought that those who broke the treaty did so largely by accident, but these men sounded like they were hunting seals, or willing to hunt them if the opportunity presented itself. That still didn't entirely explain the selkies' accusations, but it did partially explain King Fionntan's fury.

The night after that, Ceana went ashore for the first time since leaving home. She pulled herself onto the beach in a sheltered cove near a tiny fishing village, and once she emerged fully from the water, the seal-shape fell away and became only a cloak once more. Beneath it, her clothes were dry, if a bit sandy, though her hair was damp. Ceana shook her garments out and bundled the seal-cloak up in its cloth, wrapping and tying it tightly. Then she went into the village, found the inn, and traded a few coins for food and a private room, all without speaking. Onora had warned her that her speech would give away her noble upbringing if she wasn't careful, and she wanted to take no risks.

Perhaps because of that, or perhaps for some other reason, she found that being ashore alone made her feel nearly as exposed and in danger as she'd felt that morning on the rock. She couldn't miss the fact that her presence attracted attention. Some of the glances were merely curious, but others seemed eerily appraising. When she went to her room that night, she made certain to bar both window and door and to shove what furniture she could in front of each. And after she returned to the sea in the small hours of the morning, she did not go ashore again.

Still, in all her searching, she neither saw nor heard any sign of the selkies. She saw seals enough, to be sure, but none that seemed to be anything more than animals. And the more time went on, the more her awareness of the enormity of her task grew. She'd thought the selkies were numerous enough that she'd run across one sooner than later if she only looked in the right area. She'd thought, too, that through the cloak's magic, she might be able to tell the difference between an ordinary seal and a selkie in seal form. Yet time seemed to be proving her wrong on both counts.

Then, just as she began to give up hope, she heard it: the selkies' singing, carrying sweetly over the waves. She couldn't make out the words, but Ceana recognized the melody as if it were the voice of one of her own sisters. She turned towards the sound, speeding up, though the sky was already dark and she normally would start looking for a place to sleep at this point. If she could find the selkies tonight, a bit of weariness would be worth it.

The selkies' song ended before Ceana could locate the singers, but she had her heading now, and she continued on it as swiftly as she could, sending up a hopeful prayer each time she surfaced for air: *Dèanadair, let me find them! Let this be the night!*

Then came the storm. With the sky already so dark and her focus fixed on seeking signs of the selkies, she didn't notice the clouds gathering. But she felt the shifts in the water as the air and winds changed, sensed the vibrations as the first drops fell—and when she swam to the surface to investigate, she poked her face up into a deluge so dense she wondered for a moment if she were still underwater.

She managed to get a breath anyway and then dove beneath the waves again. Would the selkies be out in such weather? Would they seek the shelter of a cliffside cave? Or would they be rushing towards open waters and the storm's edge as fast as they could go?

The shore seemed more likely, so she tried to angle in that direction. But as the storm swirled up ever-shifting currents and the waves caught her up one moment and pushed her deeper down the next, she found that it was all she could do to keep moving. There was no question of searching now. Only of survival.

She struggled on through the waters, searching now not for the selkies but simply for any sign of shelter or any break in the storm. Eventually, as she surfaced once again for a damp breath, she caught sight of a looming mass off to the right that looked like the cliffs along Atìrse's shores. Perhaps there she'd find some shelter—could find a cave or cove in which the winds and waves would be less fierce. She could see a hint of something there, a bit of light—a Tùr-Faire, maybe, or a sheltered fire.

Ceana turned towards it, only to immediately realize her mistake as the currents swept her up, speeding her towards the rock wall. She had no time for prayers other than a wordless plea for help; she struggled free of the first current only to be caught by another. She tried swimming against the flow, but only managed to hold her place for a few minutes. She wasn't the only thing caught in the currents; she could see debris from what looked like a wrecked fishing boat scattered through the waters.

Her lungs began to burn, and she surfaced for air. She'd only just taken a breath when another wave crashed down on her, driving her below the surface. The next moment, something hard and heavy smacked into her, forcing nearly all the air she'd just taken in back out of her lungs. She frantically tried to swim free, but something had tangled round her, tightening with each movement. Ropes, she thought, attached to the heavy thing, which seemed to be one of the spars off a boat—but that knowledge did nothing to help her free herself.

The waves caught her and the spar and drove them towards the cliffside. Ceana couldn't help a cry of pain as the waters slammed her into the stone and the spar into her. This was it. She was going to die here. Oh, she should've stayed home —

Then she caught a voice amidst the noise of crashing waves and wailing winds: *"Hold on—we're coming for you!"*

Who was coming? Help? *Please, Dèanadair, let it be help!* A moment later, she heard a splash, rapidly followed by two more, as something or someone dove into the water from the cliffs above.

She stilled her struggling, partially in hopes that she wouldn't make her situation worse and half in hopes that if she'd been spotted by an enemy, not a rescuer, she'd go unnoticed. But a moment later, she saw a round figure—another seal?—appear in front of her. It bit at the ropes, and they loosened from around her.

Rescue after all! Ceana tried to swim free, but the weight of the spar still pinned her to the wall, and it hurt just to move. As if sensing this, the seal came up under her, pushing her towards the surface and holding her up so she could at least breath easily. Two others grabbed rope-ends in their teeth and towed the wood away.

Again came the voice, though this time it didn't seem to be directed at Ceana: *"I think she's hurt—be ready to grab her!"* Then the seal beneath her surged upward, pushing her higher. Hands reached down from above, grabbing her round her middle and under her flippers, which turned into cloak-wrapped arms as soon as her feet cleared the water. The hands pulled her up and into a cave, its entrance mere feet above the water's surface. There, they helped her sit up against the cavern wall. One of the hand-owners remained long enough to pat her back a few times as she coughed up the seawater that had made it partway down her throat, and then all rushed back to the cave entrance.

Ceana blinked water away from her eyes, gasping for breath. Her side was a mass of pain that grew worse each time she took in a breath, as bad as when she'd fallen off her horse when she was ten, and any attempt to move her left arm resulted in lightning-bolt agony racing up and down it. The pain so filled her thoughts that for several moments, she couldn't even focus enough to figure out who had rescued her.

But after a moment or two, once she could breathe again and her vision cleared, she managed to look around. A fire glowed at the back of the cave; no doubt that was the light she'd seen from the sea. More important were the people within the cave, now helping their companions out of the water. There were just over half a dozen of them, four women and three—no , four men, she realized, as another scrambled into the cave. Eight, then, plus whoever remained outside. But the important thing was that they all wore sealskin cloaks like the one that hung over Ceana's own shoulders.

If Ceana hadn't been so focused on just breathing normally, she would've broken out in shouts of praise to Dèanadair. Selkies! She'd found them at last! Three of the men and two of the women were garbed like the guards who had come with King Fionntan, and two of these men seemed to have been in the water helping Ceana. The other man and two women looked to be ordinary people—well-off ordinary people, judging from the cut and colors of their clothing, but not guards. She really had been in luck!

Then she caught sight of the final person in the group, and all thoughts of luck vanished from her mind. For standing at the edge of the cave, just free of the water, was King Fionntan himself.

Chapter 9

KING AND STRANGER

Oh no. *Not* King Fionntan. *Anyone* but him. Ceana ducked her head, trying to hide her face and avoid looking in his direction. Why, of all the groups of selkies she could have come across, all the people who could've rescued her, did *he* have to be among them? He was certain to recognize her, and then her plans would be in tatters.

Now that the last of their number was safe from the sea, the selkies gathered around her, though with her head bowed, Ceana could only clearly see their feet and legs. There followed a silent moment in which she had the odd sense that someone was saying something, though she could hear no words. Then one of them—King Fionntan *again*, oh Dèanadair *why?*—knelt before her so she could *just* see his face through her lashes. In a surprisingly gentle voice, he asked, "How fare you, maiden? Were you injured?"

Ceana briefly considered saying no, but the agony that shot through her arm as she tried to bring it up to hide the injury convinced her otherwise. Perhaps, if Dèanadair and the selkies were merciful, they'd at least make the pain stop before they accused her of espionage. So, she nodded, opening her mouth to answer—but no sound came from her throat.

What was wrong with her? She tried again, but all she could manage were a few squeaking noises. She pressed her uninjured hand to her throat, trying to stem this latest wave of panic before she ended up completely swamped.

A grave look came over King Fionntan's face. He glanced back at his companions, and again Ceana had that sense of someone speaking nearby despite the silence. Then he turned to face her again. "Do you understand my speech, maiden?"

Ceana nodded, wondering why he would ask—wasn't he speaking the language of Atìrse? But then her ears caught up with her mind and she realized that he *wasn't* speaking the human tongue at all, though she understood him as clearly as if he were. It was another tongue, similar and yet not the same. But somehow, as the strange words found her ears, their meaning overlaid them.

This must be the selkie tongue, then, the one she'd heard King Fionntan briefly speak to his party at the treaty signing. But how could she understand it? She seized on the question as distraction from both pain and embarrassment. Was it part of the cloak's magic?

King Fionntan's voice interrupted her thoughts: *"And do you understand me still?"*

Ceana started, then winced as the movement added another layer to the web of pain in her side. This time, the words had bypassed her ears entirely and simply formed themselves in her mind. What manner of magic was this? Still, she nodded again.

"That is well." King Fionntan studied her a moment, and Ceana waited to hear the fatal question: "Don't you look familiar?" Or possibly, "Haven't I seen you before?" Or, "How does a human princess have a selkie cloak and knowledge of the selkie language?"

But instead, he asked simply, "Again, maiden, are you injured? Some of my party have knowledge of the healing arts and can tend to you."

Ceana nodded and indicated her side and arm. King Fionntan stood. "Aíbinn, will you aid her? Ealar, Nes, with me. The rest of you, give the lady her space."

The group of selkies obeyed. Most retreated to the far side of the cave; Ceana could feel their eyes still upon her. One of the female guards hurried to the back of the cave to fetch a satchel that had been left there. Meanwhile, two of the male guards, one tall and burly and the other slimmer, but no less dangerous-looking, walked with King Fionntan a little way off from the rest and conversed quietly. Ceana took the opportunity to take a good look at the selkies present. She recognized the larger of the men speaking with King Fionntan as one of the guards who had accompanied him to the treaty signing. No one else looked familiar, though. King Fionntan must have returned to his home and come back out with a different group.

The lady guard, Aíbinn, returned to Ceana's side, carrying the satchel. She knelt on the sandy cave floor, already opening the bag. "Can you move your arm at all?"

Ceana nodded and managed to wiggle her fingers and bring her arm up to a more easily accessible position. Aíbinn nodded, taking Ceana's wrist gently. "I'll need to roll the sleeve up to see if it's broken or just bruised. It may hurt, but if the pain becomes too much, poke me or make whatever sound you can."

Again, Ceana nodded, watching nervously as Aíbinn slid the sleeve of her dress up past her elbow and probed her arm with careful fingers. It *did* hurt, terribly so, but she grit her teeth and squeezed her eyes shut, focusing on Aíbinn's voice: "There's much bruising here, all along the arm. If there is a break, it is not a bad one."

Footsteps came from the direction of King Fionntan and the two guards who'd gone with him. Then someone pressed something that felt like a stone into Ceana's right hand, and a new voice—male, but a bit lighter than King Fionntan's deep tones—spoke. "Hold this, maiden."

Ceana opened one eye to see the smaller of the two guards standing before her. She glanced down at what he had placed in her hand and found looked like a common river rock with a pattern of runes, lines, and dots carved on it. As she watched, the pattern began to glow with a faint blue light. What might this be?

She gave the guard a wary, questioning look, and he seemed to catch her meaning. "It'll do you no harm." He touched the stone's surface briefly, and the lights flickered to green, then back to blue. "It...it ensures you carry no curse that can spread to others."

Did he think she was cursed? *Was* she cursed? Was that why she'd lost her voice? Ceana wished she could ask him, but before she could think of a way to try to do so without words, Aíbinn's fingers pressed down in a particular spot in Ceana's forearm. The pain spiked, and Ceana couldn't help letting out another squeak. Aíbinn paused. "That hurt worse than the rest?"

Once more, Ceana nodded, her breath coming in swift, shuddering gulps. Aíbinn continued to probe the area, more gently now. "There may be a fracture here, but I don't think there's a severe break. I'll bind it to make sure the bone doesn't move out of place and that it doesn't grow worse."

From her bag, she produced bandages and two short, flat rods. With these, she swiftly wrapped Ceana's arm, ending with a long loop that she passed over Ceana's head and neck to form a sort of sling. "There. Let me check your side next—as well as I can in this company." She pressed first with the flat of her hand, then with her fingers, along Ceana's side, twice more finding places that made Ceana squeak in pain. "You may have broken ribs as well, but there's little I can do for that. Does it hurt to breathe?"

She waited until Ceana had nodded, then pulled a stoppered leather bottle from her bag. "Drink this, then. It will help with the pain." She let Ceana take the front of the bottle with her good hand, then helped her hold it up so she could take a few swallows. The liquid tasted like nothing more than weak tea, but as it slipped down Ceana's throat, a soft warmth spread through her, blanketing the pain until she barely noticed it.

Aíbinn pulled the bottle away, wedged the stopper in, and returned it to the bag. "Is that better?"

Ceana managed a weak smile in answer. Aíbinn stood. "Good. I'll talk to the...I will talk to the others and see what's to be done now. You're in no condition to travel on your own; that's certain."

She hurried to the back of the cave to speak with King Fionntan, and the guard who'd given Ceana the rock went with her. A few moments later, as if in response to some unheard signal—or, perhaps, a voiceless command from their king?—several of the group across the way from Ceana joined those in the back. Ceana let her head droop once again, watching the runes in the rock she still held flicker and glow, studying them for any hint of something familiar. If only she'd spent more time with Queen Moireach—if only she'd seen the value in learning something about magic alongside her lessons in statecraft, diplomacy, and how to manage anything from a household to a country! Then perhaps she could figure out the stone's purpose.

At least it didn't seem to be hurting her, whatever it was. The guard had said it only checked for curses, and perhaps he had told the truth. Something about the way he said it, about the way he'd hesitated, made her think it had another function as well. But even if he'd been telling only a half-truth…the ability to detect curses would be a magic well worth bargaining for. If only her own family had thought of it! She would have to remember it when she got home—if she got home.

Time went on. Now that pain no longer consumed her consciousness, weariness began to catch up to Ceana, and she felt her eyelids grow heavy. Still, she forced herself to stay alert. She couldn't fall asleep until she knew what the selkies intended to do with her. To distract herself, she attempted again to form words, but try as she might, she couldn't manage more than a squeak or a moan.

Eventually, as she watched and waited, she noticed the glowing runes turn from blue to green again, but this time they stayed green rather than flickering back to their original hue. A few moments later, King Fionntan and the group he'd been speaking with returned. Once again, he knelt in front of her, and Ceana cringed, waiting for an accusation.

But when he spoke, his voice was as gentle as it had been before—perhaps more so. "Aíbinn tells me that you are not grievously injured, and that you bear no hurt that will not heal. She said that she gave you a draught for the pain as well. Has it helped you?"

Ceana nodded, pushing a half-smile again to show her

appreciation. He smiled in return—a kind smile, Ceana couldn't help thinking; not what she would expect if he suspected her identity—and continued, "I am glad, and I am glad that we could pull you from the sea before you suffered worse. I am Fionntan, ruler of the Daoine Ròin. You have met some of my people already, but I will not weary you with full introductions now. May I know your name?"

Ceana let the smile fade from her face, tapping her throat. King Fionntan just nodded. "I understand. Do you know how to write?"

Would this give her away? But she had to communicate somehow, and even most of the farmers in Atìrse knew the basics of reading and writing, so Ceana nodded.

"That is well." King Fionntan motioned to one of the others—the same man who'd given Ceana the stone—who handed him a wax tablet and stylus. King Fionntan held out the stylus to Ceana. "Will you write out your name on this?"

Well, that was a solution. Between this and how the selkies had reacted to her inability to speak…Did they deal with this problem frequently? Did selkies commonly lose their voices due to injuries or curses or some other cause? She'd have to try to find out. Ceana set the rock aside, took the stylus, and waited for the king to hold the tablet where she could reach it. Then she traced out the false name she and Onora had selected.

King Fionntan turned the tablet to read what she'd written there. "A lovely name. Welcome to our camp, Maid Kenna. May I ask why you travel alone in such weather as this?"

Ceana gestured for the tablet again. Now came the tricky part! She had no way to know how well the story she and Onora had concocted would work, so she'd have to dole it out in bits and pieces, telling no more than necessary. So, in the wax she wrote, *I was lost.* Then, in a sudden burst of inspiration, she added, *I heard the singing and hoped for help.*

A brief, frantic thought seized her: if the selkies had their own spoken language, did it have a written form as well? Had she given herself away by writing in the human tongue? But she could do nothing about it now, for King Fionntan was already reading what she'd written.

He looked up again a moment later. "And help you have found. Now, I think I can guess a little more of your past, if you will allow me to do so?"

Ceana made a "go-ahead" motion. Thankfully, King Fionntan seemed to understand her meaning. "Thank you. Now, do I guess aright that you were brought up on land?"

Without even thinking, Ceana tensed. *How did he* —

But before she could spiral further into panic, King Fionntan's kind voice called her back. "Do not fear to answer, Maid Kenna. There is no shame in however you answer. I—and my people—simply wish to understand how best to aid you."

That was a strange thing to say. Everyone knew selkies couldn't live long on land. But then his words from the disastrous treaty meeting rang again in her head: *kidnappers and slavers*, he'd called her people. And since she couldn't speak, perhaps it would be better to let him make his assumptions and see what she could learn from what he guessed. So, slowly, she nodded.

"I thought as much." A bit of sadness crept into King Fionntan's expression. "And this is your first time transformed, or nearly so, is it not?" He waited for Ceana's hesitant nod, then went on, "You found the cloak hidden away, or else were given it by a family member who said they could no longer use it. Which?"

Ceana held up two fingers—Onora had told her that the most believable lies were mostly true—and again, he seemed to understand, though the sorrow in his look grew. Then he shook it away. "Who in your family gave you the cloak?"

He handed her the slate without being asked, and Ceana didn't hesitate this time before writing, *Grandmother*, and passing it back. He glanced at what she'd written and then nodded. "So, your grandmother gave you the cloak and told you to go to the sea and seek the selkies. Had she or anyone else told you of your nature before that?"

Ceana shook her head. Did he truly not recognize her, then?

He seemed to think her a genuine selkie. She supposed that she did look different now than she had when he'd met her before—face free of faery potions, garbed in a grubby dress rather than royal finery, and with her hair falling out of a braid instead of elegantly pinned up. Hope again rose in her heart. She could salvage this. Perhaps Dèanadair had blessed her after all.

King Fionntan nodded solemnly. "Where was your home, Maid Kenna?"

What to say? She and Onora had originally planned to say she came from the easternmost side of Atìrse. But now...that would almost certainly seem unbelievable. So instead, Ceana gestured south, the way she'd come, and then held up three fingers. With her other hand, she made a tiny circle, hoping Fionntan would catch on that she meant a small village.

"Three days south of here?" A measure of astonishment entered King Fionntan's voice, and the brows of several of the gathered selkies went up. "You are a brave lass indeed, Maid Kenna, to make such a journey alone. But you need not travel further unguided and unguarded. My party returns to Emain Ablach on the morrow, and we would be honored to bring you home—if you will join us."

A blessing indeed! Ceana didn't have to fake the smile she offered Fionntan or the eagerness in her nod. If he was offering her escort to the selkies' home, he must really believe her claims—small wonder, since he'd supplied most of them himself—and she'd suffer no more days of searching and nights of uncertainty.

He returned her smile as he stood. "So be it. Rest well, Maid Kenna, for tomorrow will be your homecoming-day."

Chapter 10
JOURNEY TO EMAIN ABLACH

Ceana slept better that night than she had any night since leaving home. True, her arm and side ached, despite the soothing effects of the tonic Aíbinn had given her. True, the cave floor was hard and rough, even with the blankets the selkies had provided her for cushioning—blankets many of them disdained to use, simply wrapping themselves in their cloaks and lying down by the fire. True, most of the selkies were strangers. But it was warm and dry, and Ceana felt far safer with King Fionntan's people than she had alone, or even when she'd gone ashore the other night. If the selkies learned who she was, there would be trouble. But even the little she had seen and heard of King Fionntan told her that he was a good king, just as her father was, and she had no doubt that his company would match his character.

So, she slept soundly through the night, until she woke the next morning to find that Aíbinn's tonic had worn off and her injuries were once again making themselves known. She groaned and gingerly got up, untangling herself from both cloak and blankets. The fire had died down in the night, but sunshine brightened the cave mouth, and she made her way towards it.

A single guard stood at the entrance to the cave, hand on his sword. Ceana recognized him as one of the two King Fionntan had initially spoken to the night before—Ealar or Nes. She opened her mouth to bid him good morning and ask which he was, but once again, no sound came out.

Why could she still not speak? Ceana sat down on the ledge at the cave entrance, her legs dangling over the edge. The spray from the waves dampened her dress and feet, but she took no notice. True, her inability to speak had helped her yesterday—but would it last? What if she'd stayed in seal-shape too long? What if she could never speak again? What would she do?

Sighing, she turned her focus out over the open sea and the rippling waves. A haze of dawn's pink tones still lingered at the horizon, though the sun was already climbing. Thinking on that, she sent up a silent thanks to Dèanadair that the selkies weren't inclined to rise and set out before the sun.

For some time, she sat there, watching the waves and letting her thoughts flit from one question to another, tracing and retracing steps in case she'd come across something she missed the first time. She barely noticed when the guard turned towards someone coming out of the cave, or when he walked away from his post. But she very much noticed when King Fionntan's voice came from just behind and beside her. "Might I sit by you, Maid Kenna?"

Ceana looked up and nodded, patting the stone beside her. It was kind of him to ask—he was the king; he could sit where he liked. And, of course, that meant she couldn't easily say no to him, even if he was more likely than anyone else here to identify her.

He sat, putting a hand on his sword to hold it up so it wouldn't hit the stone. "How fare you this morning, maiden?"

Ceana shrugged—but the movement hurt arm and ribs alike, making her wince. Still grimacing, she held up a hand and waggled it a bit.

"Ah." King Fionntan gave her a sympathetic grimace. "Your injuries still pain you, no doubt. Hopefully our journey today will not be too much for you. It is not short, and we must complete it today, for there is no good place to rest for the night mid-route. Still, pain is often less in seal-shape than this form, if that is any comfort. And should you find yourself struggling, you need only nudge Aíbinn or me, and we will help you along as we may."

Ceana offered a smile by way of thanks. She hadn't even considered what the journey to the selkies' home from here might entail, but the hope of lessened pain was certainly welcome. Hopefully Aíbinn would give her another draught of the tonic that had helped last night as well.

She and King Fionntan sat in silence a few more minutes. Then, he spoke again. "You said you hailed from a town three days south of here. That is still in Lord Arran's lands, is it not?"

Was it? Ceana thought a moment, trying to gauge her current location in comparison to the maps she'd studied, attempting to remember whose banners had waved in the town where she'd spent a night. Eventually, she nodded. If it wasn't in Lord Arran's lands, it was, at least, close.

King Fionntan's expression grew grave. "I see. In your town, do you believe there were others like yourself and your grandmother? Other selkies?"

Ceana shrugged, then gave him a questioning look, hoping he wouldn't interpret it the wrong way. A selkie on land long enough to bear a child, long enough to become a grandmother, seemed a strange thing. Yet Fionntan seemed to suggest that it might happen multiple times even in a small town.

However, he simply sighed, frustrating her hopes of answers. "I understand. I can hardly expect you to have spotted others when you only just learned of your own heritage. Do not concern yourself with it—but if you remember aught at all, let me know. Will you do that?"

Ceana nodded, managing a smile, which he returned. "Good. I must go now and rouse the others—we have already lingered later here than we often would, so we might rest after the storm—but I will send Aíbinn to you to check on your arm and make sure you have breakfast."

With that, he stood and headed back into the cave. As promised, Aíbinn emerged not much later, carrying her medicine bag in one arm and an oatcake and a portion of dried fruit in the other. She handed the food to Ceana and helped her take another draught of the pain-dulling potion, then unwrapped the bandage she'd applied the night before so she could inspect Ceana's arm. Ceana endured it, focusing on the pleasure of proper food.

After a few minutes, Aíbinn pronounced that Ceana's arm was, as far as she could tell, beginning to heal. She splinted it once more, this time without the sling, explaining as she worked: "It'll do you no good to wear it when you're transformed, and it'll only make it harder to swim. By now, your arm ought to have healed enough to use it gently." Ceana strongly suspected that the royal physician would have disagreed with that, but she had little choice but to trust Aíbinn. All the same, she kept her injured arm close to her chest and supported it with her unbroken one as she waited for the rest of the selkies to gather at the mouth of the cave.

All were assembled before long, though a few were still yawning. At King Fionntan's orders, two of the guards jumped into the sea below. They reappeared some ten minutes later in seal form, and Ceana heard the voice of one of them in her head as she'd heard the king's the night before, declaring the nearby area free of danger.

With that signal, the other selkies followed into the water: first the rest of the guards, and then the ordinary folk. It was a strange thing, watching them. Both times Ceana had transformed up to this point, she had been fully underwater before the change occurred. Yet if she looked closely, she saw that the selkies' cloaks began to gather round them the minute their feet touched the water, and by the time they were halfway under, she could see both seal and human forms at once, one overlaid on the other

She was so caught up in watching that she didn't notice when only she and King Fionntan remained. The king offered a hand to her. "Come, Maid Kenna. The others tell me the waters are calm and clear today; you need not fear returning."

He must have thought she was frightened, not that she'd been too busy staring to think about what else was happening around her. Ceana blushed despite herself, but took his offered hand.

He lifted to her feet with seemingly no effort at all. "Let us join the rest. See, they have made a space for us." He indicated the water below, where Ceana could see that the selkies had indeed moved aside to leave a clear area for people to jump in. "Can you make the jump yourself, or do you need aid?"

Ceana gave him a tentative smile and a shake of her head, hoping he'd understand that she needed no help. He seemed to, for he released her hand and stepped aside to give her room.

Pulling her cloak closer around her, Ceana stepped to the edge of the ridge. Below, little waves made ridges in the waters. It was only a few feet down, hardly any distance at all. She'd jumped off much higher heights when she was a child, free to play along the shores of the sea and the inland lakes. She could do this.

Taking a deep breath and holding it, she stepped off into open air. As her legs hit the waters, a sudden frantic thought occurred to her: what if the cloak failed? What if her drop was too sudden and she was drowned or else exposed before King Fionntan and all these people? But a moment later, she felt the warmth of the cloak enclose her, and her vision cleared, and she became a seal once more.

King Fionntan dove in a moment later, and the company set off. While a few shot away—to scout, Ceana guessed, just as her own father would send outriders ahead when he traveled—the rest assembled themselves, apparently according to some prearranged plan. Ceana didn't even have enough time to worry about figuring out her place or keeping up before they swept her up with them. She found herself positioned at the front of the group between the king and Aíbinn—though she wouldn't have identified the latter had Aíbinn not identified herself via the same strange mental speech that many of the selkies seemed to use. The selkie man who wasn't a guard swam on King Fionntan's other side, with another guard by him. Then came the selkie ladies, and the remaining two guards last of all.

Much to her relief, Ceana discovered that she could still swim well enough. Propelling herself along with her rear fins caused her only a little extra pain, though she feared it would build over time. Steering, which required her front flippers, was another matter. While Fionntan had spoken truly when he said that being in seal-form decreased her overall pain, her left limb responded stiffly and with limited motion, and any movement too forceful overpowered both the pain-dulling draught and the effect of the seal form.

King Fionntan and Aíbinn must have noticed this, however, for they both started helping her along: pressing into her and nudging her on the right path when she struggled to change direction, or sliding partially under her so they could almost "carry" her through the waters. Ceana wished time and again that she could express her appreciation for their help—but try as she might, she couldn't replicate the selkies' mental speech any more than she could mimic their speech the night before.

So, she was left to try to smile—as much as a seal could smile—whenever she caught their eyes and to listen as the others talked—when she could, anyway. She could feel a sort of pressure in her head as if there was sound around her that she couldn't hear, and she guessed that many of the members of the group were talking in a way that didn't include her. She couldn't help wondering, were they doing it on purpose? Or did her false cloak mean she couldn't hear them?

She thought it probably the former, as she could hear others perfectly well, even if they weren't speaking directly to her. King Fionntan, Aíbinn, and the pair on Fionntan's other side seemed to be carefully including her in the conversation, even if she couldn't reply. Sometimes they addressed her directly, but more often, they talked around her.

Listening to them, she soon gathered that Aíbinn was a friend of King Fionntan's as well as one of his guards, and that Aíbinn's elder sister was Lady Mairearad, an advisor to the king—Ceana thought back to the treaty meeting, recalled the lady selkie who had accompanied King Fionntan, and decided that she and Aíbinn did indeed look alike. Aíbinn had a second sister as well, Uaine, and she, too, seemed to be a close friend of King Fionntan. The three of them had grown up alongside the king, Aíbinn explained—or, rather, she and Uaine had, while Mairearad had been old enough that she often watched over the others until all were old enough to look after themselves. They were, in many ways, the closest thing he had to siblings.

The selkie man on King Fionntan's other side spoke little, but from what he let drop and what the others said about and to him, Ceana gathered that his name was Donnchadh, and that he was a poet or bard of some form. She wondered to herself if he had composed any of the songs she'd often heard the selkies singing and resolved to ask later.

The final guard was Ealar, and he had told Ceana to hold the strange stone. He seemed to have some specialized position within the ranks of the selkie guard, though Ceana couldn't quite figure out what. He wasn't a healer—that was Aíbinn's duty—but she thought whatever he did must have something to do with magic or curses.

As they traveled and as she listened, Ceana noticed another oddity in their speech. Like her grandmother and the faeries, they made a distinction between formal and informal address—but either the selkies used the informal far more liberally than Queen Moireach did or else all four of those by Ceana were very good friends indeed. Aíbinn, in particular, used the formal *you* only for King Fionntan and Ceana, and more than once, she seemed to start to use *thou* for King Fionntan, only to change at the last minute, as if remembering that it would be improper to address the king in a familiar manner in public.

On and on they journeyed. Though no one commented on their pace, Ceana couldn't help a sneaking suspicion that she was slowing the group down. She gave thanks that at least she'd traveled on her own so long before meeting the selkies; otherwise she would have had to stop at least a dozen times. As it was, they paused only twice, bobbing at the surface with neither land nor rocks in sight.

Eventually, however, as day crawled towards evening, a familiar shape appeared on the horizon: a large, conical island of craggy rocks and steep cliffs. Ceana had seen it many a time on voyages with her family; Teine-Falamh, it was called. Her father had told her once that it meant *fire-barren*. Once upon a time, it had supposedly been green and fertile, but then Dèanadair had grown angry with the people who dwelt there and smote the land so fire burst up from the ground below and rained down on it from the sky, and everything burned for a hundred years until only glassy rock and ash remained.

Of course, Ceana's mother had later told her that the island was more likely the remains of an ancient flame-mount. Many Tryggestrend adventurers had come across such islands in their adventures—though, she admitted, it was strange that so little grew there after all this time. For that reason, Ceana had always suspected that there was something different about Teine-Falamh. But what the selkies wanted with it, she couldn't imagine—there was no hospitable place upon it.

And yet, as they neared the island, she could hear and sense the excitement and relief growing among her companions. Confirming her thoughts, King Fionntan said to her, *"We are nearly home, Maid Kenna. The island before us is Emain Ablach, and it has been home to the Daoine Ròin for many generations now. It may look unwelcoming now, but do not be deceived—you will find it a pleasant place indeed."*

Ceana could make no reply, so she just nodded as best she could. If she were going to hide a civilization, she supposed a lifeless island said to be cursed by Dèanadair would be as good a spot as any. But how such a life could be pleasant, she couldn't imagine. An unwelcome thought crept in the back of her mind—perhaps she had been blessed indeed to avoid marriage to King Fionntan, if this would have become her permanent home.

They drew closer and closer to Teine-Falamh, and Ceana's doubts grew and grew with every moment they traveled. She couldn't even see a cave such as they'd sheltered in the night before, not even a welcoming shore on which they could climb out. Was this some trap or scheme? Had Fionntan seen through her after all and decided to lure her to some isolated spot where he could leave her to die?

The scouts rejoined the group when they were nearly to the island's shores. Not long after that, the whole group surfaced for a breath. Again, Fionntan's voice entered Ceana's mind: *"Breathe deep; the dive before us is long. But if you follow close by Aíbinn and me, all will be well. Trust me."*

The dive? Oh, if only she had a voice with which to ask questions! But all she could do instead was take as large a breath as she could, then follow as the rest of the selkies dove beneath the waves once more. Down, down, down they swam, until the waters grew dim. To their left was the open sea; to their right, so close Ceana could almost touch it, was the dark stone of the island root.

Then Ceana spotted a faint glow below, so weak that she never would have noticed it if not for the enhanced vision of her seal form. As she drew closer, she realized that it came from the rocks—that there were runes painted and carved *into* the rocks, their placement seemingly random. Had the selkies carved them here? For what purpose?

Nearer still the group came, until suddenly, the selkies darted into what looked like a crevice or cave in the stone. Ceana followed, wondering how much long she could stay under the water before her lungs burst and she drowned.

The crevice led into a winding tunnel, nearly pitch-black. In some places, the walls drew so close together that only one selkie could pass at a time. In others, Ceana swore she could see glowing eyes watching from crevices in the rock walls. But any time she quailed, King Fionntan's voice came to her, reassuring her that all was well and that they would soon be home.

And, gradually, the tunnel widened, and a light appeared up ahead. It shifted grey to green a moment later, as they emerged into what seemed to be a small lake, with the sky and sun visible through the waters above. The group turned swiftly towards that light, and Ceana followed eagerly.

Then they broke the surface, and had Ceana been in human form, she would have gasped. As she'd thought, they swam in a calm, round lake with waters of a brilliant blue-green. The waters lapped on sandy golden shores, which rose up to rolling green hills and what looked like buildings set on and among the hills—many buildings, from what Ceana could tell, and quite a few people in those buildings. Beyond was a green blur, but it held the suggestion of trees.

King Fionntan's voice sounded in her head once more, full of all the pride and love Ceana often heard in her own parents' voices when they spoke of Atìrse. *"Welcome, Maid Kenna, to Emain Ablach."*

Chapter 11
ARRIVAL

Ceana was still marveling at this new land when the rest of the selkies made for the shore. She followed, paddling along at the surface where she could continue to stare. How could such a beautiful place have remained hidden all this time? How had no one found it before now?

She reached the shore a few minutes behind the main group. They had already shifted and were brushing the sand from their clothes by the time Ceana hauled out and her seal-shape fell away into the cloak. Heedless of propriety or anything except the loveliness around her, she rolled onto her back and stared up at the sky, which was a far more brilliant blue than any she'd ever seen before. Dèanadair certainly hadn't cursed this land—if anything, He'd blessed it!

She sat up after a moment or two and looked around. Her earlier guess had been correct; a village—perhaps even a whole city—lay around the lake, fading into a forest almost as vibrant as those in Tìrsheun County, where the woods overlapped with the faery lands of Tìr Soilleir. The buildings looked to be well-made, some of wood and some of black stone, and many people, all garbed in the selkies' distinctive sealskin cloaks, were going in and out and about. Even from here, Ceana could hear the murmur of friendly greetings and friendlier conversations.

After a few minutes of staring, she picked herself up, wincing a little as she jostled her ribs. She'd made it at last to the selkies' home; now came the real work of integrating herself with them and gathering information. It was a good thing they sounded so friendly; she doubted such an isolated location would have an inn, and she could hardly rely on the hospitality of local nobility as her family normally would while traveling. She'd have to see if she could beg lodgings with a kindhearted family, perhaps trading service of some kind for a place to sleep. Of course, how much work she could do with a fractured arm, she wasn't sure.

Perhaps some of the selkies who'd brought her here would have an idea of who to ask. She needed to thank them anyway. Gathering cloak and skirt away from the sand, she made her way up to the dispersing group. King Fionntan, Aíbinn, Ealar, and a few others remained, conversing together, but they stopped and turned as she approached. King Fionntan smiled and addressed her, "Not as forbidding within as it is without, is it, Maid Kenna?"

Ceana laughed at that, then tested her voice. Still nothing but a squeak came out, so she just nodded. Then, to show her thanks, she curtseyed to those there—a deep dip for King Fionntan, and then a briefer one for the others. Straightening again, she paused, trying to think how to signal that she wanted to know where to find room and board.

King Fionntan spoke again before she could come up with anything. "I am glad you think so. Now, I do not doubt that you are weary from travel. Aíbinn has agreed that she and her sisters will host you until long-term accommodations may be found. Before that, though, if you are not yet too tired, 'twould be best if you saw a healer to ensure you have not aggravated your injuries with today's exertions. Is that agreeable to you?"

Ceana nodded again, not even bothering to hide her relief. Solving all her problems at one stroke went far beyond *agreeable*!

"Excellent." King Fionntan turned, beckoning her to join him. "Now, your road lies alongside mine a little longer, so I will see you and Aíbinn to the healer before we part ways."

Ceana could think of no objection, nor could she have made one if she'd thought of it, so she followed as bid. Initially, she tried to stay just a step or two behind Fionntan out of respect, but after he slowed down twice to let her catch up, she gave in and walked beside him. His insistence made her heart and mind race with panic—only a noble ought to have the right to walk beside a king! Did he suspect after all?

Yet, as they walked and he talked, her fears eased. Though the day had just turned to evening, the streets were still full of people, many of whom stopped to bow or curtsey as King Fionntan passed. Even those who did not bowed their heads respectfully. The king returned the courtesy with smiles and, often, with greetings. Ceana couldn't help wondering how he knew so many of his subjects by name. True, the selkies were a much smaller people than Atìrse, but King Seoras hardly knew everyone in the royal city by name, nor did Onora know the inhabitants of the village nearest her castle with such familiarity.

In between these greetings, King Fionntan told her of Emain Ablach's origin. It had, he said, been discovered by Artair, the first king of the Daoine Ròin—though he had not been king when he found it. He had been only a selkie warrior, ordinary save that his seal-cloak and seal-shape were pure white. But he had left his family and band to seek a refuge for them, somewhere where they could dwell safe and separate from the human kingdoms. Long he searched until, following the words of a faery prophetess, he had found the passage in the roots of the fire-mount. He wormed his way through what was then a far tighter tunnel and came at last out into the lake. Then he saw the golden shores and the green hills, and he knew that he had found a good place.

And so, Artair returned for his family and their band, and he fought the band's leader until the rest agreed to follow him. He saw them settled, and then he and a few others set out to draw other bands of selkies to the island, convincing some with words and others with blows. As time went on, some came of their own accord, and eventually they built the town and named Artair king over all the Daoine Ròin. From him was King Fionntan descended, and thanks to him, the seal-folk *were* a proper people, not just a loose collection of wanderers.

His speech left Ceana with as many questions as it did answers. Yet it also brought peace into her thoughts, at least for the moment.

If he suspected her identity, he wouldn't speak like this—not so openly, not with tones so warm. Perhaps, despite their manner of speech, selkies stood less on ceremony than humans did—what she'd already seen would bear that out, as even Fionntan's guards seemed to treat him as a friend as much as they did their king, though they still addressed him respectfully. Or perhaps this was simply his way of showing welcome and hospitality to a stranger.

Friendly though the people were, though, Ceana couldn't help but notice that nearly every adult bore some fashion of weapon. The guards had their spears and knives and sometimes swords, of course, but many who wore no armor or emblem still carried a blade or a spear. In fact, there seemed to be an uncommon number of swordsmen among the common folk. Ceana had thought the guards who came with Fionntan to the treaty signing to be among the elite, or else drawn from the nobility, but now she questioned that guess. And even many of the women wore long knives on their belts, and some of them carried spears as well. Did they fear attack at any moment? Or were they prone to fighting among themselves?

She was still wondering when they reached the healer's shop, which stood just off one of the main thoroughfares, some twenty minutes' walk from the water when you allowed for the time taken up by greeting passers-by. Ceana expected Fionntan to leave her and Aíbinn there, but instead he ushered her into the small main space and rang the bell hanging by the door inside.

Ceana had been in healers' shops only rarely—usually, the royal physician or one of his assistants attended on her—so she looked around with interest. The space was well-lit, with wide windows at the front and on the left wall. Chairs were set against the walls in the front part of the room, while the back wall was entirely taken up by shelves containing all manner of jars, pots, and packets, as well as hanging dried herbs. A work counter separated the two halves of the room, while a curtained doorway in the back corner led to whatever lay beyond.

Through this doorway, there appeared a small, birdlike man. Unlike most of the people Ceana had seen here, he wore no cloak, just a common tunic and hose. Grey speckled his thinning dark hair, and he wore a pair of crystal spectacles perched atop his sharp nose. Upon seeing Fionntan, he made a quick bow. "Your majesty! A pleasure to see you in my shop! What—*oh!*" His gaze lit on Ceana, and his whole expression brightened. "The singing—it was a success, then?"

"Indeed," Fionntan replied. "This is Maid Kenna, who hailed most recently from Atìrse—Arran's territory." He added the last in a meaningful tone. "She was caught in a storm searching for us and suffered some broken bones in her arm and side when she became trapped between wreckage and a rock wall. Lann Aíbinn has tended to her enough for the journey, but I would have you see that all is well and provide what you can to speed her healing." To Ceana, he added, "This is Ninian. He has served as a healer, physician, and apothecary for many years, and there is little he cannot cure. He will tend to your injuries."

"Alongside the usual ministrations, of course?" Ninian asked. Without waiting for an answer, he went on, "'Twill be my pleasure to serve, as always."

"I do not doubt it," Fionntan replied. "As always, do what is needful, and send for whatever payment you require from my treasury. I must be on my way, but Maid Kenna will stay with the Northwaves sisters, and you may pass along any instructions for care to Aíbinn." He turned to Ceana. "I bid you good day, Maid Kenna. It has been my pleasure to meet you and bring you home. If there is aught else you need, or if you recall any others of our kind from your hometown, you may send word to me."

Ceana curtsied by way of thanks and farewell. Fionntan then bid goodbye to Aíbinn and set out with Ealar in tow.

Once he had left, Ninian beckoned Ceana towards the curtained door. "Well, Maid Kenna, come into my treatment room and I will see to these broken bones of yours. Never fear; I don't bite."

Aíbinn sat down in one of the chairs. "Go on. I'll be out here if you have need of anything."

Ceana did as she'd been told, wondering what Ninian had meant by *other ministrations*. Still, perhaps she could ask about her inability to speak—surely a healer would have some idea.

The back room was as bright as the front had been. Cupboards and counters lined the walls, save for one space that held a hard-looking bed and a few chairs. A seal-cloak hung on a hook on the side of one of the cupboards; Ceana assumed it was Ninian's. Perhaps he took it off so it wouldn't get in the way while he worked.

Ninian gestured towards the chairs. "Have a seat, Maid Kenna. I'll first make certain that you're healthy aside from the injuries his majesty told me about, and then I'll take a look at that arm and side of yours. Agreed?"

Seeing no reason to disagree, Ceana nodded. She sat and watched as Ninian pulled a wax tablet and a stylus from a drawer. He set both on the seat next to her. "These should help if you've any questions. Now, let me see what I can see."

For the next fifteen minutes, Ceana followed the healer's instructions as he inspected her eyes and throat, as he pressed his fingers to her wrist and the side of her neck, as he used a reed to listen to her heart. Only once did she protest, when he produced a long needle from a drawer and took hold of her good hand. "Right, I'll just be needing to take a drop or two of blood."

Ceana squeaked in panic and tried to pull back, but he kept a firm grip on her hand and pressed the needle to the ball of her middle finger. "Never fear, lass. You'll come to no harm from this." Setting aside the needle, he squeezed her finger so a drop of blood welled up. "I've a magical test or two that wants doing; they'll tell me if you've any kin in Emain Ablach and ensure there's no curse laid upon you. I do it for all who come from the human lands." He let a few drops of blood fall into the vial, then released her hand and passed her a bit of cotton. "Here you are. Just press that to your finger while I set this aside."

Ceana obeyed, holding the cotton to her finger while Ninian capped the vial. He continued to talk as he set it on one of the counters and pulled bandages and rods from a drawer. "From all

I can tell, you should have naught to worry about. You're a whole and hale lass, far better off than some I've treated. Unless you've suffered other hurt his majesty knew naught about?"

He turned and quirked an eyebrow at Ceana expectantly. Ceana hesitated, debating whether or not to ask about her voice. After a moment, she tapped her throat and made another of the squeaks that seemed to be all she could manage. Then, remembering the tablet, she scratched out, *"Can't talk,"* and held it up for Ninian to see.

"Ah, I should've guessed." Ninian shut the drawer again with an apologetic chuckle. "Sorry, lass. The last few newcomers I treated, they asked someone on the way in. Seems I'm a bit rusty. I'll explain while I have a look at your arms and ribs, eh?"

Ceana nodded amiably; she couldn't exactly protest. Ninian returned to her chair and began unwrapping the splint Aíbinn had made. "You've noticed by now, I'd wager, that you have no trouble understanding our speech, even if it's not the tongue you grew up with. Do I guess aright?"

Again, Ceana indicated that he had. Ninian continued, "Good. Now, no doubt when you were a wee lass, you had to learn to speak the human tongue. That's not so for us selkie folk. We're half of magic, you understand. Our language is given to us, as the faery folk's is to them. For the bairns raised hearing it, it comes in gradually, but you're a full-grown lady, or nearly so—seventeen or eighteen summers, I'd guess?" He finished unwinding the bandage and pushed her sleeve up past her elbow.

Ceana held up five fingers three times, then only two. Ninian gave a satisfied nod, gently probing her arm. "As I thought. How many months 'til you turn eighteen?"

Wincing at the pain, even with the distraction of the conversation, Ceana held up five fingers and then one. He went on, "Six months. And you've transformed how many times in your life?"

She hesitated, wondering if he meant shifting both ways or only one way. As if guessing her thought, he added, "It's seal to not-seal I'm after."

That helped. Ceana did a quick mental calculation and then held up three fingers: once entering the village, once in the cave, and then once this morning.

"Hardly at all, then." Ninian released her arm and went to a different cupboard, from which he removed a jar of what looked like whitish ointment. "Your arm must not have had a bad break; it's already beginning to heal. I'll apply a little of this to speed it along and help with the pain and then wrap you back up. You should be right as rain in a week or so."

Ceana couldn't help giving him an incredulous look. He chuckled, uncapping the jar. "The selkie side of your blood's awake now, lass. You'll find you're a bit heartier and hardier than you were a month ago, and quicker to heal as well. And that brings us back to your question." As he spoke, he applied the ointment to Ceana's arm near the break. "As I said, our language is given to us. But you first put on a cloak as a nearly-grown woman, not a bairn in arms, so all the language you should know is coming in at once, and it's a bit more than your mind can handle."

He finished with the ointment and began re-splinting Ceana's arm. "And, on top of that, the cloak you've got isn't properly your own, which means all the connections don't come in quite right. As you transform back and forth again and again over time, your voice and your human speech will eventually come back. If you want to hurry it along, you can make a point of shifting seal and back at least once per day—but not more than three times in one day, mind you, or you'll make things worse. Once your voice is back, you can change as much as you like, but until then, don't overdo it."

That was reassuring, but a question remained. With one of her arms in Ninian's hands and Ninian standing so close, trying to write would be difficult. Instead, Ceana tapped his arm to get his attention. Then she touched her throat and the cloak round her shoulders, hoping he'd understand her meaning: what about the seal language?

Ninian knotted off the splint. "Never fear; you'll find your voice in our tongue as well, both the spoken form and the cainnt-inntinn—that's the speech of mind to mind. No doubt you heard a bit of that on the way here."

Again, he waited until Ceana confirmed she had before he continued. "There's a slim chance your voice in our tongue come in on its own over time as well." He looped another length of cloth around the arm and then behind Ceana's neck to make a sling. "But if it doesn't, don't fret. Most have to wait until they've a cloak that's properly their own to speak in our language, especially the cainnt-inntinn. Once I finish those tests I mentioned, we can see about getting you yours. Now, which side did you say hurts?"

Ceana indicated her injured side, and Ninian began probing it gently, still talking. "In the meantime, don't worry yourself about it. Most folk here are used to newcomers having to communicate in writing and gesture—and I'd keep mostly to that, if I were you, even after you can speak the human tongue again. There's folk enough here who understand it, but only by necessity, and many who learn it vow not to use it within Emain Ablach except at need."

He lifted his hands and brushed them together as if dusting them off. "Your ribs will heal as well, I should think, though you'd best avoid overexerting yourself until they do. I'll give you some of the ointment I put on your arm; apply it every morning and night for the next eight days. It'll help with the pain and speed up the healing. You can apply it to your arm as well once a day; have Aíbinn help with undoing and redoing the splint. You can remove the splint for a short while to apply the ointment and bathe, but don't keep it off long. And make sure you wear the sling for the next few days, at least, save when you shift. Any other questions?"

Ceana shook her head, offering a thankful smile, and stood. Ninian stepped out of her way and handed her the jar of ointment. "There you are, then. Just come by again in a week so I can see that all's healed properly. Sooner, if anything hurts more than it ought. And remember not to go swimming during storms after this, lass!"

He laughed as he said the last sentence, taking the sting out of the reprimand, and Ceana managed to laugh as well. She pulled her purse from her pocket, intending to offer payment, but Ninian held up a hand as soon as he saw what she held. "No need for that. King Fionntan will pay; he always does, any time a new selkie comes home. Save your coin in case you need it later."

Ceana bowed her head and tucked her purse away again. King Fionntan was a generous ruler, to be sure. She wasn't sure how often this sort of situation came up, but it was a kind action nonetheless, and more than many nobles would have done.

She made her way out into the front room again, Ninian following after. Aíbinn, who'd been lounging in one of the chairs, hastily stood up. "All done?"

"She'll be right in a week or less," Ninian replied. "You did well in your treatment, and you can tend her a little while longer, as I'm told she's staying with you." He briefly repeated what he'd told Ceana about tending to arm and side, ending with an admonition to come to him if anything went wrong. Then, once he'd confirmed that they both understood and that Ceana had no further complaint, he sent them on their way.

Chapter 12
THE SISTERS

Outside, the light had turned golden with evening's onset. Aíbinn set off up the road with a long, swinging stride. "Come along, then, Kenna. I've sent word to my sisters to say I'm home and bringing a guest, so they'll wait on us for dinner."

Ceana hurried along next to her hostess, clutching her jar of ointment. Aíbinn didn't seem to be aiming for speed, but her gait was such that she probably could have left Ceana behind in minutes without even trying. Aíbinn, however, didn't seem to notice, and she was as talkative a guide as Fionntan. As they walked, she pointed out the homes of particular friends of hers and recounted past adventures: explorations of the island and the seas around it, training in the guard, and so forth.

Their path turned upwards, and the buildings, already spread fairly far apart, grew fewer. Ahead, at the top of a grassy hill, a largish stone house came into view. Though well-built, it had the irregular shape of a residence that had originally been far humbler, but had since been expanded. There was no courtyard as Ceana would have expected; rather, the road led right up to the door, and the space around it had clearly been...well, not cultivated into a proper garden, but certainly coaxed into producing far more flowers than there were elsewhere, with paths worn between not-quite-beds and bees buzzing amid the blossoms.

Aíbinn gave no attention to any of this, of course, but strode straight to the door and inside, pausing to hold it for Ceana. "Here we are. I'd guess my sisters are already at table and waiting on us. I'll show you where to wash up and then we can join them."

She guided Ceana to a small room off the entryway with soap

and a basin and pitcher of water. There, she allowed Ceana to wash her face and hands before doing the same herself. Then, she led the way down a hall to a smallish, but well-appointed dining room. The table was already laid with a tureen of soup and a dish of roasted fish.

Though the table clearly seated eight or ten, only four places were laid, and only two currently occupied. Ceana recognized the lady at the head of the table as the selkie noblewoman who had come to the treaty signing, and she fought a new surge of panic. Fionntan hadn't recognized her, but what if this lady did? Yet as she turned to face Ceana and Aíbinn, her face held no horror, no suspicion, not even a hint of recognition, just curiosity.

The second selkie appeared no older than Ceana, perhaps even a little younger. She was fair-haired where her sisters were dark, and though Ceana could see the resemblance between the three, she was also struck by the thought that, in another setting, she might have mistaken this girl for one of her own sisters.

The older of the two stood, pushing her chair back. "Aíbinn, I am glad thou art back safely! Is this the guest of whom thou sent word?"

"She is!" Aíbinn replied. "This is Kenna, once of Atìrse. Kenna, this is my elder sister, the Lady Mairearad."

Ceana remembered just in time to curtsey—after all, she was no princess here, and therefore everyone probably outranked her. No one seemed to take much notice, though, and Aíbinn went on, indicating the younger girl. "And this is my younger sister, Lady Uaine."

Lady Mairearad stepped forward, extending her hands in a gesture of welcome. "Be welcome to our home, Kenna. We are glad to host you as long as you have need. Come, please, and be seated. I've had a spot laid for you next to Aíbinn, as you know her already."

For what seemed the thousandth time that day, Ceana smiled and dipped her head in a nod. She went to the seat indicated and waited until the others had sat before sitting herself and then glancing about for a cue.

Lady Mairearad folded her hands in front of her. "It is our custom, Kenna, to open each meal with a prayer to Dèanadair. I believe this is the custom in the human lands as well?" She waited for Ceana's confirmation, then launched into prayer without preamble. "Maker of all, we gathered here thank Thee for that which Thy hands have provided—for open sky above and fertile ground below and free waters all about and for the food laid upon our table. We thank Thee too for those who prepared the food and those whose company will sweeten our meal. And we thank Thee always for Thy protection over those who go forth from our land, for Thy laying of the path to bring them safely home again. In all these things, we praise Thee; so may it be."

Aíbinn and Uaine echoed the last phrase, and Ceana mentally did the same on reflex. As Lady Mairearad rose once more and began to serve out the soup, Uaine leaned forward. "Aíbinn, how went thy journey? How was the singing?"

"Well and well." Aíbinn passed a bowl of soup to Ceana and claimed the next for herself. "We kept further out from shore than we sometimes do, but we were in the right place for Kenna to hear us and find us. Were you all caught by the storm a few nights ago?"

"We saw it building in the distance, but it passed us by," Uaine replied. "It struck thy company, then?"

"Late in the night of the singing, yes. Else we would have been home sooner—we had to spend the night in a sea-cave on the Atìrsen shore so we would be sheltered. But it's well we did so, or Kenna wouldn't have found us."

She launched into an account from her perspective of the events of the night when Ceana had found the selkies: of how two of the other guards had spotted a seal figure being tossed about and battered by the waves and wreckage, how they had heard the cry for help amid the storm, and how Fionntan had been the first to leap into the waters to save the stranger.

Here Lady Mairearad interrupted to *tsk* in the same way that Sorcha often did when she thought a younger sibling was being foolish. "Our king needs to learn more caution. He has guards about him for a reason. It wouldn't do for him to be hurt or worse when others could take the risk." But though her words were critical, she spoke fondly.

"Thou canst tell him that—again." Aíbinn laughed. "I doubt he'll listen to you any more than he ever has on that matter. As I was saying, he freed her from the ropes while Nes and Tam pulled the wreckage away. Then he had to get her into the cave, but the rest of us could help with that. Once he found she couldn't speak, he had me treat her arm while Ealar ensured she was no spy."

Ceana paused mid-sip of soup, glancing at Aíbinn, who seemed not to notice. How had Ealar confirmed she wasn't a spy? Had that been the true purpose of the stone he'd asked her to hold? Perhaps it did more than just detect curses—perhaps it didn't detect curses at all. The Daoine Math couldn't lie outright, but Ceana had never heard of any such limitation upon the selkies...

Aíbinn finished her tale while Ceana was still thinking, and by the time Ceana focused again, conversation had shifted to discussion of people she didn't know as the sisters traded news of this and that friend or acquaintance. Ceana did her best to follow what they said anyway, but without a voice and the ability to ask questions, she found herself struggling. And now that she was indoors with half a proper meal in her stomach, the last week of long days had started to creep up on her, and she struggled more and more to pay attention to anything in particular.

The meal at last came to an end, after soup and fish and honeyed fruit to finish it all. By then, weariness had overwhelmed everything, even hunger, and she knew it showed. She knew, too, that it was rude of her to let it show so clearly—to nod over her plate and to periodically stare off into nothing when her mind lagged too far behind her body—but she couldn't help it.

Her hosts must have noticed, for when the plates had been cleared by a rosy-cheeked maid, they exchanged a look, and Ceana again felt the pressure of an unspoken conversation happening around her. Then Uaine pushed her chair back and smiled at Ceana. "I'm sure you're tired after your journey. If you'd like, I can

100

show you where you can bathe while a room is prepared for you. Otherwise, you can join us in the withdrawing room upstairs."

A bath! A bath sounded *heavenly*. While she didn't feel nearly as grimy as she'd expected after a week with no chance to wash—perhaps because she'd spent so much of it in the water—it had still been far too long. Ceana held up one finger and nodded, trying not to let too much of her eagerness show and knowing she was failing as much as she'd failed to conceal her weariness through the meal.

"Come with me, then." Uaine gestured for Ceana to follow her out into the hall. From there, Uaine led the way down the hall, pausing to fetch a towel, a washcloth, and soaps from a cabinet. As they walked, Ceana carefully pulled her necklace off and tucked it in her pocket, making sure to stay precisely behind Uaine as she did.

After a few minutes, they reached a descending flight of stone steps. This ended in a small space with passageways leading left and right, lit by gold-glowing stones set here and there in the walls. The passages looked as if they were at least partially natural stone, rather than something constructed.

Uaine indicated the left passage. "If there's ever trouble and you need to get into open waters quickly, that way leads to our bolt-hole. It's shorter than the main tunnel, don't worry—though sometimes it leads into the Muir Soilleir instead of the mortal waters, so you have to be careful when you come out the far side."

Muir Soilleir—like Tìr Soilleir? Was this the home of the sea-faeries? Ceana supposed it must be, and she was too tired to ask further. In any case, Uaine had already turned to the right and announced, "This way is our bathing chamber."

Ceana trailed after, noticing that, as they walked, the air grew warmer and moister, and the stone walls and floor of the tunnels glistened with moisture. A moment later, they emerged into a mid-sized cavern whose walls were thickly set with the glowing stones Ceana had noticed in the passageway. In the center of the room lay an irregularly shaped pool of steaming water at least twice as large as Ceana's bed at home. From somewhere came a sound of burbling as if from a fresh spring. Benches were carved into some of the cavern walls, and steps had been shaped leading into the pool.

Uaine set the supplies she'd been carrying on one of the benches. "We're fortunate enough to have a hot spring under our home, so the water is always warm. You can stay and soak as long as you need; Aíbinn always says it makes her feel better after she's been traveling or training hard. Do you need help with your dress?"

Ceana hesitated, then nodded. Undressing would be difficult with only one arm, after all. She couldn't help wondering, though, at the fact that Uaine offered to help her herself. A noble in Atìrse would have left that task to a servant—if they even came near enough a bathing chamber to offer. The household staff must be small indeed, unless this was some particular selkie custom.

She'd have to ask later—not having a voice was *so* inconvenient! For the moment, she pulled the sling off from over her head and set it aside. Next, she removed her cloak, pushing it over her head with one arm and hoping she wasn't doing something frightful— Ninian was the only selkie she'd ever seen not wearing a cloak. But when it fell to the floor, Uaine only commented "There's a hook there if you prefer to hang your cloak. Some people don't like folding them, since it makes the cloaks easier for someone to grab. That would never happen here, but it's easier to maintain a habit than restart it."

Easier to steal—was that a common problem, then? Ceana felt the answer should be obvious, but she was too tired to fully consider the implications just now. So, she hung the cloak up and picked at the laces on her kirtle until Uaine could help her pull it over her head. Then Uaine folded the kirtle and set it aside while Ceana sat down to remove her shoes and socks. Last of all, Uaine helped her out of her shift. "Do you want me to undo the splint now?"

Ceana thought a moment, eyeing the knots, and then shook her head. She could probably remove it herself, and it would be better to keep it on as long as possible. Uaine nodded and picked up the stack of Ceana's clothes, minus her cloak. "I'll take these upstairs to be washed, then —"

The necklace! Ceana hastily shook her head and held up a hand, hoping her expression looked less like panic and more like "Don't trouble yourself." She then pointed at herself, waggling a finger to, she hoped, indicate that she'd take them later.

Uaine's lips pursed. "It's no trouble, really—I'll send a servant down with something for you to wear as soon as they're done cleaning up dinner."

Oh bother! Having to communicate without words when she was this tired was *extremely* unfair. Desperately, Ceana mimed putting her hands into pockets, then rubbed her fingers together as if there were a coin between them.

Understanding dawned on Uaine's face. "Oh, is your purse still in your pocket?"

Ceana nodded once, then gave her a hard look. Uaine hesitated. "And...other things? Personal things?"

Again, Ceana nodded. On a stroke of inspiration, she gave an exaggeratedly furtive glance back and forth, then mimed writing. Uaine's brow furrowed. "What...oh. Do you have a private diary, then?" She set the pile back down. "We'd not look at it, I promise, but if it makes you more comfortable, I'll leave these so you can get what you need from them. And I'll still send someone to bring you something clean to wear. I think most of my things will fit you, and if not, you can make do with something of Mairearad's. Will you be all right on your own?"

Ceana smiled reassuringly, picked up soap and cloth, and stepped into the water. As she did, she couldn't help gasping at the warmth. Uaine had said it was a hot spring, but Ceana hadn't quite believed her until just now. She made her way deeper in and found that someone had carved a ridge like a seat all the way around the pool except by the steps. She sank onto it with a contented sigh, letting her eyes close. Imagine having such comfort every time one took a bath!

She must have dozed off then, with the water lapping around her and her broken arm propped up on dry-ish ground, because the next thing she knew, there came the sounds of footsteps in the hall outside, followed by the sound of someone knocking on stone. Ceana forced her eyes open and glanced towards the door. The maid who'd cleared the table was peeking around the doorway, a bundle of white clutched to her chest. As Ceana caught her eye, she smiled apologetically and asked, "May I enter? My lady Uaine sent me with clothing for you."

Ceana nodded, sinking herself a little deeper into the water, and gestured to the bench by where she'd hung her cloak. The maid hurried in, deposited her bundle, and made for the door again, pausing only long enough to confirm that Ceana didn't need anything else—not that Ceana could have communicated it if she did. Once the maid had gone, Ceana turned to the business she'd come here for. Washing herself one-handed was tricky at times, but she managed well enough. And after she'd unwound the splint and deposited both bandages and sticks at the pool's edge, she decided that her arm did indeed hurt less than it had six hours ago.

In any case, she managed to finish her ablutions and dry herself off without too much difficulty, though she carefully avoided using her injured arm more than she could help. Then she wiggled into the linen shift that had been left for her and replaced the necklace around her neck. She draped her cloak over all, so as to hide the necklace, and wrapped the sling around her arm and neck to give her broken limb some support. The towel and cloth she hung up, and the soaps she left on the bench, hoping that was correct—she'd never had a bath without either servants or sisters on hand to make sure things were put back in their proper places.

At last, she picked up her pile of clothes and made her way up the steps. The house was quiet now, the hall only dimly lit by the evening light filtering through the windows. Distantly, Ceana could hear the sound of someone talking—one of the sisters, she thought—and, lacking any other direction, she headed towards it.

Following the voice, it didn't take her long to find her way upstairs to the second floor and what she guessed to be a guest room. Aíbinn and Uaine were within, Aíbinn helping a maid finish making the bed and Uaine sitting off to the side. Ceana stopped in the doorway and squeaked to let them know she was here.

Uaine immediately turned and jumped up. "Oh! You're done already; we thought you'd be a little longer, or else we would've sent someone for you. We're just finishing here. How was your bath?"

Ceana smiled and then held up her injured arm. Aíbinn let her side of the coverlet fall. "You need re-splinted, don't you? Uaine, help Ailis finish while I see to Kenna's arm. Kenna, sit down. Where'd I put the ointment?"

Uaine and Ceana both hurried to do as Aíbinn had said. A moment later, Aíbinn came to Ceana's side, splinting materials in one hand and ointment in the other. She pushed Ceana's sleeve up and began rubbing on the ointment in a businesslike manner. "This room is yours as long as you're staying with us. Uaine is just next door, I'm across from her, and Mairearad is in the big room at the end of the hall." She finished with the ointment and began wrapping Ceana's arm. "If you need anything, just ask. Or get us, at least, and we'll figure out what you need. Tomorrow we'll have something you can use to communicate better."

Ceana offered a grateful smile in lieu of thanks. No mention of the sisters' parents! And no sign of them at dinner either! Was Mairearad mistress of this house, then, as Onora was mistress of her castle? They didn't seem well-off enough to have multiple residences, nor did the selkie island seem large enough for that. Something must have happened to their parents, then. She'd have to at least find out—without asking—if they were still alive and simply absent or if they were dead. Of course, not being able to speak did reduce the risk of making a carelessly callous comment ...

Aíbinn tied the ends of the splint tight. "There! If you'd like, you can borrow a robe and join us in the withdrawing room, since it looks as if the bed is finished. Or you can stay here if you'd rather rest."

Ceana shook her head and indicated the room and then, more specifically, the bed. She'd have time to sit with them and try to glean information later; tonight, she needed sleep. And Onora had warned her that it wouldn't do to push too much immediately; better to leave a little time for people to grow comfortable with her.

"We'll leave you be, then." Aíbinn stepped back. "As I said, let one of us know if you need anything."

"Yes, do," Uaine added. "If you care to break your fast with us in the morning, Mairearad and I eat a little after the second bell. Otherwise, you can simply go to the kitchens as Aíbinn does when she leaves for guard duty; we'll make sure Cook knows you may drop by. Oh, and there's a robe for you in the wardrobe; in the morning, we can find you some proper clothing."

With that and a flurry of other reassuring comments, Aíbinn, Uaine, and the maid, Ailis, departed, leaving Ceana alone. Ceana waited until the door shut, then went straight to the bed and crawled under the covers. So far, the selkies had been astonishingly welcoming. Now she could only pray that their friendliness continued—and that she could keep her cover long enough to do what she'd come here to do.

But she needed rest before she could do anything else. And so, with a tired sigh, Ceana closed her eyes and let weariness overcome her once again.

Chapter 13
SETTLING IN

When Ceana woke, the first thing she heard was hard rain drumming on the roof. When she went to the window and cracked the shutters, all was wet and grey and cloudy without. Praise Dèanadair that she'd found the selkies when she did! This wasn't half as bad as the storm had been, but she still wouldn't have liked to be out in it.

She shut the window again after a few minutes of watching the rain. With the sky so dark, she had no way of knowing the time. Were her hosts already up and going about their day? Or had she woken before them? She'd heard no bells to tell her which it might be; she'd just have to look around the house to see who or what she might find. So, she retrieved the robe Uaine had left for her and wrapped it around herself, then put her cloak on over that. Thus garbed, she slipped out of her room.

Where to go from here? She recalled Aíbinn's description from the night before: the sisters' bedrooms were all to the right. She'd check there later if she didn't find anyone at breakfast. Across from her appeared to be another spare room—no surprise there, but no help either.

To the left, then. She passed the stairs and peered in the door at the far end of the hall. Here, she found a large, open room with a double-sided hearth in its center. Heavy folding curtains hung in line with the hearth, gathered on either side of it, ready to divide the room into smaller sections for warmth or privacy. On the nearer side of the room were worn and comfortable-looking chairs and couches clustered around the fireplace, along with instruments set on stands, a spinning wheel in the corner, and a small bookcase near one window. Tapestries on the walls depicted scenes Ceana recognized from ancient legends and the priests' teachings; when Ceana inspected one of these more closely, she found the work to be of mixed quality. Perhaps it had been made while the sisters were still learning their craft.

The far side was mostly empty save for a few more chairs; most likely, it was spare space to be used as needed. In any case, Ceana guessed this was the withdrawing room Uaine had mentioned the night before. More importantly, it held neither people nor breakfast, so further investigation would wait.

With that thought, Ceana returned to the steps and headed downstairs. When she poked her head in the dining room, she found it empty, the table unlaid. Had she missed breakfast? Or was she up so early that the servants hadn't had time yet to set places?

The kitchen would be the best place to find out. Ceana continued down the hall until it ended in a set of doors, from which came voices: one singing, two others talking. The doors were slightly ajar, so Ceana nudged them open and stepped inside.

As she expected, she found the kitchen within. A massive wooden table dominated the center of the room, and here two women sat, discussing what sounded like plans for the next week's menu and what supplies they needed, occasionally referencing something written on a pair of slates. A third woman bent over a basin against the far wall, singing to herself as she washed dishes. None of them, Ceana noted, wore cloaks. Were they not selkies? Or had they merely removed their cloaks so they could work more easily?

None of the women seemed to have noticed Ceana yet, so she took the opportunity to survey the rest of the room. A great hearth took up most of the near wall, aligning—she suspected—with both the fireplace upstairs and the one in the dining room. An oven was set into the wall next to it, though Ceana could only just make out the opening from where she stood. Racks holding barrels, baskets, and bags of foodstuffs and supplies, along with pots, pans, and other cookware, lined two of the walls, interrupted occasionally by windows and smaller tables to provide additional workspace.

In the far wall were more windows and, near where the dish-maid worked, a small door, currently propped open to admit fresh air. Rain splashed on the doorstep and on the plants in the garden beyond—tidier than the one in front, but also clearly more utilitarian. Apparently, there wasn't enough wind to carry the rain into the house. Next to the door, hooks on the wall held three sealskin cloaks, answering the question she'd pondered a moment ago.

As Ceana stared, one of the women at the table happened to glance up. Her gaze met Ceana's, and she immediately broke off what she'd been saying. "Lass, how long have you been standing there? You must be our new guest. Kenna, isn't it?"

Ceana nodded, and the woman stood. She was decidedly round and a bit red-faced, with a friendly smile and warm, dark eyes. Her hair was swept up under a neat cap that matched her light blue dress, but a few brownish curls poked out around the edges. "I'm Dorie, the cook here; you can call me Dorie or Cook as you like. Have you had breakfast yet?"

Ceana shook her head. Dorie clucked her tongue. "Well, that won't do. Sit yourself down and I'll find a bit of something for you." She hopped over the bench and hurried towards one of the rack-lined walls.

Ceana obediently sat down at the side of the table nearest the door. She glanced at the other maid and was surprised to see the same girl, Ailis, who'd cleared the table and helped make the bed yesterday. This must be a truly small household indeed, if they made no distinction between kitchen maids and housemaids—or perhaps last night, they'd simply had to make do with the staff on hand?

Ailis offered Ceana a smile in return for her curious stare. "Lady Mairearad's already gone out, if you were looking for her—she had a meeting with his majesty at his keep—and Lann Aíbinn left for her rotation long before that, but Lady Uaine is still at home and said you might find her in her chambers once you've broken your fast."

Well, that answered a few questions. Ceana smiled gratefully back at Ailis. A moment later, Dorie returned, bearing a wooden plate in one hand and a mug in the other. "Here we are, lass. No porridge left, and it'd have gone cold by now anyway, but there's scones still, and one of my scones with a pear and a bit of cheese is a fine way to start the day all the same."

She set the dishes before Ceana and returned to her conversation with Ailis, pausing only to slide a jar of honey over to Ceana. Ceana didn't hesitate but tucked in eagerly. Dorie was right—a scone drizzled in honey was nothing to complain about. Mirren certainly would have approved. As for the rest of the meal, the pear was perfectly juicy and paired very well indeed with the hard, flavorful wedge of cheese. To wash it all down, Dorie gave her a cup of cold tea that tasted faintly of basil and berries.

Ceana stayed a little while after finishing her food, listening to Dorie and Ailis talk. But at last, she carried her dishes over to the maid at the washbasin and then headed back into the main part of the house to explore a bit more before she joined Uaine.

Investigating the rest of the ground floor didn't take long. Several doors were locked, but beyond the unlocked ones she discovered a receiving room hung with tapestries of much finer make than those upstairs, a crafting room that held a loom, another spinning wheel, and racks for fabric, yarn, thread, and supplies, as well as a table and assorted chairs, and another guest bedroom, this one larger than those above. She guessed there had to be a study behind at least one of the locked doors; surely even a selkie noble needed a private place to work and meet with people. The other locked rooms she felt less certain of, but she supposed she'd figure out their use eventually.

With nothing more to explore, she made her way upstairs to Uaine's room. The door was open, but she rapped on the frame anyway. Uaine's voice came from within. "Come in!"

Ceana stepped inside to see Uaine kneeling by a chest of clothes. Nearby, the wardrobe doors stood open. A few dresses had been laid out on the bed, all fairly simple kirtles, but clearly well-made.

Uaine excitedly beckoned Ceana over. "Oh, good, you're up! Have you had breakfast yet?" She paused, waiting for Ceana to nod, then went on, "I've been looking for things that might fit you—washing day isn't until tomorrow, and you can't go about in a shift and a robe all of today."

No, she certainly couldn't, especially not if she wanted to start finding things out. Ceana laughed and was pleased to find that she could do so aloud. Then she tapped her arm in its sling, making a questioning face.

"Your arm? Never fear; Aíbinn taught me how to wrap a splint." Uaine twisted so she fully faced Ceana instead of looking over her shoulder. "Is it bothering you?"

Ceana scrunched up her face and fluttered her good hand in a so-so motion. The pain had decreased since the day before, but it still hurt enough that she'd welcome another application of Ninian's ointment.

Uaine stood. "I'll take care of it in a moment. Do you like any of the things I've laid out? If I'm to redo your splint, I may as well help you with your clothes at the same time."

A good point, especially since it would be harder to put on the splint with a sleeve over it. Ceana turned to look at the dresses laid out on the bed. All three were in good condition, though clearly not new. One was a pale rose pink with a square-cut neck, trimmed in white and darker pink. The second was of sky-blue material, trimmed and decorated in green and yellow, with a slightly finer cut. The last was forest green with mint trim, cut a bit differently than the others and with more wear along the hem. Perhaps it had originated with one of the other sisters instead of Uaine?

Her host still waited for an answer, so Ceana indicated the blue dress. Uaine scooped it up, along with a stack of what Ceana guessed were the proper underlayers. "Oh, lovely—I thought you'd like that one. It looks like just the shade for you. Come along, then."

She bustled Ceana back to her own room, where she first tended to Ceana's arm. Her hands were less deft at wrapping the bandages than Aíbinn's had been, but she managed. Then she helped Ceana change out of her nightgown and into a fresh shift and kirtle, pausing in between so Ceana could apply ointment to her side. Ceana couldn't help wondering again *why* Uaine would take on such a task—she was a noblewoman, as far as she could tell, and she had staff. Even a noble without much money usually wouldn't stoop so far. Of course, Ceana and her sisters had occasionally helped each other when they wanted time away from their servants' watchful eyes, but that was different—they were family.

Once Ceana was dressed again and had draped her cloak back over her shoulders—the one part of the process Uaine seemed unwilling to assist with—Uaine pulled a small slate and a lump of chalk from her pockets. "Before I forget, here's something to make up a little for your not being able to talk. Mairearad and Aíbinn are planning to find a tablet for you before they come home—one for you to keep, not just to borrow—but these should do in the meantime. I'm sorry we didn't have something better; we haven't hosted a newcomer since Màirearad took over the household, and we weren't as prepared as we thought."

Ceana took both chalk and slate gratefully and scratched out her reply: *"Thank you. More than good enough."*

"Oh, good." Uaine stepped back towards the door. "And once your voice is back, you can talk to me, even if you don't have your own cloak yet and have to use the human language—unless you're planning to vow never to speak your old tongue again. I know some people do."

Ceana hastily shook her head, unable and unwilling to keep the alarm from her expression. That would be a foolish vow indeed! Though, she couldn't help wondering what could drive someone to make such an oath. Ninian had mentioned it as well; he'd said that many selkies who learned the human tongue swore not to speak it on the island. She could understand why they wouldn't often use it; they'd have little reason to do so, save when—apparently—they collected lost partial-selkies who couldn't speak the selkie tongue. But why swear it?

All questions she'd have to find answers to later. But right now, Uaine was talking again. "Oh, good. It wouldn't help with Mairearad and Aíbinn—they both took the vow—but it would be something for you, and it would let me practice without leaving the island." She turned and made for the door. "You're free to do as you wish—to explore the house or the town or just to keep to yourself. I'm sure this will take a great deal of adjustment. But if you wish to join me as I attend to my tasks for the day, I'd be happy for the company."

Ceana didn't even have to think about that. She followed Uaine at once; hopefully, shadowing her, she'd learn something. Even if she didn't, it would be better than wandering around with no real direction.

And so, Ceana spent the rest of that morning and much of the early afternoon trailing after Uaine. Most of Uaine's tasks were familiar to Ceana: overseeing the servants and setting them their work for the day, taking inventory of goods and foodstuffs to determine what needed to be replenished, discussing menus for the next few days with Dorie, keeping record of household accounts, and so on. Ceana had learned them all the same way she'd learned statecraft, history and geography, etiquette, and the like.

The fact that *Uaine* was responsible for all this, rather than Mairearad or Aíbinn, did strike Ceana as a bit odd, especially after Uaine mentioned that she'd just turned seventeen a few months ago. When she asked about it over lunch, which they took in the kitchen, Uaine explained how Aíbinn's duty in the Guard kept her out of the house most of each day, while Mairearad had her ever-growing responsibilities in the king's court. And so, as a result, the household fell more and more to Uaine.

"Not that I mind," Uaine was quick to add. "If it were really too much for me, Aíbinn would resign from the Guard. King Fionntan offered to let her off when Mairearad's duties started keeping her away from home more—it's only the men who are required to serve a turn in the Guard, after all, and Aíbinn had finished two of her three years anyway. But Aíbinn likes being in the Guard, and the servants help if I'm overwhelmed or uncertain. Besides, I'll be doing this sort of thing most of my life, more than likely. It's good to start now."

Ceana nodded approvingly at this, even as she ran through the implications of Uaine's words. She noted the way Uaine had almost left off King Fionntan's title—apparently, Aíbinn hadn't exaggerated when she said her family was close friends with the king. She caught, too, the hint of resignation in Uaine's voice as she spoke the last sentence. It hadn't sounded quite like a complaint, merely a suggestion that running a household wasn't the life Uaine would choose for herself if she had the option.

Ceana commented on neither of these, however. Instead, she wrote down a different question: *Do many women serve in the Guard?*

She held the slate up so Uaine could see, and Uaine thought a moment. "Some do. Perhaps a fifth of the Guard is made up of women, maybe a little less. Aíbinn could tell you better than I. The king tries to make sure that their duties are mostly near the island, though he usually has at least one lady in his honor guard any time he leaves Emain Ablach. Is it truly not so in Atìrse?"

Ceana shook her head and quickly scribbled her reply: *No. Only men. Elsewhere, maybe.* True, there were women who knew how to fight as well as a man could, and King Seòras had ensured that all of his daughters learned the basics of how to defend themselves. Ceana had even heard of female soldiers and guards in other countries. But never in Atìrse.

Uaine sighed. "You're fortunate, then. Athair used to say that the chief reason women were originally allowed in the Guard was that there were too few men to refuse them. That was in the *very* old days, though, and things are better now. Or they have been better, at any rate." A look of worry flitted across her face, but she shook it away and pushed a smile. "You don't want to hear about politics, though, and I think we're both nearly done with our meal. We'll need to be back to work in a moment."

Oh, but Ceana *did* want to hear about politics! All the same, she wasn't sure if she could press the topic without giving herself away, so she returned her attention to her meal. She'd ask later, when the time was right.

The right time didn't come at any point that day. But in the late afternoon, when Uaine's duties were mostly done and only her weaving remained, Ceana finally found an opportune moment to ask something else she'd been wondering about. She wrote her question out on the slate and then held it up, squeaking to catch Uaine's attention.

Uaine turned, skimming what Ceana had written. "A safe place to practice seal-shape? You could go out to the lake—no one would take any notice of you. People go in and out there all the time. But since it's so wet and dreary, you could use the entrance to our bolt-hole instead. I told you where it was last night, I think, but I should show you properly anyway."

She once again led Ceana down the stairs, this time taking the left turn at the bottom. This side of the hall continued to slope downwards for some distance, and here and there, Ceana noticed other openings off of it—storage areas, Uaine explained. At last, they came to a cave-like stone chamber, about the same size as the room for the hot spring. In the center glimmered a pool of still, dark water a bit smaller than the one for bathing.

"This is it." Uaine gestured at the pool. "It's very, very deep, and there's a tunnel partway down that leads out. I think I told you last night, though, that sometimes it exits into the Muir Soilleir, so I'd not try to take it until your arm is better and you're more used to the waters around here. But the pool is wide and deep enough for a little exercise, at least. Oh, and make sure you take your sling off before you start. Do you need anything else?"

Ceana shook her head, then held up a finger. On her slate, she wrote, *"Muir Soilleir—faeries? Like Tir Soilleir?"*

"Yes, exactly so. I've heard Muir Soilleir is more dangerous because it's less predictable, though I don't know if it's true. It's always land-dwellers who've said it." Uaine let out a little laugh. "Just don't go down the tunnel out by yourself and you'll be fine."

That hadn't been Ceana's worry, but disillusioning Uaine would be more effort than it was worth. *"In Tir Soilleir now?"*

Uaine pursed her lips, fidgeting with the edge of her belt. "Yes? Emain Ablach is in both worlds at once. I don't really know how to explain it, but if you come in through the sea tunnel, you find yourself here, but if you managed to climb the outside of the mountain and come down that way, you wouldn't find us. In any case, that's why we don't have to worry about returning to the sea every day while we live here. We can stay on land for a week or two at a time if we want to, and someone in Tir Soilleir proper can stay ashore for months or years."

Well, that was a relief. No one would question it if Ceana didn't go down to the sea every day. She supposed she ought to have guessed as much, since Uaine made no indication that *she* intended to go out. *"Thank you,"* she wrote. *"No more questions."*

"I'll leave you to it, then." Uaine turned to go. "When you're done, you're welcome to join me in the workroom. I'll most likely be weaving until dinner."

She vanished back into the hall. Ceana waited until her footsteps faded, then removed the sling from around her neck and set it aside. She walked to the edge of the waters and peered down. The dim light revealed nothing at all of what might lie within, nor did there seem to be any indication of a slope or anything other than a straight drop.

Ceana hiked up her skirt, then sat down on the edge of the pool, wrapping her cloak around herself, and let her legs hang down into the water. It was almost bitterly cold, as if drawn from the wells of winter itself. Again, she stared down into the blackness for several long moments. Then, steeling herself, she pushed herself forward, off the stone and into the pool.

The change came more swiftly this time, and Ceana didn't even have time to think before she was a seal again, catching herself from a deep dive with swift, strong flippers. She turned upright, breaking the surface again so she could get her bearings. Then she dove again and began circling the pool. Even with her more sensitive vision, the low light provided little enough to see—just shadows, really.

Still, she managed to find what she assumed to be the bolthole Uaine had mentioned. It lay not too far down, but it was even darker within than in the main pool. The entrance seemed large enough that it would be easy for someone of Ceana's size to enter, though she imagined it would be a tight fit for any particularly large seals. But perhaps it grew wider further in.

Satisfied, she returned to the surface and took a long breath. Then she dove deep, deep, *deep*, until she'd reached a depth no light could illuminate and she thought she'd been underwater about half the time it had taken to enter Emain Ablach. Only then did she turn and swim back, forcing herself to take her time and not rush upward.

She repeated this several times, until she felt confident that she could manage the trip back out on her own if and when it became necessary. Then she struggled out of the pool and onto the stone floor of the chamber. Her seal-shape fell away into the cloak, and she sat up, testing her voice.

Once again, all she could manage were coughs and squeaks. Well, Ninian had said it would take time, so time she would have to give it. With a sigh, she stood and made her way back upstairs to find Uaine.

Chapter 14
FINDING A VOICE

Mairearad and Aíbinn returned that evening, bringing with them a set of folding wax tablets and a slim stylus. Ceana accepted these gratefully, glad to set aside the dusty slate. Dinner that evening was far more pleasant—while Ceana still couldn't participate much in the conversation, since she couldn't easily write and eat at the same time, she could at least listen more closely now that she felt less tired.

Over the next few days, Ceana began to find a new routine. In the mornings, she rose early enough to catch Aíbinn on her way out and have her splint adjusted and more ointment applied. During the day, she trailed after Uaine, wandered the house and grounds, or did her best to assist with the ever-present tasks of spinning, weaving, and sewing—not that she could do much of any of those with only one arm. In between, she asked questions as she could, though she avoided any particularly sensitive topics for now, recalling the instructions Onora had given her.

As a result, most of what she learned shed no light on the questions she really wanted answered, though she did find out quite a lot about the practicalities of life in Emain Ablach. Most interesting was the discovery that although selkies might go about their own homes without a cloak, and though they might remove them when doing work that the cloak would interfere with, no selkie would leave their cloak both unattended and unsecured—*not anymore*, Mairearad had said, her tone dark and sad—nor would they leave it in the keeping of anyone they did not absolutely trust, or go so far from it that they couldn't run and fetch it in under a minute. Most wore their cloaks at almost all times; some even slept in their cloaks. But the *why* for all of this remained unspoken, and Ceana dared not ask, not yet.

Though she was fairly certain she was free to go and do as she wished, she kept mostly to the sisters' estate. She wasn't quite sure why; she knew that if she went down into the village, she'd likely learn more than she could from Uaine and the servants. But each time she thought about going among the main selkie populace, she found herself finding excuses to put it off.

And, of course, each day, she made her way down to the bolt-hole pool. After the first day, she forced herself to jump in, not just slide off, and to try to take as deep a breath as she could as she leapt. To see how far down that first dive would take her. Onora had warned her: *make sure you have a way out if everything goes wrong. And make sure you know it well enough to take it quickly.* So, Ceana practiced, just in case, and after she came out of the pool each day, she tested her voice, straining to pronounce even a syllable.

She'd been in Emain Ablach four days when she finally managed to croak out, "Hello?" Her voice came out strange and scratchy and dry from disuse, but it was *her* voice all the same. At once, she reached under her cloak for the necklace Onora had given her. Her fingers found the activation symbol, and the metal grew slightly warm against her skin. Bending her head, she whispered, "I'm safe. I'm safe with the selkies. Don't worry."

With that, Ceana released the symbol again and waited as the warmth faded. If Onora hadn't heard the message, it would remain stored in her mirror until she called it forth. She wouldn't reply, Ceana knew, unless 'twas about an urgent matter. But she would know Ceana was safe and not lost at sea, and that was the important thing.

That evening, Ceana made her way to the dining room, brimming with quiet excitement. She had no intention of revealing that her voice had returned—not yet, at least. Uaine had said Mairearad and Aíbinn had both vowed not to speak the human tongue, and so Ceana would avoid antagonizing her hosts until she learned *why* they would take such an oath. Perhaps at some point she'd tell Uaine, but in the meantime, keeping silent would also protect her. It would be harder to accidentally give something away if she couldn't talk and could only write.

Upon reaching the dining room, she found Uaine and Mairearad already there. Uaine, oddly enough, occupied Ceana's usual chair, and an extra place had been set across from her. Were they having guests? Ceana cleared her throat, then made a questioning noise.

Mairearad glanced over. "Good evening, Kenna. Is aught amiss?"

Ceana made another uncertain noise and then held up five fingers, nodding to the table. Uaine's eyes went wide. "Oh, I should have told you—we've a guest tonight. I'm sorry; I forgot you wouldn't know. You're across from me, next to Aíbinn."

A little warning would have been nice! But unexpected guests had been a familiar occurrence at home, if not a common one, so she'd manage. Ceana took the seat Uaine had directed her to and pulled out her tablet, writing *"Who?"*

Mairearad started to answer, but she was interrupted by the sound of the front door opening and then swinging shut again. A moment later, Aíbinn's voice called down the hall, "Here we are!"

Ceana turned to face the dining room door to see Aíbinn appear. And just a step behind her was the last person Ceana had expected: King Fionntan.

A panicked squeak escaped before Ceana could stop it. She immediately dropped into a curtsey—oh, yes, warning would have been *very* nice indeed! Then she could have feigned illness and spent the evening in bed, rather than sharing a meal with one of the few people who might actually *recognize* her. Granted, Mairearad had seen her in Atirse as well and had yet to realize who she was...

Meanwhile, Mairearad stepped forward, extending her hands in welcome. "Good evening, Fionntan. I am glad thou couldst still come."

"As am I—though thou ought to know it would take much to make me stay away," Fionntan replied. He turned to Uaine and added, "Good evening, Uaine. I've missed seeing thee at the keep these last days."

Uaine bowed her head slightly. "Good evening, Fionntan. I am sorry; I wished to stay with our guest."

"I understand. Thou wert only being a good hostess." Fionntan now addressed Kenna. "And speaking of that guest, good evening to you as well, Maid Kenna. How fare your injuries?"

Ceana patted her splint and fluttered a hand, giving an awkward smile. She fumbled her tablet around and managed to write, *"Little better every day."* Or, at least, they hurt a little less each day, which she hoped was the same thing.

"I am glad to hear it." King Fionntan circled the table and took the empty seat by Uaine, while Aíbinn claimed her usual place.

Once all were seated, Mairearad turned to Fionntan. "Wilt thou open our meal?"

"Gladly," he replied, and launched into a prayer. Ceana barely heard what he said, however, for she was too busy with a prayer of her own: *Dèanadair, help me; don't let him recognize me; don't let me give myself away.*

The prayer ended, and food was served. Mairearad turned to Ceana. "Since Uaine failed to tell you, you should know that King Fionntan joins us for dinner once a week, just as we eat at court once each week."

"'Tis our family dinner," Fionntan added, laughing a little as if at some joke Ceana didn't know. "As I believe Aíbinn has told you, these ladies are as good as family to me."

Ceana nodded. Aíbinn had indeed mentioned that on the way to Emain Ablach—though she would have guessed anyway by the fact that Mairearad addressed him as *thou* and not *you*. She hadn't expected that to mean Fionntan would simply drop in for dinner, but it did make sense. No doubt he appreciated the fact that he could have a private meal. Even if the selkie court was more casual than the Atìrsen court, proper court dinners after a long day could be exhausting, but to miss one without another engagement would be terribly rude.

Fionntan now turned to address Uaine. "Since I have not seen thee in some time, how dost thou fare? How goes the weaving thou told me of last week?"

Uaine cheerfully launched into an update on her weaving work and her various projects, and the conversation continued from there. Ceana listened without making any attempt to participate, slowly eating her fish and roasted vegetables and keeping her head a little ducked. Fionntan talked and laughed with the sisters with obvious warmth, and Ceana wasn't sure how to join in—wasn't sure if she *should* join in—couldn't help feeling that if she tried, she'd be revealed as an intruder, one way or another.

But her ears pricked up when, as they were transitioning from the savory main meal to the sweet after-course, Uaine asked, "If thou wilt forgive my asking, hast thou heard anything of Atìrse or the human realms? Mairearad told me thou wert worried."

Fionntan shook his head slowly. "No sign of retaliation, Dèanadair be praised. Whatever offense I caused through my reaction to their attempted alliance, it was not enough to drive them to open violence—not yet."

"I still say I would be surprised if it did," Mairearad said, ignoring the concoction of fruit and cream that had been laid before her. "Thy outburst was unfortunate, but we both signed the treaty, and I believe King Seòras is too canny to break it and make war over so small a slight."

"Wise words, and on them I hang much of my hope these days." Fionntan sighed. "I would not trust my cloak to so mercenary a man, but at least I may trust him to act in accordance with his nature."

Mercenary! Her father! Ceana hastily shoved a spoonful of peaches in her mouth before she could say or do something unfortunate. Enemies or not, how could Fionntan speak of him in such a way? He wasn't *mercenary*! Practical, to be sure, and wise and noble enough to do the needful thing even when the doing was difficult, but that was hardly the same!

Aíbinn made a face as if the cream in her bowl had gone sour. "We ought to have expected it. He's already seen to it that he'll have descendants on every mortal throne. It was only a matter of time before he made a move for thine."

They didn't know him. Ceana stared at her bowl, focusing very hard on not letting her emotions show. They didn't know him. They only knew his deeds. But to mistake his hard work ensuring peace for Atìrse for *conquest*—!

Fionntan nodded, scooping up a bit of peach without bringing it anywhere near his mouth. "Aye, we should have, but I never imagined even he would be so bold." Grimacing, he went on, "I only hope any anger he does feel hasn't landed on his daughter's head instead. He cannot think much of them, if he so lightly forces them to trade their home and hearts for the completion of his plans."

At this, Ceana's restraint gave out. Before she realized what she was doing, she let out a squeak of indignation.

All eyes turned on her, mingled shock and worry reflected on their faces. Ceana felt her face burning. Oh, she was in it now! And she'd have to find a way to explain how she knew the thoughts of the princesses and the policies of the king. But she couldn't let this go on any longer. No wonder they had rejected the alliance, if they had such a skewed view of her father and his intentions! And if this was how they thought of all humans—She snatched up her tablet and wrote in the largest letters that would fit: *"NOT FORCED!"*

Fionntan and Mairearad traded glances, while a look of pity slid onto Aíbinn's face. Uaine alone seemed uncertain. Fionntan spoke, his voice gentle, "Maid Kenna, whatever you have been told, I fear it may not ..."

But Ceana shook her head, smoothing out the wax of the tablet with the flat end of her stylus as quickly as she could. The moment she had enough clear writing surface, she scribbled out a message, hoping her hastily-invented story would hold. *"Cousin serves in castle. Sees royal family. Hears much. Princesses CHOOSE. Can say no. HAVE said no."*

She slid the tablet forward, holding her breath as Fionntan and Mairearad both leaned forward and Aíbinn twisted her head to read it. Uaine, the one person without a good view, left her seat to hover behind Mairearad and read over her shoulder. She looked up while the rest still studied the tablet. "What do you mean, they've said no?"

Ceana hesitated, uncertain if the others were finished reading. A moment later, Fionntan pushed the tablet back to her. "Aye, Maid Kenna, what mean you by this?"

Again, Ceana smoothed out the wax so she could write. *"King 1st asked P. Linnhe to wed Glassraghey noble. She said no. Asked to stay in Atìrse. Married to Tirsheun noble now. Cousin heard all."*

She had to write very small on both sides of the tablet to make it all fit, and she wasn't sure how legible the sharp letters were in the end. But she passed the tablet back anyway, and again, all bent to read it. As Fionntan's gaze slid along the words, his expression shifted from concerned to a mix of surprise and contemplativeness. Mairearad pursed her lips thoughtfully, while Aíbinn looked as if her eyebrows would fall off her face if they rose any higher.

At last, Fionntan passed the tablet back. "You have given me something to think on, Maid Kenna. If this tale of your cousin's is true, then King Seòras is owed more credit than I have given him. But I would like to know; does your cousin carry you many tales of the royal family?"

Oh, bother! What was she to say? Ceana nodded, praying that this wouldn't land her in worse trouble.

"I see," Fionntan said thoughtfully. "Later, once you are settled, would you be kind enough to come to my keep and share more of what she has said?"

No. Oh no. She couldn't—but she couldn't *refuse* either. Not without raising suspicions. And how could she miss such an opportunity? If she could convince Fionntan that her father and family were honorable people, perhaps he'd rethink his response to the offer of an alliance.

So, Ceana nodded once again. *Dèanadair, I beg you, don't let this make things worse. Don't let me expose myself. And please, please, let me be able to tell Fionntan what he needs to hear.*

Chapter 15
EXPLORING EMAIN ABLACH

The next morning at breakfast, Ceana had a question waiting on her tablet for Uaine: *"Do you attend court often?"*

Uaine yawned and blinked at the words, stirring berries into her porridge. "A few times a week, yes. If you're feeling bad about what Fionntan said yesterday, you needn't. I don't mind staying with you."

Ceana shook her head and took back her tablet to write another message: *"You can go. Don't worry for me."*

"I couldn't." Uaine frowned. "I mean ..."

Ceana gave Uaine her most encouraging smile and cleared the tablet so she could write, *"I don't mind. Would like to explore village and island on own, if allowed?"*

"On your own?" Uaine's brow furrowed. "It's allowed, certainly. But are you sure you wouldn't rather have a guide so you don't become lost? I know the island looks small when you approach, but there's plenty of places to go astray."

"I'm fine. Don't want to trouble you." Besides, Ceana needed to find somewhere private where she could send Onora a longer message and tell her what she'd learned at dinner the previous night. That would be hard to do if she had a guide she'd have to slip away from.

Still, Uaine clearly wasn't reassured. "If you're just going down to the village, I suppose you'd likely be all right. But if you plan to explore further, I really would feel better if you had someone with you. I'd hate for you to become lost. Besides, sometimes creatures from deeper in Tìr Soilleir wander in on the faery paths, and even if your side is doing better, you're in no condition to have to run from one."

Ceana hesitated, then wrote, *"Does that happen often?"*

"Not *very*, but enough, and it's more common if you end up far from town, in the less-traveled parts of the island." Uaine straightened up. "Why don't you just go down to the village today, or over to the orchards? And I'll ask Aíbinn if she or one of her friends can show you some of the other parts of the island. Will that be all right?"

Hiding her disappointment, Ceana nodded. It was better than nothing. She was *supposed* to be talking to the common selkie folk and learning what she could about them, after all; that had been her original plan. And if there was a risk of running into beasts and monsters, it would be better to know where she was running— better still to have someone who knew how to fight to defend her.

So, late that morning, Ceana set off down the path from the house towards the village, her wax tablet and stylus in one pocket and a small purse filled with coins in the other. Some of the coins were those she'd brought from home, as she'd confirmed with Uaine that many merchants would accept human currency. Gold, silver, and copper remained precious no matter who had shaped them. But Uaine had also topped up Ceana's purse with selkie coinage, requesting as she did that Ceana run a few errands while she was out.

Ceana found the town just as bustling on this day as it had been the evening she arrived. For some time, she just meandered through the streets, looking around and trying not to call attention to herself. No one seemed to take particular notice of her, though, aside from the occasional person who smiled at her or bid her "Good morning," as she passed. No one, that was, until Ninian's voice hailed her. "Maid Kenna, be that you?"

Ceana stopped and turned. She found Ninian standing in the door of his shop, leaning out slightly to watch her. He stepped out onto the doorstep and raised a hand in greeting. "How's the arm and side, lass?"

Ceana made the so-so motion that had, over the last several days, become more or less routine. Neither hurt much, even though she'd been a little concerned that the walk to the village would jostle her ribs. The ointment Ninian had given her was truly far better than anything available at home.

Ninian nodded and beckoned her over. "Come and let me check your arm, if you've a minute. I'm having a slow morning."

He stepped back into the shop as she approached. She followed him in and offered her arm, pushing the sleeve up to her elbow. Ninian inspected the splint, nodded once in approval, and then began unwrapping it in a businesslike fashion. "Settling in well, are you?"

Ceana nodded, unable to write with one arm in Ninian's hands. Ninian set the splint materials aside and probed her arm with careful fingertips, pausing when she winced and hissed in response to pressure on a particularly sore spot. "Are you applying the ointment as I told you?"

Again, Ceana nodded. Ninian frowned at the arm and continued probing, more gently. "You seem to be healing, though not as quick as I'd expect. Still, could be reason for that." He began wrapping up her arm once again. "How's your voice?"

Ceana hesitated. Should she tell him? She hadn't even told Uaine yet...Would he frown on her admitting she had her voice back? He'd been the first to warn her about speaking the human tongue, after all.

Ninian tied off the end of the splint. "I'll not ask you to speak if you don't care to, lass. I know there's enough who come here who'd like to leave their pasts behind. I only ask as a physician, no more."

Well, that was all right, wasn't it? So, Ceana nodded and spoke in a hoarse whisper, "It came back a little yesterday."

"Good. Keep practicing the shift. Staying too long in one shape or the other isn't particularly healthy—though you'll always cope better than most if it's necessary." Ninian dusted off his hands.

"Had any other trouble?"

Ceana shook her head, hesitated a moment, then asked, "How do I learn to speak like everyone else?"

"You know already, lass. It's a matter of bridging the space between your mind and tongue. As for how that's done, well, it's another's right to explain, and I'll not step on their feet." A thoughtful frown crossed Ninian's face as he stepped back. "But if you want to try hurrying things along, find a book or other writing in our tongue and try reading it aloud. It occasionally helps—not often, but occasionally. Perhaps one or two folk in every ten who try."

Well, that was better than no chance at all. Did the sisters have any books? Ceana didn't remember seeing many, but there had been some locked rooms, and of course she hadn't poked into anyone's bedroom. "Is there anything else I could try?" Her voice cracked at the end of the last word, and she frowned at herself.

Ninian rubbed his chin thoughtfully. "There's a potion we use on dire occasions, but 'tis only a last resort. 'Tis faery-made, and we've a limited supply, so we keep it for those who've had a bad shock and need the extra help. In your case, your only trouble is that you don't have a cloak of your own yet."

Oh well. She'd make do, then, and continue to take refuge in the fact that writing instead of speaking made it a little harder for her to give anything away—though only a little, as last night proved. "Thank you anyway."

"No trouble, lass. I hope the reading helps," Ninian replied. "Make sure you come back in four days or so, as I told you before. And when you come, bring Lady Mairearad with you."

Ceana tried to ask, "Why?" but ended up in a coughing fit instead. Ninian shook his head sympathetically. "Don't overdo the talking just yet, lass. It'll take time before you can give any long speeches, same as it'll take time before you can use this arm of yours to its fullest extent even after it's healed."

Oh, *good*. She hadn't lost her voice again as soon as she'd found it. Ceana gave a weak smile, then fished her tablet from her pocket and wrote, *"Why bring Lady M?"*

"For one thing, because she's your host and your guardian for the moment. For another ..." Ninian turned away. "I expect I'll have news for her as well as you. So don't forget, understood?"

Ceana nodded to his back. After several more coughs, she managed to say, "Thank you. Good day." And with that, she left the shop and returned to the sunlit street.

Emboldened by her encounter with Ninian, Ceana set about the errands Uaine had given her. Word must have gotten out that the three sisters had a guest, for no one batted an eye at the words on the tablet she offered as introduction: *"I'm Kenna. Staying with Northwaves. On errand for Lady U."* Most simply nodded and asked what the sisters needed, at which point Ceana found herself relieved that she *couldn't* speak—interacting with tradespeople as a customer had never been a skill she needed. But with no voice, she could disguise all awkwardness behind having to write what she had to say. Most seemed to be familiar with the sisters' needs anyway, and they provided a price promptly and promised to have their goods delivered to the estate in an appropriate time. Then they sent her on her way again with a smile and a comment about how they hoped that she was settling in well and that they'd see her again sometime.

Out of all of them, only one, the weaver, pressed further into Ceana's story, asking where Ceana had come from and how long she'd been in Emain Ablach. But even that proved to be more interest than distrust, as the weaver followed up these questions by asking after several cousins of hers who apparently lived in a town near the one Ceana had claimed to be from. Ceana could only shake her head and shrug, though she made a mental note to come back later if she could come up with a story that would cover her lack of familiarity with the woman's relatives. Perhaps her lack of hostility towards Atìrse meant she be might be more willing to answer questions.

By the time she finished all Uaine's errands, Ceana's stomach was growling. But she found herself unwilling to return to the estate now that she'd finally left—and, in any case, hadn't Uaine mentioned orchards somewhere? That might be private enough for her to contact Onora.

So, instead of going back, she bought two hand-pies and a glossy black plum from a pair of market stalls and then made her way to a shaded bench she'd noticed earlier. There, she sat and watched people go by. Most of those she spotted were either men old enough that their working days were behind them or women of varying ages, some alone, some in small groups, and some carrying or trailing children. Oddly enough, many of the very young children wore no cloaks, and Ceana wondered why. Did selkies not receive their cloaks until a certain age? But, no, other children of the same age wore cloaks that looked like lighter and softer versions of those worn by their parents.

Ceana had finished both pies and started on her plum when a young woman approached her bench, leading a cloakless boy of four or five—her son, Ceana guessed, for she could see a sharp resemblance between them. In her other arm, she bore a heavy-looking basket, and a sling wrapped around her shoulder and chest held a dark-haired baby. The woman smiled wearily at Ceana. "Excuse me; might I sit here?"

Ceana nodded, scooting over to make room and patting the space beside her. The woman sank onto the wooden boards with a sigh of relief, releasing the boy's hand and setting down her basket. "Thank you. I'm Bryn, by the by. I don't think I've met you before." The boy tugged her sleeve, opening his mouth, and Bryn answered him before he could even speak. "Yes, you can run back to your friends, but stay where I can see you."

The boy turned and dashed off, joining a gaggle of similarly-aged children who seemed to be playing some game involving chasing each other up and down the street.

Bryn settled back onto the bench, sighing in a way that suggested she wished she had half as much energy. Ceana took the opportunity to pull out her tablet so Bryn could read the message written there.

"Oh, you're a newcomer, then. Welcome." Bryn wrapped her arms around the baby in her sling, brushing her thumb over the child's cheek. The child, who couldn't have been more than a few months old, was wrapped in its own cloak of soft golden-white. It stared at its mother with huge, dark eyes, sucking determinedly on its fingers. "From where do you come?"

"*Atìrse. Town on w. coast.*" Ceana didn't bother to give the name; she wasn't even sure if Bryn would know it.

"Ah. My husband was born in northern Atìrse. Of course, he remembers little of it. He was only Rígán's age when he and his mother escaped." Bryn gestured towards her son as he chased another boy past a fruit-seller's stand.

"*Escaped?*" Ceana wrote. Again, she recalled what Fionntan had said at the treaty signing, how he'd called humans *slavers and kidnappers*. Just how literal had his words been?

"Aye." Bryn tilted her head. "As you did, I'm sure."

Ceana gave a little shrug. "*Grandmother gave cloak. Told me to go to sea. Didn't understand 'til in water.*"

"Ah. I understand. You must have been blessed to have such an easy time leaving." Bryn looked down as her baby removed its fingers from its mouth and reached up, making tiny questioning noises. "Yes, I'm here. You're all right." She bounced the child a few times, turning back to Ceana. "I'm sure that the Northwaves are treating you well, but if you ever have need of anything, even just someone to talk to, my husband and I keep a farm outside town, and our doors are open."

"*Thank you.*" Ceana made a mental note to try to visit sometime when Bryn's husband was home—maybe even the husband's mother, if she still lived. Then she could ask in private what Bryn had meant by *escape*. In the meantime, she scribbled a different question on her tablet: "*Why no cloak for your son?*"

Bryn laughed wryly. "Because he knows well enough to stay out of the water if he doesn't have it on, and 'tis easier to catch a child on two legs on dry ground than a pup in the waters, at least until I can safely leave Màiri alone for a moment and change myself."

She nodded down at the baby in her arms, who had started to fuss quietly. "His cloak is in my basket should he need it."

Ceana imagined trying to chase a slippery seal pup through the waters while carrying a baby. She had only to consider it briefly before deciding that Bryn was undoubtedly right.

Bryn's baby's fussing grew louder. Bryn sighed. "Ah, she must be hungry. Do you mind ...?"

Ceana stood at once, offering an understanding smile. As quickly as she could, she jotted a reply: *"Will go. Nice meeting you."*

She wasted no further time in setting off again, eating her plum as she walked. Uaine had mentioned orchards, and that seemed like a good place to go next. But somehow, despite her best intentions, she instead found her steps leading downhill. A few minutes later, she'd reached the edge of the village and stood on the shores of the lake in the island's center.

Compared to the village, the lake was quiet and peaceful; only a few people sat or walked along the shores. As Ceana watched, one pair of people who had been eating lunch stood, tucked away their belongings, and then walked into the waters. They vanished a moment later beneath the surface.

No one had seemed to pay them any mind. Ceana considered this a moment, then followed the path down to the water's edge. Still, no one took any particular notice of her, nor did anyone speak or call out as she pulled up her cloak's hood and walked into the waves. Once she was waist-deep, she bent, dove, and felt the seal-shape wrap round her once again.

She swam a tight circle, then surfaced for a breath. Still no one called her back. And why would they? The selkies were, as far as she could tell, free to come and go as they pleased, and as far as anyone knew, she *was* just another selkie. Emboldened by that thought, she dove deep into the water, making for the tunnel to outside, or at least towards where she thought it lay. Not that she wanted to leave just now—but when the time came for her to return home, she wanted to make sure she knew the way.

Finding the tunnel entrance took some time—longer than

necessary, but Ceana continually found herself distracted by some wonder: by strange fish in brilliant hues, by oddly-shaped creatures that scuttled or crawled along the bed of the lake, by the simple play of sunbeams through the waters. But at last, she came to the opening. Just to be certain, she darted in and made her way partway down, turning and wiggling out again when it began to tighten.

Satisfied, she swam back to shore in a leisurely fashion. No one took any more notice of her leaving the lake than they had her entering it, so she made her way back up to the village. There, learning from her past mistake, she stopped again at the fruit stall where she'd bought the plum, introduced herself, and asked after the way to the orchard.

The fruit-seller proved amenable enough, pointing Ceana in the correct direction and warning her to take no fruit without noting whose trees it grew on. The Northwaves family owned some of the trees, he told her, and drew their symbol, a wave with a star over it, on her tablet. As long as she was their guest, they'd likely not mind her picking a piece or two of fruit, if she found any that was ripe. But any trees not marked with that symbol belonged to other families, or else to the king, and picking from them would be stealing—though, the fruit-seller added in a whisper, if the fruit had already fallen, it was unlikely anyone would begrudge her taking it.

Ceana thanked the man and went on her way. Guided by his directions, she managed this time to navigate the streets with no trouble, and before long, she found herself walking between somewhat untidy rows of fruit trees. Nearly every one of them, she noticed, had some symbol carved into the trunk, and many had bands of color painted on them as well. Here and there amid the trees, men and women worked, pruning and tending the trees. Some nodded to her as she passed, while others ignored her.

She walked through the rows for some time, but nowhere in the orchard could she find a spot secluded enough to risk contacting Onora. At last, she returned to the village and wandered around it a bit more. Now that she wasn't overcome by the newness of everything, she felt that there was something odd about it. It took her some time to realize what: there was no Tur-Faire, nor even any sign of a chapel.

The lack of such a place made no sense. The selkies seemed as devoted to Dèanadair as anyone in Atìrse. How, then, could they have no place of worship? No place devoted to Him? There had to be one *somewhere*.

The question troubled her all the way back to the Northwaves' house. And that evening over dinner, when Uaine asked how her visit to the village had gone, Ceana wasted no time in her reply. "*Village was well. Where is your Tur-Faire?*"

She passed the tablet to Uaine and felt the pressure of unspoken conversations between the sisters. It had become a familiar sensation by now, as the sisters had discovered that the easiest way to keep conversation moving without leaving Ceana too far behind was for one person to read what she'd written and tell the others. Only when Ceana said something truly shocking, as she had the night before, did they all read it for themselves.

A moment later, Uaine passed the tablet back. "We haven't one. Only humans have Tur-Faires and chapels and such."

No Tur-Faire? Ceana couldn't keep her disbelief from her face. Beside her, Aíbinn laughed. "You look as if you think we're all heathens because we don't have a building just for worship, as if Dèanadair's creation isn't grander than anything we could make. When the weather's fair, we gather on the lakeshore or the hills to sing and listen to His word. Or, if there's a storm or 'tis too cold to meet outside, King Fionntan opens the great hall of the keep, if the whole community is to gather, or people meet in their homes. There's such a gathering in three days' time, if you wish to come with us."

How strange! Ceana tried to imagine meeting for worship under the skies and found she couldn't picture it—though, she supposed, Aíbinn did have a point. In any case, she wouldn't have to imagine it if she saw it for herself. "*Would like to come,*" she wrote. Then, she smoothed the tablet and wrote, "*What if you* need a priest other times? Or you want to pray or contemplate?"

She showed the tablet to Aíbinn this time. Aíbinn's brow knit, and as far as Ceana could tell, she didn't even wait to tell the others what Ceana had written before she replied. "Do humans believe you can only pray and think about Dèanadair in a particular building?"

Ceana managed a little laugh. *"No. Just helps sometimes."*

All three sisters breathed sighs of relief. Uaine shook her head. "If we want to pray or contemplate or study, we just find somewhere quiet and do so on our own."

"The royal keep does have a small room specifically set aside for prayer and contemplation," Mairearad cut in. "'Tis meant just for the king, his kin, and his highest officials. I rarely see it used, though, and I think 'tis there for symbolic reasons more than anything else."

"True, there is that." Uaine picked up a slice of bread from her plate and tore off a bit. "I suppose it might be nice to have a public place specially set aside for the things of Dèanadair, but not if it makes thee feel as if thou canst do those things nowhere else."

"It is nice," Ceana wrote back, thinking of the Tùr-Faire where she and her grandmother had visited. Perhaps they could have done the same thing anywhere—Dèanadair was everywhere, after all, not only in the Tùr-Faire—but there was something special in being able to go and sit in His presence in a place dedicated to Him. *"What about priests?"*

"If you need a priest, you go find one and hope he's not so busy with his other work that he can't stop to talk," Uaine replied. "All our priests play another role as well so they can support themselves. No one is *only* a priest."

Ceana wrinkled her nose. *"Why?"*

Uaine looked to Mairearad, who set down her fork. "Long ago, the Daoine Ròin didn't have enough people for anyone to *only* be a priest. Anyone who could work, hunt, or farm needed to do so, even the king himself at times. Now, we could spare a few people to devote themselves to the sole service of Dèanadair, but 'tis dangerous for such a man to depend too much on the gifts of his neighbors for his daily bread. Many believe such practices are how humans went astray, as their priests feared losing their wealth more than they feared Dèanadair.

Ceana made an *"Oh"* face as she considered this. The priests she knew best certainly had no such fears. Deòrsa, the head priest at the Tùr-Faire nearest the royal seat was one of King Seòras's advisors, and Ceana had heard her father say that he could always count on Deòrsa to tell him when he was being a fool, even when no one else would. And it was well known that the priest at the Tùr-Faire Ceana had visited before leaving Atìrse had once marched up to the castle, demanded to see its lady, and then lectured the woman he believed to be Onora about how her behavior honored neither her heavenly nor earthly father. Of course, that had been during the time when an imposter had temporarily tried to take over Onora's castle—and had succeeded until Onora managed to expose her and have her executed.

And yet, Ceana knew, not all of Atìrse's kings had been like King Seòras, and not every queen had been like Onora. Perhaps under other rulers, the priests had been more fearful. Perhaps the selkies had reason to be concerned.

Ceana was still thinking on this when Uaine spoke up. "Is it true that, in Atìrse and other human lands, there are people who aren't priests, but who still leave the rest of society to fully dedicate themselves to Dèanadair?"

Ceana nodded, hastily smoothing out her tablet so she could write her reply. *"Contemplatives. Luchd-faire, properly. Why?"*

Uaine hesitated, as if trying to choose her words carefully, and Ceana noticed Mairearad also giving Uaine a sideways glance. At last, Uaine said, "I know the reasons why our priests have to be more than just priests, and why we can't have people like the contemplatives in the human land. But sometimes I wish we could—that we also had a choice to forgo all else in order to fully serve the Creator. And sometimes I wonder how humans can act in the ways they do when there are so many among them who are dedicated to Dèanadair and no one else." She gave a little shake of her head. "But I'm sure you don't want to think about that. I'm sorry to have brought it up."

A moment of uncertain silence descended on the table. Then Aíbinn cleared her throat. "Kenna, Uaine mentioned you'd like to see the rest of the island. I can show you around tomorrow, if you like."

Ceana nodded, even as she wrote out a reply: *"If it's no trouble?"*

Aíbinn waved away the concern. "No trouble at all. I'm due a day off, and I never mind a ramble. We'll leave at the second bell."

That seemed to settle it, for Aíbinn started recounting a story of something that had happened during her shift on Guard duty that afternoon. Ceana set aside her tablet and applied herself to her meal, thus far untouched. It had been a good day; she'd learned quite a bit, even if it wasn't all what she originally wanted to know. Perhaps tomorrow, she could learn something more.

Chapter 16
STORIES OF THE SEAL-FOLK

At second bell the next morning, Ceana and Aíbinn set out from the back door, down a narrow, grassy path that led away from both house and village. They passed at first by fields green with summer's growth, then through open meadows where, to Ceana's surprise, flocks of sheep grazed, attended by shepherds and sheepdogs. After several minutes of staring and wondering, she tapped Aíbinn's shoulder and, making a questioning noise, pointed at the nearest flock of sheep and at the pointy-faced collie watching them.

Aíbinn gave her an odd look. "What? I know they've sheep and dogs where you come from. What's so strange about these?"

Ceana shook her head and pulled out her tablet. Balancing it awkwardly on one arm and trying to keep it steady as she walked, she wrote *"How HERE?"* For good measure, she added her best attempt at an illustration of the tunnel.

Aíbinn studied the tablet a moment and then laughed. "*Oh!* No, they don't come through the sea tunnel. They're brought in through Tìr Soilleir, on the faery paths."

On faery paths? Ceana's heartbeat quickened, and she scribbled out: *"Magic sheep + dogs????"*

"No, no." Aíbinn shook her head. "Not usually, anyway. The sheep are always ordinary. The dogs mostly are as well, though I think every now and then there's one that's a bit enchanted. We pay the Daoine Math to provide new stock every so often. Technically, that means they're all the king's property, and the shepherds just tend the sheep for him, and they receive the dogs on loan to help them do that, but I've never heard of anyone having their flocks or dog taken away unless they were mistreating the creatures."

So, the selkies had trade relations with the Daoine Math? Ceana supposed she wasn't surprised. They had to have allies *somewhere*—and there was that stone that Ealar claimed detected curses and which certainly had *some* magical property. What else were the selkies trading for? And what were they trading in the first place? She'd have to find out somehow—would Aíbinn know? Or maybe Lady Mairearad?

Before she could decide whether or not she wanted to ask now, Aíbinn pointed ahead. "There's the Southwood. It's riddled with faery paths, and some of them are still active, so if you decide to go there, be careful. The old entrance to the main path—from when there *was* a stable, open path between here and the mainland—is inside as well. I could show you, if you like?"

Ceana considered this, weighed curiosity against the chances of ending up on a magical path to who-knew-where or running into a faery beast, and then shook her head. But she seized the opportunity to write another question: *"How long path closed?"*

Aíbinn glanced at the tablet as she turned away from the wood. "Oh, a few generations now. One of our old kings ordered it destroyed when the humans started making alliances with the Daoine Math. He feared that humans would find out and use it to invade. Now we just have temporary paths. It's safer, even if it does mean we can't communicate as easily with Tìr Soilleir." She sighed, and a flicker of sadness crossed her face. Then she shook herself, pushing a smile again. "But as far as we've heard, the humans have never tried to invade, so we're safe for now. Still, be careful. If you feel like wandering the forests, try the Dawnwood instead. It's safer; the worst you're likely to find are territorial ravens."

Ceana nodded and gave a little laugh to signal she'd understood. With that, the conversation and their footsteps both turned away from the Daoine Math and treaties. Aíbinn, true to her word, showed Ceana a great deal of the island, most of which was taken up by the two forests. The rest, aside from the village, consisted of more fields, farms, and meadows. They paused for a lunch of apples, cheese, and bread in one of these meadows, this one clear of either sheep or shepherd. Ceana gave thanks for the rest; even with the effect of the ointment, the hours of constant walking made her side ache.

Midway through the afternoon, they reached the tall cliffs that marked the edge of the island's livable space. The sheer face of dark stone seemed to emanate heat—but moreover, the closer Ceana drew to the rock, the more she felt she ought to move away. She said as much to Aíbinn, in a message that took her a full three minutes to compose, and Aíbinn nodded. "Something terrible happened, long ago, and the rocks still echo with it."

"*What?*" Ceana wrote, and the legend she'd been told repeated itself in her mind. Had it been true after all? *Had* the island been cursed?

But Aíbinn just shrugged. "No one knows. It's worse on the outside—but only above the waterline. Under the waves, it's just ordinary rock. Some people, though, think that whatever happened is what brought the island halfway into Tír Soilleir." She glanced at the sky. "We'd best start making our way back. Otherwise, we'll miss dinner. If you're ready?"

Ceana nodded reluctantly. She still had no idea where she could safely talk to Onora. But at least she was beginning to know her way around, and maybe after this, she could explore on her own. And in the meantime, she had plenty more to discover about the selkies and their home.

Now that Aíbinn had shown her around, Ceana saw no reason not to explore further on her own. So, the following day, after a brief dip into the bolt-hole pool, she left a message with the servants for Uaine and ventured out alone along the path she and Aíbinn had taken. She walked for some time, waving to those she passed and occasionally pausing to greet those who hailed her. She kept one side of her tablet marked with her introduction, using only the second side for conversation—not that she lingered long enough to talk much. Most of those she saw were working, and she had no intention of keeping them from their tasks.

Yet, every so often she came across a group of fieldhands who'd sat down for a rest or a shepherd sitting and watching his flock. By many of the fields, too, she spotted someone sitting beneath a tree or by a rock or bush, a staff, spear, or sling close at hand. Sometimes their hands were occupied by carving, mending, or another small task; other times they merely sat and watched. Ceana wondered at this; those sitting seemed as able as those in the field, and neither Uaine or Aíbinn had mentioned brigands or bandits in the dangers of wandering the island alone. Nor did the watchers seem to be in charge over the groups, for some were just barely out of childhood.

Not knowing the reason didn't stop her from approaching them, though, no more than it stopped her from approaching anyone else she saw who wasn't busy. With a hand raised in greeting, a shy smile on her lips, and a request to sit and talk ready on her tablet, she'd step off the path. And in nearly every case, those she approached welcomed her willingly enough and, once she introduced herself as a newcomer, they were happy to answer her questions.

Though Ceana itched to jump straight to the questions she'd come here to find answers to, she kept her conversations to more neutral topics for now. She asked about her companions' lives, about what it was like to live on the island. She asked if they'd always lived in Emain Ablach and if they ever left.

The answers she received were remarkably consistent. Most had lived in Emain Ablach all their lives, and they rarely went far from their homes—though, Ceana soon learned, the selkies had a different definition of *far from home* than she did. Even those who claimed to be homebodies had traveled as far as Atìrse's northern and northwestern shores at least once or twice, traveling, as they said, "with the singing parties, like the one that brought you here." A six-hour swim was an acceptable day trip to them; a two- or three-hour swim was barely worth blinking at. The *adventurous* travelers were those who made the dangerous journey all the way to Atìrse's southeastern shores or to Tryggstend in the north, either of which meant nearly two weeks out and another two weeks back.

Even though most of those Ceana spoke to were native to the island, one or two in every ten were transplants: some from human lands and some a life of wandering the seas. Wherever they hailed from, however, few had anything ill to say about their current home. The closest anyone came was a comment from a wanderer-turned-shepherd, who commented between puffs on a pipe, "I'll never get used to living surrounded by walls—mountain walls, house walls, and the like. True, the island's bigger here inside than it is out on the mortal side, but the walls are there just the same. There were no walls in the open seas, just the waters and the skies and the rocks. But there's nothing to hunt you here, and life outside was getting to be nothing but being hunted."

Ceana scribbled back her reply at once: *"Hunted by what?"*

The shepherd snorted, then coughed. "Everything but the fish, more or less. Whales, sharks, sea serpents, deeps-dragons, humans. But the seas 'round the isle are safe, and a pretty lass like you shouldn't worry about such things."

He'd say no more on the subject, much to Ceana's frustration. She'd seen herself that there were some who still hunted seals, or *would* hunt them if the opportunity appeared. But that still didn't fit with King Fionntan's accusations.

Indeed, life on the island seemed peaceful enough. Much of it, in fact, greatly resembled life in Atìrse, and Ceana wondered again why selkies and humans would be at odds when they were so similar. There were differences here and there, of course. Mothers spoke of teaching their children to swim as well as walk, laughing at how their little ones sputtered and shrieked when first introduced to the water and how eagerly they took to it once they realized that being wet wouldn't kill them. Men told of hunting fish and eels, not deer and rabbit; the brave among them hunted sharks, lesser whales, and dolphins the way the men of Atìrse did boar or wolves. Children exulted over evening visits to the lake when the day's work was done and outings in the seas around the isle after worship each week.

Even those watching over the fields were no indication that danger lurked nearby. Ceana asked about them the third time she stopped to talk, and in answer, the boy who'd been sitting gestured into the branches. Draped there, out of sight from the road, were many silvery-grey seal-cloaks. "Someone has to watch over the cloaks," he explained. "'Tis harder to work with them on, but no one wants to leave their cloak unguarded, so we take it in turns to make sure no one disturbs them." With a reassuring smile, he added, "Not that anyone would, here on the island. You're safe here. We just try to keep in practice."

Indeed, Ceana thought, much of what they told her seemed meant to reassure her that she was *safe* here, that her future here would be a happy one. More than once, someone commented that at least no selkie ever went hungry, no matter how hard the winter or how well or poor the harvest. Whatever happened on land, the sea would provide. The mountain walls provided shield from storm and foe alike, and the deep-sea tunnels, and the king's watchful Guard further kept enemies away. Most importantly, they said, humans couldn't come here—didn't even know about the island's secrets. And they would never find out, for no selkie would ever let the secret slip.

Many of those Ceana spoke to couldn't carry on long conversations. They'd talk with her for perhaps thirty minutes, then return to their work. But when she could speak with someone for a longer time, she gradually turned the discussion from life in general to asking what the king and nobles were like, making reference to a kind king and a far less kind local lord in her homeland.

This proved a welcome topic, and the selkies spoke of King Fionntan and the nobles in as glowing terms as they did their homeland. "He'll do his father proud," many said, with as much warmth as if King Fionntan were their own kin. "He's young, aye, but wise already and growing wiser, and he served his turn in the Guard just like any other man before he took up the crown."

Others had more personal stories. One farmer spoke of an encounter with King Fionntan: "'Twas some four or five years ago, in early spring, when I was checking the fence 'round my property for damage. A part of it fell and caught me underneath. Broke my leg right badly and trapped me under the stones. I might've laid there all day if his majesty hadn't happened along with some of the Guard. King Fionntan—well, Prince Fionntan, then—stepped in and started clearing away the stones the moment he saw me. He ordered one of the Guard down to the village to fetch Ninian and had the rest help free me and make sure I wasn't dying." Chuckling, the farmer added, "And once all was said and done, he even stayed to rebuild my fence and make sure my stock stayed where they were meant to. Can't imagine any human king going so far."

Others had similar, though less dramatic, accounts of how King Fionntan had seen their needs met. One woman told of how Fionntan had settled a dispute between her and her neighbor over the stream that ran near the border of their properties; another man spoke of how, one winter when his crop had failed and sickness had struck his household, Fionntan had quietly ensured they had food and firewood enough to last until the spring.

Even those without such stories, however, spoke of having met King Fionntan or his father. Ceana couldn't hide her surprise at this—but, the selkies were quick to explain, the selkie court wasn't like the human court, where common folk rarely met those who ruled them. Anyone could visit the king's court, and most of the nobles and even the royalty made it their practice to speak to those who came, even if only to greet them, however high or low their rank.

It made sense, Ceana supposed. There were far fewer selkies than there were people in Atìrse. But she wondered at it all the same, and she wondered too what it would be like from the other side. If she could interact so freely with her own people, if she could ask them directly about what concerned them and what they thought of various matters, would that make ruling easier? She felt it would in some ways, though perhaps it would make it more difficult to be objective.

Ceana might have kept wandering and talking to people until sundown, she was so caught up in hearing the seal-folk's stories. It was strange to walk alone, with no guards or attendants, and stranger still to feel so *safe* while doing it. It was nothing like her visit to the village during her travels here, as she'd feared it might be. Then, she'd been in her own country, yet she'd feared for herself the whole time. Here, she was a stranger and, in some ways, an enemy, even if the people she spoke to didn't know it. Yet everyone she met welcomed her with open smiles, cheerful words, and hands quick to offer help when she needed it.

At last, however, evening and dinnertime drew near. As the light turned golden and the sky began to dim, she found fewer and fewer people out. And though her frequent stops meant less jostling to her arm and side, her injuries were beginning to pain her after a long day on her feet. So, she turned back towards the Northwaves home with many a sigh.

When she returned, she found Aíbinn and Mairearad debating whether or not to send out someone to search for her. All three sisters made quite a fuss when they found she'd returned—or, rather, Uaine and Aíbinn made a fuss, while Mairearad simply sighed and said, "You are our guest, and you may do as you choose, of course. But if you would do the courtesy of warning us next time you plan to stay out so long, so we might know not to worry that you've become lost, we would appreciate it."

Ceana apologized, of course, and promised that she'd warn them next time—if there was a next time. Sooner or later, she'd not be able to impose on their hospitality anymore. She'd have to find lodging elsewhere, though she still wasn't sure *how*. All the same, she couldn't really regret any part of her day. She'd learned so much, even if it wasn't strictly what she'd come here to learn. And now that she'd made the acquaintance of so many people, she had no doubt she'd learn more in the days to come.

Ceana thought to spend the next day as she had those before it, exploring Emain Ablach and talking to the selkies. But when she roused herself, she found the house all a-bustle as the sisters and their servants prepared to go—somewhere. A brief mental calculation reminded Ceana of where: the worship service that the Northwaves sisters had mentioned. A little more thought and Ceana realized that it would be the day of worship in her homeland as well. So, Ceana allowed herself to be caught up in the bustle, and when the sisters set out, she joined them, wondering what selkies' worship might be like.

As it turned out, the answer was *decidedly odd*. Not unpleasant, to be sure, and certainly not heretical in any way, but...odd, all the same.

It wasn't just that the service was outdoors, though that was strange. Those in attendance all gathered at a point on the far side of the lake from the Northwaves' home and the royal keep. Here, the hillside had been carved out and rocks arranged to form a sort of amphitheater. There were many places all over the island like this, Uaine told her, for not all the selkies in Emain Ablach attended the same worship, and the locations changed month to month, sometimes even week to week.

Nor did the oddness solely come from how people acted so casually, sitting or standing as they pleased or even moving about from one seat to another. Many had brought small handiwork with them, with which they busied their hands during the service. Ceana spotted men and boys with carving knives and bits of wood and women and girls with drop spindles, knitting, embroidery, and more. She couldn't help thinking that Mirren would be jealous; she always hated having to keep her hands still during worship at the Tur-Faire.

Part of the strangeness, certainly, was the amount of singing involved in the service. It seemed that someone started up a new song every five or ten minutes. Some were familiar to Ceana: old, traditional hymns handed down through the centuries from before Atìrse's Dark Days. Others had tunes Ceana recognized, but words entirely unlike those she knew. And still others were completely unfamiliar. She hummed along as best she could with all the songs, whether she knew them or not, and wished she could sing with the others.

In between the songs, people either read from Dèanadair's Word or spoke about what had been read—and here Ceana discovered another oddity. Rather than a single priest to lead the service, read the Word, and expound on what it contained, there seemed to be half a dozen people all working in concert. One would stand up and read, and then after a song, someone else would stand and speak. Then another person would speak on the same passage after the next song, and then yet another person read the next section of the Word, and so on it went.

Ceana supposed that, if anyone could be a priest, it made sense for multiple people to lead the service. Yet she couldn't help wondering how they organized it all. Who decided who would speak and who would read and who wouldn't do anything? Or did the speakers simply stand on impulse as they felt led? From the style of some of their oratory, Ceana suspected the latter—though she tried to be fair and remind herself that all of them had other work during the week.

After the service, people lingered for some time, chatting and socializing. Ceana tagged along with the Northwaves sisters briefly before wandering away to greet some of the people she'd met in her explorations of the last two days. She was glad to find that many of them recognized her in return and even seemed glad to see her again. But she didn't linger long in any one conversation—having to write what she wanted to say made keeping up with discussions in a crowd, where people were constantly interrupting, exceptionally difficult. So, Ceana contented herself with a litany of *hello, how are you, hopefully I'll see you again soon* and wished over and over that she could speak the selkie tongue.

With this thought in mind, Ceana asked Mairearad about books in the selkie language that afternoon. To Ceana's immense delight, Mairearad needed no persuading. Rather, she led Ceana to her study and took from one of the shelves a copy of the Holy Word, beautifully crafted and clearly a prized possession. "Here. 'Tis the best of days for it, and perhaps having the new and familiar together will be an encouragement to you."

Ceana wasted no time in either thanking Mairearad or in retreating to her room upstairs where she could read in the sunlight. And, to some degree, it *was* encouraging to find that Dèanadair's words were still the same even in another tongue. And it was comforting, too, to discover that she could read the selkie language as long as she didn't think too hard about it. The letters were the same, as she'd noticed already in the last week, and though the words were different, the meanings slipped into her head as she read.

When she tried to read aloud as Ninian suggested, however, the sounds stuck in her throat. At one point she managed a whole syllable—only to choke on the next and end up in a coughing fit. She tried one passage and another and another, searching for something easy enough to manage, but every attempt had the same result.

Writing in the selkie language went no better. Logically, Ceana knew, if she could look at a word, see the letters that formed it, and understand its meaning, she ought to be able to write it. But whenever she tried to focus enough to say that *this* letter made *this* sound, and *this* selkie word meant *this* human equivalent, her thoughts slid uselessly about, making her feel as if she were trying to climb a hill covered in ice.

Eventually, she gave up and joined the Northwaves sisters in the solar. She sat by Uaine on the couch, listening as they chatted. Again she wished she could speak—again she wondered if she should tell the sisters that she'd regained her voice in the human tongue, even if she remained voiceless in the language of the selkies.

But there was Mairearad and Aíbinn's vow to consider. Until she knew *why* they would take such an oath, she'd keep her tongue behind her teeth and satisfy herself with her tablet. At least the Northwaves sisters were patient with her need to write instead of speaking—at least they did their best to include her in their conversations when they could. She had to be grateful for that.

After a while, the sisters' discussion turned towards the next night and their weekly dinner at court. They'd missed the week before for Ceana's sake, as none of them had wanted to leave her alone on her first full day in Emain Ablach. But tomorrow, they would return. "And, of course, you're welcome to come too, if you like," Uaine told her. "It's always such a lovely evening, and I'm sure you'd enjoy it."

Ceana hesitated. It *did* sound like a lovely evening, and after all she'd heard, she certainly wished to see the selkie court for herself so she could see how it differed from the Atìrsen court. But would it be too much of a risk?

The sisters must have taken her hesitation for nervousness, for Uaine added at once, "You needn't worry about anything. Anyone who wishes to attend court can, no matter who they are. I'll lend you another gown, and Mairearad and I can tell you everything you'd need to know to feel comfortable."

"Yes, and we'll all teach you the dances, if you don't know them already," Aibinn cut in. "Even if you don't dance, though, it's worth coming for the food and the company. The royal cooks know their business better even than ours."

"Oh, *yes*." Uaine looked over to Mairearad, who was composing a letter and only half-participating in the conversation. "Kenna should come, shouldn't she?"

"If she wants to, certainly." Mairearad set the pen in its holder and looked up, addressing Ceana directly. "You don't have to join us if you prefer not to. But we would be glad if you came."

She couldn't resist all three of them at once. And when else would she get such an opportunity? So, Ceana nodded and wrote on her tablet, *"Will come. Can dance already."*

Of course, it might not even matter. She was to return to Ninian's tomorrow with Mairearad, and she had a guess now as to why he wanted them both. No doubt he'd found out that she had no kin here, and he needed Mairearad, as her host, to know so she could decide Ceana's fate. What would happen to her then? Would she be thrown out? Perhaps if she could convince them that she was related to one of the selkies who dwelt outside Emain Ablach, she could stay on the island, though she doubted she'd be able to remain as the Northwaves' guest for long. And no matter how open the court might be, she didn't think she was bold enough to go on her own.

Whatever happened, though, there was nothing she could do about it now. She'd just have to wait and see what the next day would bring.

Chapter 17
BLOOD TIES

The next morning dawned grey and damp and threatening rain. Even so, Ceana set out for the village promptly at second bell, accompanied by—to her surprise—both Mairearad and Uaine. Both seemed to know something Ceana didn't, though neither would say precisely what. When she tried to ask, Mairearad shook her head firmly and said, "Simply a guess that could be wrong. I'll tell you later, if need be," in such a big-sisterly way that Ceana promptly tucked her tablet away and shoved aside any thought of prying further.

Nearly half a dozen other people were already in Ninian's shop when the three of them arrived. Ninian himself was nowhere to be seen, though Ceana could faintly hear his voice from the other room. A young man trying and failing to grow out his beard stood behind the counter, measuring powders, tinctures, and ointments from large jars into smaller ones.

Since Mairearad and Uaine were nobility, Ceana thought she'd be seen next anyway. But her companions seemed to have no such expectations—or, at least, they made no complaint when Ninian and the man at the counter continued to attend on the other patients and customers first.

At last, the shop cleared out, and Ninian beckoned the three of them towards the door into the back room. "Welcome, ladies. How fare you today?"

Ceana gave a cheerful nod, while Mairearad and Uaine assured Ninian that they were well and asked after his own welfare. Ninian simply waved the question away. "I'm the same as I ever am. Maid Kenna, do your injuries still pain you?"

Ceana touched her wrist, then held her first finger and thumb close together, almost touching, to indicate just the *tiniest* bit of pain. Then she touched her side, brought her fingers a bit further apart, and wiggled her hand. That neither hurt more seemed a miracle, given how recently she'd been injured.

Ninian's brows drew together anyway. "Hmm. Well, have a seat and let me take a look." To Mairearad and Uaine, he added, "If you like, you can pull the chairs to the side and sit as well, or you can stand. I imagine this won't take much time."

"I will stand, thank you." Mairearad positioned herself towards the side of the room, and Uaine followed suit. Ceana sat down in the middle chair, loosed her arm from the sling, and held it out for Ninian.

He pushed her sleeve up and began unwrapping the splint with swift, practiced hands. "How's your supply of the ointment? Still using it regularly? Have enough left?"

With her arm in Ninian's grasp, using her tablet was out of the question. Ceana glanced towards Uaine, giving her a look that she hoped said *help me.*

Uaine looked puzzled a moment, but then perked up. "There's still half a jar left of what you gave her. Aíbinn or I apply some of it every time we change her splint."

"Good." Ninian probed Ceana's arm. "Let me know if what I do hurts, lass."

Ceana nodded, then squeaked when Ninian's fingers produced a spark of pain. Ninian stopped. "Here? How much pain? Less than a week ago, more than a week ago, or same as?"

Ceana pointed downwards. Ninian went on probing her arm. "Less. That's good. From what I can tell, you've still a little healing to do. Keep your arm splinted and keep using the ointment, though you can stop using the sling. Come back in four or five days so I can check on it." He began wrapping her arm once again. "And you said your side still pains you? Less or more than last week?"

Once again, Ceana pointed downwards. Ninian nodded. "I guessed as much. Not much else I can do for it, then, but tell you to keep using the ointment and be careful about how much you jostle it. You'll be all right in the end."

Uaine gave a little cough and then asked, "Is it bad that Kenna's still injured? Shouldn't she be better by now?"

Ninian tied off the end of the splint and released Ceana's arm. "If she were a full-blooded selkie, I'd worry that her arm's not well. Her side I'd expect to have another two or so weeks to heal even then. But from what I can tell, Maid Kenna has a few more generations than most between herself and her closest selkie kin, and that means she'll take a bit longer to heal." He took several steps back and turned so he could address both Ceana and the sisters at once. "And speaking of that, I've some news for the three of you."

Neither Mairearad nor Uaine seemed surprised by this, though Uaine's expression did light up a little with eager anticipation. Ceana leaned forward slightly, wondering what Ninian might have to say and, just in case her best guess was right, mentally preparing all her wavering explanations as to why she seemed to have no selkie relatives.

Ninian cleared his throat. "Maid Kenna, as you'll recall, when his majesty first brought you in, I took a drop or two of your blood to test for curses or connections to anyone here in Emain Ablach so that if you had kin here, we could bring you and them together. In this case, it seems Dèanadair's already done the work for us. The Northwaves ladies are the closest kin to you to be found in Emain Ablach or among any of the wanderers who've come here for treatment."

Ceana froze in the middle of reaching for her tablet. Family *here*? Among the selkies? Surely the test had been wrong—how could that *be*? It couldn't. Surely she'd know if any of her ancestors had been selkies; there were records of who had married whom going back generations upon generations.

But Mairearad smiled and nodded like she'd expected as much, while Uaine clapped her hands together, beaming excitedly. "Oh! Kenna, thou hast been our sister all along! How wonderful!"

"Cousin," Ninian corrected. "And a distant one. As I said, there's at least a few generations between you. But, yes, family all the same." He turned to face Ceana. "You've asked a few times now about our language—usually, it's through your kin bringing you properly into the community that you get it, though others can do the same if necessary. I'll leave it to Lady Mairearad to explain the specifics once you have some time to adjust to the idea—from the look on your face, it looks as though that may take you some time."

Ceana nodded, pushing a smile and internally smacking herself for having let her shock show so plainly. She fumbled for her tablet and wrote, *"Just surprised. I like the Northwaves, though."* She still didn't understand how they could be related. Maybe there had been a mistake with the test, or maybe it was another effect of the cloak's magic. She'd have to ask Onora to investigate, or maybe ask Onora to ask their grandmother about it. If anyone had any chance of knowing, it would be the old queen. But if it was only a mistake, she thanked Dèanadair for it.

Ninian finished reading the tablet. "That's good to hear. On that topic, have you tried reading aloud as I suggested?"

"Tried. No help." Ceana made a face, then added, *"Yet."*

"Well, keep at it, though I imagine it'll not be long 'til you have a cloak of your own and your troubles will be sorted," Ninian replied. "And how's your voice otherwise?"

Ceana glanced hastily at Mairearad and Uaine, but saw neither had reacted to Ninian's question. *"Fine,"* she wrote. Not that she'd spoken much, but she *could*, if she really needed to.

"I'm glad to hear it." Ninian looked around at all three of them. "Unless any of you've any other questions for me, I think there's naught else for me to do for you. As I said, lass, come back in a few days so I can check on your injuries, or sooner if the pain in either grows worse."

Ceana flipped to the other side of her tablet and wrote, *"Thank you."* She stood, glancing at Mairearad and Uaine.

Mairearad gathered her cloak around her. "Thank you as always for your work, Ninian. Kenna, if you're ready, we'll return home. It seems we have quite a bit to discuss."

When they stepped out of Ninian's shop, they found that the grey clouds had given way into a steady drizzle. The three of them pulled up their hoods and made their way through the streets, which were far emptier than they had been on Ceana's past visits to the village, and up the path to the Northwaves house. Even with hoods and cloaks, they were soaked when they finally reached the house, and their shoes were all a mess of sticky mud.

At the door, Mairearad and Uaine stopped to take off their shoes, and Ceana followed suit. From there, Mairearad led the way into the dining room, where a fire had already been lit. The three of them all pulled chairs over to the hearth and clustered round it, and for quite some time, they all sat in silence: Mairearad solemn and thoughtful, Uaine quietly excited, and Ceana still processing what Ninian had said. Why had his tests claimed she was kin to the Northwaves? And what did *kin bringing you into the community* involve? It sounded like a weighty thing indeed.

Finally, Mairearad gave herself a little shake and then spoke. "So, Kenna, you are our cousin. I hold you under no obligation to us, either as kin or as guest, but if you wish to claim us, we gladly claim you in return. Either way, we'll do what we can to help you find your place here."

She paused, glancing towards Ceana. Ceana pulled her tablet from her skirt pocket to write her reply: *"You are kin. You are kind. Why wouldn't I claim you?"* As long as claiming them didn't somehow bind her to the island, at least.

Mairearad's expression twitched into a smile. "I am glad to hear that. In that case, you are welcome to continue living here as long as you want. As you've surely seen, we have space aplenty. You can keep your current room, or move to another if you prefer, and whichever you choose, you can feel free to make the space your own. What we have is yours, and if you need something we don't have, we will do what we can to get it for you."

Ceana nodded and scribbled out a quick, *"Thank you."* After a moment's thought, she added, *"I like the room I have."*

"Then it's yours," Mairearad replied. "Other details, we can work out over time, but I would like to speak of making our kinship known officially. When we dine at the court tonight, we will introduce you as our cousin, and that will do for now. But there is also a ceremony to officially adopt you into our family, to claim you in the sight of Dèanadair and all the community, so you can receive a cloak of your own and fully claim your heritage. How long until you turn eighteen?"

"*Six months,*" Ceana jotted down on her tablet, and held it up for Mairearad to see. That must be what Ninian had referred to. Bother! It was probably a step further than she could safely take if she wished to return home after this—after all, she wasn't sure she really had selkie heritage to claim. And even if she did, what if this ceremony meant she couldn't live long-term on land in the human realm anymore?

Uaine made a face. "Oh! Just a few months ahead of me! I had thought thee younger than me, and that I should be older than someone at last."

"Alas," Mairearad said, drily. "Thou wilt have to suffer being the youngest by one more." She rolled her eyes, then turned her focus back to Ceana. "The adoption ceremony will have to be repeated once you come of age, unless you wish to wait out the full six months and do it once for all—or unless you somehow find a husband before that time."

Ceana couldn't help an alarmed squeak at the idea. Mairearad held up her hands. "Don't fear; 'twas only a joke. We don't expect you to do any such thing. The more important thing to consider would be the ceremonies. Usually, when the two would be so close, the family would have one small, private one and one large, public one. Given our rank, though, it would be expected for both ceremonies to be public ..."

Oh, Shepherd's Paths, no! Public attention was the last thing Ceana needed—especially when she didn't even know the full extent of what such a ceremony would mean. It seemed dishonest, at minimum, to formally join someone's family when she had no intention of staying. And—the thought now occurred to her—if she received, as Mairearad said, a cloak of her own, would she be turned into a selkie in truth? Unable to go further than a day from the sea? That would mean trouble indeed when she returned home.

Mairearad *had* said they could delay. Ceana hastily smoothed out her tablet and wrote, *"No need for two ceremonies. Can wait until 18."*

She showed the tablet to Mairearad, who read it and pursed her lips. "Are you certain? Most who wait are within three months of their age of majority—even then, many hold the ceremony twice anyway. It is not unheard of, but...'tis a long time to be silent."

Ceana turned her tablet over so she could reply. *"Am sure. Don't want fuss. Need time to adjust."* And six months would be more than enough time to figure out what she needed to know, especially since she needed to be home before the end of the summer.

Mairearad hesitated a moment longer, then bowed her head slightly. "Six months it shall be, then. If nothing else, it will give us all time to get used to each other and to make the proper arrangements."

"And time enough for thou to decide if thou wishest to be sister to us as well as cousin," Uaine added, a hint of stubbornness in her tone. "For if we adopt thee, it is no more difficult to claim thee as one than it is the other. And we have so little other family remaining here, it is a shame that thou shouldst be so far estranged."

"Don't pressure her, Uaine." Mairearad stood, shaking her head. "A cousin need not be estranged simply because the relation is more distant. Now, I have things I must attend to before lunch." She started to depart, but paused by Ceana's chair. "Truly, Kenna, welcome to the family. I am glad everything worked out as it did."

Ceana gave her an answering smile. Indeed, the way things had worked out could hardly have been better—save for the fact that if she were caught now, the scandal would be far greater. *Please, Dèanadair, protect me. Let me not be found out, either now or after I return to Atìrse. For if I am discovered, nothing but trouble will come of it.*

Chapter 18
AT THE COURT OF KING FIONNTAN

That evening found the three of them—Mairearad, Uaine, and Ceana—dressed in finery and ready to dine at King Fionntan's court. Uaine had, as promised, lent Ceana another of her gowns, this one a rich green, and a few pieces of jewelry to go with it. It almost made Ceana feel as if she were back home.

She had wondered in the days leading up to this how they would get to the royal keep. Most selkies, whether noble or common, seemed to walk everywhere in Emain Ablach, and she'd seen no horses during her exploration, only a few donkeys and sturdy ponies. Yet, to walk any great distance in evening court finery would be a risky prospect, especially with the roads a muddy mess from the day's drizzle.

Her fears were allayed, however, when they stepped out of the house and found there an elegant little pony cart, just large enough for three passengers. A shaggy-maned pony stood in the harness, its reins held by a bearded selkie man—a gardener and general handyman, as Ceana recalled, though she couldn't remember his name. The Northwaves household's solitary footman, Sean, stood by the cart, ready to help the ladies into it. Once they were settled, the gardener handed the reins to Mairearad, and off they went, following the path some distance down towards the village, and then cutting over onto a road Ceana had never taken, through a copse of trees whose branches met overhead in a tangled canopy. This joined in with another road after some time, this one clearly well-traveled, and not long after that, Ceana spotted the royal keep through the trees.

It was a strange sight, to be sure, as if a fragment of a castle had been dropped into the island. The main part consisted of an old-fashioned, defensively-built keep, square but with one corner chopped off to hold a set of double doors that now stood open. At the back of the keep, two wings extended, each about half the height of the central part but twice as long. From the look of it all, Ceana wondered if the keep hadn't been built first, and then the wings added on when the builders were sure the island wouldn't be attacked in the next month.

Mairearad drove the cart up to the space in front of the main entrance, where a man dressed in grey and green took the reins and helped them out of the cart. Then he led the pony and cart away, while Mairearad straightened her skirts and cloak. "Here we are. Aíbinn will meet us just inside, and then we will enter the great hall together."

She led the way towards the door. Uaine grinned at Ceana. "Come along, then. Remember, thou art our cousin, and even wert thou not, thou wouldst be welcome. But if thou feel overwhelmed, tell one of us—or tell one of the Guard or a servant, and they'll show thee somewhere thou canst rest and take air." Then she followed Mairearad.

Ceana hurried after them, doing her best to ignore the twist in her stomach. All the people most likely to recognize her in one place! What was she thinking? But Mairearad hadn't recognized her yet, nor had Fionntan, and if they hadn't, surely no one else would. Even so, she sent up a silent prayer: *Dèanadair, protect me.*

Aíbinn was, as promised, waiting just inside the doors, dressed in what looked like a more formal version of her Guard outfit, with polished leather armor decorated with embossing, her tunic tucked into a long skirt of the same shade to suggest a dress, and silver and gold bands glinting among her braids. A torc much like the one Onora had given Ceana hung around her neck, but rather than being wrapped in wire, it had wavy etchings all along its shape.

She waved as they approached her. "Hello! I thought you three would never arrive."

"The path was all over mud." Mairearad pulled Aíbinn into an embrace. "How went thy day?"

"Oh, same as ever." Aíbinn shrugged. "And thine?"

"We received some good news." Mairearad stepped back and beckoned Ceana forward. "According to Ninian the healer, Kenna is kin to us—a distant cousin, he said, but he could find no closer relatives."

"Oh?" Aíbinn turned to Ceana. "Welcome to the family, cousin. Does this mean thou'll stay on with us?"

Ceana nodded, offering a smile. Before she could think to take out her tablet and add anything more, Aíbinn had pulled her into a hug. "Good! The house is too empty these days, with only the three of us in it." She stepped back just as swiftly. "I think King Fionntan will wish to hear of this. Come along!"

Catching Ceana's arm in hers, she led the way further into the Great Hall, past clustered groups of selkies laughing or talking together. Their garb varied from brightly-colored court dress, pearls, and jewels that wouldn't have looked out of place in Ceana's own home to what was clearly peasants' best, made of rougher fabrics with little adornment, but clearly crafted with no less care than the richer garments. Quite a few groups they passed included both nobles and peasants, and Ceana recalled what she'd been told about even the lowest-born folk being welcome to visit court.

They reached the back of the room, where a high table sat upon a dais. No one sat yet at the table, but King Fionntan stood to one side. A line already formed in front of him of people who wished to speak with him before dinner. In Onora's castle or at the royal seat, such a receiving line would have been marked out well prior to the start of the evening, with a heavier concentration of guards stationed near it. Here, it seemed to be forming naturally, and the only extra guards were those who flanked King Fionntan.

Aíbinn pulled them into the queue and waved in the direction of King Fionntan—or perhaps towards his guards, as they both nodded to her. Ceana took advantage of the pause to survey the room. On the whole, were it not for the proliferation of sealskin cloaks and the variance in the room's occupants, it could have been the great hall of any older Atìrsen castle. Lanterns hung on hooks on the walls and wheels of candles suspended from the ceiling supplemented the slivers of evening light that could slip through the narrow windows. The walls were hung with tapestries, some woven and some embroidered. Tables occupied the center of the room, with places laid ready for diners, though no one had yet taken their seats save for one selkie who might have been mere days from seeing a full century of life. To one side of the room was a great hearth, large enough that Ceana could have stood up inside it. Only a small fire burned there, however; the night was warm enough that, with the number of people present, anything larger would've been far too hot.

They reached the front of the queue, and Lady Mairearad stepped forward and curtseyed, offering King Fionntan her hand. "Good evening, your majesty."

"Good evening, Lady Mairearad." King Fionntan made a partial bow and briefly kissed the back of Maireard's hand in a very polite way. "I'm glad you and your sisters and guest could be here tonight." He turned and offered a hand to Aíbinn, and they clasped wrists in the way of warriors. "Lann Aíbinn, you are aware you aren't on duty tonight?"

Aíbinn laughed. "Aye, but why run all the way home to dress up when I can simply wear my formal uniform and have spare time to inspect the kitchens before the feast?"

King Fionntan raised an eyebrow. "Ah, so if we're short a pie or two, it seems I know where to start my own investigation." He turned next to Uaine. "Lady Uaine, good evening."

"Good evening, your majesty." Uaine dipped into a curtsey. "How are you this night?"

"Very well." King Fionntan kissed Uaine's hand as he had Mairearad's. "Can I count on you to open the dancing with me tonight?"

"Only if you don't throw my sister in the dungeon over a

missing pie," Uaine replied, rising from her curtsey. "But you know you hardly need to ask."

King Fionntan inclined his head gravely, though his eyes danced with merriment. "For you, Lady Uaine, I shall show mercy to any pie-thief."

At this point, Mairearad cleared her throat and tugged Ceana forward. "If I may interrupt, your majesty, may I present our cousin, Kenna of Northwaves?"

"Your cousin?" King Fionntan echoed, turning his attention from Uaine to Ceana and Mairearad.

Ceana took this as her cue to dip into the deepest curtsey she knew. Halfway down, the thought came to her that a peasant wouldn't know how to curtsey in such a way, but—too late! Another bit of knowledge to attribute to her court-serving cousin.

She glanced up to see a smile on King Fionntan's face. As she began to rise, he bowed over her hand and brought it to his lips as he had for Mairearad and Uaine. "It is my pleasure to meet you anew, Lady Kenna. You are fortunate to have found such a family as these sisters—you know already that they are as dear to me as if they were my own kin. And as they are welcome to visit my keep at any time, so too are you, if you desire."

Ceana could only smile and make what she hoped came across as an appreciative squeak as King Fionntan released her hand and continued to speak, "In fact, there is something to that end that I would ask you—but later, as there are others whom I must greet just now."

It was a gentle hint, but a hint all the same, and the sisters could clearly identify it as well as Ceana could. They moved off to let the next person in line speak to the king. Then Uaine looped her arm through Ceana's and pulled her away to meet some of her other friends, while Mairearad and Aíbinn both vanished into the crowd.

The next twenty minutes were a blur of names and faces as Uaine seemed determined to introduce Ceana to not only her close friends but also everyone she had a friendly acquaintance with, whether noble or common. Ceana did her best to commit them all to memory, but even after a lifetime of practice, she only felt confident about three-quarters of them at best. Much to her relief, a herald blew a blast on his horn before too long, signaling the start of dinner, and Uaine and everyone else made for their seats.

A few minutes later, Ceana found herself seated at the high table, several places down from King Fionntan, with Uaine on one side and a plump noblewoman about the age of Ceana's parents on the other. The noblewoman introduced herself as Lady Derbáil, but once she discovered Ceana couldn't speak, she proceeded to focus all her conversational efforts on her equally round cousin, seated across from her, and her nephew, a thin fellow a few years younger than Ceana who kept looking over his shoulders as if wishing he were sitting anywhere else. As half of Lady Derbáil's conversation with him seemed to be focused on recommending this or that young lady to the nephew's attention and inquiring what he thought of each one, Ceana felt she really couldn't blame him. She did her best to give him a sympathetic smile whenever he looked her way, though only when she felt certain Lady Derbáil wouldn't see and take it the wrong way.

As this was only an ordinary court dinner and not a feast, only three courses were served. Ceana had already become acquainted with the selkies' cuisine over the last week, so little of the food placed before her came as a surprise. Every course included at least one form of fish, whether stewed or roasted or baked into a pie, and Ceana partook of these dishes cheerfully. They were familiar foods, most of them, that might have been served at her own father's table—or Onora's, at least.

Less welcome was the presence of so much shellfish: broiled crabs split in half so the eater could dig the meat out of various crevices, unpleasantly chewy grilled oysters, and so on. The selkies seemed to consider these delicacies, or at least highly enjoyable, though Ceana couldn't imagine *why*. She knew people in Atìrse ate such things as well, but they rarely found their way onto noble tables. And having gotten a good look at the still-living creatures during her journey, she had no desire to put them in her stomach.

But even avoiding the shellfish, there was more than enough food for Ceana to eat her fill: soups and stews, baked and stewed fruits, pies both savory and sweet, and a different sort of bread for each course. And Ceana had to admit, King Fionntan's cooks could easily match the skill of those employed by her own family back home.

Between each course, a group of musicians stood to play and sing a ballad about a particular selkie king of legend, who'd roamed the seas protecting his people, and who had fought a great deeps-dragon in its lair. They sang the ballad in two parts, ending the first half just as the king entered the lair, and had the food not been so *very* good, Ceana felt she might have been too caught up in suspense to eat a bite.

At last, however, the meal came to an end. Servants hastily cleared the lower tables, and those sitting jumped up to help move board and bench and make space for dancing. As the musicians readied their instruments to play the first tune, King Fionntan stood, made his way down the table, and offered his hand to Uaine. "Ready, my lady?"

Uaine stood and took his hand. "Ready."

They made their way to the floor, and other couples gathered and followed. Much of the high table emptied; Ceana spotted Aíbinn arm-in-arm with Ealar and Lady Mairearad accompanying a dark-haired gentleman with a neatly trimmed beard and somewhat questionable mustache. The young man opposite Ceana took this as an opportunity to scuttle away—not, Ceana noted, to find a partner, but to disappear into the crowd around the edges of the floor. After a few minutes, however, all were assembled. The band looked to the king, instruments poised, and King Fionntan raised his hand with a smile, signaling them to begin.

The musicians took their cue, launching into a jaunty tune. Ceana leaned forward, watching the dancers. This was a couple's dance, with each pair dancing on their own, and Ceana was relieved to see that it strongly resembled some of the dances she knew. Not that it really mattered—as a stranger, she would likely receive few invitations to dance—but the familiarity comforted her all the same.

Even with most of those present dancing, she could easily pick out particular couples from the crowd. Ceana soon found herself watching Uaine and King Fionntan as they stepped, hopped, and spun, chatting all the while. She could tell from the way they moved, from how they anticipated one another's movements without breaking stride or conversation, that they were frequent partners. Each movement flowed into the next as smoothly as riverwater in its course, all with no apparent effort on either person's part. Ceana tried to imagine dancing with so familiar a partner, but couldn't begin to fathom it. As a princess, she'd been expected not to show particular favor to any one person—an expectation that hadn't been hard to live up to. After all, entanglements were foolish when you expected your marriage would be arranged.

Not that it had worked out like that in the end. Perhaps if she'd paid a little more attention to her dancing partners, rather than focusing on distributing her time evenly among them, the prospect of choosing her own husband would have been less daunting.

The music shifted, and the couples on the floor broke apart and rearranged themselves into new pairings. Now, Fionntan escorted Aíbinn, while Uaine danced arm-in-arm with the poet who Ceana had met on the way up—she couldn't remember his name. Mairearad, somewhat to Ceana's surprise, remained with her original partner. How curious! Mairearad hadn't mentioned being betrothed, or even having a sweetheart, but what else could two dances in a row signify?

This next dance was a group dance, performed by sets of four couples in a square. It, too, bore a startling resemblance to those Ceana knew—though, then again, perhaps that wasn't so surprising. Everyone here acted as if it was quite ordinary for people in the human countries to discover they were part selkie and come to Emain Ablach to live. Surely some of those people brought knowledge of dances—and, in any case, many of the steps she'd learned had been around for generations and generations.

Perhaps some dated back to the days when humans and selkies were still friendly.

The dancing went on, couple's dances alternating with group dances. Mairearad, despite some of Ceana's predictions, did not partner exclusively with the man with the questionable mustache; King Fionntan claimed her attention for the third dance, and after that, several other selkies, some noble and some wearing formal versions of the Guard uniform, drew her away. Uaine and Aíbinn, for their parts, seemed to have no trouble finding a new partner for each tune. And King Fionntan, of course, was clearly dancing with each lady in turn, as was proper for his position.

Even recognizing that, though, Ceana couldn't help starting in surprise when, several dances on, during a slightly longer break between songs, he stepped back onto the dais and approached her seat. "I'm surprised to find you still sitting, Lady Kenna. Do you not dance?"

Ceana managed a little laugh as she pulled out her tablet. She wrote her response, *"I dance. No one has asked."*

"Allow me to set that right, then." King Fionntan bowed and offered his hand. "Will you join me for this next dance?"

Ceana stood and curtseyed in return, then took his offered hand with a smile that she hoped would suffice for an answer. He seemed to take it as it was meant and led her down to the dancing floor. "I've been told this next dance is just like one common in human celebrations, though I don't know what it's called in those lands. In any case, I think you'll have no trouble with it."

Ceana nodded confidently, listening for the opening strains of the song. As the band launched into the first stanza, she breathed a sigh of relief. Yes—though the words were unfamiliar, the tune was the same as "Stars on the Breeze," and she'd known the steps for that particular song since her first dancing lessons as a little girl. So, she followed King Fionntan's lead confidently, matching his every step and turn through the first several measures.

A laughing smile broke across his face. "Well, Lady Kenna, I see that you do indeed dance. You must enjoy it, to do it so well."

Another girl might have flushed at that—but Ceana had spent enough of her life being complimented to not read too much into it. She nodded cheerfully, adding a little flourish to the next few steps. If only she could speak! Couple's dances, even the fast ones, were so much more pleasant when you could converse during them.

They danced a few more measures in friendly silence, until another couple, who seemed to have abandoned the intended steps in favor of making up their own, careened towards them, and Fionntan neatly guided Ceana to the side without breaking from the tune. Once they were back in regular step again, he said, "Regarding what I said earlier, my lady—I did not exaggerate when I said you are welcome to come to court whenever you wish. Many here would welcome a new face. And to that end, I still wish to speak with you about what you told me the other day, and about your cousin and what she has said to you. If you are yet willing to do so?"

Again, Ceana gave a nod. She'd nearly forgotten about King Fionntan's request, she'd been so caught up in exploring the island and meeting its people. What a relief that she'd been given warning enough to come up with what she could and couldn't reasonably know from her fictitious cousin.

"Good." King Fionntan stepped into another turn. "Would you perhaps come in three days' time, at the third bell? I know not what plans you may have already made, or what plans the Northwaves sisters have involving you, but I wish to not delay too long."

If the sisters had plans, they'd said nothing about them to Ceana. So, Ceana nodded agreement yet again. Better indeed to speak sooner, before she had enough time to either forget or overthink, and when she could have the most time possible to change King Fionntan's mind about her family and humans in general.

"I will look forward to it. But if anything changes, send a messenger, and I will understand." As the music drew to a close, they made their way through the final steps, and then King Fionntan bowed and released her hands. "It has been a pleasure dancing with you, Lady Kenna. I hope to do so again sometime."

Ceana curtsied in return and fished her tablet from her skirt pocket. She had just enough time to scribble, *"My pleasure; hope the same,"* before King Fionntan turned away to find his next partner.

She started to turn away and go back to her seat, but before she could take a step, one of the noblemen approached her to ask for the next dance. Ceana accepted willingly enough, and soon found herself no more lacking for partners than she'd ever been at home. Each time a dance ended and her partner bowed away, another fellow stood ready to claim the next. Some were nobles—not many, though; there seemed to be only four or five noble families among the selkies. Many were guardsmen, starting with Ealar and continuing through what must have been half the company, all of whom had apparently heard the news from Aíbinn already and were eager to tell Ceana what an excellent family she'd fallen into. And more than a few were tradesmen or peasants whom she'd met in her exploration of the island. They approached with a little more caution than either nobles or guards, but from what Ceana could tell, it was caution born of the fact that she was a newcomer to the island and the court, not because of any difference in rank, for she saw them ask other young noble ladies with far less hesitation both before and after her.

Eventually, however, she grew weary and returned to her seat to rest. Lady Derbáil and her cousin were still sitting and chattering together. Ceana initially ignored them in favor of the platters of nuts, cheese, and fruit and pitchers of water and mead that had been left out on the table for those who, like her, needed a break from the dancing. But she pricked up her ears when she caught a familiar name in their conversation.

Lady Derbáil's attention was focused out on the dance floor, and she gestured towards it. "Look, there, young Sir Cianán dancing again with Lady Mairearad. What is that, the sixth time tonight?"

"Seventh, by my count," the cousin replied, popping a walnut into her mouth.

"Seven times!" Lady Derbáil clucked her tongue. "'Tis a wonder he's not asked for her hand yet, he puts on such a display any time he sees her."

"'Tis hard, in their situation," the cousin replied mildly. "One parent gone, the other so far away—perhaps he is waiting until he can ask properly. Or perhaps he *has* asked by letter, and he's still awaiting a reply."

Lady Derbáil let out a sniff. "If he plans to wait for that, both he and Lady Mairearad will be old and grey before they wed. All know that Lady Mairearad is the head of the Northwaves these days, practically speaking, and her hand is hers to bestow as she wishes." She took a long sip of wine, then added, with a significant look at her cousin, "No, I imagine it's not her *family* he's waiting on, not in that way."

"I can't imagine what you mean." The cousin refilled her cup with mixed mead and water and then pulled one of the platters closer so she could contemplate its contents. "But, then, I never could be bothered to attend as closely to these things as you do."

Ceana stifled a laugh at the touch of reproof in the cousin's tone, but Lady Derbáil seemed entirely unaffected. "I mean his majesty, of course. Everyone knows he'll marry one of the Northwaves ladies—he has eyes for no other women on the island, within or without the court."

"Oh, is *that* what you meant?" The cousin slid the platter away, having restocked her own plate with cheese and assorted berries. "I was under the impression that it was only the youngest he fancied."

"Lady Uaine certainly does seem to be his majesty's favorite," Lady Derbáil agreed, a bit begrudgingly. "Even so, he is very fond of Lady Aíbinn, and some say he's only waiting for her to finish her service in the Guard before he makes his intentions known. But he is close to Lady Mairearad as well, and marrying her would be the wisest choice, especially in these unsettled days. And so, Sir Cianán is caught in uncertainty until his majesty makes his choice."

"If you say so." The cousin shrugged and picked up her cup. "But I doubt our king would prevent Lady Mairearad's happiness for some slight advantage—that's the sort of thing the humans do, not our kind. If anything, I would think he's waiting for Lady Mairearad to be wed before he claims the hand of one of her younger sisters. And in any case, it's *their* business, not any of mine."

"It shall be our business in time, if his majesty doesn't make a decision." Lady Derbáil clucked her tongue again. "He ought to be wed with an heir on the way by now, given his position."

"Derbáil, *really*." The cousin sighed and set her cup down again. "He only lost his father a year ago, and he has nearly ten years before he *has* to choose a bride. Let him be."

"I'm merely saying —!" Lady Derbáil grumbled, then perked up again as her gaze caught another figure amid the dancers. "Oh, is that my nephew? Can you see who he's dancing with? I don't believe I recognize her at all ..."

Having no interest at all in Lady Derbáil's nephew, Ceana turned her attention back to the dancers. King Fionntan had evidentially danced with every woman he needed to, and now he escorted Uaine once again. They truly *did* look well together! Ceana thought again of how friendly the two of them were, how Uaine visited King Fionntan at court so often and how he had seemed to genuinely miss Uaine's visits when Ceana had kept her away. How he had asked Uaine first to dance tonight.

Ceana sighed. How inconsiderate she'd been when she suggested trying to arrange a marriage alliance between Atìrse and the selkies! She'd thought that just because she knew of no official betrothal, that King Fionntan had no particular plans. But if the selkies had no practice of marrying for duty, of course he would wish to wed his best friend.

There truly would be no marriage alliance, that much was clear now. Ceana bid the last lingering shreds of that idea a regretful farewell. But perhaps there could still be an ordinary alliance, if she could only figure out why the selkies disliked and distrusted humans so—if she could only find a way to change their minds.

Chapter 19
QUESTIONS AND ANSWERS

Three days later, in the mid-afternoon, Ceana returned to the royal keep as King Fionntan had requested. The paths were still nearly as muddy as they had been last time she came this way, and by the time Ceana arrived, she was thoroughly grateful that Uaine had loaned her a pair of proper boots, not just shoes, even if they were a bit small.

The keep doors stood open once again, with guards posted on either side. They held up their hands as Ceana approached, but Ceana was ready. She held up her tablet, on which she'd written, *"Lady Kenna of Northwaves—King wishes to see me."*

At that, the guards nodded and waved her on. One commented as she passed, "His majesty is in the library. 'Tis on the second floor; any servant can direct you."

Ceana nodded her thanks and continued on her way. It was strange that they'd simply let her wander, but perhaps they didn't have enough servants to spare to send someone with her—or maybe they were more trusting of their own people. She paused to ask directions from a passing servant, who directed her to the nearest staircase and told her to look for the largest set of doors in the hallway.

Upstairs, she could easily spot the library—not just because it was the only room with double doors, but also because no other room had a guard in front of it. Ceana recognized him as Nes, one of those who'd been in the group that rescued her, and she smiled and waved at him as she approached.

He nodded and smiled back. "Welcome, miss—sorry, I hear 'tis lady now. King Fionntan's expecting you." He leaned back and called into the room, "Lady Kenna is here, your majesty." Apparently without waiting for a reply, he gestured for her to go inside.

Her father's guards would never have been so informal! The arrival of any visitor would have required that the person be properly announced and acknowledged. But perhaps King Fionntan had responded through the selkies' mental speech to Nes's rather casual announcement.

She wasn't here to analyze selkie court etiquette, though, so Ceana followed Nes's guidance and stepped inside. The library was small compared to that in her own home, and its shelves held far more maps and scrolls than proper books. King Fionntan sat at a table against one of the walls; across from him waited an empty seat with a stack of parchment and a pen sitting in front of it.

Ceana paused and curtseyed to him. He stood. "Welcome, Lady Kenna. How fare you this day? Not too tired after the other night, I hope?"

Smiling, Ceana shook her head. Then she extended a hand towards him with a questioning expression that she hoped would be interpreted as "And you?"

He seemed to catch her meaning. "I'm well." He gestured to the empty chair. "Please, sit."

Ceana did as he'd requested. He, too, sat back down and spoke again. "I know you have your tablet, but I believe pen and paper will be easier. No doubt having to stop to smooth out the wax every few sentences is tiresome."

Oh, he didn't know the half of it! Ceana nodded emphatic agreement. Then, after a moment's hesitation, she pulled out her tablet anyway and wrote, *"Can talk in human tongue now. Might be easiest."* She slid the tablet across to him, hoping she'd not committed some grave offense. She knew that Mairearad and Aíbinn had vowed against the human language...but King Fionntan had spoken it at the treaty meeting, and *perhaps* that meant he was

178

less opposed to it than they were.

But no, she could see the shadow passing over his face already. He passed the tablet back to her and said, his words careful and precise, "Lady Kenna, perhaps you have heard of the vow that many of us selkies take? Those who make it swear not to use the human tongue within the borders of Emain Ablach save at great need. In its strictest form, which I have sworn, that vow includes having the human language spoken to us. If you would prefer to answer in speech, I can find another to speak with you on my behalf, someone who has not taken the vow or who has sworn a lesser version of it. But I had hoped to converse with you personally on these matters."

Ceana bowed her head in understanding. So much for her hopes! All the same, if King Fionntan felt humans had wronged his people, she couldn't blame him for despising their language. No doubt he had been displeased indeed to have to speak it at the treaty meeting. Writing would be safer for her anyway. She scraped the tablet smooth, then wrote, *"I will write. May I ask a question?"*

She spun the tablet around, smoothing the other side while Fionntan read her latest message. He nodded. "Ask what you will."

She had hoped he would say as much, and had already started on what she wanted to say. She finished the last few words and turned the tablet again. *"Why writing, but not speech?"*

She saw him read the question several times, brow furrowing. "Why...Why does the vow allow for reading words written in the human language, but not speech in that tongue? Is that your question?"

Ceana nodded. King Fionntan nodded slightly. "I see. You are not the first to raise that point. There are some who make no distinction, who will not even read the human tongue. But for most of us ..." He indicated what she'd written. "The language is of humans, but the letters came first from our people. It is a slim justification, but it is enough, and some allowances must be made. This is the one with which most of us can live."

Slim justification indeed—but without it, she truly would have no way to communicate, so she certainly wouldn't protest. Instead, she turned her tablet again to show her latest question: *"Why vow?"*

King Fionntan stared at the question, chin in his hand, his expression contemplative, as if searching for the right words. At last, he spoke. "There are many in our history and our present who have suffered at the hands of humans. There are many folk here in Emain Ablach, full-blooded selkies and half-blooded alike, for whom any reminder of their time in human lands is as painful as a knife in the back. We cannot keep out every trace of humankind—not without abandoning the safety of this home and forsaking the ability to walk upon land. Nor can we provide them the justice they deserve without provoking a war we cannot win. But we can keep the human language, the language in which so many were ensnared and abused, from our mouths and ensure those voices cannot reach this place. And so, we do."

He paused, then went on. "I do not know if you have lived a kinder life than some who come here, or if you simply have a greater capacity for forgiveness than most. No one will force you to take the vow. Not everyone does, and no one will stop you from speaking your old tongue. But if you must use it, do so in private, where you will not be readily heard."

Ceana bowed her head slightly. *"I understand,"* she wrote. She itched to ask just what kind of horrors would cause such a reaction, but somehow, it didn't seem like the right time. So, instead, she pulled a sheet of parchment and the pen towards herself and wrote at the top of the page, *"Ask your questions, please. I am ready to answer."*

And for the next two hours, that was exactly what she did. King Fionntan plied her with question after question, all centering on the royal family: their goals, their plans, their attitudes towards the selkies and other nations, their relationships with one another. Ceana did her best to answer each with just enough information to perhaps lower Fionntan's suspicions without giving away secrets or sharing something she should have no way of knowing. Only what could be construed as castle gossip, tidbits overheard while working, or nuggets shared by an overexcited princess—only this she wrote, as well as she could manage.

Every question brought a new struggle. Keeping her family's confidence was no hardship; she was used to that. Yet telling King Fionntan as much as she could in a bid to turn his trust would have been nearly as easy. Balancing the two...Ceana took grateful refuge in the fact that she was supposedly recounting secondhand knowledge that she'd have to think about to recall, for otherwise, her struggle to decide what she could and couldn't say would certainly have given her away. She wished with everything in her that she'd thought to spend some time in the past two days preparing rather than wandering the island and talking to people.

King Fionntan didn't make things any easier. After she wrote down her answer to each of his questions, he would study her words for what seemed like an eternity. And then, when he at last passed the paper back, he had a way of picking up particular details and asking the most inconvenient follow-up questions, questions that made her wonder if he was learning far more than she thought she was sharing. Again and again, she prayed silently that Dèanadair would guide her pen and protect her from revealing too much.

In all her answers, she did her best to emphasize the good character of King Seòras and her family and the fact that Atìrse wanted only peace. Why had King Seòras married one of his daughters to this person or this family? Because it would ensure peace for Atìrse. What kind of agreements stood between Atìrse and a particular other nation? Treaties promising friendship, mutual trade, and aid in times of trouble.

The easiest questions to answer by far were those about the character of her family members—Ceana only had to stop herself singing their praises. King Fionntan, understandably, took the most interest in her parents and Onora, though he asked about the others as well. Even so, with all Fionntan's questions, she managed to write nearly three pages about her father before she could catch herself. Thankfully, she restrained herself better when it came to Onora, focusing on her preparation to become Atìrse's next ruler and her desire to imitate the best qualities of their forebears while avoiding any reference to Onora's *other* role in helping King Seòras and Queen Isla rule.

All the while, Ceana nervously awaited one particular question, uncertain whether to hope Fionntan didn't ask it or hope he did. But her hopes mattered not at all, for after a long series of queries about the princesses' marriages and the goals of each, Fionntan returned the paper to her, saying, "What of the youngest princess? You heard the discussion between your cousins and myself the other day about her and about the fact that King Seòras offered me her hand. Know you aught of what his intention might have been?"

Ceana stared at the paper in front of her, her quill poised over the inkwell. What to say? How much *could* she say? At last, she dipped her pen and slowly wrote, *"Heard it was the princess's idea. Not the king's."*

She slid the paper to Fionntan, and he read it silently—several times over, if Ceana was any judge. Brow furrowed, he passed the paper back. "What interest has Atìrse's youngest princess in my people or in me?"

Oh, if he only knew! Ceana ducked her head, focusing on writing her reply and hoping that her hair would hide any trace of her thoughts on her face. *"Think she wants to serve her country as her sisters did. Maybe thought marriage alliance with you was best choice, didn't realize it would anger you."* She hesitated a moment, then added, *"Heard she felt awful when she realized she'd offended you. Was afraid you would end the whole treaty."*

It was probably the closest she'd ever be able to come to an apology. It wasn't enough. But it was better than nothing, so she handed the paper to Fionntan again.

He read more quickly this time, then sighed. "A desire to serve, I can respect, but 'twould have been better had she found another path to do so. Still, she is the youngest; perhaps 'tis no wonder if she is more naïve than others in her family."

Oh! Ceana had to lower her head again, lest Fionntan see her face reddening. It was hardly *naïve* to think that the people you'd coexisted with and had a treaty with for generations upon generations might be open to friendship. But she couldn't think of a way to say as much without revealing the depth of her knowledge, so instead she wrote, *"Would you have ended the treaty? She wasn't the only one afraid."*

As he read her words, Fionntan's expression softened. "Ah. Were you one of those?"

Ceana nodded, keeping her eyes down. Hastily, she scribbled, *"Some friends thought you might declare war. Didn't know what to believe. Still not certain."*

Fionntan shook his head. "You have no need to fear. Angry as I was—angry as I still am, in many ways—I would not take that step unless 'twas truly necessary. Too many lives would be lost; too many we cannot afford to lose. Imperfect as the treaty is, it is still the best protection we have." He paused. "I know little of what circumstances you left behind, but...are there still those in Atìrse who you care for?"

Were there! Ceana's thoughts darted to her family, to her friends among the nobility and to those among her family's guards and servants with whom she'd been friendly. *"Many,"* she wrote, her hand shaking a little, *"Family. Friends. As you said, I had a kinder life than some."*

She paused at the end, long enough that her pen dripped a blot of ink on the page. Hastily, she handed the paper to Fionntan and cleaned the nib before she could drip any more.

When she looked up again, Fionntan was studying her closely. "If I may ask, Lady Kenna, what led you to seek us out? Most of those who come to us are fleeing something. Others have lost everything else and hope to find a new home and answers here. Those who are happy on land rarely leave it. So why did you?"

How to answer that? She couldn't exactly say that she'd come to find out *why* the selkies had refused the alliance. After long thought, she wrote, *"Maimeó gave me the cloak. Told me to go to the sea. And I wanted to understand why you sang and what it meant."*

As Fionntan read, he nodded slowly. "I see. Why did your

grandmother give you the cloak?"

That, at least, was a little easier to answer. *"She had been protecting it. She said she felt it was time to pass it on."* This felt a bit too personal—time to change the subject, just a little. *"Would the cloak have worked the same for others in my family? For my cousin? My sisters?"*

She had to squeeze the last words onto the very edge of the page in the tiniest letters. Fionntan squinted at them, his face taking on a thoughtful expression. "'Tis hard to say for sure. If I may ask, do your parents yet live?"

Ceana hesitated, then nodded. Would saying as much give something away? She wasn't sure. But claiming to be an orphan felt like one lie too far for her to carry off.

"I see." Fionntan's gaze drifted to her cloak. "After two generations—even after one generation, in some families—it is hard to say how much the selkie blood will bear out. Within any family, some will be more like our people, and some will be more human. If your grandmother gave you the cloak, no doubt she believed you were the most selkie out of all your kin; that you were the person for whom it would work the best. It would seem to me that she chose wisely."

Again, Ceana blushed, though she didn't try to hide it this time. Picking up her tablet, she wrote, *"Do you have more questions for me?"*

Fionntan stood. "Many. Yet I have already kept you here a good two hours, and I can tell you are growing weary. I would be a churlish man indeed if I forced you to continue. Perhaps you will be good enough to return in ..." He paused. "Not a week from today, as I have already made plans that afternoon, but six days from now, this same time?"

Six days. Surely that would be enough time to think more about what she could and couldn't afford to say and what she wanted Fionntan to know. Enough time to prepare so she wouldn't hesitate on every question. So, Ceana nodded agreement.

"Excellent." Fionntan offered her his hand. "Come, then. Your cousin, I believe, will be off-duty soon. Shall we seek her out so you need not walk home alone?"

Ceana smiled, took Fionntan's arm, and stood, sliding her tablet into her pocket. Then they made their way out of the library and through the halls. The meeting had gone well, she thought. Hopefully, some of what she'd said had been enough to start Fionntan thinking about Atìrse as less of an enemy—she could only pray that it hadn't also been enough to reveal she wasn't who she claimed to be. At least Fionntan didn't seem suspicious yet. She'd just have to make sure that didn't change.

The next day was the day on which Ninian had instructed Ceana to return so he could check on her arm. Ceana had intended to make a brief trip to the village, then spend the rest of the day deciding what she could tell King Fionntan next time she met with him.

But instead, at breakfast, Mairearad announced that, as Ceana was part of the family now, she ought to have some new gowns of her own, and so, after Ceana's visit to Ninian, Uaine was to take Ceana to the tailor's shop in the village to pick out colors and be measured. Ceana tried to protest, but Mairearad simply waved her concern away, saying, "You are our cousin, and you cannot spend the rest of your life wearing cast-offs. It would reflect poorly on us, besides being unfair to you."

Against this, Ceana could find no argument. She consoled herself with the fact that at least the gowns could be adjusted to fit Uaine or Aíbinn after she left—and if she happened to stay long enough to use any of the dresses first, well, it would be nice to wear something that was *hers* again.

As the morning progressed, she couldn't help enjoying herself. Uaine chatted the whole way down to the village, telling Ceana of the tailor, Master Lachlainne, and his assistants, and what fine work they did. He and his workers had made the blue dress Ceana wore just now, along with many more of the sisters' gowns in the last few years. "Since Màthair left and Mairearad and Aíbinn are at the keep so much, it's really too much for the servants and me to do on our own," Uaine explained. "And I'm far better at weaving and spinning than at stitching. Mairearad does lovely stitchwork, but she's *so* busy."

Ceana would have liked to ask what Uaine meant by saying her mother had *left* and where she'd gone. But they reached Ninian's shop just then, and so Ceana's question was left behind. Happily, Ninian pronounced her arm healed enough that he could remove the splint, though he instructed her to use the ointment a few days more and to return again in two weeks. Ceana still couldn't fathom what miracle had led to such swift healing, but she thanked Dèanadair for it anyway.

As he finished, Ninian asked again after her voice and after the Northwaves' plans for an adoption ceremony. When Ceana told him of her decision to wait, however, his expression darkened. "Are you sure 'tis what you want, lass?"

Ceana nodded. Uaine had stayed outside, so she felt no compunction about speaking her reply. "I'm certain. I want time to adjust. Is something wrong?"

"Perhaps. Perhaps 'tis nothing. As a healer, 'tis my business to worry either way." Ninian shook his head and fetched a fresh jar of ointment from a cupboard. Handing it to her, he added, "But if you find yourself having trouble of any sort, with your voice or anything else, come straight to me."

Ceana promised she would and then departed. Ninian's words cast a faint grey cloud over her good spirits, but then again, she'd never met a healer who *didn't* fuss more than necessary. In any case, she'd surely be gone long before any trouble arose.

She and Uaine went next to the tailor, and Ceana quickly forgot all about Ninian's worries. She'd never visited a tailor's shop before; her family's tailor had always come to her. Master Lachlainne was a large man of a shape that suggested his table was as well-laid as the king's, but he was courteous and professional and made Ceana feel instantly at ease. Uaine clearly knew him well, for she and he chatted in a friendly manner through the whole process of taking measurements, choosing styles and materials, and arranging payment.

After the stop at the tailor's, there were other errands to run. To Ceana's surprise, Uaine attended to these herself, rather than sending a servant—but, then again, there probably weren't enough servants in the Northwaves household for that to be practical. And it wasn't as if Uaine hadn't performed far more menial tasks already.

When they returned to the Northwaves house, Ceana again thought to plan for her next conversation with Fionntan. But somehow, she instead found herself in the workroom with Uaine, winding yarn one-handed while Uaine worked her loom and chatted about this and that. She spent a great deal of time telling Ceana stories of when she, Mairearad, and Aíbinn were all much younger, as if to make up for the fact that Ceana hadn't been there herself.

The sisters' parents featured frequently in these stories, and their presence in Uaine's recollections made their absence in the present all the more glaring. What *had* happened to them? Uaine had said that their mother had "left." Did she mean that literally? Or was it a euphemism for her having died? And what about their father? None of Uaine's stories gave any hint as to what might have happened to him.

Fionntan's words from the day before slid back into Ceana's thoughts: *"There are many in our history and our present who have suffered at the hands of humans."* Were the Northwaves among those of whom Fionntan spoke? Had Ceana's own people been responsible for whatever happened to Uaine's parents? Was that why Mairearad and Aíbinn had made their vow?

Ceana resolved to ask the first chance she had when all three sisters were together. She knew she could just ask Uaine, but perhaps if she put the question to all three at once, she'd learn more—Mairearad, as the eldest, would no doubt know the most details, while Aíbinn seemed the least likely to shy away from potentially sensitive topics. Perhaps it would even be the opening

Ceana needed to find out what she'd come here for in the first place.

That evening, she waited patiently through dinner, listening as the sisters traded accounts of their days and writing out answers to the questions directed at her. She'd long since gotten into the habit of participating very little in mealtime conversations with multiple people; she couldn't write and eat at once, and when she tried, it often took so long to write what she wanted to say that the conversation had moved on before she finished. The Northwaves did their best to not leave her behind, true, but with all three of them present, that was easier said than done.

After dinner, the sisters moved upstairs to the solar: Mairearad at the spinning wheel, where she picked up the work she'd started the night before, and Aíbinn and Uaine each on one of the couches. Ceana, after a moment's thought, sat down by Aíbinn.

Conversation drifted, and before long, Ceana saw Uaine reaching for a book. That usually meant she planned to offer to read aloud, and if she started that, Ceana would lose her chance. So, hastily, Ceana tapped Aíbinn on the shoulder and passed over her tablet, on which she'd written a question that took up both sides: *"Wondering: what happened to your parents? Said they're both gone? All right to ask? Don't need to answer if not willing."*

Aíbinn read the questions silently. A long pause followed in which Ceana wondered if merely asking had been offensive—though she also felt that strange pressure around her that meant the sisters were speaking mentally. At last, Aibinn passed the tablet back to Ceana. "Thou canst ask anything thou wishes, of course. 'Tis only natural thou'd want to know about thy kin."

What a relief! Ceana smoothed out the wax and wrote, *"Thank you. I worried if they were dead, would be painful for you."*

Aíbinn glanced down. "Thou art sweet, but no fear. We have done our grieving, the three of us."

"Aíbinn, thou willst give Kenna the wrong idea if you go on like this," Mairearad cut in, shaking her head a little. "Thou willst convince her that both Athair and Màthair have taken the Final Path." She glanced up at Ceana and raised an eyebrow. "Though perhaps you already thought as much."

Ceana nodded and wrote her reply on her tablet: *"Yes—not dead?"* She then showed it to Aíbinn so she could pass the message along.

Mairearad replied a moment later. "No, only Athair. He passed on some six years hence. Ninian said 'twas a problem with his heart."

"It wasn't the first trouble he'd had," Aíbinn added. "I remember he'd had spells before that when he'd have to sit down because his chest hurt and he felt like his head was spinning and he couldn't breathe right. I don't know if Uaine remembers —"

"I do! I was *ten*; I knew something was wrong as well as the rest of you," Uaine protested. "He had one of his spells on my name-day celebration, and I was so upset, and then he made that silly comment about his heart being so excited for me that it got all worked up, and then I cried because I thought 'twas my fault."

"Oh, thou didst. I'd forgotten." Aíbinn shook her head. "He and Màthair were at the castle when it happened. They were on their way to meet with the old king and queen, and Athair just collapsed. We were lucky Ninian was there already, or else he would have been gone before we could even reach him to say goodbye."

Ceana tried to imagine losing her father in such a way; the mere thought made her feel sick and small. *"I'm sorry."*

Aíbinn offered a sad smile. "Thanks. 'Twas hard at the time, but as I said, we've done our grieving."

How could you ever stop mourning such a loss? But Ceana kept that thought to herself, instead writing, *"What of mother? Gone, not dead? Not expected to return?"*

She showed her tablet to Aíbinn, and all three sisters brightened, one after another. Uaine spoke the quickest, her voice rich with pride. "Màthair is King Fionntan's ambassador to the Daoine Math."

Oh, that *would* explain it. Of course, the selkies would need a permanent ambassador stationed in Tìr Soilleir, since they had such strong ties to the faery folk and traded with them so frequently. The only reason Atìrse could manage without a permanent ambassador themselves was that Thrice-Great Uncle Diarmad filled that role in all but title. But since time didn't always work properly between Tìr Soilleir and the mortal realm, agreeing to live there full time might well mean never seeing your home again. How brave of the former Lady of Northwaves! But, too, how hard for the sisters, who would have to grieve another parent's loss.

But she couldn't say any of that, no more than she could tell Fionntan all she wished he understood about her family. Instead, she wrote, *"That's wonderful. Must be very proud."*

All three sisters nodded. "Fionntan's father used to say Màthair was one of the best diplomats he had," Uaine said. "Though I think Mairearad is probably nearly as good."

Mairearad flushed. "I doubt that. I'm still young, and as you'll recall, my first major diplomatic assignment ended with Fionntan storming out of the meeting after threatening to end the treaty we'd just renewed."

Aíbinn shook her head. "That was King Seòras's fault, though, not thine. Fionntan's told me that thou and Lord Muir did a marvelous job salvaging things before you left." She turned her focus back on Ceana. "Màthair was very good, though, especially considering that she was a wanderer before she met Athair. She spent the first twenty years of her life rarely interacting with civilization or even changing from seal-shape, but she could outthink and outtalk anyone."

Oh, that was interesting! Ceana could hardly get the words down fast enough: *"How did she and your father meet?"*

Mairearad smiled fondly, her hands slowing a little on the wheel. "Athair had gone out with a singing party, and he stayed behind an extra night—his sister had recently gone missing in that area, and he hoped to find her. Màthair, while seeking a place to rest for the night, overheard his singing for his sister and thought it the loveliest thing she'd ever heard. She approached, offered to help him search, and then said she'd swim back to Emain Ablach with him so they'd have safety in numbers. After that, she simply kept finding excuses not to leave until he finally proposed."

Uaine made a face. "Thou could tell it better than that—the way Athair always did."

Mairearad shook her head. "Kenna merely asked how they met—and thou art too old for bedtime stories."

"'Tisn't *bedtime stories*; 'tis one of the greatest stories in our family history, and thou ought give it its proper telling." Uaine spun towards Ceana. "Dost thou not agree, Kenna?"

Ceana shrugged and wrote, *"Would like to hear in full sometime. What happened to sister?"*

Aíbinn glanced at the tablet. "Athair never found her. Eventually, we all assumed she was either dead or gone for good. Her picture's in our family's section of the Halls of the Lost, if thou'd like to see it."

"Kenna should go there in any case," Mairearad cut in, her hands picking up speed once more. "If her relation is on Athair's side, or on the known part of Màthair's side, mayhap she would recognize them. I should like to know our connection."

"We could go after the next service," Uaine suggested. "The current meeting place isn't far from the Halls."

"Excellent idea." Mairearad nodded decisively. "Unless you object, Kenna?"

On one hand, if they expected her to identify some shared relation, that would be nearly impossible. On the other hand...it sounded like quite a bit of their extended family wasn't represented, so she had an easy explanation when she couldn't tell them who she was related to. So, she nodded and wrote, *"Happy to go."* Perhaps it would even give her some answers about why Ninian thought them related.

Mairearad gave a decisive nod. "Then we shall go. And now, Uaine, since thou art dissatisfied with how I relate family history, thou canst tell Kenna of some of our other ancestors and relations."

Uaine gave Mairearad a pleading look. "Me! Why, when thou canst tell everything so well?"

Aíbinn raised a hand. "If neither of you wants to, I'll tell her

191

about Eisia and Aerdon —"

"*No!*" both Mairearad and Uaine chorused at once. Uaine added passionately, "Tell Kenna another time; if I hear that tale one more time, I shall *scream*. It's horrible." Directly to Ceana, she added, "Eisia and Aerdon were siblings, many generations back. They got lost in the deepest and darkest parts of Muir Soilleir, and went through all manner of terrible things trying to find their way home, and I don't understand at all why Aíbinn likes telling the story so much."

"It is a bit over-told, and perhaps a bit frightening for some," Mairearad agreed, more tactfully. "Very well, since there seems to be no other way to keep the peace, I will do the telling."

Aíbinn huffed in annoyance, while Uaine fairly crowed, "Oh, yes! You should tell Kenna about Great-Grandfather and Queen Aisling, if you're not going to tell her about Athair and Màthair properly." To Ceana, she added, "He saved her life! It's terribly dramatic."

"Thou wilt give away the ending before I begin? Now who tells the story poorly." Mairearad clicked her tongue, adding another mass of wool to her spindle. "This tale is from many years ago, when our grandfather was a young boy and our father not even a twinkle in the sun's eye. One day, Great-Grandfather was out patrolling the waters around Emain Ablach ..."

Chapter 20
REVELATIONS

The next day passed swiftly, and soon the day of worship came. Ceana sat through the service, alternately fidgeting with impatience and internally scolding herself for her restlessness. She *shouldn't* want to rush through time spent praising Dèanadair and seeking His wisdom—but she couldn't deny that she wanted to know what answers she might find in the Halls of the Lost.

At last, the service came to an end. Ceana and the Northwaves sisters lingered only long enough to greet a few people before they left. To Ceana's surprise, they made not for somewhere in the hills but for the lakeside. From there, Mairearad led them into the water and along the shore until they reached an area where there was no sandy bank, just a steep, rocky slope leading down into the lake. Here, they dove and entered an underwater tunnel, like the entrance to the island but far wider. Ceana could see other selkies a little ways ahead of them, and when she glanced back, she noticed still more coming in after them.

The tunnel sloped steeply downward, then upward. At last, they emerged from the water into a stone chamber, dimly lit by lanterns hanging from hooks in the stone walls. A little way ahead, the chamber bent; a much brighter light came from around the corner.

The Northwaves sisters headed towards the light, and Ceana followed. The day before, Uaine had told her a little about what to expect. The Halls of the Lost were where selkies kept record and memory of those who had either taken the final path or were assumed to have done so. It wasn't *precisely* a graveyard, as it was a place to remember the missing as well as those who were confirmed dead, but it was similar. However, the exact nature of the Halls was, Uaine had said, better seen than explained.

Around the corner, Ceana found another chamber, its walls lined with shelves full of books and scrolls. In the center of the space, a large staircase descended into the earth. Mairearad gestured to the shelves. "These hold a record of all those memorialized here, sealed with enchantments to ensure age touches them not. Similar enchantments are laid throughout the Halls; their provision is part of our treaty with the Daoine Math." She started down the stairs, Aíbinn close behind. "Follow me, and stay close. The Halls are large and winding, and you may easily become lost if you stray."

Ceana stepped after her, Uaine keeping step beside her. As they descended, the air grew warmer and stuffier, almost suffocating. The seal-cloak didn't help; though it was light enough that it didn't bother her outside, in here, it became one layer too many. Ceana found herself fussing with it, trying to unobtrusively move it this way and that in an attempt to not overheat.

Her motions must not have been subtle enough, for Uaine leaned over and whispered to her, "Once we reach our family section, thou canst remove thy cloak if thou art uncomfortable. 'Tis considered part of our home."

Thank Dèanadair! Ceana gave Uaine a grateful look and forced herself to stop pulling at the cloak. She could endure a bit longer now that she had relief to look forward to. Strange that the sisters didn't have the same trouble—but perhaps part of the magic of a true seal-cloak was that its wearer would never be too warm because of it. Or, equally likely, the sisters were just used to it.

The staircase ended in a larger cavern with many passages leading off in various directions. More lanterns were set in the walls, and when Ceana held her hand by one, she felt no heat—no doubt they were magical lanterns, then, so there would be no risk of fire and little fear of their going out. They cast a dim, golden glow over the space and reflected off the glassy walls.

Mairearad set off down one of the passages, walking confidently even though Ceana could see no marker to differentiate this tunnel from any other. As they walked, they passed openings here and there in the walls. Some of these led to other passages, darker than the one they were currently in, and some seemed to lead into caverns, though most of the cavern openings were curved in such a way that Ceana couldn't see much of the interior from the tunnel.

As they approached one such opening, a figure stepped out of it. In the dim light, it took Ceana a moment to recognize him as King Fionntan. Mairearad, Aíbinn, and Uaine all dipped into curtsies, and Ceana followed suit a moment behind them.

King Fionntan made a gesture to dismiss the formality. "Good day to you, ladies."

"Good day, your majesty," Mairearad replied. "Visiting your parents?"

"Indeed." King Fionntan nodded. "And you?"

Mairearad gestured to Ceana. "Kenna wished to know something of her kin here, and I hope that she might recognize someone well enough to determine how we are related."

"Ah. A wise endeavor," Fionntan replied. "Would you care for company on your way home after you are done? I am glad to wait in the main cavern until you are ready to leave."

Mairearad wavered a moment. "We would hate to keep you, your majesty ..."

King Fionntan shook his head, a smile flickering on his face. "It is no trouble for me. In truth, I ask because I would enjoy having the company of someone other than my guards."

"Then we can hardly refuse you," Mairearad replied graciously. "But if you feel you need leave before we are finished, please, do not let us hold you back."

"And do not let me rush you. I am happy to wait." King Fionntan stepped to the side. "After all, down here, no one can ask after matters of state."

With a final bow and a few more murmured words, the sisters and Ceana continued on. They passed another four openings before Mairearad turned in at one of the caverns, saying, "Here we are."

Ceana followed and found herself in a long, gallery-like hall. Unlike the main passages, it was lit not by torches, but rather by veins of glowing crystal that ran through the rock walls. This light fell on numerous paintings and statues hanging on the walls or set throughout the chamber. Here and there, Ceana spotted odd, rectangular seams in the floor and the lower parts of the wall. In the center of each seam, carved letters formed names—perhaps marking actual burial places?

Mairearad raised a hand and swept it out to indicate the room. She spoke in a hushed voice. "This is our part of the Halls of the Lost. Every member of our family who has been lost to death or currents or uncertainty, all those of whom we have record, is represented here in painting or sculpture. Some are buried here; others lay to rest elsewhere. If you would like, I can tell you a little something of each of them, or you can look on your own and ask questions."

"You tell," Ceana wrote in reply. *"Please."*

Mairearad nodded and headed further into the cavern. "Come, then. These closest to the entrance are our oldest ancestors; better to start with someone a little more recent." About halfway down the cavern, she stopped before a pair of paintings. "Here. These are our great-great-great grandparents—mine and my sisters', that is. They may be yours as well, of course, but of that we cannot yet be sure. 'Twas they who built our home in its current form ..."

Ceana followed, removing her cloak and keeping it folded in her arms. At first, she attended closely to Mairearad's words, but as they moved down the line of relations, her attention waned, and she spent more and more time simply studying the pictures and statues, only half-listening to what the sisters said. The frames and stands of most of the pictures were carved and painted with runes—perhaps anchoring the enchantments of preservation Mairearad had mentioned. Ceana recalled seeing similar runes on some of the very oldest artworks in her family's palaces.

Mairearad had said that these enchantments were part of the treaty with the Daoine Math, and Aíbinn had said that much of the selkies' livestock also came from trade with the faery folk. What were the *selkies* providing the faeries in return for all this? They had to be doing something, but what could the selkies get that the Daoine Math couldn't acquire far more cheaply and easily either on their own or from humans? Pearls, perhaps? But even if all the selkies did nothing but dive for pearls all day, surely that wouldn't be enough. She needed to find a way to ask Mairearad that sometime…

The pictures and statues ended well before the cavern did, probably to leave space for future generations. As Mairearad talked on, having gotten all the way to the sisters' grandparents, one of the last paintings caught Ceana's eye. The figure there looked strangely familiar—though, perhaps that was only her imagination?

She edged her way over and stared up at it, searching the thin face, the huge, dark eyes, the silky black hair. Yes, she knew those features—or, rather, a version of those features, thirty years older and worn with melancholy. But how? What was a portrait of Lord Arran's wife doing on a wall full of Northwaves family members?

Ceana scribbled a question down on her tablet and cleared her throat to catch the sisters' attention. Once they'd turned, she pointed to the painting and held up the tablet to show them what she'd written: *"Who is this?"*

All three sisters clustered round. "That's Aunt Eilidh," Uaine replied, a breathlessly hopeful edge to her voice. "Athair's sister, the one he was looking for when he met Màthair. Do you…do you know her? Is she related to you?"

Ceana shook her head. Eilidh. That couldn't be a coincidence, could it? She adjusted her grip on her tablet as she wrote her reply, only to realize that it was her pen hand shaking. *"Not related. Looks like a noblewoman. Wife of Lord Arran. Same name."*

When Ceana looked up again, Mairearad's face had gone very pale, while Aíbinn's was flushed. Aíbinn pushed forward to stand directly in front of Ceana. "This noblewoman is the wife of Lord Arran. She has the same name as our aunt. Do you know where she came from?"

Did she know? Ceana thought for a moment. She'd had to memorize hundreds of lists of who was related to whom among the nobility of various lands. Lady Eilidh, though...she wasn't in the lists. *"I don't know. No one does. Lord Arran traveled to Gormthall, came back with her."* Some speculated that she was the illegitimate daughter of some Gormthaller nobility, of course, but Ceana wasn't about to spread that rumor to the selkies. Bad enough that it was so widely repeated in Atìrse.

"So close," Mairearad whispered. "All this time, she was so close. If only Athair had known ..." She shook her head and focused on Ceana again. "Is this lady still alive? Well?"

Ceana nodded. *"Alive. Well. Always seems sad."*

"Well, no wonder!" Aíbinn exploded. She spun to face Mairearad. "We should tell Fionntan. She's so close—there has to be something we could do."

"Not close enough." Mairearad's hands clutched the edges of her cloak. "Not close enough to mount a rescue. And it's not as if demanding her return would work any better than it has in the past."

What were they talking about? Ceana glanced from one sister to another, scribbling down a question. She cleared her throat and held up her tablet once more. *"I don't understand. You think Lady E is your aunt? Lord A & Lady E often travel so far from shore, selkie would die. Couldn't get to sea often enough. How?"*

Another look passed among the sisters, mingling confusion and astonishment. Then, speaking slowly, Aíbinn asked, "You... you don't know?"

Emotion overcame years of royal training, and Ceana gave Aíbinn an exasperated look. Of course, she didn't know! If she knew, she wouldn't be asking!

"Oh my...you *don't* know." Now it was Aíbinn's turn to pale. "You said your grandmother gave you the cloak, didn't you? What did she tell you about it?"

"She told me to take it and go to the sea." Ceana's hand shook again, despite her best attempts to keep it steady. *"Said it was from*

her mother's mother. She'd been told to keep it safe until time to use it." All true—hopefully they weren't truths that would expose her.

Once more the three sisters exchanged glances, and this time the glances carried with them the weight of unspoken communication. The silence stretched on unpleasantly long. At last, Mairearad spoke. "It is true that our kind cannot spend too long away from the sea under normal circumstances. But a selkie who is bound to a human in marriage has no such limitation."

Well, that explained some things. Namely, how there could be so many part-selkies around. *"That doesn't sound bad."*

"It was meant as a blessing, once," Mairearad replied, bitterness and regret lacing her tone. "But just as the selkies are given access to the land, so the humans who marry them have the freedom of the seas through their spouses' cloaks. And that, it seems, is a freedom and power many covet enough to turn to cruelty to get."

But that meant...that meant...Ceana couldn't make the thoughts come together. Couldn't bring herself to put it together. *"What are you saying?"*

"What she's saying," Aíbinn replied, taking over from Mairearad, "is that there are many in the lands of men, Atìrse especially, who will kidnap our people and steal their cloaks and force them into marriage—because whoever holds a selkie's cloak has power over them, and they can use the cloaks to take seal-form like we do. It doesn't happen as often as it did in the bad old days before the treaty. But the treaty didn't *stop* it like we thought it would. And no matter how often we go out and sing, no matter how much we search, there's always someone lost."

No. Ceana took a step back, her cloak suddenly heavy in her arms. That couldn't be true, could it? Her people wouldn't...they wouldn't do something so awful, would they?

But she thought of Lady Eilidh and her sad, grieving eyes. She thought of Fionntan's words: *We have no need of friendship with kidnappers and slavers.* She thought of the hunters she'd encountered on the way to the island—they'd sounded just as eager to catch a selkie as a seal.

If all this was true...no wonder the selkies hated Atìrse. No wonder they had refused the alliance, if Atìrse couldn't even keep the treaty. But why hadn't they told someone? Surely if they had told her father—

Unless...

Oh no.

Ceana looked down at the cloak in her arms. Queen Moireach thought it merely enchanted to work like a selkie's cloak. But she hadn't known where it came from or who made it. And Ninian's tests said that Ceana had selkie ancestors ...

Ceana didn't realize she'd let the cloak fall until her tablet and pen clattered to the ground beside it. She took two stumbling steps back as Mairearad reached out to her, lips moving with words that were lost amid the ringing in Ceana's ears. She couldn't be here. She shouldn't be here. She needed air.

She turned and ran from the room, out into the twisting passages. Where was the path outside? She turned this way and that, pushing past people until she made another turn and found no one to block her path. On she rushed, even as the passages grew darker. Was this the way? Everything looked the same, and there were no voices to guide her except those behind her, but those had already faded.

She turned down another passageway, but two steps around a curve plunged her into darkness. Her foot caught on something, and she tripped, sprawling face first on the ground. She lay there, breathing hard.

She should have known. How could she have known? If only she had realized; if only *someone* had realized. If her father and mother only knew, if Onora only knew, they would have done something, surely.

They needed to know. Ceana wiggled herself closer to the wall, fumbling for the necklace Onora had given for her. She felt along its length and pressed her finger to the trigger rune. "Onora," she whispered, "Onora, I found out—Onora, the selkies—they—we—"

She couldn't get the words out. Her voice broke into sobs, and no matter how she tried, she couldn't get it under control again. And so, for a long, long time, she stayed there, weeping for all she hadn't known.

Chapter 21
A KING'S COMFORT

Ceana might have stayed there, still weeping, for the rest of the day—possibly, if she had her way, the rest of her life. Eventually, though, she heard her name being called, echoing as if from far away. She sniffled and pressed herself deeper into a curve in the side of the passage. By now, her tears had subsided into occasional hiccupping sobs.

The voice calling her name came again, closer this time. King Fionntan's voice, she realized. What was he doing, looking for her? She tried her best to keep quiet. Oh, how he must hate her! Or, not her as he knew her, but her real self.

She could hear his footsteps now. Could still hear him calling her name—not just aloud, but in thought-speech. She couldn't face him, though. She couldn't ...

His voice and footsteps drew closer still. Out of the corner of her eye, she could see the glow of a torch that cast dim light over the passage and threw King Fionntan's distorted shadow on the wall. "Lady Kenna?" he called again. "Are you here?"

Ceana pressed her lips together, but another sob welled up and escaped her despite her best efforts. King Fionntan moved closer, coming just around the curve of the tunnel. "Lady Kenna?"

Ceana curled into herself, burying her face in her arms so she could just *barely* see the hallway. She couldn't speak, and her tablet was back in the Northwaves' part of the Hall, along with her cloak—*not* her cloak. It was the cloak of some long-ago selkie who'd been stolen and forced into marriage for the satisfaction of some ancestor of Ceana's. Oh, if only she could remove all trace of whoever it had been from her blood! If only she could clean herself of that taint—but, then, she would still be princess of a country where such things were practiced, even if only secretly.

If only she'd known ...

King Fionntan moved forward, drawing level with her position. "Lady Kenna? Are you well? Your cousins said that you fled after they told you about their aunt."

Ceana didn't reply. She couldn't reply; even if her voice *wasn't* gone, she wasn't sure she'd be able to form words.

King Fionntan stood still a moment. Then, he sat down across from her. "Your cousins are worried about you. You went so fast, they couldn't find you, and they feared you would be lost down here."

He waited, and when Ceana still failed to respond, he added, "I worried as well. They said that you took what they told you...badly. I know you said you had a kinder life than some. I suppose it was a shock to learn the truth of your heritage."

A shock! That was putting it lightly! Ceana sniffled again, shutting her eyes. Oh, she should never have come here!

Another long silence. At last, he spoke again. "I know that you left your tablet behind. But if you are willing, please, speak to me. I will listen."

There was something strange in the words. It took Ceana a moment to realize what: he had spoken not the selkie tongue, but the human language.

That made her pull her head up and open her eyes so she could give him a questioning look. "Your vow?" she managed to mumble, her voice hoarse.

Sitting against the wall, knees bent and torch held in one hand, Fionntan shook his head. "I swore not to use it *save in great need*. And, my lady, I can see that your need is great indeed."

How could he be so *kind*? How? How, with what her ancestors and her people had done and were doing to his people? Despite her best intentions, she started sobbing all over again.

Fionntan waited, silent and patient. At last, she managed to control herself enough to choke out, "We didn't know! We didn't know! Oh, I'm so sorry."

"Lady Kenna, you have nothing to apologize for." Fionntan leaned forward a bit. "I understand that it was a surprise to learn ..."

"You don't understand!" Ceana fought to keep from wailing outright. "We didn't *know*! All this time, you've been suffering horrible things, and we didn't even realize. We didn't see it. We weren't *looking* for it. We've just been wondering why you seemed to hate us, even though you have every right to."

"No one hates you, Lady Kenna," Fionntan replied, his voice gentle and patient. "You are one of us. You are of my people, and that will not change."

"But three weeks ago, I wasn't. Three weeks ago, I was as human as anyone else I knew. Three weeks ago, I didn't know selkies and humans could marry—I thought they could, because the faeries and humans can marry, but I didn't know." Ceana took several deep breaths, trying to rein in her tongue before she said something she'd regret. "Three weeks ago, you hated me, just as you hate everyone in Atìrse. And you're right to, but *we didn't know*."

"You keep saying *'We didn't know,'*" Fionntan said, slowly. "Who is *we*?"

"*Everyone*! All of Atìrse, except the people doing it. *No one* knows." Ceana shook her head. "If we would have known, we would have done something, but we didn't, so we couldn't, and now ..."

"No one knows," Fionntan echoed, his voice hollow. "How sure are you of this?"

"If people knew, we would have done something. My *family* would have done something." Ceana could feel her voice breaking, and her throat already ached with the effort of talking so much after being mostly silent for so long. "But no one knows! Everyone thinks the treaty is about not hunting seals so we don't hurt your people by accident—even the royal family thinks that."

"Did your cousin tell you that?" Fionntan leaned forward. "Are you certain?"

Ceana could only nod and sob. Fionntan rested against the

wall, staring ahead for several long moments, his face strangely blank. But at last, he shook himself. "This...changes things. You are full of surprises, Lady Kenna." He leaned forward, coming up onto his toes, knees still bent under him. "But know this. You *are* of my people. You were of my people three weeks ago, though you didn't yet know it, and you will be of my people as long as we both live. If what you say is true, then I cannot blame you for what you did not know."

"But—But I should have known," Ceana managed to hiccup. "I should have found out, somehow."

"If Atìrse cannot remember the reason why the treaty was first made, then you may have been hard-pressed to discover anything, even if you had all the scholars of the lands to aid you," Fionntan replied. "Do not lay blame upon yourself for that which you had no hand in. I do not. And I surely do not hate you, no more than your cousins hate you. This secret has robbed you of your heritage, and that, too, is a grievous evil."

Ceana sniffled. "I wish I didn't know part of it. Whoever stole away a selkie, I wish I could cut out every trace of him from me."

"Yet if he had not, you would not be here. None of us are our ancestors, and neither is my bloodline free of sinners." Fionntan stood and offered his hand. "Come, Lady Kenna. You have spent enough time in this dark place. If you still wish for solitude, I understand, but please, take it in the sunshine so your dark thoughts will not consume you."

Oh, why did he have to be so kind? Ceana wanted to protest simply on principle of misery, but she couldn't bring herself to argue—not with those dark eyes looking at her, not with his hand outstretched to her. And, she had to admit, his advice was good; it was the same sort of thing her parents or Onora might have told her—*had* told her on more than one occasion when she was younger.

So, she wiped her eyes and took his hand in her good one. He lifted her to her feet easily and, when her legs still shook under her, wrapped an arm around her, supporting her. "There," he said, switching back to the selkie tongue. "Come. Let us find your cousins before they fear us both lost forever."

Ceana managed to push a wobbly smile. "That would be tragic for your people, your majesty, if you were lost on my account. They're lucky to have a king like you."

"By Dèanadair's grace, I had good teachers to learn from." Fionntan started back down the passage the way he'd come, still with one arm around Ceana and the torch in his other hand. "Would that I have had more time to learn before I took the throne. Often I think 'twould be better if my people had a more experienced ruler."

"You are honorable and noble and kind, and you *listen*," Ceana replied, choking a little on the words. "I don't think they could ask for better."

"Could they not?" Fionntan glanced down at her. "You say *they* could not. Yet you are, as I said, of my people as well. I know you speak highly of King Seòras. Do you wish you still lived under his rule? Would *you* ask for better?"

How to answer? She *wasn't* properly of his people, selkie blood or no. She was still a princess of Atìrse, even here, and she could hardly choose against her father. Yet, had the alliance gone through—had she married him—she *would* have been under his rule, not that of King Seòras. And that was hardly an unpleasant thought. So, she replied, "I would not. King Seòras is a good king, but so are you."

"Thank you for your kind words and your confidence. I hope I do not prove your trust ill-placed." As they walked, the murmur of voices slowly became audible from ahead. Fionntan stopped walking. "Are you well enough for the company of others, my lady?"

Ceana caught the meaning hidden in his words; once they were in public, it would be impolite for her to continue in her tongue and questionable for Fionntan to be noticed listening to it. She nodded. "I am. Thank you for listening. I am sorry to have made you hear and speak in a language you hate."

"Nay, my lady." Fionntan shook his head. "I do not hate the human language itself, only that it has been used for so many generations to enslave my people. So long as it remains the language of slavery, I will not lightly let it enter my mouth or my ears, unless to refuse it would mean a greater harm to one of my people."

A flicker of regret crossed his face. "Perhaps, I admit, 'twas rash of me to take so strict a vow. Perhaps if I had sworn only to keep it from my lips...Still, what is done is done. But, Lady Kenna, should there come a day when the vow is no longer taken, when I may speak either tongue with a clean conscience, I will rejoice, for on that day, Dèanadair will have worked a miracle, and there will be no more selkies kept in bondage."

Fionntan started walking again, though he moved slowly and kept his arm around Ceana. "In the meantime, though...It pleases me little that you are left voiceless for so long. Mairearad said you chose to wait until you reach the age of majority to be officially adopted, but will you not reconsider? If you fear the idea of a public ceremony while you are still adjusting to life here, I will speak to your cousins, and we will do all we can to ensure it is as private as possible."

Oh *no*. She couldn't do that. That would just tangle this whole matter up even worse. "Let me...let me think on it." The voices from up ahead were growing louder, so she said no more.

Fionntan nodded gravely. "If you decide you would prefer it, simply tell me so, or tell Mairearad yourself. I doubt she would refuse. And I will see, too, if I can find some who know the human tongue but who have taken no vow, with whom you can speak freely."

Ceana could think of no response but to nod. Of course, she had no intention of going through with the ceremony—the more she thought about it, the more it seemed a step further than a princess of Atìrse could reasonably go, even if she were in disguise. All the same, she appreciated Fionntan's concern.

A little further on, and they were back in the main cavern. Mairearad, Aíbinn, and Uaine were all clustered near the staircase, watching the passages. Uaine let out a cry almost as soon as Ceana and Fionntan emerged, and all three sisters rushed over. Within moments, Ceana found herself pulled from Fionntan's arm and into Uaine's embrace. "Oh, thank Dèanadair, thou art all right!"

She released Ceana, only for Aíbinn to swoop in to take Ceana by the shoulders and look her up and down. "*Art* thou all right? Thou ran away like thou had seen a ghost, and we lost track of thee. We've been searching for thee all over, with his majesty's help. Thou hast not injured thyself?"

Ceana shook her head, offering a half-smile and holding up her hands in what she hoped would come across as a don't-worry gesture. From just behind, Fionntan said, "She seems to be well. Only alarmed by what she did not know."

"Good!" Now Aíbinn hugged Ceana, though far more quickly than Uaine had. "I'm sorry thou had to find out in such a way. We truly thought thou already knew. Most seem to."

"Most do," Fionntan agreed. "Yet, perhaps, not as many as we believe. Some of what Lady Kenna said after I found her has given me much to think about."

"Thank you for finding her," Mairearad said. Though she had hung back a step behind her sisters, and though she made no move to embrace Ceana as they had, her voice was thick with relief. "Had she remained lost, I know not what we would have done."

"You need not thank me. I am glad I was here to help." Fionntan rested a hand on Ceana's shoulder for a moment, but removed it again almost as quickly.

Mairearad turned to Ceana and handed her the wax tablet and pen. Ceana noted with a guilty twinge that the frame was cracked where she'd dropped it. "Here are these," Mairearad said. "And here is your cloak."

She held out the seal cloak, but Ceana hesitated. She opened her tablet and slowly wrote, *"Not really mine, though. Belongs to your family."*

"It belongs to *our* family," Mairearad replied, voice firm and gaze steady. "Unless you have decided to disown us."

Ceana hastily shook her head. *"Don't feel as if I should wear it. Not after what you said."*

"The person it originally belonged to can no longer use it. Whoever she was, she has taken the Final Path, and the cloak she has now can never be spoiled or stolen." Mairearad stepped forward. "I have no doubt that she would be glad to see it used to bring the daughter of her daughters back home. When you have a cloak of your own, we will bring this one back here and lay it to rest in place of the one to whom it belonged. Until then, wear it, and do not despair."

She gently settled the cloak over Ceana. The weight of it and what it meant still hung heavy on Ceana's heart and shoulders, yet she couldn't help but feel that Mairearad's words had lightened that weight, just a little. She bowed her head; then, feeling that and the written word insufficient response, she wrapped her arms around Mairearad in a hug.

Mairearad gently returned the embrace, rubbing Ceana's back the same way Onora often had when Ceana was younger. "Truly, Kenna, we are glad you are not lost." She made a noise that might have been a held-back sniffle, then straightened. "Come, then. It is high time we returned home."

They made their way back up the staircase and out into the light of day. Ceana blinked in the warm, bright sunshine. After all she'd just learned, she almost felt that it should be storming outside. Yet, even so, warmth seemed to lift a little more of the weight on her shoulders.

They continued onward, taking seal-shape to cross the lake and then walking up the path from the village. The others talked as they walked, though not chatting as enthusiastically as they sometimes did. Everyone else seemed in nearly as somber a mood as Ceana. But Ceana couldn't miss the fact that one of her companions almost always seemed to have a hand on her arm or her shoulder, as if to make sure she didn't run away again—or, perhaps, to remind her that they were there.

At the doorstep of the Northwaves home, they stopped, and Fionntan made a slight bow. "Here I must leave you and return to my keep. But, Lady Mairearad, if you will, I wish to speak with you and some others late this afternoon or tomorrow morning. I will send a messenger with details once I speak to the others who need be present."

Mairearad bowed her head. "I am happy to come at your convenience, your majesty."

"Thank you." Fionntan turned to Ceana. "And, Lady Kenna, I believe we had agreed to meet a few days from now. Are you still willing to do so?"

Of course. Fionntan had more questions about Atìrse. Ceana nodded and wrote, *"I am willing."*

"Then I will look forward to seeing you then." Fionntan lastly addressed Aíbinn and Uaine. "As for the two of you, I have no doubt that I will see you again sometime soon."

"Certainly—we'll be at court dinner tomorrow. And surely thou art still coming to dinner in three days?" Uaine asked. "Has anything changed?"

"Nothing has changed save my faulty memory," Fionntan replied, laughing. "Until then, if I do not see you sooner. Good afternoon to you."

The sisters chorused their goodbyes. Then, with a final raised hand of farewell, Fionntan turned and made his way back down the path.

Uaine looped her arm through Ceana's and pushed the door open. "Well, come along then. After this morning, I'm sure you must be starving." And with that, she led the way inside, pulling Ceana with her.

Chapter 22
SISTERLY INTERFERENCE

None of the sisters seemed to want to leave Ceana alone for long all that afternoon and evening. They didn't crowd, but no matter where Ceana went in the house or garden, one of them would appear nearby a few minutes later. Or, when she retired to her room, after fifteen minutes or so, a knock would come on the door, followed by the voice of one of the sisters asking if she were all right.

Ceana had been annoyed by this at first, but her frustration didn't last long. Too much solitude felt strange, used as she was to having a gaggle of sisters around, even if their number had been dwindling over the last eight years or so. And she couldn't exactly blame them for worrying, the way she'd run off earlier.

She had needed solitude then. Now...now, she didn't know what she needed. But quiet company seemed to help all the same.

Her mood improved slightly as the day went on. It was hard to be truly morose on such a beautiful day; even the newly-discovered guilt hanging off her soul couldn't keep the sunshine from shining or the breeze from rustling through the green leaves and playing through her hair. It couldn't stop the bees from buzzing round the purple and golden flowers that filled the meadow-garden, and it couldn't stop the wrens and finches from chirping or flitting amid the tree branches or perching on Ceana's windowsill.

Nor could the guilt quite keep away the repeating memory of what King Fionntan had told her: "*You were of my people three weeks ago, though you didn't yet know it, and you will be of my people as long as we both live.*" If only that were true; if only he knew! Had he not refused the alliance, she could have been happy with him. Yet, knowing what she knew now, she could hardly blame him for his reaction. He must have thought her father—her family—all her people—heartless and mercenary indeed. No doubt he saw them openly trying to trap him in the same fate as so many of his people, claiming to offer friendship with one hand while actively breaking the treaty in the worst way with the other.

Oh, if only she'd known ...

By that evening, she was almost back to her usual self. Or, at least, she had managed to go a solid three hours without crying, which she decided was close enough. Dinner had passed, and she was about to ask Mairearad for another story of the Northwaves ancestors—*her* kin as well, in truth, it seemed—when the necklace warmed around her neck and she heard Onora's voice in her ears, breathless with worry: "Ceana? I just got your message; what's wrong?"

Her message—*oh*. Ceana wondered how long she'd held onto the necklace while sobbing. Hopefully not the *whole* time ...

In any case, she needed to answer Onora, or else Onora would worry and possibly even tell their parents about what Ceana had done. And that would ruin *everything*. Besides, Onora needed to know about what Ceana had learned. No, not just Onora. Everyone needed to know. Everyone in their family, at least, to start, and the nobles and the rest of the country after that.

But where to go? Only she could hear Onora as long as no one else touched the necklace, but anyone would be able to hear her talking. Ceana still hadn't found a truly good place for a conversation where she wouldn't be disturbed. Certainly not that she could access tonight. Tomorrow, maybe...

Onora's voice came again: "Ceana, if you can hear this and you can't talk, tap twice on the activation rune."

Oh! Trust Onora to know what to do in these situations. Ceana reached up and played at adjusting her sleeve, carefully tapping twice on what she hoped was the correct spot as she did so.

She must have hit the right place, given the relief in Onora's reply. "Thank Dèanadair. I still need to know what's happened. Tap once if you'll be able to speak tonight; tap twice for within an hour of sunrise tomorrow."

Within an hour of—oh, that was cruel! Or, no, not cruel. Nowhere near cruel, really. But still far too early. Tonight...oh, perhaps if she called from the bathing chamber, that would do. So, she tapped once and felt the necklace grow cool. And later that evening, when the Northwaves sisters were going to bed, Ceana gathered her things and made her way down to the chamber beneath the house.

Once down there, she sat down on one of the benches built into the wall, where she could keep an eye on the door, and touched the rune. "Onora?' she whispered.

"I'm here," came the reply, steady and familiar. "Ceana, what happened?"

"I found out why the selkies don't like us." The mere thought made a lump swell up in Ceana's throat. "Oh, Onora, it's *terrible*. They're right to be angry."

There came a pause before Onora replied. "Tell me everything."

So, Ceana did. Everything she'd learned, everything she'd been told, everything about what humans had done to selkies and how the selkies reacted, everything that had happened since she left home, she poured out to Onora. At certain points, she had to speak through sobs as the grief and guilt welled up within her once more.

When she finished, silence followed, and Ceana wondered if she'd somehow lost hold of the rune at some point. But then Onora spoke again, her voice fierce. "That can't be."

"It *is*." Ceana swallowed hard. "I saw the picture. It looked just like Lady Eilidh. And why would they have lied?"

"I don't know," Onora replied, "But it can't be right. I'd know about it if it were true. My agents watch for anyone breaking the treaty; surely something so wide-spread as this would leave some trace for them to find."

"It sounds to me as if it's been going on for generations; they probably know how to keep it secret. Or maybe some of your agents are in on it." Ceana wished she hadn't said the last sentence as soon as it left her mouth, but there could be no taking it back.

"If they are, it'll be the worst mistake they ever made. I'll have them in the dungeon for treason—or executed." Another pause; Ceana could almost see Onora calming herself. "I'm going to investigate this here. I have a few people I know couldn't be involved; I'll have them look into Lord Arran and Lady Eilidh and dig into the oldest records we can find. I'll see if Maimeó can find anything as well; perhaps she can write to Thrice-Great Uncle Diarmad and find out if the Daoine Math know something about this. There should still be some old enough to remember the time before the treaty. And in the meantime, I think you should come home."

"What?" Ceana caught herself and forced her voice back down to a whisper. "Why?"

"You've found out what you needed to. We know why the selkies are angry at us, or why most of them think they're angry with us. And it sounds as if you're spending your time with the nobility and royalty. That wasn't the plan. If anyone finds out who you are, you're certain to be accused of espionage, and there's only so much we can do to help you."

Onora was right. And learning that an Atìrsen princess had snuck into their home would do nothing to improve King Fionntan and the other selkies' opinions of humans. On the other hand, the thought of leaving now made Ceana ache inside the same way she did when she had to say goodbye to any of her sisters. "I'm...I'm not ready to leave. I think if I stay a little longer, maybe I can change people's minds and make them realize that not everyone was aware of what's been done to them. Or maybe I can identify other people who've been kidnapped."

"I don't know." Onora had been using her most big-sisterly voice, but Ceana could hear it wavering. "If something happens to you..."

"I'll be careful," Ceana pleaded, fairly clutching the necklace. "Please, Onora." A sudden thought occurred to her, and she seized

216

upon it. "If I leave now, it'll look more suspicious. If nothing else, people may worry and come looking for me. If I wait, people will start thinking less about me, and I can make an excuse that will ensure they won't wonder initially if I disappear."

Onora gave a long sigh. "Very well. But you need to be careful, you need to stop attracting attention—*especially* the king's attention—and you need to check in with me regularly. At least once every other day, understood? You don't have to do more than tell me you're alive and safe, but let me know that much. And, for Dèanadair's sake, be careful what you say to King Fionntan!"

"I will—all of it." As if Ceana didn't already know that! But at least she'd be able to stay here to keep telling him things. "Thank you. I won't let you down."

"You'd better not, or I don't know how I'll explain this to Athair and Màthair," Onora replied. "I'll let you go now before anyone notices you talking. Goodnight, Ceana."

"Goodnight," Ceana whispered back. Then she took her finger off the rune, ending her side of the conversation. And, since she was down here anyway, she set about taking a proper bath.

***

By the next morning, Ceana felt a little better, though the previous day's tears and discoveries had left her so exhausted that she didn't get up until well after breakfast. Even then, her heart and limbs were too heavy for her to do much. She spent much of the day sitting outside, watching the bees and thinking. Uaine had helpfully supplied her with knitting needles and yarn for stockings, which Ceana worked at intermittently, not wanting to overtax her arm.

Her thoughts kept going round and round in circles, though that was an improvement over the knots they'd been in yesterday. At one point, she found herself trying to think through everyone she'd ever met, wondering how many of them had selkie blood. How many of them were, in fact, selkies held captive on land? Some said that everyone in Atìrse probably had at least a drop or two of faery blood; perhaps the same was true regarding the selkies.

She still felt too tired and heartsick to attend court dinner that evening, though she insisted the Northwaves sisters go without her. She would be fine on her own, she told them again and again. She'd not do anything rash. She'd read a bit and then go to bed early. There was no reason why they should miss a pleasant evening simply because she'd had a shock.

Eventually, they conceded, and Ceana was left with the house to herself. She thought about contacting Onora again, now that no one remained to overhear—not even the servants, in fact, for they had the night off. But Onora was no doubt busy with her own affairs, and the fact that Ceana wanted to hear her voice again didn't seem reason enough to bother her.

So, instead, Ceana did just what she'd told the Northwaves sisters she'd do. She read a little, trying futilely to force the selkie language through her throat. Then she went to her bed before the sun had even fully set and curled up amid the covers. She fell asleep well before her thoughts could start spiraling again.

She half-woke, briefly, at the sound of footsteps and hushed speech in the hall. Faintly, she heard Aíbinn say, "All right; 'tis decided. Uaine will ask her tomorrow, and if she's agreeable, we'll go on with the plan."

"I *hope* she's agreeable," came Uaine's voice in reply. "'Twould solve everything so nicely and be good for both of them as well."

"I know." This was Mairearad, serene and patient. "Now, hush. Too loud and one of us will wake Kenna. Dèanadair knows she needs her rest."

The voices stopped after that. Ceana wondered what they could have been talking about, what this *plan* might be. She'd have to ask tomorrow, if Uaine didn't bring it up.

But as she slipped back into sleep, the memory faded from her mind. And when she woke, she'd forgotten it altogether.

"What thinkst thou of Fionntan?"

Ceana looked up from her pen and paper and glanced at Uaine. For nearly half an hour now, she'd been absorbed in trying to figure out what she could tell Fionntan the next day and writing down everything she could think of so she could study it. She'd planned to keep at it the rest of the morning, but now ...

Uaine sat at her loom, her hands busy with shuttle and thread. She seemed fixed on her work, yet her question hung in the air, and her gaze flickered to Ceana every few seconds.

Stifling a little sigh, Ceana set aside the pages and reached for her tablet. Uaine spoke again before she could write anything. "If thou wouldst rather talk, I don't mind. Really."

Ceana hesitated, then wrote *"Are you sure?"* in the largest letters she could. She held up the tablet, hoping Uaine would be able to see across the room without a sister able to silently communicate the words.

Uaine peered over in Ceana's direction, lips moving slightly as she read. "I'm sure. I told thee before that I wouldn't mind, did I not? So, unless thou hast taken the vow since yesterday ..."

Ceana hastily shook her head. She cleared her throat, then said, "Are you really sure? You aren't...bothered? F— His majesty told me some people were, and your family ..."

"'Tis all right." Uaine turned her eyes back to her weaving. "I wouldn't have offered if I minded thee speaking thy old language. I would have brought it up sooner, only I didn't know thy voice was back until just last night. Fionntan told me how thou spoke to him and a little of what thou told him. Why didst thou not tell us?"

"Oh." That was...Well, Ceana hoped it was good. She was a little surprised Fionntan had told anyone about making an exception to his vow for her, but then again, since he was so close to the Northwaves, it was probably no different than her telling Onora or Mirren things. "I just...I knew Mairearad and Aíbinn had made the vow, and Ninian warned me that people here wouldn't like it if I used the human language, and I didn't want to offend any of you."

"Thou wouldst not have offended us simply by telling us

that thou canst speak again." Uaine started weaving the shuttle through the warp threads once more. "Fionntan and Mairearad are worried about thee, thou knowst. Neither is happy that thou must remain silent so long. Hardly anyone waits more than a month for adoption, once their kin are found, and most have their cloaks within a week or two."

Ceana frowned slightly; had Fionntan spoken to Mairearad about moving up the ceremony after all? But, as if reading Ceana's thoughts, Uaine hastily added, "Fionntan said he asked thee about changing the date and thou said thou wert not certain, and he told Mairearad she wasn't to push thee on it. But he also suggested that I might remind thee that thou canst talk to me. And if 'tis an important matter, Mairearad and Aíbinn can make an exception— as Fionntan no doubt would do again, if thou wert in need."

"I don't want to make them make exceptions, though." Ceana toyed with her stylus, sketching little lines along the edges of the wax. "Not lightly, anyway. I appreciate Fionntan doing it yesterday. It was very kind of him. But they made their vows for a reason."

"I don't think any of them would do it lightly," Uaine replied. "They just don't want thee to be left hurting when they could help thee." With a shake of her head, she added, "Thou hast not answered my question, though! What thinkst thou of Fionntan?"

"He is kind," Ceana answered, almost without thinking. Then she caught herself and added, "Why do you ask?"

"I wish to know, 'tis all." Uaine suddenly seemed to find that her current row of weaving required a great deal of attention. "So, you say he is kind? Aught else?"

"He is...noble. Honorable. A good king and a good man." Ceana fiddled with her stylus. Why was Uaine asking this? People said she and Fionntan had some sort of understanding; perhaps she wanted to know if Ceana approved? But Ceana was a newcomer! What she thought of Uaine and Fionntan marrying hardly mattered. "I wouldn't think you'd need to ask me. It seems you know his majesty very well indeed."

Uaine nodded. "We're old friends, indeed—nearly family. I've known him all my life. But thou art kin, and I wish to know thy opinion."

"Well, you know it now." Ceana began making cross-marks on all the little lines she'd sketched on her tablet, trying to decide whether or not to broach the topic of Uaine and Fionntan's *understanding*. She supposed she might as well, just to be certain. "I thought...Well, I've heard some say that you and he are...committed to each other?"

"Have you?" Uaine gave a shaky little laugh. "I suppose some people might say that. 'Tisn't really anything, though."

Ceana turned to fully face Uaine again, sitting up straighter. "Are you, truly?"

"Only in a sense. 'Tis nothing so serious as a betrothal, if that is what thou art thinking." Uaine finished her row, glanced up, and sighed when she met Ceana's gaze. "Fionntan is required by law to wed by the time he turns three-and-thirty, or else the nobles will choose a bride for him. About two years ago, he and I were talking—complaining to each other, really. I'd just reached the age to start thinking about men and marriage, and the old king kept hinting to Fionntan that he wanted to at least meet the lady Fionntan *intended* to marry before he died."

Uaine changed thread colors and started another row. "We were both quite cross—neither of us fancied anyone on the island, really, and yet we both knew we'd have to marry eventually. Then we came round to promising that if neither of us fell in love before Fionntan *has* to wed, that we'd just marry each other, so at least we'd each be bound to a friend. Of course, someone at court caught wind of part of the story, and now half the island knows we made *some* sort of promise to each other, even if they don't know the proper details."

Letting out a huff, Uaine pushed the row she'd just done back into the rest of the weaving. "It's only a last resort, though. If Fionntan finds someone before then, though, he's still free to marry her, and the same is true for me—and truly, I *hope* he finds someone to love. Just because he was fond of no one *then* doesn't mean that's true *now*."

Ceana considered the way Fionntan had danced with Uaine at court the other day. She was no great judge, but Fionntan seemed to have already found someone to love very much indeed. Perhaps he delayed only until he could collect on their promise. But she said none of that, only, "I suppose not."

"Exactly." Uaine wove her shuttle through another row. "So, thou likest him? Thou enjoys his company?"

Ceana considered the question. Had her previous answer not been clear enough? "Why would I not?"

Uaine gave a little shrug. "I know not. But I wished to be certain."

Ceana waited Uaine to say more, but no further comment came. Uaine returned her full attention to her weaving, and so after a few minutes, Ceana turned back to her papers. Why *was* Uaine acting so strangely today?

Whatever the reason, it was probably none of her business, and Ceana had other things to do than pry into Uaine and Fionntan's love life. She had confirmation of a preexisting arrangement between the two of them, and that was all she needed to know.

Chapter 23
PLANS MADE

What a relief it was to be able to speak again! Even as often as she'd wished to be able to speak in the last weeks, she'd not truly realized how much she missed it—not until today, when she could talk without fear of giving offense, without fear of being overheard. She still had to be careful, of course. It would be far easier to slip up when she didn't have to write everything. But even that couldn't sour the taste of freedom on her tongue.

Still, she didn't complain about going back to her tablet when Mairearad and Aíbinn returned home—though some of whatever strangeness had taken hold of Uaine seemed to have caught them too. Ceana felt the pressure of unheard mental conversation around her all evening, and Aíbinn and Uaine closeted themselves in Uaine's room soon after dinner. She could hear their hushed, serious voices any time she went near the door, though she couldn't make out what they were saying.

The next day brought an end to her self-imposed exile, for she'd promised to meet with Fionntan a second time that afternoon. She'd thought more than once about sending him a message and asking to delay, to give her more time to think—but now that the day had come, she knew she couldn't put it off. Hiding in the Northwaves' house would do nothing to right what her people had done wrong. Talking to Fionntan, on the other hand, might do some good.

When she reached the keep, she was once more directed to the library, where she found Fionntan waiting. He stood as she entered and offered her a smile. "Good afternoon, Lady Kenna. How fare you today? Better than the last time I saw you, I hope?"

Ceana smiled back and nodded. She pulled out her tablet and wrote, *"Better, yes. Still shaken."*

"I understand." Fionntan pulled out the other chair from the table and gestured for her to sit. "Perhaps I should have picked a better place for our meeting. The library is convenient for most of my discussions; it is secure, and I like to think that being surrounded by the wisdom of the generations has some value. But it is, I know, a dark place as well, and if you are still troubled, we can move to a place with more sunlight."

Ceana shook her head and sat down in the offered chair. *"I don't mind. Like what you said about wisdom of ages."* It was a lovely sentiment—as if merely being in the presence of so much recorded and preserved knowledge could convey wisdom. And, of course, being near the books meant you could read them when you needed them without sending someone dashing down the halls to fetch what you wanted.

Fionntan took his own seat across the table. "Did you have the opportunity to read much before coming here?"

Without thinking, Ceana nodded. Then she caught herself—a peasant wouldn't have access to the royal library as she had—and hastily wrote, *"Some. Family had a few books. Borrowed more whenever I could."*

"And here?" Fionntan asked.

"A little," Ceana wrote back. *"Reading the Word. Ninian says might help voice. Mostly exploring, though. Trying to learn about island and people."*

"A wise practice." Fionntan slid paper and pen over to her. "And just now, I wish to learn as well, of your former people. A few days ago, you told me much of the royal family. But, if you will, I also wish to know of some of the other nobles. Has your cousin told you much of them?" Upon receiving her nod, he went on, "Good. Now, Lord Arran is our nearest Atìrsen neighbor."

Ceana instinctively scrunched up her face. Even without the knowledge of the selkies' history, if she'd known *that*, it probably would've been enough to explain the animosity. Fionntan must have noticed, for he raised an eyebrow. "I take it he has endeared himself no more to his people than he has to us?"

"*Some think much of Lord Arran,*" Ceana wrote, on paper this time. "*And some admire the beauty of vipers. Has argued with the king often about the treaty between selkies and Atirse. About other things as well.*"

"Argues in what way?" Fionntan asked.

"*He thinks Atirse should end the treaty.*" Ceana hated that she had to write the words. "*He thinks there's no gain in it.*" She paused. "*His wife is a selkie.*"

"Mairearad mentioned that you said as much to her." Fionntan stared at the words she'd written, fingers slowly tapping the table. "It would seem he has reason to want the treaty ended."

He did. His opposition to the treaty did indeed make much more sense now. If only she'd spoken more to Lady Eilidh! If only she'd found a way to learn of her history and where she'd come from! "*He must.*" A thought occurred to her. "*I ran into hunters on my way here. I thought they were hunting seals, but perhaps they were hunting selkies. They were in Lord Arran's lands.*"

Fionntan's expression darkened. "That does not surprise me. Of those of the lost who have returned to us, most are fleeing his lands—as you were yourself, if I recall your story aright."

Had she? Ceana tried to remember where the village she'd referenced as her home had been. "*Yes. But I lived close to the border.*" Hastily, she added, "*Will you try to rescue Lady Eilidh?*"

Fionntan sighed as he read her question. "If we can. We have rescued others before. But 'tis no easy matter, and 'twill take much careful planning and as much information as we can gather. To that end, Lady Kenna, what else know you of Lord Arran?"

What else did she know of Lord Arran? For a moment, Ceana wished that she had simply brought with her the papers of everything she could afford to tell Fionntan. But, then again, the more time she spent answering his questions, the more opportunities she had to ask her own. And despite Onora's warning, she couldn't help enjoying the chance to spend time in his company. He *was* everything she had told Uaine, and since he and Uaine were already at least somewhat attached, there need be no question of propriety, nor of him expecting anything more than friendship.

So, Ceana dismissed all thoughts of simply handing over her notes to Fionntan—that would end things far too soon. Instead, she picked up her pen, called to mind what she had recorded for herself earlier, and started writing.

Fionntan's inquiries didn't end with Lord Arran—not that Ceana had expected them to. Over the next few hours, he asked about one noble after another. Some were those Ceana would have expected: the counts who ruled Atìrse's three non-royal counties and some of the particularly influential lesser lords. Others were less expected, but made sense once Ceana gave the matter some thought: nobles with ties to Lord Arran, or whose territories bordered the sea, or who had strong connections to other lands and therefore an interest in seafaring even if their holding had no shoreline. Despite the gaps in the selkies' knowledge, Ceana had to admit, they seemed to be reasonably well-informed about who was and wasn't important.

Midway through their conversation, there came a knock on the library door. Fionntan glanced up, brow furrowed, as the door opened and a guard stepped inside, a maid and a manservant just behind him. The maid carried a covered tray, while the manservant held two cups and a pitcher. "Two of the servants for you, your majesty."

Fionntan beckoned the two inside. "Yes, come in. What have you here?"

Both stepped forward and bowed, the maid placing the tray on the end of the table as she did. "Lann Aíbinn said you would want refreshments, your majesty." She uncovered the tray to reveal an assortment of tarts, some of which looked to be filled with sweet fruit and nuts, and some whose appearance suggested a savory filling. The manservant stepped up beside her to set a cup by Fionntan and another by Ceana, then filled each with a golden-hued liquid from the pitcher.

Fionntan raised an eyebrow. "Lann Aíbinn said this, did she?"

The maid nodded. "Yes, your majesty. I assumed she spoke on your behalf; was it not so?"

Fionntan glanced at Ceana. "Lady Kenna, do you desire refreshments?"

Ceana, for lack of a better idea, gave a little shrug and a smile that she hoped Fionntan would interpret as 'not opposed to the idea.' Fionntan turned back to the maid. "It would seem Lann Aíbinn has decided to start anticipating my orders rather than just relaying them. Thank you; you may go."

The servants bowed themselves out of the room. Fionntan faced Ceana once more. "Well, Lady Kenna, you may help yourself. I am afraid that the tarts are merely last night's leftovers, but I assure you that they taste as well the second day as they do the first—my cooks know their business."

Ceana nodded, though she reached for her glass rather than a pastry. The golden liquid proved to be a mild cider with a light taste; very pleasant on the whole. Ceana fancied it would have been better enjoyed outdoors in the sunshine, but she would hardly complain about it. She then picked up her tablet and wrote, *"I didn't ask Aíbinn to ask."*

"I never thought such a thing of you, my lady." Fionntan chuckled. "If anything, I imagine it is intended as a reprimand to me for not thinking to offer you refreshment myself, for which I apologize."

"No need to apologize." Ceana offered a shy grin, uncertain how Fionntan would take it. *"'Tis here now."*

"True, and next time, I shall be a more considerate host," Fionntan replied. "And now I suppose I ought to pause my questioning so you can have a chance to eat."

"I can write one-handed." It was annoying, true, but more manageable with something like the tarts than with a proper meal. *"What else do you want to know?"*

Their discussion went on late into the afternoon, long after the tarts were gone and the cider pitcher dry. At last, however, there came another knock on the door, swiftly followed by the appearance of Aíbinn. "Still up here? You'll miss dinner if you linger any longer, and you know how cross Mairearad will be—*especially* with you, your majesty, keeping our cousin from her meal!"

"'Twould seem that keeping Lady Kenna fed is a significant worry for both you and she." Fionntan raised an eyebrow at Aíbinn. "Especially as you took it upon yourself to order refreshments up here for her benefit."

Aíbinn gave Fionntan a too-innocent look, tucking her hands behind her back. "'Tisn't my fault if you failed to be a proper host, your majesty. I'm only thinking of your benefit."

"And how many of those tarts did you steal before the tray found its way to me, Lann Aíbinn?" Fionntan shook his head and stood. "One thing, however, is true; if I keep any of us here any longer, Mairearad won't forgive me for a month. Shall we depart?"

He offered his arm to Ceana, and Ceana, after a moment's hesitation, took it. In another circumstance, it should've been Aíbinn he escorted, but of course, Aíbinn was still on duty. So, they made their way out of the library, down the stairs, out of the keep, and down the path towards the Northwaves home.

Ceana had expected Aíbinn to walk with them and carry most of the conversation. Yet, to her surprise, as soon as they were off the main road to the keep, Aíbinn moved ahead, weaving side-to-side along the path and poking at bushes with her spear. Then she fell back again, now harrying the shrubbery behind them.

She continued to orbit Fionntan and Ceana, passing them now and then but never pausing long enough to have a conversation, and mostly staying too far ahead or behind to talk to. One glance at Fionntan's face told Ceana that he was as surprised by this as she. After a few minutes, Fionntan called out, "Aíbinn, what art thou doing?"

"Guarding thee! Thou canst never be sure what's lurking in the bushes!" Aíbinn emphasized this by an especially enthusiastic bush-poke that sent a grouse whirring away in a panic. "What dost thou think I'm doing?"

"I have no idea," Fionntan replied, bemusedly. "But I should think thou couldst guard just as well while walking with us as ahead and behind."

"Certainly not! One must stay alert, thou knowst well." Aíbinn stabbed another bush. This one yielded no birds or other creatures. "I'm just doing my duty."

"Thy duty," Fionntan echoed, his tone now drier than the earth after a month without rain. "And art thou aware of some special circumstance that requires this extra vigilance? For I have heard of none."

"Sir Bhaltair says I'm to be more attentive to my surroundings," Aíbinn called back. A bit too innocently, she added, "Anyway, thou hast Kenna for company."

"So I do," Fionntan murmured, too quietly for a proper reply. He glanced down at Ceana. "Lady Kenna, I believe your cousin is up to something. Do you agree?"

Ceana glanced ahead at Aíbinn, then nodded. What Aíbinn's purpose might be, she couldn't fathom, but this hardly seemed like *normal* behavior. Anyway, Ceana had given enough flimsy excuses of her own to recognize them from someone else.

"As I thought." Fionntan shook his head, his expression one of friendly exasperation. "Whatever she is about, I imagine we'll have no luck getting it out of her before she's ready to tell us. Unless you have some inkling?"

Ceana shook her head emphatically, then pulled her tablet from her pocket and, carefully balancing it, managed to write, *"No idea. Ignore her?"* That tended to be the safest solution when her sisters were acting exceptionally strange...not that she'd needed to use such a solution in quite a long time.

"I think that may be a wise idea." Fionntan's gaze followed Aíbinn a few minutes more as she circled back behind them, no doubt to terrorize more bushes. "In the meantime, we may as well enjoy the walk."

Aíbinn's strange behavior continued the whole way to the

Northwaves house, though she did become less dramatic with her bush-stabbing as time went on. By the time they reached the house, she had settled into merely following some ten feet back and occasionally making a half-hearted poke at the leaves. Meanwhile, after a few fitful attempts at conversation, made more difficult by the fact that Ceana had to stop walking in order to write anything longer than a few short words, Ceana managed to start Fionntan talking about his favorite spots on Emain Ablach, a topic that required very little input from her and was extensive enough to carry them all the way to the house.

When they reached the house, they found Uaine and Mairearad waiting as expected— though not quite *where* expected. Uaine had shifted across the table to the seat beside Aíbinn's, leaving Ceana's usual seat—*Uaine's* usual seat when Fionntan visited, so far as Ceana could tell—open.

Aíbinn went straight to her chair, but Ceana paused at the edge of the table, caught Mairearad's eye, and gestured to the two seats with a questioning hand and a furrowed brow. Mairearad gave a little laugh. "Oh, I should have warned you. Uaine and I thought 'twould be simpler to have only one of you move."

That was...true, actually. Still...Ceana glanced at Uaine questioningly. Uaine gave a bright smile. "'Tis all right. Besides, 'twill make conversation easier if thou canst simply show Fionntan thy tablet, and then he can tell the rest of us what it says. He's far more likely to notice than Aíbinn." This comment earned a cry of protest from Aíbinn, to which Uaine responded with a too-innocent, "What? 'Tis true!"

In the midst of the resulting sisterly squabble, Fionntan shook his head and pulled out the chair beside his and said quietly and wryly, "Come, Lady Kenna. It seems that oddness has infected more than one of your cousins. 'Tis a good thing some of us still have our wits."

Ceana nodded agreement and sat. Fionntan and Mairearad both took their seats as well, and Aíbinn and Uaine followed suit a few minutes later, neither one of them looking the least bit contrite.

Then, at Mairearad's prompting, Fionntan blessed the meal and the servants began serving.

Ceana had hoped that, at this point, the sisters might begin acting normally again. And, thankfully, Fionntan set them on a fairly safe conversational path by first asking after Uaine's various projects and, when that topic ran dry, mentioning that he'd had word from the Daoine Math to expect a group of messengers and traders in just three weeks.

The announcement sent a shock of visible excitement through the sisters. "Did Màthair send any message for us?" Uaine demanded, dropping her utensils on her plate with a clatter.

Fionntan shook his head. "The missive came from one of the Daoine Math, not from your mother. But I was told to expect a great company, so I have no doubt a message will come—and much more, no doubt. The message said 'twould be a large group."

"I wonder what they'll bring." Aíbinn leaned forward, a wild grin on her face. "Do you all remember when the one trader brought the fiddles that played themselves? That was a marvel!"

The conversation turned to recollections of wonders brought by faery visitors past—everything from moonshine cloth to seeds that grew to full maturity in a day—and hopes for what this new group would bring. Ceana listened in awe, noting the most useful or magnificent items to tell her family about later. Atìrse traded with the Daoine Math as well, but it seemed that the faery folk were keeping their greatest wonders back. What might it take to change that?

Eventually, the conversation settled into a lull around the same time they all finished with their main course. As the servants cleared these dishes and laid out bowls of fruit crisp and little pitchers of cream, Aíbinn said, a bit too casually, "By the by, Fionntan was telling Kenna of the nicest places in Emain Ablach on the walk home. 'Tis a pity she's hardly seen any of them yet."

"Oh, it is!" Uaine jumped in, sounding almost as concerned as if Aíbinn had announced Ceana had never eaten anything but bread and water before now. "Fionntan, thou and I should take

Kenna on an excursion someday soon. Maybe to the spring in the Dawnwood? 'Tis always especially pretty there in summer. Can we?"

"Thou art welcome to take thy cousin where thou willst," Fionntan replied, raising his eyebrow slightly. "Thou hardly need my permission."

"I'm not asking thy permission; I'm asking thee to *come*," Uaine protested. "'Twouldn't be the same without thee."

"That sounds like an excellent idea," Aíbinn said. "Thou shouldst go, Fionntan!"

Fionntan shook his head. "I cannot simply traipse about willy-nilly anymore. I have duties as king to attend to."

Mairearad gave a gentle shake of her head, putting a hand on Fionntan's arm. "I know thy duties as well as thee, Fionntan, and thou canst spare a day. 'Twould do thee good."

"So you all come at me together?" Fionntan turned to Ceana. "What say you, Lady Kenna? Are you going to join your cousins' side?"

Ceana hesitated, then wrote, *"Sounds nice. Sure Uaine or Aíbinn can show me if you can't."*

Fionntan must have told the rest of the table what Ceana had said, for Uaine immediately exploded into protest. "Kenna, 'twould not be the same without Fionntan! Do tell him thou'd like him to come. Thou said just this morning that thou dost enjoy his company."

"And 'tis one of his favorite places," Aíbinn added. "'Tis only right he come along to show it to thee."

Why were they so insistent? But Ceana turned her tablet and wrote, *"If the place is special to you, would be nice for you to come. Don't want to impose."*

At the same moment, Mairearad urged, "Go, Fionntan. Thou canst use the rest and the sunshine, to be sure, and thou canst take a message-mirror in case any trouble should arise."

Fionntan fell back in his seat, holding up his hands in a gesture of surrender. "Very well! Since you are all so insistent, we will go.

When do you wish to make this excursion?"

"Six days hence?" Mairearad offered. "I've heard several folk say to expect rain in the next days, but surely everything will be dry again by then."

Aíbinn and Uaine chorused their agreement that six days from now sounded excellent to them, and Ceana nodded acceptance. Fionntan bowed his head gravely. "Six days it shall be, then, providing the weather does not turn." Despite his reluctance, a smile appeared on his face. "No doubt you are all right, and I will find myself glad of it afterward."

"Of course you will," Aíbinn exclaimed. "We're thy friends. Would we ever steer thee wrong?"

Chapter 24:
WISHES

Ceana had hoped to use the next day to search out a good place to speak to Onora in private, away from the Northwaves house and anyone else who might overhear, now that she had a little more to say. But the day dawned grey and heavy with a cold, miserable rain that showed every inclination of staying around all day.

So, instead, Ceana whispered a message to Onora to say that she was well, but couldn't talk today, as she had done twice already, and then moped her way downstairs. She couldn't help but feel cheated out of her hopes of a productive day. Though she tried to make herself useful in the workroom, her arm ached so she could barely use it more than she could when it had been splinted, and her ribs pained her as well even with the effect of the ointment. Whether she'd slept on something wrong or if she'd somehow overexerted herself in the last few days, she wasn't sure, but apparently even miraculously fast healing could be set back. And the little she managed to get done wasn't the work she'd *wanted* to do; neither spinning nor sewing would satisfy her soul today.

She was still in a mood as grey and gloomy as the sky outside when there came a knock on the front doors. With Uaine in the middle of a particularly intricate bit of weaving, the task of answering fell to Ceana. She trudged down the hall and opened the door just a crack.

A messenger stood there, carrying a small, rectangular bundle under his sodden cloak. "Lady Kenna?" he asked.

Ceana nodded and opened the door a little more, wondering if he would want to come in. But instead, he pulled out his bundle and held it out to her, keeping it under the shelter of first his cloak and then the roof. "For you, from his majesty."

What was this? The pinpricks of curiosity were just enough to rouse Ceana from some of her gloom. She took the package and offered a smile at the messenger, then gestured questioningly inside.

The messenger shook his head. "No, thank you, m'lady. I've more ground to cover yet today. Good day to you." He touched his hood, then turned and made his way down the path. Ceana watched him go until he was out of sight, then shut the door and turned her attention to the parcel, which was wrapped in thick, waxy cloth to keep the water off. What would Fionntan have sent her? She stepped over to a small table placed in the entryway so she could unwrap the cloth.

Within she found an elegantly bound book and a piece of folded paper on top. Ceana unfolded the paper and read the short message:

Lady Kenna,

    While I understand that you are largely learning the ways of Emain Ablach by meeting its people, I thought perhaps you might like to read something of our history. If nothing else, it may be some diversion on days such as this one. You may keep it as long as you like; your cousins have often borrowed books from the royal library to supplement their own collection.

                                      — *Fionntan*

Oh! That was kind of him. More eagerly now, Ceana opened the book to its title page, which read *A History of the Daoine Ròin, the Seal-Folk*. A bit dry, perhaps, but it would be instructive in more ways than one.

Ceana spent much of the rest of that day and the next reading, as the rain continued to pour down with only brief breaks in which the sky remained clouded over. She learned, through the pages, of the days of old when the selkies had no land to call their own but rather roamed here and there or lived along the coasts of the human lands, sometimes alone and sometimes in villages, even though they were themselves not human. She read of how the humans and selkies would willingly intermarry in those days, binding themselves in a true union that gave the selkie freedom of the land and the human freedom of the seas and bestowed upon both the ability to communicate with the other's people.

"Two souls, cleaved to each other, sharing one body, one breath, and one blood, forever united in the sight of the Maker and equal in standing beneath him," the book said of these unions. Ceana found herself wishing she had lived in such days, or else that such days would return. 'Twas certainly a more appealing idea than the discord that marked the present-day.

As she read on, she learned of the cause of the split, as human folk turned away from Dèanadair and bowed to other gods: to Celaldir the Free and Amuna the Oracle, to Guleòr the Lord of Plenty and his wife, Rivelia, the Mistress of the Endless Night. The priests of these gods taught that selkies were a lesser people, to be used rather than welcomed as friends, and so the rituals of union were corrupted. And the selkies fled the human lands, living for a while ever on the move—until the first king of the selkies discovered the passage into Emain Ablach and led his people to dwell there, safe from human discovery, as Fionntan had told her on her first day in Emain Ablach.

And there they remained, even when humankind remembered Dèanadair and burned the instruments of their pagan worship to ash. For selkies still vanished from the seas, and too many humans still remembered the perverted ritual, and the treaties that the Daoine Ròin signed with the human kingdoms did little to stop it. But the selkies grew in friendship with the Daoine Math, and so long as they kept far from human shores as much as possible, they began to grow and flourish once more.

On the third day, the rain still fell—but Ceana had finished the book cover-to-cover, and Fionntan had requested she come speak with him again. So, she wrapped the book securely once more, pulled on a pair of boots borrowed from Uaine, and set out for the royal keep.

When she arrived, her boots and the hem of her dress were

thick with mud. But the guards recognized her and let her in without question, and a servant directed her upstairs to the library once more. There, she found Fionntan waiting. In addition to the usual pen and paper, a steaming pitcher and two thick-bodied cups sat on the table.

Fionntan stood to greet her as usual. "Lady Kenna, welcome. I wondered if you would come or not, with the weather."

Ceana gave him a quizzical look. Once she reached the table, she pulled out her tablet and wrote, *"You're the king, you asked me to come."*

A slight smile tugged at the corners of Fionntan's mouth. "True, but surely you have seen that we are far less concerned with rule and rank than many human kingdoms are. I would not have blamed you if the rain had kept you away."

Ceana shook her head. *"Would never."* Regardless of whether or not she could have refused to come without giving offense, she couldn't pass up a chance to try to change Fionntan's mind on humans. Besides, she was coming to enjoy these meetings, tiring though they might be.

"Well, I thank you, and I am glad you have come." Fionntan pulled out her seat for her, then picked up the pitcher. "There is hot mulled wine here, if you wish some to warm you after your walk." He waited for Ceana's grateful nod, then poured some into each cup.

What kind of king poured drinks for one lesser than himself? *A good one*, replied something deep in Ceana's heart. But now wasn't the time to dwell on that thought. From her bag, she removed the book Fionntan had lent her, wrapped in its original waxed cloth. She set it on his side of the table, unwrapping it partially so he could see the note she'd written before leaving: *"Thank you for lending me this. I'm glad to know now what I never learned at home. I enjoyed reading it, even when it made me sad."*

It took a moment for Fionntan to read the note, during which Ceana took long, slow sips of her wine, savoring the way it brought warmth back to her insides after the chill of the rainy walk. Finally,

Fionntan replied, "You're welcome, Lady Kenna. I'm glad you gained some pleasure from it. I hardly expected you to finish it so quickly."

Ceana gave a rueful smile before writing, in the smallest handwriting she could manage, *"Arm & side still hurt sometimes. Reading lets them rest."*

"Ah. I understand." Fionntan nodded at her arm. "How much longer do you expect 'twill be before your injuries are well again?"

"Not certain." Ceana shrugged. *"Barely hurt at all until three days ago."*

"Well, 'tis a blessing that you were improving until then. 'Tis hard to live when all you do is pain—though I'm certain I need not tell you that." Fionntan passed her the paper and pen. "Though whatever hurt you bore two weeks ago seemed not to stop your dancing when you visited court."

Ceana had to laugh at that. *"Dancing is worth pain. Still stopped much sooner than normal."*

"Ah, I see," Fionntan replied. "Then shall I expect to enjoy your company in the dancing again the next time your cousins come? I was sorry to see that you did not accompany them last time."

"Was still tired when they went. I will be there next time," Ceana wrote in reply. *"I am happy to dance with you, if you wish."*

"Not if *only* I wish it," Fionntan corrected, leaning in slightly. "If you do not care to dance, you may refuse, Lady Kenna. I will bear you no ill will."

As if that were why she wouldn't turn him down!. She underlined *"I am happy to dance,"* then smoothed over *"if you wish."* Then she tapped the papers before her, giving Fionntan a questioning glance. Surely Fionntan meant nothing but friendship by the question, but habit drew her to redirect his attention anyway.

"Ah, yes." Fionntan nodded. "You're right; we should begin. I have a few questions that I thought of while reading your answers from our last two conversations ..."

That morning's session proved far more difficult than the last two had been. Fionntan had clearly been rereading her answers *very* carefully, picking up on details she didn't realize she'd included and holes and questions she hadn't known she'd left. Answering him without revealing too much was, Ceana thought, one of the hardest things she'd done since arriving in Emain Ablach.

She had some respite when, about an hour in, a servant arrived with a tray of small cakes, fruit, and cheese. At that point, she set aside her pen, and Fionntan ceased his questions, and they ate in friendly silence.

Ceana had finished off two cakes and what she estimated as half an apple when Fionntan spoke again. "You said that the history book taught you some things you never learned at home. And the other day, you said...you said you didn't know selkies and humans could intermarry. Is that truly so?"

Ceana nodded and reached for her tablet, but Fionntan shook his head and pushed a fresh sheet of paper towards her. "Write on this, please. I would like...I would like to have record of it, to think upon."

Well, this was a safer topic than what he'd been asking about. *"I don't think anyone knows. I didn't. I thought they could. Humans can marry the Daoine Math. Why not selkies? But I wasn't sure, and I never heard of anyone doing it."*

Fionntan was silent again for several moments. "I see."

Ceana hesitated, then wrote again without waiting for a question. *"I wish the old, old days would return. Before humans turned from Dèanadair. When humans and selkies were at peace."*

"So do many," Fionntan replied, his voice soft. "And for those who do not, it is because we have lost hope of any such peace returning."

"Do you truly believe there is no hope?" Ceana prayed he'd answer *no*, he didn't believe it. But he had said *we* ...

Fionntan stared at the paper, but the look on his face said he didn't truly see it. "In Dèanadair, there is always some hope...but in this case, 'tis only the hope that He would work some miracle. In order for the peace of the oldest days to return, humans would need to cease persecuting us, and we would need to see evidence that the change was genuine before we began to trust." He turned and looked at her. "You lived your life among humans. Do you believe such change is possible?"

Ceana nodded without hesitation. *"If people knew, they would change. They would be as horrified as I was. They wouldn't let it go on."*

"And yet, in order to affect anything, the nobility and the royal family would have to be convinced to act. And they are motivated to protect their own." Fionntan shook his head. "I am sorry to burden you with this, Lady Kenna. Are you ready to return to our earlier questions?"

"It is no burden," Ceana wrote back. *"And yes, I am ready."* Or, at least, as ready as she could be.

She remained with Fionntan another hour and a half, answering his questions as best she could. At last, however, the time came to depart. He sent her on her way in a covered, pony-drawn cart, with a smile of thanks and another two books, both full of tales of heroes and legends among the seal-folk. "Keep them as long as you like," he told her when he handed them to her. "I know not when the rain will cease, and perhaps they will provide some relief—or distraction, at least—whenever your injuries pain you."

Ceana had thanked him and assured him that she was confident that the books would be great relief indeed. It was kind of him, after all, to be so generous with the contents of his library, and she could not spend all of every day working or walking. And when she returned to the Northwaves home, Uaine seemed pleased as well by Fionntan's generosity, though Ceana wasn't quite sure of why she was so excited.

By the following morning, the rain had finally stopped, though the sky still hung low with grey clouds. Uaine and Ceana took the pony cart down to the village to run errands and check on Ceana's dresses. While they were there, Ceana took the opportunity to stop at Ninian's again. Though the pain in her arm and side had receded again, she wanted to take no risk that something might have gone wrong.

Thankfully, when Ninian had inspected her arm and pressed her side, he found no sign of trouble. "'Twas only due to the rain, more than likely," he told her, giving her shoulder a comforting pat. "If you've a broken bone or an old wound, foul weather can make it ache the same as it does the bones of us old folk." He chuckled at that and went on, "Be careful, don't push yourself too hard, and perhaps try not to sleep on that side when you know there's a storm coming in, and you'll be well in time."

Ceana gave him a grateful smile and stood. "Thank you. I'll take care."

As she went to leave, Ninian caught her good arm. "Before you go, lass, any more luck with the books?"

Ceana shook her head. "I can talk fine in this language. But I still can't read aloud in the selkie tongue, let alone speak it without reading."

"Ah well. Keep trying." Ninian's keen eyes studied her face. "Are you still set on waiting on the ceremony?"

Ceana nodded. "I think…I think it'll be better. It'll give me more time to adjust, and it'll make things easier on Mairearad if she only has to plan one ceremony."

"It may be easier on her, aye, if all goes right," Ninian replied—not quite agreeing, Ceana noticed. "But the further back in your line your selkie blood comes from, the more things can go wrong. My tests can't say how many generations removed you are from whoever last wore your cloak, but 'tis certainly enough to put you at risk. If you can stomach the ceremony sooner than six months, I'd recommend going through with it. In the meantime, be careful, and if aught strange happens, come and see me."

"I will." Ceana sent up a silent prayer that nothing would go wrong. She knew her cloak was old indeed—older than Thrice-Great Uncle Diarmad. But perhaps, since it had been so carefully kept, it would be all right? Anyway, she only needed it to work until she'd learned all she could and convinced Fionntan that there *was* hope of reconciliation between the selkies and the humans.

"I'll hold you to that, lass." Ninian released her arm. "I'm glad to see you settling in so well, even keeping company with his majesty himself."

Ceana flushed, though she didn't know why. "He wants to know about Atìrse, and I don't mind talking about it. And he's friends with my cousins."

"So he is, as we all know well." Ninian opened the door for her. "As I said, if anything strange happens, come and see me. Good day to you."

Ceana departed with a wave and set out to the tailor's, where she was to meet Uaine for the fitting for Ceana's new things. The tailors had made enough progress on two of the gowns for Ceana to try them on, and once again Ceana felt a pang of regret that she likely wouldn't be around to wear them—and again that the dresses would have to be modified again for Uaine after all the work to fit them to Ceana. But such was life, and she could do nothing to change that.

Though the dresses were coming along well, neither could be worn out and about yet. So, that evening found Ceana once again dressed in finery borrowed from Uaine as she followed her cousins into the keep for court dinner.

They arrived later than they had the last time, and so had no time to talk to Fionntan before the dinner. And, somewhat to Ceana's relief, she found herself seated not by Lady Derbáil this time, but rather with Aíbinn on her right and a few young knights of the Guard to her left and in front of her. She recognized some of these as men she'd danced with on her last visit to court, and one of them—the one directly across from her—was Mairearad's Sir Cianán. They all welcomed her into their conversation cheerfully, even boisterously, and a little prompting from Aíbinn was enough to launch them all into stories of their escapades and adventures, which ranged from pinching pies after practice—apparently Fionntan's concerns last week were founded in reality after all—to fending off whales and sharks who came too close to the island to, in one case, fighting a crew of Tryggestrender raiders who thought to use the mortal-world part of the island as a stopping point.

The storytelling, thankfully, needed no significant input from Ceana, save for the occasional nod or gasp or do-go-on noise. And if they were exaggerating just a little on the more heroic aspects of their exploits, well, Ceana was hardly inclined to correct them.

Sir Cianán participated little in the storytelling, save to add a detail here or there. He was decidedly the oldest in the group—the same age as Onora's husband, Ceana thought, just as Mairearad was about the same age as Onora—and seemed a little steadier than the rest. At one point midway through the third course, when a story of a shark-hunt had devolved into an argument about whose idea a particular plan had been, Ceana scribbled down a question on her tablet—*"You are close to Mairearad? How did you meet?"* and passed it to him.

He took it with a raised eyebrow of surprise, read it, and then smiled. In a low voice, he replied, "We are close, yes. We've known each other most of our lives, since we were both children."

He had a nice voice, Ceana thought. Grave and kind, more like a priest than a warrior. When he returned her tablet, she wrote, *"You are noble too? Family friends?"*

"Ah, no." Sir Cianán chuckled quietly. "My family worked the orchards and fields, and I would tend the orchard of which the Northwaves own part. Lady Mairearad and her sisters often used to play there, and sometimes she would come alone to walk or sit beneath the trees and think. She was always kind and friendly when we ran into each other, and I started finding excuses to work nearby any time I saw her so we could talk. Sometimes she would even help me. As time went on, we simply grew closer and closer. Signing on for my term in the Guard was a blessing; it kept me near her when she had fewer and fewer chances to come to the orchards."

How sweet! Ceana wouldn't have taken Mairearad for the type to marry below her station for love. Yet, she had to admit, Sir Cianán seemed an honorable man, as much so as any king Ceana had met, and if he and Mairearad had been friends a long time, it was no wonder they would wish to wed, the same way Uaine and Fionntan did. Still, a question remained. *"If not noble, how a knight?"*

Sir Cianán glanced at the question, then shook his head a bit bashfully. "Ah, a man may be knighted for service as well as nobility here. The old king was impressed with my capabilities."

"What?" one of the others cut in, apparently having caught on to Sir Cianán and Ceana's conversation. He leaned across the table to look at what Ceana had written, then scoffed, "Typical Cianán! Making it sound as if the old king just liked the look of you and leaving out that you saved his life."

"It was nothing that another wouldn't have done," Sir Cianán protested mildly.

"But 'twas you who did it," the other insisted. "Here, Lady Kenna, it happened like this —" And into the tale he launched. Ceana had no doubt that he exaggerated it as he had the others; surely Sir Cianán hadn't fought a dozen rogue selkies on his own after they ambushed the king's party, all while keeping the half-conscious king from drowning. But Cianán, though red-faced, made no move to correct them, so perhaps the story held more truth than it seemed it should.

Eventually, however, the meal ended, and the Guards abandoned their storytelling for the lure of the dance floor. Sir Cianán excused himself to claim Mairearad for the first dance, while one of the Guards asked Aíbinn and the other two scurried off in search of other ladies. One returned, a bit sheepishly, to ask Ceana if she wanted to dance, and she accepted happily, not at all bothered by the slight. As they made their way to the floor, Ceana spotted Fionntan arm in arm with Uaine again; no surprise there!

The dance was a quick one, both in length and in step, and Ceana soon found herself breathless and back on the side of the dance floor, waving to her partner as he went to find another lady. She glanced about as he departed, hoping that another Guard or one of the nobles from last week would think to ask her.

But instead, as she turned, she found herself face-to-face with Fionntan. She let out a little "eep!" of surprise and took a step back before she could recover and offer an apologetic smile.

Fionntan, thankfully, seemed unoffended. "My apologies for startling you, Lady Kenna." He held out a hand, bowing. "Might I have this dance?"

Ceana took his hand with a smile and a curtsey. But as they made their way out to the floor, she gave him a questioning look and gestured in the direction of both Mairearad and Aíbinn.

He seemed to catch her meaning, replying as they took positions and began the dance, "I do usually open the first few dances with your cousins, yes. But Uaine suggested this tune might be one you are familiar with already, and I believe I told you yesterday that I hoped to enjoy your company for a dance or two."

Ceana bowed her head slightly in understanding and gave him another smile. He went on, "I hope that your injuries pain you less today—I imagine that they must, by how well you managed that last dance."

Another nod. Ceana put a little flourish in the next few steps to demonstrate how healed she was.

"I'm pleased to see it," Fionntan replied, laughing. "And now, I suppose, you intend to dance the whole night away?"

Ceana laughed and nodded again, then indicated Mairearad and the door, hoping Fionntan would understand that she meant "Until my family needs to leave."

"Good." Fionntan held out his arm to turn her. "Then perhaps I will have the pleasure of a second dance sometime?"

A second dance? Something inside Ceana fluttered, but she immediately squelched it. There were only so many ladies here; naturally, Fionntan would dance with people more than once. And it was hardly unreasonable that she should be one of them, since she was kin to his oldest friends and to the woman he'd likely marry. Realizing he still waited for an answer, she nodded and worked a bit of a curtsey into her next steps.

"I will look forward to that, then." Fionntan sighed, a hint of a frown crossing his face. "It is a pity you cannot speak during the dance. You are a fine partner, Lady Kenna, and I only wish we could have the pleasure of conversation."

Ceana gave a philosophical shrug. It was, indeed, annoying to not be able to talk. But for now, she could do nothing to change that. She'd just have to live with it.

Chapter 25
AT THE DAWNWOOD SPRING

The next morning, thankfully, the clouds rolled away to reveal pale blue sky. Nonetheless, Ceana pulled on her boots once more and dressed in her older gown, the one she'd worn when she came to Emain Ablach. Downstairs, Uaine and Aíbinn had already eaten and were, along with the servants, busy packing bags with drinks, food, and a cloth. Ceana, who hadn't had a real picnic since she was seven, watched in interest. All involved were clearly old hands at this, even if the process did seem to involve a certain amount of sisterly bickering and I-told-you-s between Uaine and Aíbinn.

Fionntan arrived just as Uaine and Aíbinn were finishing, with Nes in tow. Aíbinn glanced around as they made their greeting, then asked, "Only one Guard today?"

"Two," Fionntan corrected. "As of this moment, thou'rt on duty."

"What?" Aíbinn protested, though she didn't sound entirely upset. "Making a lady work on her outing?"

"Unless thou wish to argue with the Counsel's ruling on how many guards I need or with *my* orders to thy fellow Guard," Fionntan replied, voice and stance and look all suddenly stern. "And I know thou would have thy spear and sword in any case."

"Well, of course. But now I have to fetch my armor as well." Aíbinn made a few grumbling noises under her breath. "What orders did you give? I heard nothing of them until now."

"Thou wilt hear the full tale tomorrow, but I have sent a fair number of the Guard on a particular mission away from Emain Ablach." In a drier tone, Fionntan added, "Specially picked for their subtlety, Aíbinn, lest thou protest at not having a chance to volunteer."

"As thou art king and friend, I will pretend I didn't hear thee insult me," Aíbinn retorted. "Very well; let me find my armor and we'll be off."

She vanished upstairs, and Uaine set about rearranging the contents of the packs. Fionntan and Nes both already carried bags of their own, Ceana noticed, which they surrendered to Uaine so she could properly distribute the load. A few minutes later, Aíbinn returned, now properly armored. She slung her pack on her back and picked up her spear from where it leaned by the door. "Ready."

The rest of the packs were distributed with each person, even Ceana and Uaine, carrying one. Ceana knew from watching that she had the lightest pack, but it still seemed a strange and unfamiliar weight on her shoulders. All the same, if Fionntan was carrying a pack, she could hardly protest at being asked to do the same.

Even with the extra weight, she could feel nothing but merry as they set off down the path away from the house. The sun above seemed to be trying to make up for lost time, it beamed down so brightly, and the color of every bush and blossom seemed brighter in the wake of the rain. Aíbinn struck up a walking song before they'd even gone ten feet, and the others, even Nes, joined in with good will. Ceana hummed along for a little while, until she found that she needed all her breath to keep up with the pace the rest of the group set.

Their path took them towards the north and east, through fields and hill country. After a while, Aíbinn tired of singing, and she and Fionntan began pointing out spots of particular interest. Occasionally, farmers and shepherds called greetings to the group, and once a sharp-eared sheepdog ran up to Fionntan, barking happily and nosing for pets. Fionntan obliged with a laugh and a scratch behind the dog's ears before sending it back to its sheepish master. After, he explained to Ceana: "All the dogs we receive spend time in the kennels at the keep while we determine who will receive one. Storm spent a little more time than some; she was the smallest of her litter and still had some growing to do before she could go to work. She and I became very friendly in that time."

They walked the whole morning, while Ceana's feet grew more and more sore. But eventually, the hills and fields gave way to forest boughs, and they walked amid leaf-dappled light on a narrow path riddled with rocks and tree roots. After the first time Ceana nearly tripped, Fionntan offered her his arm to steady her, and she took it. Uaine and Aíbinn both seemed perfectly at home, and Ceana couldn't help a feeling of squeezing inadequacy—but no one but she herself seemed to hold her awkwardness against her.

And before long, the sound of splashing, burbling water caught Ceana's ears. A bit further and they left the main path entirely, pushing along a game trail so narrow that they had to go single-file. Ceana found herself behind Fionntan, and she gave thanks that he took care enough to hold back branches until she could pass, rather than letting them whip back and hit her or shower her in dusty pollen.

Then, another turn, and there they were. Before them lay a small pond fed by a clear-running spring at one end. A small stream trailed away from the pond and swiftly vanished amid the trees. Grassy banks, speckled here and there with wildflowers, bordered the waters. All was still and peaceful, save for the songs of birds in the trees.

"Here we are, Lady Kenna," Fionntan said, his voice quiet and almost reverent. "The Dawnwood spring."

He seemed as if he might have said more, but at that moment, Aíbinn dropped her pack and exclaimed, "Here at last! Someone give me a hand with the cloth so we can eat."

The moment was broken as the bustle of preparations took over. While Fionntan helped Aíbinn spread the cloth, a patchwork of well-worn canvas, and Nes checked the surrounding bushes for anything potentially troublesome, Uaine and Ceana unloaded the food and drink from their packs.

Seeing the spread, Ceana almost felt the struggle of carrying it all the way had been worth it. There was chicken and boiled eggs and pasties filled with meat and vegetables, all carefully packed so they'd still be cool when they arrived. There was a salad of fresh-picked greens and blossoms and a jar of crisp pickled vegetables. There were juicy peaches and firm, sweet plums from the orchards and wild strawberries hanging ripe in the bushes around the spring. There were three kinds of cheese—one sharp and brilliant orange, one pale and studded with nuts, one in between and flavored with savory dried herbs—and two types of rolls, one dark and savory and one lighter, with a chewy crust and an impossibly soft interior. And to drink, they had a bottle of the light honeyed wine that Ceana had tasted the other day, a smaller bottle of berry cordial, and all the fresh, clear spring water they could want.

There were no courses in the meal, no formality. Once all had been laid out and Fionntan said the blessing, everyone simply filled their plates with what they wished, when they wished it. Ceana didn't know what to make of it at first, but she quickly found she had no objection to the arrangement—not when no one commented on her taking third and fourth pieces of the nut-cheese, or when suggestions flew back and forth of how tasty this or that was when paired with another element of the meal.

The others chatted as they ate, trading memories of past pleasures in this place, recalling old jokes and making new ones, commenting on other places they should take Ceana in the future, and occasionally interrupting to request that someone pass a particular food or demand that Aíbinn stop hoarding the candied nuts. Ceana, her hands full, couldn't join in beyond headshakes and nods and occasional expressive noises, but she felt no less welcome for that fact.

By the time they finished, even as famished as she'd been after the morning's walking, Ceana felt as full as if she'd been at a proper feast. She sighed contentedly, glancing at the cleared dishes and wondering if she ought to help clean them up. She suspected she should, but she felt uninclined to do more than sit and enjoy the breeze and sunshine.

Aíbinn, on the other hand, seemed to have no such impediment. She finished off the last bite of the roll she'd stuffed with chicken and pickles and cheese, stretched, and began gathering the dishes, brushing off crumbs into the grass for the birds and animals, and occasionally asking if someone wanted the last bite of something. The others gradually roused to help her, and before long, all but the blanket and the drinks and cups had been put away.

Once all had been cleared away, everyone sat in companionable silence for a few minutes. Then, Uaine pushed herself to her feet. "Aíbinn, wilt thou come help me a moment? I saw ripe pears on a tree just a little way back, and I'd like to gather some to bring back to Mairearad."

Aíbinn leapt up as if someone had lit a flame under her. "Aye, I'll come."

"Where was this tree, Uaine?" Fionntan started to rise as well. "The rest of us can help thee as well."

Uaine hastily shook her head, holding her hands up. "I only need one to help. Aíbinn will be aid enough, really."

Aíbinn went to stand by Uaine, ruffling Fionntan's hair as she passed. "What Uaine means is that we're having a minute of sister talk, the two of us. Nes can guard thee and Kenna well enough without me, aye, Nes?"

She winked at Nes, who nodded seriously. "This deep in the wood, we should be safe, and I'll walk the borders of this space to be certain."

Fionntan looked at Ceana, and Ceana shrugged. When she saw that they seemed to expect more of a response, she wrote, *"Wouldn't want to intrude. Happy to stay here."*

"Then I suppose we'll stay here, as we can tell when we're not wanted." Fionntan sounded a bit bemused, but not displeased. "Enjoy your 'sister talk,' the two of you."

"We will!" Uaine called, already vanishing back down the path with Aíbinn on her heels.

A few moments later, Nes stood and stretched. "I'd better walk a bit to check on things and help the digestion. Call if you've need of me, your majesty."

"Go on," Fionntan replied. "I imagine you'll be taking your time?"

"Have to be thorough, your majesty." Nes's face was solemn and serious, but his words held an undertone of laughter that Ceana couldn't figure out the reason for. He bowed, then made his way into the edge of the trees with surprising speed for someone who'd just eaten a large meal.

"And there he goes," Fionntan murmured. "I tell you, Lady Kenna, were we anywhere else, I would suspect our companions of being up to some mischief."

What? Uaine and Aíbinn—no! Ceana hastily scribbled down, *"Mischief? Are you worried there's danger?"*

Fionntan shook his head. "No, no. I meant not to worry you. This place is...special to me. Aíbinn and I found this place long ago, when I could still slip my guards to wander the island. I doubt we were the first to come upon it, but few people visit here, and it has always been a special place for me—a place to rest and think and set aside care for a time and enjoy the beauty of what Dèanadair has made. These days, I can no longer leave my guards behind, but when I do visit here, they always manage to find an excuse to give me a little time to myself."

Oh. Ceana hesitantly wrote, *"Do you wish me to leave as well?"*

She had to tap his arm to get his attention, for his gaze had drifted out over the water of the pond. When he saw what she'd written, he smiled gently and shook his head. "Nay. I am glad to share this time with a friend—assuming, Lady Kenna, that we are friends?"

"I hope we are," Ceana wrote in reply. *"I would be glad to have a friend as kind as you, your majesty."*

"Then friends we shall be." With a twinkle in his eye, Fionntan continued, "But if we are to be friends, you must call me Fionntan in private, and let the titles be. Continual majesty is too much for any man; only Dèanadair can bear it."

Ceana couldn't help laughing at that. Smoothing out her tablet, she wrote, "*True. If you are just Fionntan, then I am only Kenna. No lady.*"

Fionntan bowed his head slightly, smiling. "Gladly, Kenna."

The way he said her name, Ceana felt a momentary pang wishing that it had been her *true* name—but she shook that thought away as silly. If he were to speak her real name, it would not be with such warmth.

They sat in pleasant silence for a little while, listening to the burbling of the spring and the chirping song of the birds and the occasional rustle of leaves from Nes's passage. Then, Fionntan, who had been watching the pond, turned to face her directly. "If I may ask, as a friend and not a king...I do not think Emain Ablach is the first place you have been called a lady. Do I guess aright?"

What—did he *know*? How could he know? Had he recognized her after all? Why would he bring her here if he knew who she was? Had all of this been a ruse to make her let down her guard? What if he meant to have her killed here, alone, away from anyone—No. That was foolish. Fionntan wouldn't act in such an ignoble, underhanded manner. And, she recalled a moment later, it would be as good as declaring war for him to execute a princess so unceremoniously, even a princess who had been spying on him and his people.

Her distress must have shown on her face, for Fionntan added, "I make no accusation, Kenna. Whoever you may have been in Atìrse, whatever titles you may have worn, they are of your old life, washed away by the sea, and they do not matter here. But something in your manner and bearing, and much of what you have told me...I do not think you were a simple peasant girl."

All right. Perhaps he hadn't realized exactly who she was. She just didn't make a very convincing peasant. And surely, if he'd already guessed this much, adjusting her story couldn't hurt? It would mean living a little less of a lie, and Ceana would certainly be glad of that. *"You're right. Father is minor noble with holding in Tiran Righ near sea."* That would be a believable enough story, she hoped. There were plenty of small-time lords who fit that description, and most of them were compatriots of Lord Arran.

"I thought so," Though Fionntan's face was grave, his voice offered no reproach. "Why did you lie?"

Ceana took her time smoothing out the tablet, trying to find the right words. *"Knew about the treaty meeting. When you found me, was afraid I'd be sent away. Thought being a peasant was safer."*

"Ah." Fionntan placed a careful hand on her shoulder. "I apologize again, Kenna, for causing you such fear. I promise you that you would have been welcome no matter who you had been before. A selkie is a selkie, and all selkies are under my protection, regardless of their birth."

His words were a balm to her fears—but a stinging balm, as they reminded her of how much she still hid. *"But nobles are more at fault for what's been done to your people."*

Fionntan shook his head almost immediately. "Each person who sets out to steal one of my people does so by choice, Kenna. Their choice. Yes, the nobility of Atìrse should not be leading their people in evil—but I would be a fool and a coward to turn away those who reject such evil and seek refuge from it. One does not cast away a pearl because it came from an unwelcome bit of sand."

What? Ceana stared at him, blinking, as she tried to parse that metaphor. He just gave a wry chuckle. "Never mind. So, is Kenna the name you were born with, or one you decided to take up?"

This was an easier question. *"A nickname,"* she wrote. *"It sounded less noble than my real one. And now I would rather leave my old name in Atirse."*

"It sounds noble enough to me." Fionntan shifted to partially face the pond again, though in doing so, he ended up sitting a little closer than he had before. "And what you have told me—is that knowledge from a cousin, or from yourself?"

"Both," Ceana wrote. *"My cousin was lady-in-waiting to Princess Linnhe."* True enough. Ceana did distantly remember one

of Linnhe's ladies-in-waiting being one of their cousins. *"I served Princess Mirren for a little while."* That, she knew, was a more dangerous lie. But it was technically true, in so far as helping each other with their hair and clothes went, and hopefully Fionntan wouldn't dig too deep now that he thought she was being fully honest.

"Little wonder you knew so much," Fionntan chuckled. "I wondered how a maid with such sharp ears and loose lips as your cousin could keep her position so long."

Ceana didn't know how to respond to that, so she just shrugged and gave a little laugh. Silence fell again as they sat, staring out over the pond. After a little while, Ceana wrote, *"What gave me away?"* and passed the tablet to Fionntan.

He looked it over and thought a moment before handing it back. "There were many clues. Your knowledge of the Atìrsen court and royal family, for one, and your insistence on defending King Seòras. Your mannerisms—you curtsey like an Atìrsen noblewoman. But what you said in the Halls of the Lost is what made me nearly certain."

Ceana tilted her head, giving him a curious look to prompt him to go on. He did, almost as if he were recalling a precious memory. "You said *'We* did not know,' and you spoke for all Atìrse. You spoke of your family as if you could act to change what has been done and what is being done even now. You learned of an abuse of which you are as much a victim as we are, and you spoke as if it were your duty to see it solved. Those are the words of one noble in both birth and character, and were more of the nobility like you, the treaty might have become unnecessary long ago."

Ceana flushed despite her best intentions. *"You are kind,"* she started to write, but Fionntan's hand came down on hers before she could put down more.

"I speak only the truth," he said, his voice firm. "Kindness has nothing to do with it."

Ceana bowed her head in acceptance. Once Fionntan took his hand away again, she smoothed out what she'd written and wrote instead, *"You say this even though I lied to you?"*

"'Twould have been better had you been truthful from the start," Fionntan admitted. "But in that moment, I deem you were nothing but honest. Am I wrong?" Ceana shook her head, and he went on, "I thought as much. And so, even had I been wrong in my assessment of your heritage, had you indeed been a remarkably well-informed peasant, I would have said that you are more worthy to wear the title of a lady than many who have born it since birth."

Even with all Ceana's practice at accepting compliments, *that* was too much, all the more so because it was so sincere. She squeaked and ducked her head, burying her face in her cloak lest Fionntan see how much she was blushing.

She heard Fionntan chuckle, but he said no more—thank Dèanadair! Eventually, Ceana recovered herself enough to sit up properly and let Fionntan see her face. When she glanced up at him, he smiled back, but still didn't speak. So, she tucked her tablet away, and they sat silently together, soaking in the beauty of the space around them, until Aíbinn and Uaine came crashing down the path, their arms loaded with ripe pears.

Aíbinn immediately set about loading packs with fruit. "Well! Did you two have a pleasant time here?"

"Very pleasant indeed. Kenna and I had quite an enjoyable conversation." Fionntan shook himself and turned to help distribute pears. "And I see your picking was successful."

"'Twas!" Aíbinn tucked away the last of the fruit. "We'll have pear and cheese pie next time you come for dinner."

"I'll look forward to it." Fionntan stood, shouldering his pack, and offered his hand to Ceana to help her up. "The day grows late; shall we return?"

Ceana nodded and took his hand, intending to use it as leverage to scramble up—but he lifted her to her feet as easily as if she were a child. She looked around for her pack, but it seemed to have vanished.

"We probably should go home," Uaine agreed. She picked up two corners of the cloth. "Kenna, help me fold this and put it in

Nes's pack. Aíbinn has both of our bags folded up inside hers."

That explained it. Ceana hurried to obey Uaine's request, and before long, no trace of their picnic remained, save for a few scraps and impressions left in the grass. Then they set off, leaving the peaceful spring behind.

Chapter 26
CALLING HOME

Ceana "confessed" her new story to the Northwaves sisters that evening after dinner, thinking that it would be best if all those closest to her believed the same thing. Somewhat to her disappointment, not one of the sisters seemed surprised. Much the opposite; Aíbinn turned to Uaine with a triumphant cry. "Ha! I told thee!"

"I know, I know" Uaine grumbled. She fumbled in her pocket and then passed something to Aíbinn.

Mairearad gave both her sisters a reproving look. "Did you two truly make a bet on whether or not Kenna was nobility?"

Aíbinn shook her head quickly. "Oh, no—we wouldn't put money on *that*. Just on why she didn't tell us in the first place and how long it would take for her to tell us."

"I do hope you both see why that's not better." Mairearad sighed and turned back to Ceana. "I apologize. Thank you for confiding in us."

Ceana nodded slowly. Had *anyone* not seen through her original story? *"How did you know?"* she wrote, then held up the tablet for Mairearad to see.

Mairearad just gave a little shrug. "I am a diplomat, and part of my duty is to be observant. You presented clues enough for those who know what to look for. But if you want to know, your comfort with being served by others and sitting at the high table at court started and finished the matter for me."

"'Twas the servants for me too," Uaine offered. "Thou acted like thou art used to being served instead of serving thyself."

Oh. That was a good point. Ceana hadn't even thought of how, if she were really a peasant, she would be unaccustomed to having servants. She looked at Aíbinn questioningly, wondering if she'd have the same answer.

Aíbinn shook her head. "Oh, I knew from the first day. Thy walk is more like a noble's than a peasant's."

Even her walk gave her away? By the Shepherd's path, how did Onora's spies manage? Ceana groaned, then wrote, *"Why did you think I wasn't telling you the truth?"*

Again, she showed the tablet to Mairearad, knowing that her question would be passed to the others. Aíbinn glanced at Uaine. "Which of us shall say first?"

"Thou," Uaine grumbled. "Since thou wert closer to right."

"So I was," Aíbinn replied smugly. "I thought thou feared Fionntan would use thee as a bargaining chip, used as thou are to human politics, and I guessed thou wouldst come clean as soon as thou realized he'd do no such thing."

Was that why Aíbinn had been acting so oddly? Trying to get Ceana comfortable enough with Fionntan that she would confess? It was a strange tactic, but Ceana supposed she could understand it to some degree. She turned to Uaine questioningly and gestured for her to say something.

Uaine sighed. "I thought thou wert fleeing an arranged marriage and that thou thought we would send thee back if we found out, and that thou wouldst not tell unless thou learned thy would-be betrothed or thy family were dead."

Oh, could it be any further from the truth! Ceana couldn't help it; she burst out in laughter so hard she nearly doubled over and so loud she could barely hear Uaine protesting, "What? 'Twasn't such a bad theory, really! Why's it so funny?"

Ceana managed to control her merriment down to breathless giggles. *"Will explain later. What did Mairearad think?"* she wrote, and then held up her tablet. Yes, she'd explain later, once she had an answer that wouldn't rouse suspicion.

Mairearad shook her head and started, "I assumed you had your own reasons —"

She was interrupted by Uaine. "That's a lie! Thou told me thy theory, and 'twas nearly as exciting as mine. And if I told Ceana, so must thou."

"Oh, dear." Mairearad sighed, giving Uaine just a hint of a dirty look. "I did briefly wonder if there might have been a coup in one of the minor holdings and if you had been given the seal cloak in hopes that you, at least, might escape. But 'twas not a *serious* theory."

Ceana shook her head, still laughing to herself. *"Nothing so exciting. Sorry."*

"Strangely, I am not at all displeased to have been wrong," Mairearad replied drily. "Again, thank you for telling us. I'm sure 'twas no easy task."

No; it had been no harder than telling them her last set of claims. But Ceana just smiled in return. It was nice to have a little less to hide—and hopefully, this would make it easier for her to keep the rest of her secret.

With her arm now healed and no longer aching, Ceana decided it was high time to venture outside Emain Ablach in search of a private place to contact Onora. So, the next morning at breakfast, she nervously informed Uaine that she wished to go outside the island and asked if she'd be allowed to do such a thing.

Uaine laughed at that. "Of course, thou art allowed. Thou art no prisoner, and as thou art mostly healed, there is no reason thou must stay within the borders. Others venture forth quite often. Dost thou wish for company?"

Ceana shook her head, speaking aloud in the human tongue, as had become her practice when she and Uaine were alone. "No. Not unless you wish to come." She hoped Uaine wouldn't; she needed to be on her own to talk to Onora. But she felt it would be rude not to offer.

Thankfully, Uaine shook her head, scooping up the last of her porridge. "I've much weaving and sewing to do today, so I'll stay here if it matters not to thee. Just don't wander far and thou wilt be fine. There are always a few guards watching the waters near the island if thou should need help."

Which meant she'd have to keep an eye out for them while talking to Onora. Well, if she whispered, she should be safe enough. And maybe she could go far enough to be outside their ready notice.

So, after finishing her breakfast, she loaded her pockets with two apples and some cheese and bread left over from yesterday and set out down to the lake in the center of the island. The path was familiar by now; in the last two weeks, she'd made a habit of going down to the water on sunny days just to practice shifting. And the faces along the path were growing familiar too; many of those she passed paused in their walking or work to wave and call hello. She waved back, smiling, and continued on her way.

Soon she reached the lake. As usual, no one even glanced her way as she drew her cloak over her head and walked out into the water. She'd learned to recognize when the shift was about to begin and will it to speed along so she no longer had to wait until she was fully submerged—small blessings. She hated the terrifying moment of being underwater, holding her breath and hoping the change happened before she ran out of air.

Once shifted, she swam down and away from the village until she found the exit hole. She surfaced again there and took a good breath of air. Then, with a flick of her tail, she started down the tunnel. It seemed even longer and darker than she'd remembered—though perhaps that was merely because she swam alone instead of in the company of others.

Finally, she reached the other side and popped out into the open ocean. She immediately noticed that her vision had changed. Underwater in Emain Ablach, the colors were still as rich as they were on land, if a little darker. Here, solely in the mortal world, she could see only in shades of grey. But her sight was no less sharp for all that it was less colorful, and her lungs ached from the long passage, so she wasted no more time on reflection and instead sped upward to get another breath. Thus relieved, she set out, swimming at a leisurely pace around the island.

Here and there, she tried to haul out on the island itself. But every time she attempted it, she found she couldn't bear to even touch the stone. Whether because of a curse or natural causes, the stone *burned*, and touching it made her skin go numb. After a few tries, she gave up and turned her attention outward.

As she swam, she passed both seals and other selkies. She hadn't been sure if she'd be able to tell the difference, but now, seeing both in close succession, she found she could identify which was which with little difficulty. How, she wasn't sure. Perhaps it was something in the scent that she, with her decidedly human mind, didn't know how to describe. Perhaps it was a light of greater intelligence or expressiveness in the eyes of the selkies than in the seals. Perhaps it was some other quality. But she had no doubt which was which, even before the selkies thought-called greetings to her. She answered them with a wiggle and a wave of one flipper, since she couldn't reply in the same way.

After some searching, she discovered a group of standing stones in the water about half an hour's swim from the island, on the far side from the entrance. Once she got closer, she found that, in one of them, wind and waves had carved out a nook just above the water's surface. It took her a few tries to figure out how to fling herself out of the water and catch onto the rock so the seal-shape would fall away, and by the time she finished, she suspected that her front was bruised all over. But eventually, she managed, and she clambered up the rest of the way to settle in the nook.

Dampness coated the stone inside, and she had to brush away algae from the rock's surface. But it was secure enough, and it gave her a view of the surrounding waters so she'd be able to— hopefully—spot any of the Guard coming to investigate her. She hoped that, since they'd all seen her earlier and seemed to recognize her, they wouldn't question her presence. But one never knew.

Her stomach was growling from her long swim, so she pulled an apple from her pocket and ate it, then dropped the core in the water for the fish to eat. She wiped her hands on a handkerchief, then reached under her cloak and pressed her finger to the symbol on her necklace. "Onora?" she whispered. "Are you there?"

A pause. Ceana sent up a silent prayer that Onora would respond; she hadn't come all this way just to leave a message! Then, blessedly, she heard Onora's voice: "I'm here. Is all well?"

Thank Dèanadair! "Yes, everything's fine." Aside from Fionntan and her cousins seeing almost straight through her cover. At least none of them had realized she wasn't just a noble, but a princess! Or, at least, they had all seemed satisfied with her revised story. In any case, she wasn't about to tell Onora that; Onora would probably just order her to come straight back to Atìrse. "I'm away from the island, so I can talk a little longer. Have you found out anything?"

"My agent only just reached Lord Arran's holdings. I've heard no more from him. I'm still working on searching the archives for any records of the time before the treaty. But what about you? Have you learned anything more?"

That the king of the selkies was kind as summer when he wasn't enraged at unintentional insults. That she was a terrible spy. That the selkies danced the same dances that humans did, even if they called them different names. But none of that seemed like the right thing to say, so instead she replied, "I think King Fionntan and the selkies would consider a closer alliance if Atìrse showed we weren't going to continue breaking the treaty. Right now, they're afraid and angry because people keep hunting them and no one does anything about it."

"That's good to know, since if what they say is true, Athair *will* do something about it—and so will I. But we need proof before we can act. Do you know of anyone else who you think might be a captured selkie who we could investigate? Aside from Lady Eilidh—someone who might be easier to reach and speak to?"

"Not yet. I could ask about going back to the Halls of the Lost— that's like our portrait halls combined with a graveyard. It's where the selkies keep records of those who are gone." Ceana considered the dim cavern tunnels. She didn't dare return alone; she'd be lost in an instant. Perhaps one of her cousins would take her, if she asked...but even then, would she be allowed to enter other families' areas?

"Try, if you get the chance—one moment." The necklace, which had been ever so slightly warm, cooled again. Onora must have released the mirror on her side. Ceana sat and waited, wondering what had called Onora away. A few minutes later, the necklace warmed again, and she heard Onora's voice. "Maimeó is here as well now. She wished to speak with you next time you had time for a longer talk. I've already told her what you told me about where you think the cloak came from."

"It's not what I think," Ceana retorted, a bit more sharply than she meant to. "It's what the selkies told me, and they would know."

"They could be wrong," Onora replied, her tone bristling ever so slightly. "I'd like proof before I act on what they said."

"And yet, thou must recognize that the seal-folk would know far better than we," came Queen Moireach's voice. "Ceana, I have written to thy Great-Great-Great Uncle Diarmad to enquire what the Daoine Math know of the selkies, their cloaks, and what started the rift between our peoples. There may still be some among that people who remember the days before the treaty, and if not, there are certainly some who are only one generation removed."

"But if they knew, surely they would have told us," Onora protested, in a tone that suggested she'd made this point before and remained frustrated that no one had listened to her.

A particular note in Queen Moireach's voice confirmed as much—not only had they discussed this before, she would gladly argue her side again. "Not if they believed we already knew. Even the most grounded of the faery folk sometimes forget how short a mortal's memory may be, and we have far less communication with them than we might hope."

"The selkies thought we knew, and they're nearly as mortal as we are," Ceana offered. Then, recalling what she'd been told previously, she added, "Oh! The selkies communicate much more with the Daoine Math than we do! They have a permanent ambassador, and they trade with the faeries for goods and livestock and enchanted things. There's supposed to be a whole group of messengers and traders coming in a few weeks."

"Really?" Onora asked eagerly. "If you're still there when they arrive, see if you can find out more about them and what it would take for us to trade more with them. Do the selkies have many magic-made goods, since they trade with the Daoine Math regularly?"

"Some. They trade for normal things, too—livestock especially. They can't get it to the island except on faery paths." Should she have said that? Ceana had decided not to tell Onora about Emain Ablach's location, just in case, but...oh well. Too late now. In any case, there were abundant little islands in the seas, and Teine-Falamh was the last one anyone would think to check. "Aíbinn told me that sometimes they get faery dogs instead of normal ones, but not often."

"Aíbinn?" Queen Moireach asked. "Is this one of the cousins thou hast found?"

"Yes—didn't Onora tell you?" It wasn't like Onora to leave out details.

"I gave Maimeó the abbreviated version," Onora replied. "I didn't want to pass on information I wasn't certain of."

"Perhaps thou couldst start from the beginning?" Queen Moireach suggested gently. "I may not have the practical interest of thy sister, but I would learn of what welcome thou hast found among the seal-folk."

"I wouldn't mind hearing the full story either, if you have time," Onora added. "I feel as if I've only had pieces so far."

"I can tell you the whole thing." Ceana shifted into a more comfortable position. "Where do you want me to start?"

"Start with thy departure," Queen Moireach replied, in her queenly-command voice. "When thou walked into the sea. What happened?"

"Oh, you want the *whole* thing." Ceana gave a little laugh. "Well, I walked until I fell underwater, and I really was afraid the cloak wouldn't work, until ..."

Over the next two hours, she related, as best she could, everything that had happened since she left Atìrse, leaving out the fact that Fionntan and the Northwaves sisters had guessed she was nobility and not a peasant. She spent quite a long time talking about the Northwaves sisters, and couldn't help feeling a sense of quiet relief when Onora and Queen Moireach both seemed to approve of all three. Onora even commented that Mairearad had seemed like a wise and sensible person at the treaty meeting and that it was a pity that the two of them couldn't make a longer meeting. Ceana agreed, though inwardly she shuddered at the thought of facing the combined big-sister influence of Onora and Mairearad at once.

Often, Onora and Queen Moireach interrupted, seizing on a detail and asking for more information on it or requesting clarification on particular points. Onora, unsurprisingly, paid particular attention to anything to do with the selkie's court, governance, and guard, and Ceana strongly suspected that she hadn't been able to provide nearly as much detail as Onora would have liked, even though she did her best. Queen Moireach, on the other hand, spent nearly fifteen minutes solely on the subject of the selkie cloaks, how they worked, the effects of Ceana having used one, and how selkie heritage was passed down or passed on. Ceana *knew* she didn't answer those questions as satisfactorily as her grandmother would have liked, but she felt a bit less guilty about it—she hadn't come here to look for information on magic.

Queen Moireach also seemed very interested in the selkies' tests for curses and blood relations. She had Ceana describe the stone the selkies had told her to hold in their first encounter as precisely as possible, prompting her with one clarifying question and another, narrowing down the runes detail by detail. When Ceana could, at last, summon no more information from her memory, Queen Moireach thought for a moment, then spoke in a tone simultaneously curious and peeved. "If the runes are what thou said...perhaps it is meant to detect curses, but it seems as if it would be more aligned to detecting a magical connection between beings."

"Maybe it is," Onora suggested. "Ceana, you said that the selkies claim a marriage between a selkie and a human allows the human to use the selkie's cloak, didn't you?"

"Yes—that's what they told me. But it doesn't fully work unless the selkie wants to be married." Or so the history Fionntan loaned to her had implied. "I read in a book that there were good marriages once, where the human received a cloak of their own, and the selkie could stay on land as long as they wanted, and they could both speak the other's language."

"That would've been good news if the alliance had worked out," Onora muttered, then seemed to catch herself. "I'm sorry."

"It's all right." Ceana sighed, slumping back against the rock. "I should have known better in the first place. Even without knowing about why the selkies don't like humans...I should have realized that King Fionntan might already have plans."

"I don't think his plans were the problem." Onora sounded as if she might want to say more, but was restraining herself. "In any case, if what they told you about selkie-human marriages is true, they may have been making sure you weren't married to an unwilling selkie and trying to infiltrate them."

Ceana thought back to that night. "I think they must have been. None of them would really talk much to me until after the runes changed color."

"Find out, if thou art able," Queen Moireach said. "I would think they would have no reason to lie to thee now, as you say they truly believe thee to be one of them. If the stone is indeed for detecting a bond between selkie and human, that would lend further credence to what they say about the kidnappings."

"I'll try to find out." Ceana glanced up, noting the time. "I should go soon. People will wonder if I'm out too long."

"Go, then," Onora replied, sighing. "I have much I should do myself. Be careful, and call when you can."

"I will. Goodbye for now, Onora. Goodbye, Maimeó." Ceana waited for their answering goodbyes. Then, she let go of the necklace and shook out her hand, now quite sore from holding position so long. Once her muscles were no longer quite so unhappy, she pulled up the hood of her cloak and slipped into the water. Time to return home —

No, she corrected herself. Time to return to the Northwaves house. *Home* was Atìrse. And yet, she had to admit, she felt as at home with the Northwaves sisters and in the isle of Emain Ablach as she did in Onora's castle or even in the castle where she had grown up. True, she had lived here a far shorter time, all of it under a false identity. Yet it seemed she belonged there as much as she did in Atìrse.

What *would* she do when she had to go back to Atìrse for good? She would miss the Northwaves sisters and Fionntan, would miss the island and the lake—and most likely, she'd not even have the sea for comfort. The royal castle lay inland, and whoever she married might well dwell far from the sea as well.

That was a bridge to cross later, though. For now, she could stretch out her stay here as long as she could. Who knew? Perhaps, if all went *very* well, they could build enough of a relationship with the selkies for her to visit occasionally, somehow. They might be state visits—but no, she'd never be allowed to come here in any royal capacity. Not when she'd be recognized in an instant, and that revelation might ruin everything she accomplished here.

Maybe she could find a way to visit in secret. There had to be something she could do. But for now, she would treasure the time she had here, in this home that wasn't home and yet somehow was all the same.

Chapter 27
GROWING COMFORTABLE

The days passed peacefully, and the longer Ceana stayed, the more at home she felt, especially as the practices she'd begun in her first weeks morphed into a comfortable routine. She continued to check in with Onora every day or two, usually with just a short message to say all was well. But once a week, she'd make her way to the standing stones outside Emain Ablach for a longer chat. Sometimes only Onora answered; sometimes Queen Moireach joined the conversation as well. Ceana half-expected these calls to make her homesick, but while she frequently wished she could see her sisters or parents or grandmother again, the thought of leaving still made her heart ache. And though Onora suggested returning to Atìrse more than once, Ceana always found a new reason to stay a little longer.

Aside from her conversations with Onora, though, Ceana took care to leave Emain Ablach for a swim in the open sea every couple days. It had been Onora's suggestion originally, a way to ensure that no one had any reason to take any notice of Ceana going out to call home. However, Ceana quickly came to enjoy her oceanic outings almost as much as she'd enjoyed wandering Emain Ablach, and the more she practiced, the more at ease she felt with shifting form and navigating the waters.

Occasionally, Uaine and others joined her on these expeditions. They showed her all the secrets it would have taken her years to discover on her own: the swift currents that would speed you on your way with hardly any effort; the shipwrecks where long-fallen vessels lay to rest, algae and kelp slowly growing over their hulls; the great forests of kelp as tall as trees; the spots where one could wait and watch and often see great whales go by—not the lesser whales, which would attack selkies as readily as they would seals, but massive, barnacle-crusted creatures so immense that they would only just fit in the keep's great hall.

Ceana had been frightened the first time she saw one of the whales, even sheltered as she and her companions—Uaine, Fionntan, and two of the Guard—were in a nook amid the undersea rocks. But Uaine and Fionntan assured her that the creature was harmless so long as she stayed out of its way and that it and its kin fed on neither seals nor people but rather on tiny shrimp-like creatures. After that, Ceana looked on with more wonder—though only from a distance.

They told her, too, that though the selkies did not hunt the great whales, they kept careful watch in case one newly dead should be seen nearby. Then everyone who could be spared rushed out to harvest what they could, for nearly every part of the whale could be used: skin, bones, meat, fat, and more. Anything they took and didn't use themselves, they traded to the faery folk, who prized sea-goods of all kinds, some for their rarity and some for their use in magic-making. Much of Emain Ablach's current prosperity had come from trading sea-goods, especially from these great whales, for the sea-faeries did business with no one save in gossip, and so the selkies were the land-bound faeries' best source of such things. Ceana took note of this to tell Onora later—not just out of curiosity, but in case Atìrse might be able to trade for such things as well in some far-future day.

When she wasn't exploring the waters in seal form, Ceana continued to periodically wander the island, retreading familiar paths to meet again with those she'd befriended before and sometimes taking new routes to find corners she hadn't looked into previously. One day, she found the home of Bryn, who she'd met the first time she went to the village, and she visited there quite frequently after that.

In the course of those visits, she learned the story of Bryn's husband: how his mother had been barely out of girlhood when she was captured—not through any particular scheme, but simply by a fisherman's accident. The fisherman had taken her to his home and kept her there by hiding her cloak, only rarely using it himself. But she'd found it one day, and she'd fled the same night to the sea, carrying her child under her cloak. The journey to Emain Ablach with a pup in tow had been a hard one, but by Dèanadair's grace, she'd found her way, and neither she nor her son had ever looked back.

On other days, Ceana made her way down to the village. There, she found a seat near the market square, and watched people go by, or else visited with people to learn their stories. One of the first days she returned to the village, she spoke with the weaver again. She learned the woman's name, Teàrlag, and learned of how she had, when she was young and about to be wed, found her father's cloak one day while searching for an old gown of her mother's.

After she found the cloak, Teàrlag had intended to escape with her father. The two of them had laid their plans, even come up with a story to cover their disappearance. But the night before they were to depart, a stray arrow from a hunter struck him down. She had debated whether to stay or go—had almost stayed, for life in Atìrse for all she had known, and she cared very much for the man she was to wed. Yet the more she thought on it, the more she feared what would become of her if she stayed in a land that had treated her father in such a way. "I still miss what could have been, sometimes," she told Ceana, a wistful note in her voice. "My Seocan was a good man, or so I yet believe, and I think I'd've been happy with him. 'Tis why I've not yet wed, though I've been here many a year now. But I am happy here, too, and it does me no good to dwell on might-haves."

Ceana heard many similar stories from others in the farms and villages, and she passed each one on to Onora so her agents could investigate. Each tale increased the burden on her heart, increased her sorrow over what her people had done to the Daoine Ròin. Yet she couldn't bring herself to stop asking. She needed to *know*, no matter how much it hurt.

Even with all the time she spent wandering the island and the surrounding waters, however, she spent just as much of her time in the company of Uaine and the other Northwaves sisters. Though Mairearad and Aíbinn's duties kept them away from the house most days—more days than they used to in Aíbinn's case, or so it seemed—Uaine was at home nearly every day and always appreciated company. Many mornings Ceana occupied herself helping Uaine with the sewing or spinning—though not the weaving, for Uaine kept that task for herself. While they worked, they would talk, Ceana in the human tongue and Uaine in the selkie language, and Ceana treasured these opportunities to speak without having to limit herself to what she could write quickly enough to keep a conversation going.

It was on one such sunny morning that Uaine asked, "The other day, when thou laughed at my guess that thou wert running from an arranged marriage—why was that so funny to thee? Thou still hast not explained."

The memory almost made Ceana laugh all over again, and she had to hastily tuck her needle into the fabric of the shift she was hemming lest she accidentally stab herself. "'Twas only that I *was* meant to have an arranged marriage, but it fell through, and I was still sad about it. 'Tis part of why I was so willing to leave home. I thought being away would make my heart hurt less."

"Oh—didst thou love the man thou wert to marry very much, then?" Uaine asked, drawing her shuttle through the warp of the loom. "'Tis strange that he'd refuse you, if you and he felt strongly for each other."

Ceana shook her head. "Of course not. We'd never met before."

"And thou wert...sad? About not having to wed a stranger?" Uaine gaped around her loom. "*Why*? If Mairearad or even Màthair tried to force me to wed someone I didn't know, let alone love, I'd run away. It sounds barely better than slavery."

Easy for her to say! *Her* marriage was as good as decided; she only had to wait for Fionntan to ask the question. "Why wouldn't I be sad? 'Tis what I'd planned to do all my life. And the marriage would have brought good to both his people and mine—I hoped it would, anyway."

"But—but—" Uaine screwed up her face as if tasting something unpleasant. "You make it sound as if all that matters is what good it does for other people, and that 'twas what you expected. What if the man you were to marry was horrible?"

"He wouldn't be." Ceana shook her head. "He wouldn't have been. Athair and Màthair wouldn't ask me to marry someone unworthy of me, and they would have listened if I met him and truly despised him."

Uaine pursed her lips, switching the shafts on her loom. "I still can't understand it. What if thou married him and then found thyself unable to love him? A marriage *has* to have love in it, else 'tis doomed, and those in it are trapped."

Ceana considered this, resuming her sewing as she did so. "I don't think that I could make promises to a good man, share a home with him, and work towards the same aims as him without coming to love him eventually. 'Tis no different than any other family member, really. Y—" She paused, correcting herself. "*Thou* didst not choose y—thy sisters. Dèanadair arranged that. But thou lovest them anyway." The old-fashioned words felt strange on her tongue, even after she'd practiced them on her own the last two nights. But it was not a bad sort of strangeness, no more than the strangeness of her first transformation from human to seal had been.

"That's—*Oh*." Uaine let out a soft gasp. "Kenna! Thou said *thou*! Thou art becoming properly one of us!"

Ceana flushed despite herself. "I only thought—well, thou and Aíbinn say it to me—it seemed fair —"

Uaine tilted her head. "If thou art not comfortable with it, thou needst not use *thou* for us. We think of thee as close kin, even if thou art not by blood, and we want thee to feel welcome, but if thou dost not think of us that way yet, thou need not be ashamed of it."

Ceana hastily shook her head. "No! No! I do think of all three of you as family, even if I've only known you a few weeks. And I wanted you all to know that."

Uaine left her loom and fairly flew across the room to hug Ceana. "Oh, I am so glad! I truly do think of thee as another sister, truly I do! And I am glad thou thinkst somewhat the same of me."

Ceana returned the hug, carefully keeping her needle out of the way. Uaine let go first and returned to her loom. "Where were we? Oh—yes—thou said arranged marriages are no different from other family."

"Am I wrong?" Ceana demanded. "Thou knew no more of me when I first came here than I knew of the man I thought to marry. But thou called me *sister* when thou had only met me a week before. Why should I not be able to come to love a husband after marriage just as well as before—or better?"

"I suppose there is something in that," Uaine sighed. "Still, it seems strange to me that thou wert so *excited* for it. Didst thou have no sweetheart already? No one thou loved or wished to marry?"

Ceana shook her head, carefully stitching along the place where the shift's side-seam met the hem. "No. I knew...I thought I knew, at least...that my marriage would be arranged, so I tried not to fall in love. Perhaps Athair and Màthair would have gone along with my wishes even if I had. But it seemed safer to wait and save my love for the man I knew I would marry."

Uaine wrinkled her nose, even as her hands found the rhythm of shuttle and shafts, weft and warp, once more. "Is love really about safety, though?"

"No. But I don't think 'tis *not* about it either." Ceana sighed. "I just...I don't want to fall for someone and find he's the wrong person. Perhaps I'll never marry at all, since what I hoped isn't to be."

"Oh, don't say that!" Uaine cried. Had Ceana not known better, she would've thought Uaine was in a proper panic over her words. "Thou canst never know what Dèanadair has in mind. Perhaps thy arranged marriage fell through because thou wert meant to wed someone here. I know there are very good men indeed who must already have their eye on you."

"Perhaps." Ceana couldn't keep the doubt from her tone.

"Don't be so gloomy. If thou art uncertain and don't trust thy own heart, thou canst always ask us. Mairearad knows all about love, and all three of us know all the gentlemen here," Uaine insisted. "Thou shouldst consider it, at least. And if thou should wed a selkie man, then thy struggles with thy cloak and thy voice would be over."

"Thou art as mercenary as thou thinkst humans are! I can't marry a man just for his cloak." Despite herself, Ceana laughed. "Anyway, even if I do find someone here, I'll probably be an official part of thy family long before I feel certain enough to wed him."

"Thou canst never know," Uaine said, in a tone that very distinctly said that she thought she *did* know very well. "Just wait and see. Thou wilt find someone, and perhaps 'twill be sooner than thou thinkst."

In addition to joining Uaine at her work, Ceana began accompanying her cousin on her visits to Fionntan's keep. At first, when Uaine invited her to come, Ceana had feared that she would detract from the two's time together. But Uaine assured her that she was welcome, and so Ceana came along most days when Uaine visited the king. Fionntan always seemed glad to see them both and to have a reason for rest from the business of governing, so Ceana soon let go of her guilt at intruding. Mairearad sometimes joined them during these visits, often accompanied by Sir Cianán, and Aíbinn frequently managed to be on Fionntan's guard detail at those times as well.

Somehow, though, no matter who else was there, at some point during every such visit, Uaine would contrive to vanish for a surprising length of time, always taking with her whoever besides Fionntan and Ceana happened to be present. The first time it happened, when only Uaine disappeared, Ceana thought little of it. The second time, when Mairearad and Uaine both vanished, she found it a little odd but assumed it was merely a matter of Uaine wishing to talk to her sister in private. But after the third time it happened, when Uaine managed to remove herself, Mairearad, Sir Cianán, and one of Fionntan's guards, Ceana decided there had to be something afoot.

She asked Fionntan if he thought the same after the fifth such occurance, jotting the question on her tablet. Fionntan just smiled wryly and replied, "I did notice, and I have asked. Your cousins say they are trying to give you the chance to make up for lost time, as they have so many more years of friendship with me than you do. It does not mean that they are not still up to something, however. Do you wish me to tell them to stop?"

Ceana shook her head and wrote back, *"Only if it bothers you."* Strange though their behavior might be, it wasn't as if she minded spending time with Fionntan. He was always kind and patient with her need to write what she wanted to say—unlike some others she had met, who would cut her off as soon as they thought they knew what she meant to say, or who were all-too-transparent in their efforts to remove themselves from conversations with her when they grew too tired of waiting for her.

She saw him more often than just these visits, though. He seemed to make a point of partnering with her for at least two or three dances every time she and the Northwaves sisters dined at court, and when they danced, he always made sure to keep to yes-or-no questions. Sometimes he would make up for her inability to talk by filling the silence with stories about his day or about the other dancers; sometimes they simply enjoyed the dance and the music without the need for talk.

In addition, Ceana continued her every-few-days appointments at the keep to tell Fionntan about Atìrse. These days, they seemed to meet in the keep's gardens or under a canopy on the rooftop as often as they did in the library, and Fionntan always made sure that a drink was waiting for her when she arrived and that some sort of refreshment appeared midway through their conversation.

She remained a little surprised that he kept asking her to return. By now, she wasn't sure what could remain for him to ask her. Yet, somehow, he always had some question. On several visits, he returned to the topic of the nobles, pressing her for more information that she might not have been willing to share when she was pretending to be a peasant. In one notable meeting, rather than asking her about Atìrse, he requested that she record everything she had known about selkies and their history with Atìrse and the other human kingdoms before coming to Emain Ablach. The result barely filled a page and a half of short paragraphs, and Fionntan shook his head in disbelief when she told him that she'd known no more than that. After that, he seemed more attentive than ever in answering her questions about Emain Ablach and the selkie people or telling her things he thought she might like to know.

During one such conversation, Ceana asked what he knew of the island's nature and whether or not Dèanadair had truly cursed it. Initially, Fionntan shook his head. "You need not fear the island, Kenna. It is safe; surely you have seen that by now."

"*Not afraid,*" Ceana wrote back, making a face at Fionntan. "*Curious. Màthair told me island was old fire-mount. Others said Dèanadair cursed it. Rocks are warm. What is true?*"

"Ah. I see I misunderstood." Fionntan thought for several long moments. "I am no scholar, and perhaps the question would be better put to another. But as I understand what I was taught, both are true. Emain Ablach began as an ordinary island, with its mortal and magical sides fully separated. We think there must have been inhabitants on this side of the isle, at least, for sometimes our diggings and plowings turn up remnants of a civilization older than ours. Perhaps there were inhabitants on the human side as well. But at some point, the island became a fire-mount, and the transformation and eruption killed the inhabitants on both sides and created the tunnels that lead from the human realm to our land. A curse from Dèanadair seems as likely an reason for that as any, given that the heat of that transformation still lingers in the stones, and that the mount has never erupted since."

That seemed as good an explanation as any, Ceana supposed, and as probably as certain a story as she would get. But Fionntan's words struck a cord of a new worry. *"What if another eruption? We're inside the mount."*

"'Twould depend on the nature of the eruption. If it were only a small eruption on the mortal side, we would have a few grey days, but no more. A larger eruption might force us to find new tunnels in and out, though those we have are stabilized with magic—no doubt you've seen the runes. Still, our side would remain largely undamaged unless debris managed to enter through some airborne path. If it erupted on both sides ..." A grave look swept across Fionntan's face. "Well, there would be much destruction, and we might well have to seek out a new home."

He shook his head, resting his hand on Ceana's shoulder. "Yet it has been long since the island spat fire, and we should have warning enough of an eruption on either side to flee out through the tunnels. In such an emergency, all are to go northwest to a group of standing stones in the sea. From there, we would journey together to a safer distance until the danger ended and we could send scouts back to see what had become of Emain Ablach. Do not let fear of such things trouble you."

Were the standing stones the same as her place to talk to Onora? They must be; Ceana could think of nowhere else that would fit the description. Well, at least she'd know where to go if it came to pass! But, as Fionntan said, it probably wouldn't happen. So, she smiled in thanks and wrote, *"I won't. What more did you want to ask me?"*

With that, they returned to their previous discussion. Yet, every time Ceana came, whatever topic Fionntan began the meeting on, his questions somehow always wandered to take on a more personal nature. He asked about where Ceana had grown up, and Ceana drew on her childhood visits to various seaside holdings, combined with occasional stories from life in the royal palace, to construct something she hoped would be convincing. He asked about her family, and Ceana told him what she could about her parents or carefully shared stories of her favorite sisters, changing names and doing her best to make it seem as if she only had two sisters, not six. He asked about a thousand little details of her life, and she answered them all as best she could.

Occasionally, she worried that she said too much, that she gave away information that could reveal her true identity. She knew Onora wouldn't approve of how much she told him. Yet it was so *easy* to talk to him, especially when he answered her stories with accounts of his own upbringing, of his adventures on the island and in the neighboring seas, of his parents and the Northwaves family and others on the isle with whom he was close. And so, she kept sharing with him whatever she could, praying with every word that he wouldn't see through her further than he already had.

Chapter 28
SPECTACLE AND WONDER

"By the way," Uaine mentioned over breakfast one morning, "Aíbinn suggested that we might like to come up to the keep a little early today to watch the Guard sparring and then take lunch with her and some of her friends."

Ceana looked up from her own bowl of porridge. "Why?" The lunch suggestion made sense. But why would Aíbinn invite them to come see the Guard train?

"Why?" Uaine echoed, brow furrowed as if she didn't understand the question. "Do folk in Atìrse not enjoy displays of fighting skill? Tournaments and such?"

"We have tournaments," Ceana replied slowly. "Every holding has its Games once a year, and my family always attended." It would have been unthinkable not to—in past years, there had been all sorts of accusations thrown when the royal family failed to open and close the Games. "But I don't see that watching the Guard train is the same thing at all."

"'Tis the same concept, only less formal." Uaine tilted her head, scraping the last of her porridge from her bowl. "Hast thou truly never watched such a thing? Surely thou had a Guard company of some form in Atìrse?"

Ceana shook her head. "We had guards, but we didn't visit their training grounds save on special occasions."

"Very strange." Uaine wrinkled her nose and stood. "Well, I wish to go. Aíbinn likes when people watch; some of the others try to show off, and that gives her an advantage. Wilt thou join me?"

"I suppose." She couldn't think of a reason to object, and she was supposed to meet with Fionntan again this afternoon anyway. She might as well walk over early so she'd have company. "When shall we leave?"

"In an hour or so. I'll come and fetch thee when 'tis time." With that, Uaine swept out of the room, leaving Ceana to finish her breakfast.

An hour and a half later, they reached the keep, and Uaine led the way confidently around to the training area. This lay some distance from the main building, near the stables, screened by hedges and shade trees. To Ceana's untrained eye, it mostly looked like a group of unimpressive buildings and fences around bits of ground that were no different than their surroundings.

One of these fenced-off areas held what appeared to be a fair portion of the Guard—albeit a smaller number than Ceana would have expected. She had noticed over the last few weeks that, in addition to Aíbinn taking longer shifts, there seemed to be fewer of the Guard about than there had been when she arrived in Emain Ablach, and the smallness of the group gathered here now appeared to confirm that. Not for the first time, she wondered where they'd all gone and whether or not Fionntan would tell her if she asked. Then again, would asking be a step too close to *actually* spying?

As Uaine led the way to the area with all the Guards, Ceana noticed that there were also a fair number of non-Guards about: several young ladies whose garb suggested a variety of social stations, half a dozen boys and a few girls who all looked to be between ten and twelve years of age, and a small group of nobles. This last group, Ceana noticed with surprise, included Fionntan, who currently seemed to be ignoring the conversations around him to focus on the two Guards within the fence, who were sparring with wooden practice swords.

Uaine guided Ceana to the side of the fence where Fionntan stood and wiggled and squeezed through the others there until they were both next to him. "Good morning, your majesty."

"Good morning, Lady Uaine, Lady Kenna," Fionntan replied,

turning his attention from the sparring. "I see Lann Aíbinn must have made you the same invitation she did me."

"She must have." Uaine had kept her arm through Ceana's since they reached the keep, and now she smoothly pulled Ceana around and deposited her nearest to Fionntan. She then let go of Ceana and leaned nonchalantly on the fence. "Has she had a turn yet?"

"Several, I think, but not since I started watching—Ah, look." Fionntan nodded out into the fenced area, where one of the guards had knocked the weapon from the grasp of the other and pinned the now-weaponless man to the ground. "Heilyn's won this one. He'll challenge your sister next, I'd guess."

Out in the dirt, the winning guard—Heilyn, apparently— withdrew his practice blade and helped his beaten opponent up. They shook hands, and then Heilyn turned towards the other assembled Guard members. "Aíbinn, I challenge you. Time someone knocked that smug look off your face!"

Though his words were phrased as a taunt, he spoke without malice, and Aíbinn's answering laugh suggested neither concern nor fear. "If I'm smug, 'tis because I've fairly beaten the rest of you and barely taken a bruise doing it." She stepped forward, taking the practice weapon that Heilyn's last opponent tossed her. "I hope *your* ladylove isn't watching; I'd hate for her to have to watch you lose!"

"Ah, she'll kiss my wounds either way." Heilyn assumed a ready stance. "Come and do your worst, Northwaves."

Aíbinn spent no more time taunting; she darted in with a low strike, which Heilyn countered. Back and forth they went, too fast for Ceana to keep track of. Other Guards and onlookers called out, yelling encouragement to one combatant or the other, and Uaine added her voice to those cheering on Aíbinn.

In what seemed like moments, it was over: Heilyn on the ground, his weapon skidding across the dirt to rest just on the other side of the fence from Ceana and Uaine. Aíbinn tapped Heilyn's chest with the end of her weapon, then stepped back and reached down to help him up. "What was that about knocking the smugness off my face?"

"Seems I'll have to leave that task to another." Heilyn hauled himself up and shook Aíbinn's hand. Then he made his way back to the crowd of Guards.

Aíbinn turned, glancing around to find the practice blade. She spotted it, then raised her gaze to smirk at Fionntan. "Toss the sword back this way, your majesty? Unless you'd care to take a turn and show us all what you remember from when you were in our ranks."

Fionntan raised an eyebrow. "Is that a challenge, Lann Aíbinn?"

Aíbinn gave her own weapon a spin, laughing again. "Of course it is. So, what say you?"

Ceana held back a gasp. She couldn't imagine any of the guards in Atìrse saying such a thing to King Seòras, even when he was younger. Yet no one else seemed shocked. She caught whispers and nudges from those around her, but they all sounded eager, not concerned.

"Hmm." Fionntan considered Aíbinn keenly, hand on his chin. Then, in a smooth motion, he vaulted over the fence and picked up the sword. He gave it a testing swing and stepped forward. "Challenge accepted."

Aíbinn's smirk widened into a proper grin. She winked once at Uaine, then took a ready stance. Fionntan moved forward and did the same. For a moment, all was still.

Ceana didn't see which moved first, but suddenly, both darted forward, weapons seeking their opponents. The two wooden blades cracked against each other as they struck and parried again and again. It seemed to Ceana that Aíbinn had the advantage of speed, yet wherever she attacked, Fionntan was ready for her. And when he struck, she was quick to block or dart away—yet, as Ceana watched more closely, she could see where Aíbinn's guard shook from the force of Fionntan's attacks, while Fionntan's blocks never once faltered.

Back and forth they went, first one retreating and then the

other. But at last, Fionntan's weapon slipped under Aíbinn's guard to strike true, and she stumbled backwards. His next attack knocked her practice sword from her hand, and his last swept her legs out from under her.

Flat on her back, she gasped out a laugh. "I see your skills are still sharp, your majesty."

"I put in no small effort to keep them that way." Fionntan reached down and pulled Aíbinn back to her feet. "You fought well yourself."

"What now, your majesty?" Heilyn called. "Winner challenges the next opponent, or do you only fight old friends?"

Fionntan raised an eyebrow towards the cluster of Guards. "Eager to see if you can best your king, are you?"

"Some of us still remember serving as a Guard alongside you," another man called, a little older than some of the others—Ceana thought she recalled his name as Ardgal. "Ay, and challenging you as a fellow warrior, not as a king."

This raised an unexpected outcry as half the Guard pointed out that Fionntan's days in their ranks had only been a few years ago and that half of them had served at the same time as their king, even if it hadn't been for long. Fionntan drew the tip of his weapon through the air in a lazy arc, eyeing the group with a faint smile as if deciding who to call out.

But before he could pick, an errand boy dashed up. "Your majesty!" he yelled. "Your majesty! The Daoine Math contingent—they're here!"

Delighted whispers spread like a wave through the onlookers. Beside Ceana, Uaine let out a squeak of excitement. Fionntan turned at once, tossing the practice sword to Aíbinn. "It seems any challenge I might have made or answered will have to wait." He strode across the practice area and swung himself over the fence. "Lead on, lad."

The errand boy nodded and darted off, Fionntan following at a swift pace behind. The Guard captain called out, "You heard the boy. The Daoine Math have arrived; now get this area and yourselves cleaned up double-quick!" The end of his order was nearly lost in the ensuing scramble of the company to clear themselves and the area.

Around the ring, the crowd already streamed after Fionntan and the errand boy. Uaine caught Ceana's arm. "Come along! The Daoine Math are here; let's go see who's in the company!"

Ceana didn't have to be asked twice. She followed along with Uaine as they made their way back to the keep and through the Great Hall to the courtyard in front. Princess though she was, she'd only rarely met the Daoine Math in person, and those she had met had seemed depressingly ordinary—though she'd been assured by Alasdair, Queen Moireach, and various others with the Sight that the faeries' commonplace appearance was a glamour meant to keep from attracting undue attention or suspicion among humans. Here, among the selkies, would the faery folk wear their own faces?

They reached the courtyard, and Ceana's heart fairly leapt in wonder. Gathered there was a great company of what could only be the Daoine Math, and if they were glamoured, it was at least a far more interesting disguise than that which they wore to visit her father's court. Though all present were, at least, human-shaped, none among them could have been mistaken for humans. Some were smaller than squirrels, with wings like those of dragonflies or hawks or even bats. Some were so tall they would have to stoop to enter the keep, with skin brown and rough as tree bark or as shiny-black as the outer stone of Emain Ablach. Some were roughly the same size as humans, but were set apart in other ways, with eyes like those of cats or with vines and leaves growing from their skin and amid their hair or simply with a strange beauty and almost radiance that no human could match.

Ceana made an effort to control her expression, but she couldn't help gaping at the crowd all the same. Uaine squeezed her hand and leaned over. "Aren't they magnificent?"

Fionntan strode forward, and one stepped forth from the company to meet him, a man with freckled greenish skin and leaves amid his brown hair, garbed in a loose and flowing tunic and cape.

He bowed and did not straighten until Fionntan spoke. "Welcome, Lord Elnathi, to Emain Ablach. Too long has it been since you and your company graced our home."

"Thank you for your welcome, your majesty. You are as courteous as your fathers before you." Lord Elnathi straightened up. Even with the freckles, he had a stern and noble look about him. "What is your will regarding the stock and supply which we have brought in accordance with our treaty?"

Fionntan gestured to the side of the keep. "Let those who keep the treaty goods assemble them there for my ministers and I to survey and distribute. The appropriate price will be provided to you as soon as we see all in order. Yet not all of those with you bear only treaty goods, I dare say."

The final sentence had the ring of ritual to it. A flicker of a pleased smile appeared on Lord Elnathi's face. "Nay. Messengers and merchants come in my train. What do you command regarding them?"

"Let the messengers enter my Great Hall so that those to whom they bear word may seek them there." Fionntan gestured towards the doors behind him, then surveyed the company. "As for the merchants, once they have marked out the boundaries of the path you took here so none of my people will wander astray, they have the freedom of my courtyard for their market."

A cheer went up from both the Daoine Math and the selkies. Almost at once, the faery contingent broke apart: some carrying their burdens or guiding livestock towards the side of the keep where Fionntan had indicated, a few making for the keep's great hall, and others rushing to claim spots for the market. Several took sticks and ribbon from their baggage and began marking out a space in the middle of the courtyard. It looked much like everything else around it, but Ceana guessed that it was the path that Fionntan wished blocked off so no selkie would become lost in Tìr Soilleir. Many of the selkies hurried off too, some following the Daoine Math and others rushing out of the keep, no doubt to tell their families and friends that the faeries had come with messages and a market.

Amid all the din, Ceana could just hear Fionntan ask Lord Elnathi, "Until when may your people remain?"

"Until tomorrow's dawning," Lord Elnathi replied. "The paths are erratic of late, and the one we traveled on will last no longer than that. Yet it is the most stable path we have had in some months."

"Know you why this is?"

"It is the natural way of things." Lord Elnathi did not sound particularly troubled. "The paths are living things, in their own way, and as such they have good years and bad years. We will keep our treaty, do not fear. But, young king, for the sake of your great-grandfather I will tell you that there are some who see the patterns of the path as meaning something more, and they say that unsettled paths mean an unsettled land or else a land that will see great change soon."

"With due respect and thanks, Lord Elnathi, I pray that Dèanadair grant that they are wrong," Fionntan replied gravely. "My people have weathered my father's passing well; they do not need further trouble to come upon them."

"I said change, not trouble, young king. But you may still have your prayer answered all the same." Lord Elnathi nodded in the direction that those carrying the treaty-goods had gone. "Shall we see to business?"

"Let me gather those I need." Fionntan turned, no doubt to call upon whichever officials were involved in treating with the Daoine Math.

Uaine tugged on Ceana's arm. "Come, Kenna! The market will take some time to be set up and ready, but the messengers are waiting. I want to find Mairearad and Aíbinn so we can ask if Màthair has sent any word."

Ceana nodded agreeably and followed Uaine's lead. She would have liked to stay and watch the faery market set up, but perhaps that would be rude. In any case, she had no real objection to keeping Uaine company.

It seemed that Mairearad and Aíbinn both had the same idea as

Uaine, and they all found each other quickly in the Great Hall. Just as quickly, they split up again so they could more rapidly check with all the messengers. Ceana trailed after Uaine as she asked first one and then another: any messages for them from Lady Northwaves? Or anyone else?

Aíbinn found the right messenger first, and she called out triumphantly as soon as she had the messages in hand: "Mairearad! Uaine! Màthair *did* sent word!"

They rushed over to her. Aíbinn clutched one thick letter and three thinner ones, and she held them up for her sisters to see. "She's sent one for all of us and then one for each of us on our own, just like always. Uaine, here's yours, and one for you, Mairearad."

Uaine grabbed her letter and then circled to peer over Aíbinn's shoulder. "Open the big one, come on!"

"Keep your skin on!" Aíbinn tucked her letter into a pocket and broke the seal on the thicker envelope.

"*Not* in the middle of the hall!" Mairearad gently shepherded her sisters towards the side of the hall. "Everyone can't stop and read messages exactly where they get them; I've told you both this a thousand times."

"Sorry," Aíbinn mumbled, gaze fixed on the letter. "Can I read it now?"

"Go on," Mairearad started to say. She got no further before a glad cry rang out from across the hall, followed by Sir Cianán calling her name. All three looked up to see Sir Cianán dashing across the hall towards them, all his usual reserve forgotten, a letter in his hand.

He reached the group and swept Mairearad into his arms. "Maire, I've heard from your mother! She gave her blessing to everything!"

"Oh!" Mairearad gasped, all her big-sister bossiness falling away into delight. "Oh, Cianán!"

The next moment, she pulled his face close and kissed him soundly. Aíbinn burst out with a great laugh and grabbed Uaine in a hug, crowing all the while, "I told you! I told you! We'll have a

293

wedding before the year is out!"

How lovely for Mairearad! And what a pity that, even among the selkies, a noblewoman's wedding probably took too long to arrange for there to be much chance of Ceana attending. 'Twould have been lovely to see a selkie wedding—lovelier still for it to be one of Ceana's own kin doing the marrying.

The sisters and Sir Cianán seemed caught up in their joy for the moment, so Ceana stole away back towards the doors out to the courtyard. She would leave them to their celebration, give them space to revel. And if she could watch the faery folk more...well, she'd certainly not be displeased.

No one stopped or questioned her, and none of the Daoine Math seemed to take any notice of her. So, Ceana found a bench near the doors to the keep and sat, gazing at the bustle of activity as the merchants and traders set up their market. Some had carts and wagons whose doors and windows they opened wide before setting up tables holding samples of their wares. Others had curtained booths draped in shining, colorful fabric. Others merely spread a blanket on the ground and perhaps a canopy overhead, and still others had no set place at all, but rather carried their goods in trays and baskets rigged to their person. Ceana noted that, though the crowd of selkies grew steadily, none drew too close to the market, and she wondered what signal they were waiting for.

After she'd sat for a little while, she spotted Fionntan coming around towards the front of the keep out of the corner of her eye. She looked up and waved at him. To her surprise, he veered towards her. "Are you enjoying the spectacle, Lady Kenna?"

Ceana nodded enthusiastically and pulled out her tablet so she could reply, *"Never saw anything like this in Atìrse. It's amazing."*

"Is it not?" Fionntan turned to look at the market, a smile spreading across his face. "Even as many times as I've seen it, the splendor never grows stale. Yet I would not have expected it to be so strange a sight. Does not one of Atìrse's princes dwell in Tìr Soilleir, and did not the old queen of Atìrse grow up partially among the Daoine Math?"

So! Thrice-Great Uncle Diarmad's marriage was common knowledge in Atìrse, of course, but the fact that Queen Moireach had spent her summers in Tìr Soilleir until she married and assumed the throne was not. It wasn't exactly hushed up, but it also wasn't considered polite to talk about, and Ceana certainly hadn't told Fionntan. Had the Daoine Math told the selkies, then? *"Prince Diarmad is wed to a lady of the Daoine Math. But we have only occasional traders, and they wear glamours."* After a moment of hesitation, she added, *"Maybe they remember what we have forgotten."*

"Perhaps so." A shadow passed over Fionntan's face for a moment. "But this is no fit day for me to ply you with questions of statecraft and politics. And, in truth, I came to find you—there is something I think you should like to see among the treaty-goods. Will you come, or are you busy?"

Something he wished to show *her*? Ceana fairly leapt to her feet. *"Not busy. What is it?"*

"Come, and I'll show you." He offered her his arm, which she took, and then led her back the way he'd come. They wove amid livestock being herded into rapidly-constructed temporary pens by selkie and faery herders, piles of bags and boxes of unknown goods, and officials trading money and papers. At last, they reached a small building that Ceana guessed was a kennel—or, at least, she recognized the mid-sized dog run set up outside it, fenced in with woven net strung between poles. A few of the Daoine Math were there, along with a few selkies and three collie pups, each no more than a few months old.

"Aìbinn told me that you were curious about the faerie dogs." Fionntan stopped at the edge of the run and called out, "Geansaidh, come and show Lady Kenna what you showed me earlier, if you will."

One of the Daoine Math, a short woman with skin like jade and hair black as a raven's wing, walked over, scooping up one of the pups, a fluffy creature with pointed ears and face. It squirmed excitedly in her arms as she stepped out of the run. "Lady Kenna, is it? You look not like one who'll be working with our dogs."

Ceana shook her head as Fionntan replied, "Nay, but she is a noble of the Northwaves family, and she is newly come to the island besides. Thus far, she has only heard secondhand what the dogs you breed are capable of. I did not think you would want to miss a chance to demonstrate."

Geansaidh's eyes, dark as her hair with no white in them at all, twinkled. "Well, I'll not deny that, your majesty." She turned to address Ceana directly. "As his majesty's not yet made proper introduction, I'm Geansaidh. I or one of my kin have bred most of the dogs on this island, going back as long as there've been dogs here. And this little one is Priobadh, Prio for short." She set the dog on the ground—leashless, Ceana noted, though there was a collar around the pup's neck.

Prio pranced around Geansaidh's legs, yipping excitedly, until Geansaidh snapped her fingers and pointed down. "Sit."

Prio sat, though his tail still wagged with enough force to move his whole rear end. Geansaidh snapped her fingers again. "Release."

Prio was up again in a moment, and when Geansaidh pointed away, he darted off like a shot, tearing across the courtyard. Geansaidh waited until he'd run some ten feet away, then let out a short whistle. "Prio, fast to me!"

The dog wheeled about and gathered himself as if about to jump. Then, quick as his name would suggest, he vanished and reappeared at Geansaidh's feet. Ceana gasped. One moment, he'd been ten feet away, the next here. Magic indeed!

Geansaidh bent, fondled Prio's ears, and slipped him a bit of dried meat from her pocket. "Good boy." She straightened again and handed Fionntan a ball made of knotted cloth. "Here, you give him the next command. Help him get used to hearing it from the mouths of your folk."

Fionntan nodded, weighing the ball in his hand. Then, he tossed it, calling as he did, "Prio, fast fetch!"

Prio perked up, gathered himself again, and vanished. He reappeared across the courtyard, at the peak of a leap, intercepting the ball in midair. He landed, spun, and was back to them in a blink, leaping around Fionntan's feet with the ball held triumphantly in his teeth.

Fionntan knelt, trading the ball for another treat that Geansaidh had handed him. "Good boy, Prio."

"He'll be able to do it with larger than that, once he's older," Geansaidh added. "Give him a few months and he'll have no trouble bringing you a whole sheep. Could demonstrate with one of the lambs we brought, but only if his majesty warns their breeders first. Else they'll tell me off for frightening their flock."

"I think the ball was sufficient demonstration." Fionntan stood again, though not without giving Prio a last pat. "As I've said before, your dogs are the best of the best."

Geansaidh's eyes sparkled again. She turned to Ceana. "What of you, silent lady? Care to try?"

Ceana hesitated, then touched her throat and her cloak and shook her head.

"Ah, you're that new?" Geansaidh asked. "He's not trained in the human tongue, but I can tell you the commands in my language and you can try with those, if you're of a mind."

Ceana nodded shyly. She listened carefully as Geansaidh told her the commands—*sit, release, fast, come, fetch*—sounding out each strange word. She almost feared that she'd have the same trouble she did with the selkie language, but though she stumbled a little, she could speak the commands clearly enough for Prio to obey. In between, she scratched behind his ears and ran her fingers through his silky fur and let him snaffle bits of treats from her hands.

Finally, however, Geansaidh picked Prio back up. "That's enough of a demonstration for now. Let me get him back in the kennel so he can rest. He'll be wanting to flop down and nap soon enough, I deem."

"Of course," Fionntan replied, bowing his head. "Thank you for the demonstration." He turned and offered his arm to Ceana once more. "I imagine the market will be ready to open soon. Let us return there—I would hate for you to miss any of its wonders."

Chapter 29
THE FAERY MARKET

As they were walking back, there came a horn call through the air, clear and silver as a highlands river. A cheer swiftly followed it, rising from many throats. Ceana glanced up at Fionntan for an explanation, and he smiled. "That was the signal; the faery market is open."

Sure enough, when they reached the front courtyard, Ceana spotted seal-cloaks among the booths and stalls and selkies moving from merchant to merchant. By the keep doors, her cousins waited, Mairearad on Sir Cianán's arm.

As she and Fionntan reached them, Uaine waved. "Kenna! There thou art; I was about to send Aíbinn to find thee."

"I apologize for stealing her away," Fionntan chuckled. "Geansaidh had brought one of her magic hounds, and I thought Kenna would wish to see it. I'll leave you four to enjoy the market; I need to see what messages have come for me."

"But you'll find us later, will you not?" Uaine insisted. "You'll not miss the market yourself?"

"Not in a thousand years,
  but every wonder will not vanish if I wait until the first rush is ended." Fionntan stepped back, bowing slightly. "I'll see you all later."

He headed into the keep. Once he had left, Mairearad turned to face Uaine, Aíbinn, and Ceana. "Well! Remember, the market is here 'til tomorrow dawn, so don't rush, but don't wait too long either. Aíbinn, Uaine, you know the rules, but since Ceana doesn't: if you buy food, know what it is you're buying; if you buy anything living, it's your responsibility to care for, not a servant's; and take care if you decide to buy from any merchant who takes anything but the usual forms of currency. What they ask may be a higher price than you think. Kenna, any questions?"

Ceana shook her head. It wasn't as if she'd be able to purchase much herself anyway. She only had a few coins left over from her last trip into the village, and while she might be able to ask for more, she wasn't sure how much she was really entitled to as a distant cousin. And they had already been so generous ...

"Then go on. We'll meet back here at dinner time." Mairead said.

"We'll see thee then." Uaine grinned mischievously. "Wilt thou and Cianán be seeking wedding jewelry at the market?"

"If we are, 'tis no affair of thine." Mairearad gave Uaine a little push on the shoulder. "Go. Enjoy thyself, and leave me to do the same."

Uaine just laughed and caught Ceana by the arm. "Come on, Kenna. We'll leave the lovebirds be. There's the whole market to explore."

Ceana made no argument, but followed Uaine eagerly as she rushed towards one of the openings into the market and plunged in amid the booths and stalls. As soon as they passed the bounds of the market, the chatter and shouts of people and the bleats and barking of livestock and dogs all faded to a pleasantly muffled tone. Music floated through the air like pennants in the wind, overlaying all other noises. Ceana spotted its source almost immediately: a pair of faeries of the same sort as Lord Elnathi, one playing a harp and one a set of pipes. Each had a drum on their back, and these kept the beat of the melody, though Ceana could see no hands striking them.

Ceana might have stopped there for some time, trying to figure out how the drums were being played, but Uaine tugged her away. "Come along; don't block the entrance. Art thou hungry?" She didn't even wait for an answer before pulling Ceana to a nearby stall manned by a group of dark-haired, cat-eyed faeries tending an astonishing array of pots and griddles suspended over a channel of flames. The faeries must have recognized Uaine, for they called out to her as she approached and joked with her in their cheerful, clipped accents. Ceana followed none of it, but she nodded when it seemed appropriate, and a few minutes later, she and Uaine were walking away again with something that Ceana supposed was food in hand—at the very least, she'd recognized the shredded cabbage and carrots and thin pieces of chicken, which had then been rolled up in a sheet of something papery-thin and partially translucent and folded into an oblong bundle. The outer part seemed to be edible, or at least Uaine bit into hers without hesitation, chatting about how some of the Daoine Math had come all the way from the other side of the world, originally, so far away that even by the faery paths, their journey took a full week on foot.

Ceana gave her meal a skeptical look after that; no wonder it looked so strange, if it was from somewhere so distant. But when she bit into it, the flavor was pleasantly salty and vinegary, and the vegetables were crisp, and before she knew it, she'd eaten the whole thing.

From there, she followed Uaine through the paths of the market, eyes wide as she took in all the wonders. There seemed to be even more people here than Ceana had realized, enough to make a whole city on their own. Yet, though there were people on both sides of almost every booth, the space didn't feel crowded, and room always remained for people to sidle up to each seller's space and gaze at the wares. Ceana wondered at this—and then she recalled what Queen Moireach had told her about how the faery realm shaped itself to suit its inhabitants, and she wondered more if perhaps the faery market did the same thing.

Almost as wonderful as the sellers were their wares. Some sold beautiful marvels: glass and gemstone animals that moved as if alive, everlasting roses that constantly bloomed and refolded, changing color with each rebirth, and wonderfully fashioned instruments that played themselves. Others' goods were far more practical, though no less magical: pots and pans of silvery metal that would never tarnish and that cleaned themselves on command, embroidered tablecloths that would recreate the last meal served upon them in response to their owners' word, shoes that would never wear out and would carry the wearer seven leagues in a single step. Ceana was tempted to try on a pair of these, but Uaine warned her away, saying that this particular merchant would hike up the price if you accidentally took a step while testing them—and that he had a habit of trying to trick buyers into doing just that.

Of course, there were also many merchants selling goods with which Ceana was more familiar. She spotted five separate sellers of message-mirrors, three of which also offered to enchant customers' normal mirrors for them. There were sellers of serums and creams for beautification and ointments and tinctures meant to heal injuries, prevent or drive off infections, and so forth. And, of course, there was jewelry of a hundred different styles, with equally as many enchantments, and other jewels and adornments that weren't enchanted at all, but were crafted with all the skill that could be gained by a craftsman for whom two hundred years was an unusually short life.

Wherever they went in the market, though, there was always music. It seemed that they couldn't turn a corner without finding a new group of musicians, playing and singing as if nothing else in the world mattered. Some sang in the selkie tongue; others in their own language; but neither was less lovely. And the more Ceana listened, the more she wondered if the musicians' songs were part of whatever caused the market to sound the way it did. Near a musician, the music and the merchants could be heard clearly enough, but no conversation rose so loud as to hinder hearing or thinking or even pleasure. Yet the further one went from a musician, the louder the crowd seemed and the harder it became to actually converse with anyone.

Many musicians kept hats or instrument cases open at their feet, inviting passers-by to show their appreciation—although, Ceana noted, not all seemed to take exclusively coins, no more than the merchants did. Many among both musicians and merchants would take shells of a particular type, those that were especially well-formed or whose insides were lined with pearlescent material, as readily as they did gold and silver. Ceana spotted a few merchants, too, whose booths held signs to say they accepted stone from the island walls as payment. And, of course, there were those who called out that they'd trade trinkets for strands of hair, gems and treasures for memories, or, in one case, good fortune for a kiss. Though this last sounded to Ceana more like a festival game of some kind, the pair of Daoine Math strolling the market and calling out their offer seemed serious, and the one selkie who Ceana saw take them up on it stumbled away as if she were drunk. After that, Ceana took care to not so much as make eye contact with the pair the next time she saw them, and she kept well away from the rest. Even growing up without a faery market to visit, she had learned enough from her grandmother and her teachers to know better than to give bits of herself away.

At first, Ceana kept close by Uaine, hesitant to stray too far lest she become lost or accidentally do something wrong and trade away something she didn't intend. But as time went on, she became more and more bold about browsing stalls on her own. On one occasion, she wandered over to one of the sellers of message-mirrors and was debating whether or not she could get a pair and leave one with Uaine when she left so they could keep in touch. She'd have to think of an excuse to explain why she'd left, rather than simply leaving, but maybe she could say she'd decided to take up a wandering lifestyle …

As she contemplated a nice little pair of silver-rimmed, palm-sized mirrors, the stall owner's voice pulled her attention away. "Have I not seen thee before, lass?"

Ceana startled and drew herself up, half in defense and half in surprise at being addressed in such familiar style by a stranger. She revised her second concern the minute she looked at the man, whose bark-brown face was rough with the passing of years and whose hair was so white that he had to be old even for a faery—no doubt she seemed a mere child to him. But his question remained. She pulled out her tablet and wrote, *"Don't think so."*

"Ah, half-blood art thou? Grew up in human lands? I have clients in Atìrse and Glassraghey, and I travel there every so often." Before her eyes, his form shrunk and smoothed out and his skin changed shade until he stood in front of her in the shape of a human man, tanned and travel-worn, though still with white hair and beard. "Perhaps this face is more familiar?"

Oh, she *had* seen him before! Once, when she'd been visiting Onora's castle soon after Onora's marriage, this merchant had come through. Onora had gathered herself, her husband, and her cat and had shut all of them in her office with the man for what seemed like ages. The merchant had stayed on as long as the royal family had, though he'd remained mostly in the rooms he'd been allotted. Supposedly he'd been enchanting message-mirrors, though Ceana had seen surprisingly few for how long he'd worked. Now, of course, she guessed that Onora had commissioned a large number of mirrors for her agents from him. Perhaps he'd even made the necklace Ceana wore now.

But she could reveal none of that, so she gave a little shrug and wrote, *"Was Atìrsen noble. May have met once. Don't remember."*

"Perhaps 'tis only that," the merchant murmured, resuming his natural shape. "Is thy birth family a client of mine?"

"Don't know," Ceana wrote, then stepped back. *"Should go find my cousin. Good day."*

She hurried away before he could reply, sending up a silent prayer: *Dèanadair, let him mention that to no one else.* She didn't quite trust that he'd not remember who she was, and if he told Fionntan or the Northwaves sisters or *anyone*, it would all be over for her. At least she'd not told him her name—but there weren't many other still-mute half-selkies on the island, and if he offered a description of her, it wouldn't be hard for people to figure out who he meant. *Please, Dèanadair...*

She'd just caught up with Uaine again when another horn call rang through the air, this one as golden as the first had been silver. Uaine looked up and set aside the cloak pins she'd been inspecting. "Oh! That's the call for dinner. We should go."

Ceana gave Uaine an inquisitive look and tapped her shoulder to get her attention. Once Uaine turned, Ceana wrote, *"Dinner?"* and passed over the tablet.

"We'll walk and talk." Uaine again took Ceana's arm, and they set off through the stalls. Ceana noticed as they went that many of the merchants were covering their goods with cloths or closing curtains around their stalls. "When the Daoine Math come with their messengers and their market, the king always provides the evening meal for the visitors and all the market-goers. It's like court dinners, but less formal."

The selkie court dinners were already so informal; how could they be less so? But she followed Uaine anyway, down paths that seemed far shorter than they'd been when the two of them had entered the market—as if the place were trying to direct them and everyone else out as quickly as possible. Across from them, the doors to the keep stood open, and golden light spilled from within. Daoine Math and selkies alike streamed inside.

Uaine and Ceana joined the river of people, and as soon as they were within the keep's hall, Ceana saw what Uaine meant. In the center of the room, several tables had been pushed together, short end to short end, and laden with food for people to take freely. None of it was as fine as what would be served at a proper feast day, but Ceana knew by now that Fionntan's cooks could make the simplest meals taste like the grandest banquet—and she'd bet everything in the market that a nicer meal had been prepared and served separately for Fionntan, Lord Elnathi, and a few select high-ranking individuals on either side.

Once people had served themselves, they could drift to one of the other tables or back outside. Uaine and Ceana opted for the former, having filled their plates with roast seabird in mushroom sauce, roasted and seasoned vegetables, thick slices of still-warm bread, hard cheese, and candied nuts. Aíbinn and a half-dozen other members of her Guard company soon joined them, laughing and chatting and comparing newly-acquired treasures and trinkets. One young man had bought himself a dagger that the seller swore would never grow dull, even without sharpening, regardless of what it was used to cut. Another sheepishly revealed that he'd already spent most of the little he had to share on preserved delicacies from far-off lands. Yet another showed off a matched pair of rings—heartbeat rings, he said, for himself and his bride-to-be, another Guard, so neither would ever have to wonder if the other was safe and well. The concept seemed very romantic, and Ceana wondered if Mairearad and Sir Cianán had also purchased a pair.

Aíbinn, for her part, said little, but it didn't take long for Ceana to notice that her braids were now full of short pins, each with a tiny star-shaped gem on the end. When she asked about them, Aíbinn grinned. "Aren't they lovely? They hardly cost a thing, but look!" She touched one, and a moment later, all of them lit up. "They're practical as well; they provide just enough light to see by in a dark space. But what have thou and Uaine found?"

Ceana shook her head, while Uaine launched into a long ramble about this, that, and the other thing that she was thinking of purchasing. Aíbinn listened good-naturedly until Uaine began repeating herself, then interrupted, "All right then. Kenna, what about thee? Hasn't anything caught thine eye?"

Ceana just gave a little shrug and wrote, *"Lots of nice things. Don't want to spend too much."*

"That's why thou must bargain—that and the Daoine Math think it's rude to buy *without* trying to negotiate. And even then, thou should have enough to get something...unless Uaine forgot to give thee thy spending money." Aíbinn turned to give Uaine a pointed look.

Uaine flushed. "I...might've? Sorry." She dug in her pocket until she found a money pouch, which she handed to Ceana. "Mairearad gave it to me earlier, and I was so excited that I didn't realize I hadn't passed it to thee."

Ceana gave her a reassuring smile and peeked inside the bag. Inside she found a mix of coinage and the pearlescent shells that many of the merchants seemed to accept. Enough to buy one or two truly nice things or a fair number of trinkets, she guessed. She needn't spend all of it, but...she certainly could get *something* to remember this night by.

After they finished their dinner, Ceana and Uaine returned to the market, this time in company with Aíbinn and several other members of the Guard. Now that she had money to spend, Ceana paid quite a different kind of attention to the merchants' stalls and booths. Most of these were open again, and the food-sellers seemed never to have closed. In fact, the number of food merchants seemed to have increased, particularly the strolling sellers of sweets and pastries who wandered about, calling out their wares and the wonderful properties they held.

Despite her best intentions, Ceana found herself unable to entirely resist these treats. From a goat-legged man with little horns poking through his curls she bought a tiny golden-apple tart laced with nectar-sweet honey. From a green-skinned woman wreathed in flowers she purchased a sugar-rose that melted in her mouth with a flavor Ceana could only describe as the essence of springtime itself. And from a night-dark man with brightly-hued feathers growing amid his braids, she bought a mug of a rich drink that he called *chocolate*, creamy and bitter-sweet. At each merchant, however, she she made sure to ask what effect their wares might have on her, and only once they had promised that the food offered sustenance and sweetness and nothing more did she buy and partake.

In between these treats, she poured over other merchants' wares, trying to decide what treasure was most worthy of being brought away. She didn't have to think long before buying a set of little pins like Aíbinn's, but shaped like tiny flowers instead of stars. The maker assured her that the enchantment would last for at least a hundred years, and as Aíbinn had said, they cost so *very* little. But other decisions were more challenging, and so caught up was Ceana in her debating that she barely noticed the sky growing dark and the lamps hung along the paths coming to golden life.

But she noticed when the world around her suddenly *shifted*, reorienting itself and making her head spin. She stumbled a few steps, wondering if she'd accidentally found her way onto the path to Tìr Soilleir—but, no, there stood the booth she'd been looking at in front of her, and there were Uaine and Aíbinn and Aíbinn's friends still nearby, and none of them seemed at all panicked.

Yet, though they were all still there, the market had changed around them. Rather than on a path lined with booths, they stood at the edge of an open space ringed with merchants' stalls, with openings here and there showing glimpses of paths like the one they'd been on. As Ceana stared, a band of Daoine Math stepped forward and struck up a jaunty dancing tune. Almost at once, several selkies skipped forward into the center of the circle to start a reel, and more rapidly followed.

Still a bit shakily, Ceana made her way over to Aíbinn. She tapped her shoulder and wrote, *"What happened?"*

"The sun went down," Aíbinn replied, raising her voice a bit to be heard amid the music, which now seemed determined to remain just a little louder than most conversations. "There's always dancing at the market center once night falls, especially during short markets like this one. It helps everyone stay awake."

Ceana pursed her lips as Aíbinn's words struck chords within stories she'd heard from Queen Moireach. *"Isn't that dangerous?"*

Aíbinn shook her head. "No. It's not the sort of dance that traps people, mistakenly or on purpose, and no one's going to accidentally dance a hundred years in one night—not when all the merchants here are the ones whom that would hurt most. The only enchantment is to make everyone a little less tired, and anyone can buy perfectly safe potions here with a much stronger version of the same effect."

Before Ceana could ask more, one of the Guard dashed up. "Aíbinn! Come dance with me!" He grabbed her hand and tugged her towards the floor. Another Guard seemed to have claimed Uaine's attention, for they were already in the middle of the crowd.

Ceana hung back, hesitant—but when another of Aíbinn's Guard friends offered her his hand and an inviting smile, she couldn't think of a good reason to refuse. Aíbinn said it was safe, and how many other chances would she have to dance among the

Daoine Math without fear?

So, she let herself be drawn into the dance, and soon she and her partner were stepping and spinning to the music with right good will. Ceana quickly realized what Aíbinn had meant about the enchantment in the music. All the soreness seemed to vanish from her feet within minutes of joining the dancers, and her legs, which had started to ache a little while ago, felt as fresh as if she'd just gotten out of bed.

The musicians flowed from one song to the next with hardly a pause, and Ceana had no time to search for another partner—nor did she have any need, for her first partner spun her out straight into the arms of one of his friends without any interruption to the steps. That gentleman did the same at the end of the next dance, and in that fashion, Ceana was passed from one partner to another until, several songs in, the hands that caught hers were keenly familiar ones and she looked up into the face of Fionntan.

He spun her round with a laugh. "There you are, Lady Kenna. I should have known 'twould be amid the dancing I'd find you. Are you enjoying the market?"

Ceana nodded, giving him a curious look. He drew her in from her spin and into the next steps. "Are you wondering what need a king has to visit the merchants himself? Believe me, the crown does not make one immune to the wonders of this place, nor to the pleasure of seeking out its treasures for oneself or for one's friends."

Well, she couldn't argue with that. If this market visited her father's court, she'd be no less eager to browse there as a princess than she was tonight as a noble. So, she bowed her head with a little laugh to signal that she understood.

For the rest of that dance, Fionntan spoke of the merchants he had visited and asked if Ceana had seen them yet and what she had thought of this or that among the wares. He was still talking when the song ended, so they danced a second dance together.

When that one reached its final notes, Ceana expected to spin away to someone else. Instead, however, Fionntan steered them towards the booths and stalls that encircled the dancing square. "If you don't mind?"

Ceana shook her head—she still had shopping to do, after all, and she had no opposition to doing it in Fionntan's company rather than Uaine's. So, she let Fionntan guide her out of the dancers and to the ring of booths, where he let go of one of her hands—though only one. "May I give you something, Lady Kenna?"

What was this about? Ceana nodded hesitantly, and Fionntan reached into his pocket. In a moment, he'd pulled something out and slipped it on her wrist. Only then did he release her other hand. "What do you think of that?"

She drew her hand closer to see a narrow bracelet of sea-blue stone and shimmering silver set in an intertwining pattern. If she looked very carefully, she could just see tiny runes etched into the underside. Pulling her tablet from her pocket, she wrote, *"It's lovely."*

"I hoped you would think so. These go with it." Fionntan now produced a silver stylus and a folding wax tablet made of the same blue stone, edged with silver. "Put the stylus to the tablet as if to write and then let go."

Ceana gave him a suspicious look—was he teasing her?—but she put away the old tablet, took the new one, and did as she was told. Then she gasped as the pen remained standing upright. Fionntan touched the bracelet. "If you are wearing this, the stylus will write for you according to your wish. Try it."

Would it really? Ceana thought for a moment, then imagined writing *"Thank you"* on the tablet. As Fionntan had said, the stylus moved of its own accord, forming the letters in a hand very much like Ceana's own. She gasped again and touched the lines.

"Do you like it?" Fionntan asked, a hint of eager uncertainty in his voice—strange, for a king. "It cannot replace your voice, and you have to have a hand free for the tablet, but perhaps it will make things easier for you until you can speak again."

"I like it very much." Ceana flipped the stylus, focused, and found that it would smooth the wax for her as well. Again, she turned the stylus over. *"But surely this is too great a gift."*

"Not so great, not for a friend." Fionntan pressed the tablet towards her. "Please, don't argue over it. There's always someone selling these at the market. I simply happened to see the booth and think of you."

Ceana's heart made a strange little jolt at those words—but that was silly. Fionntan was kind, and he called her friend; it wasn't so odd that he would want to give her a good gift. *"Thank you for thinking of me. I wish I had something for you."*

"You must think me intensely mercenary if you believe I give gifts in order to receive something in return," Fionntan chuckled. "But the pleasure of your company for a little while longer will be thanks enough, if you insist—unless you wish to dance further."

Ceana shook her head. *"No. I planned to stop and browse more. Would be glad to do it with you."*

"Then let us go." Fionntan offered his arm, and together they strolled slowly along the ring of booths and through a break in the ring to the outer path.

The night drew on and on. Ceana wandered the market, sometimes in the company of Fionntan, sometimes with her cousins, sometimes with all of them at once. She pored over the merchants' wares again and again, bargaining with a few sellers to purchase mementos. Every so often, any time she and her friends grew too tired, they returned to the center of the market and there were refreshed in the dancing.

But eventually, the dark sky above started to lighten, and the merchants began packing away their wares and folding their stalls and canopies into bundles and baggage. At last, nothing remained but the blocked-off path. Then, as the first rays of the rising sun's glow began to show on the horizon, they unblocked the path and filed down it in twos and threes. Lord Elnathi departed last of all, bowing to Fionntan as he went.

As he vanished and the last traces of magic faded from the air, Ceana yawned, the effects of a full night of no sleep catching up with her. Fionntan put a hand to her arm, steadying her. "So, you've had your first faery market."

Ceana nodded, too weary to form words, with or without the help of the enchanted stylus. A little way away, her cousins were collecting themselves and sleepily arguing about whether it would be better to walk home or call for the pony cart. Ceana hoped they decided on the latter, though she wasn't sure she'd last the whole way home without falling asleep in either case.

Fionntan spoke again, pulling her away from thoughts of her bed. "I'll not keep you much longer, but there is something else I wished to ask you. In two weeks' time, two singing parties will set forth for Atìrse's shore, and I plan to join one of them. I wondered if you would like to come with me—and the others, of course."

Oh, she had to come up with a proper answer now. Ceana shook herself, blearily considering the question. *"Can't sing,"* she managed to write, after more thought than such a short reply should have required.

"I know. But I wish you to hear the singing from our side, even if you cannot join in. 'Twill not be a long trip—only a little further than to where we first found you." Fionntan looked down at her, gaze strangely eager. "Will you come?"

A part of her mind that sounded very like Onora tried to protest, to insist that this was dangerous. But that part was muffled by weariness and by the look on Fionntan's face—and, anyway, this would be an opportunity to learn something. So, she nodded and wrote in reply: *"I'll come with you."*

Chapter 30
SEEKING WHAT'S LOST

In the end, walking won out, and so Ceana and her cousins stumbled home with only enough energy left on their arrival to undress and collapse into their beds. The next thing Ceana knew, the sun was streaming through the nearby window onto her closed eyelids, and Onora's voice was in her ears, hissing her name with furious urgency: "Ceana! Ceana, are you there?"

Ceana moaned and fumbled for the necklace. It took her several minutes to find the rune and press her finger to it so she could mumble, "What is it?"

Onora's voice lost a little of its urgency, replaced with worry. "Are you all right? Is this a bad time?"

"'Tis fine. I just woke up." Ceana yawned, burrowing more into her blankets and keeping her eyes tight shut. If she was lucky, if anyone heard her, she could pass her whispers off as talking in her sleep. Besides, she was decidedly *not* ready to get up. "What's wrong?"

"Far too much. You were right about Lord Arran." The fury had returned to Onora's voice, even more intense than before. "My agent just told me this morning what he's learned. Lady Eilidh *is* a selkie, and she absolutely did *not* marry Lord Arran willingly. No wonder she always looked like she was mourning someone! She's been captive for years, and you know Arran's castle overlooks the sea. Every day, faced with what she's lost—and he *taunts* her with it."

That sounded like Lord Arran. But before Ceana could reply,

Onora went on, "And there are others—my agent is still working out how many of Arran's people are actually human and how many are captured selkies and how many of his friends and close allies are part of his schemes. We don't know exact numbers yet, but neither my agent nor I like what we've found so far."

"I *told* thee," Ceana insisted, waking up a little more despite her best intentions. "I didn't think they'd lie about something like that."

"I—Wait." Onora paused, and when next she spoke, her tone held utter bewilderment. "Did you call me *thee*? Shepherd's paths, Ceana, you're turning into Maimeó." Another pause. "Of course, there are far worse people who you could turn into."

Ceana pulled the blankets all the way over her head, trying to block light out and sound in. "Sorry. I'm just *used* to it now. What art thou going to do? Hast thou told Athair yet?" She should probably switch back—but she'd *just* woken up, and thinking about pronouns was really too much effort just now.

"Not yet. My agent thinks there's something more going on, and I want to be able to bring Athair the full story when I tell him. And besides —" Onora's tone took on a grim note—"Once Athair knows, he *has* to act, and it's harder for him to keep things secret than it is for me. Lord Arran and his people may retaliate against the selkies they've captured if they get wind that they've been discovered."

That, too, sounded like Lord Arran. Ceana imagined, just for a moment, what his vengeance might be like, and the mere thought made her sick to her stomach. "We need to make sure the selkies will be safe."

"Exactly," Onora replied, and Ceana could almost see the steel in her face. "My agent is trying to find their cloaks; barring that, he's looking for a way to evacuate them all or move them all to an easily defensible location so they'll be safe until we can reach them. I've identified several other agents as undoubtedly trustworthy, and I've sent them up to help him. You said that the selkies have a way to create new cloaks for those who don't have one?"

Ceana considered. She'd been told of the adoption ceremony that would give a half-selkie a cloak of their own, and she'd been told of the old version of the marriage ceremony that would bring a human into the selkie fold and vice versa. Surely one of those would work for a full-blooded selkie who'd lost their cloak? "I think so."

"Good. If we have to evacuate them without their cloaks, there's always the risk that Lord Arran and his men will destroy the cloaks before Athair's forces can get there. But if that's not going to cut anyone off from their home forever, we can focus on making sure they stay alive."

Having seen how the people of Emain Ablach acted, Ceana doubted that any of the captured selkies would agree to go far without their cloaks. But perhaps the risk of a threat to their lives and the promise of freedom would be sufficient motivation. "Should I try to find a way to tell someone here? Maybe the selkies here could help. They've mounted a few rescue missions before."

"There's no way you can tell them without revealing who you are. If I thought it would do any good, I'd look for a way to send word myself. But I doubt they'll believe we're well-intentioned." Onora sighed, long and low. "More likely, they'd suspect us of trying to draw them into a trap with false promises."

"They might not. I think...I think some of them are softening a little." Fionntan might be, at least. "Surely there's some way I could let them know?"

"That may be, but I don't think they'd believe enough to act unless we'd already made some significant gesture of change and goodwill. And if you reveal your identity, that's a step in the opposite direction. Once we have a plan, maybe you can find a way to make sure there will be selkies in the right place to receive the rescues, but don't tell them more than that. If you want to help, try to go back to the Halls of the Lost you told me about and look for anyone else you recognize."

"All right." Much as Ceana wished it were otherwise, she had to admit Onora had a point. And at least there was *something* she could do to help. "Thou'rt not going to tell me to come home?"

"If you're staying within the island and being careful, you may be safer there than you would be here. From what my agents can tell, Lord Arran and his people still don't know where the selkies live, though they'd *like* to know. And in the chance that he hears something and retaliates against more people than just the selkies... well, I'd rather you were there."

"What—What meanst thou?" Onora's words weren't quite making sense; surely she wasn't saying that Lord Arran would—would try to—not against his own king and future queen! "Dost thou really believe ..."

"I will put nothing past a man willing to write off a whole race of people as *things* to be used and abused." The steel had returned to Onora's voice now, steel and fire both. "I don't plan to give him a chance to try anything. Neither will Athair. If all goes to plan, we'll have him in chains and facing trial before he realizes what we know. But only Dèanadair sees the future, and I want you out of harm's way as much as possible."

"I'll stay safe. I promise." Better *not* to mention that she had agreed to go with the singing party. That wasn't really *unsafe*, though. She'd be with Fionntan and some of his Guard, and from what she could tell, the singing parties didn't go on shore. "Please be careful thyself too. Thou and Athair and Màthair and everyone."

"We will." Onora sighed. "I should go, but I wanted you to know what's happening."

"I appreciate it." Ceana tightened her grip a little on the necklace. "I love thee."

"And I love you too. Until next time."

Ceana waited, but Onora said nothing more. Well, at least others knew the truth now. And Onora was clever. Surely, she and her agents would figure out how to free the selkies. Still, Ceana rolled over and whispered a prayer to Dèanadair: "Please, guide her and protect her, her and her agents and all the selkies on shore. Don't let the worst come to worst, whatever else happens." Then, having placed the matter solidly in Dèanadair's hands, she rolled over and attempted to go back to sleep.

Ceana wasted little time in following Onora's request. Though the Faery Market had thrown everyone's schedules into confusion, the next day brought a return to routine. So, when everyone was present at dinner, Ceana wrote, *"Would like to go to Halls of Lost again. Allowed?"*

She passed the tablet to Mairearad, who read it silently. "You're certainly allowed to go back whenever you would like. Still, it is difficult to navigate if you've not been there before. Can you wait until I can go with you and guide you?"

Ceana nodded. She smoothed out the wax of the tablet, pleased that she could do so with it still in Mairearad's hands—Fionntan's gift truly *was* lovely!—and wrote, *"Will wait. Why you, not Uaine?"*

"I've been there the most times," Mairearad speared a bit of fish. "If you prefer to go with Uaine, I understand, but I do go every few weeks just to see that all is well. If you can wait a week or, I'll be going there anyway."

"A week is fine," Ceana wrote. Hopefully, that wouldn't make too much difference to Onora's plans. She smoothed the wax again and added, *"Would like to see spaces for other families too. Allowed?"* She didn't see why it wouldn't be—it was a graveyard, more or less, and no one objected to having one's family's gravestones looked at.

Mairearad hesitated. "Typically, entering another family's cavern isn't done without an invitation. Why do you wish to look?"

Unexpected. Then again, the Halls of the Lost were a little more personal than a normal graveyard. *"Want to look for anyone I recognize. Maybe can identify someone who's captured & living."*

"Well ..." Mairearad contemplatively ate several bites of fish, gazing off into the space just above the table. "As long as you are careful to disturb nothing and no one, I think that should be all right. But do not speak broadly of it; if you see anyone you know, tell me so I can decide how to let their family know."

Ceana gave thanks that she hadn't had to come up with a false excuse. After all, she *did* want to look for anyone she recognized;

the fact that she would be passing that information to Onora was beside the point. And Mairearad's condition seemed reasonable. *"I will. Thank you."*

"Of course." Mairearad returned her attention to her meal, then paused again. "If you are in earnest about trying to identify those who were captured, not killed, speak to Fionntan. He could give you proper permission, even a royal order. If you are doing it to help others here, I doubt he would refuse you."

"Oh, that's a good idea!" Uaine chimed in. "Thou canst ask when thou art at the keep tomorrow."

"Will ask," Ceana wrote in reply. Since her last planned meeting with Fionntan had been supplanted by the Faery Market, Fionntan had sent a messenger that morning to reschedule for the following afternoon. He'd mentioned in the message that he'd be glad to walk with her back to the Northwaves home, since his weekly dinner with the sisters had also needed to be rescheduled. Ceana thought that a bit odd. After all, he'd made a habit over the last weeks of having her to the keep the day he came for dinner and then walking back at the same time she did. Why mention it specifically now?

Mairearad gave a nod. "'Tis settled, then. Who knows, if he gives his blessing, he may even send some others with you to make note of who you recognize and ensure no one raises contention over your presence there. Perhaps he'll even come with you himself."

Ceana gave Mairearad a befuddled look—why would the king trouble himself with such an errand? Surely there were others he could send instead. And why did Mairearad's tone have that meaningful note to it?

Unfortunately, she had no chance to ask before Aíbinn changed the conversation with a mischievous question: "So, Mairearad, *did* thou and Sir Cianán find your wedding jewels at the Faery Market the other night?"

Mairearad flushed, but kept her head held high. "We did. As Màthair has given her blessing, we have no intention of delaying long enough for the next market to arrive."

"I knew it!" Uaine crowed. "I saw thee and him looking at rings and necklaces and things. Have you two set a date yet?"

"Not yet." Mairearad sounded as if she were fighting to sound casual. "But we have spoken in the past and agree that an autumn wedding would suit us both well. Cianán is speaking with his family today to ask their thoughts. He may also join us tomorrow night for dinner, if his conversation with his kin goes well."

"He might?" Aíbinn asked, dropping her fork in her excitement. "He hardly ever dines with us!"

"He and I prefer to spend our time together at the keep." Mairearad arched an eyebrow at her sisters. "I suggest that both of you think on why that might be and what that might mean for tomorrow."

"Oh, Fionntan's here. Thou knowst we won't get in too much trouble." Aíbinn waved a hand dismissively and then picked up her fork. "Have thou and he decided anything else?"

From there, the conversation turned fully to wedding plans, of which Mairearad seemed to have a surprising number, considering how short a time she'd been properly betrothed. Ceana reclaimed her tablet and mostly just listened, though occasionally she managed to squeeze in a comment about her own experience with her sisters' weddings or a question about selkie wedding customs.

For the most part, however, she kept her stylus still and silent, taking in all she could learn and, periodically, imagining Uaine and Fionntan discussing all these things some future day. The thought made something inside her twinge oddly, but she did her best to tamp the feeling down. Her best guess as to what it could be was sadness that she'd not be there to see those days—but she'd have to go home long before that time came, and there could be no getting around that.

⁂

The next day, when Ceana arrived at Fionntan's keep, the maids directed her up to the rooftop again. As usual, she found Fionntan waiting for her with a pitcher of watered honey-wine and a short stack of paper at hand. He took her hand in greeting, bending over it as she curtseyed in a way that would not have been amiss had they been meeting as king and princess, not king and lesser-cousin-of-a-noble-family. "Good afternoon, Kenna. How fare you today?"

"Very well. And you?" Ceana had prepared her tablet before she came in, arranging it in her off-hand with the stylus poised, and now she gave thanks she'd done so. It was *so* nice to not have to fumble it out and write something—especially as Fionntan seemed to have forgotten to let go of her hand. Instead, he stared into the air between his face and her hand as if trying to remember what he was going to say.

She gave his hand a little tug to bring him back to reality. He hastily released her hand and glanced at her tablet. "My apologies. Yes, I am well. Have the tablet and stylus been useful?"

Ceana erased the *well* and underlined *Very*, then added, *"Bracelet is also lovely. Thank you."*

"I'm glad they please you." A strange smile spread over Fionntan's face. "Though as far as the bracelet goes, I find that half the beauty in any particular piece tends to be reflected from the wearer, rather than being inherent to the adornment itself."

Ceana couldn't help a little laugh. *"You are very kind."* It was a strange thing to say to her—it would have been better addressed to Uaine—but perhaps Fionntan was just in an odd mood today. *"Should we sit and begin?"*

"Ah, yes." Fionntan took a step back and pulled out Ceana's chair for her. Only then did Ceana notice that the chairs were both on the same side of the table this time. She gestured questioningly at the second seat as she sat.

Fionntan stepped to his chair and set a hand on it. "The chairs? I thought 'twould be easier to converse if we were both on the same side of the table, rather than having to pass a page or tablet back and forth. Unless, of course, you are uncomfortable sitting side by side with a king?"

It would hardly be the first time she'd done it, even in much more formal settings than this. But Ceana could hardly say that. So instead she shook her head with a smile. *"I never mind sitting by a friend.*" Then, turning the tablet to the unmarked side, she added, "*Besides, sat by you at the spring.*"

"True. That was a pleasant afternoon. Perhaps I should make time to do things of that sort more often. Assuming I can call upon your and your cousins for company again, of course?" He asked the last with a raised eyebrow in her direction.

"*Am sure none of us would object,*" Ceana wrote. It had been Uaine and Aíbinn's idea in the first place, after all, and as for herself—Well! She'd certainly not complain about seeing more of the island's wonders before she had to someday leave.

Fionntan nodded thoughtfully. "Then I shall have to arrange another excursion. Is there anywhere on the island you have heard about and would particularly like to visit?"

Ceana shrugged and smoothed out her tablet again. "*Wherever you think best.*"

Again, he nodded, staring off into the distance as if searching the hills for the ideal spot. Ceana waited for some minutes, expecting him to turn to the questions he'd called her here for. But when he showed no indication of beginning that part of the interview, she wrote "*May I make a request?*" on her tablet, then tapped him on the shoulder so he would know to look.

He glanced down with a start. "What? Of course. Of what do you have need?"

"*Not need,*" Ceana hastily wrote. Then, more slowly, she wrote, "*I am visiting Halls of Lost with Mairearad soon. Would like to look in other family's halls for anyone I recognize. Maybe I can help find people.*"

She stopped there, though she kept the stylus ready to offer further persuasion or assurances that she'd disturb nothing and no one. But instead, Fionntan nodded at once. "Of course. If you are willing, I would be glad for you to make such a search and tell me of anyone whose condition you can confirm. 'Twould provide closure to many families, and perhaps would give us a chance of some rescue attempts."

Hopefully any rescue attempts wouldn't interfere with

Onora's efforts. Ceana would have to do her best to keep abreast of any planned rescues so she could warn Onora. Perhaps, if all went very well, Onora's agents could, as individuals, win over the selkie rescue parties, and they could assist each other.

That thought reminded her of Lady Eilidh. Turning her tablet, she wrote, *"Thank you. Any news of Lady Eilidh? Trying to rescue?"*

A cloud settled over Fionntan's expression. He turned away, resting his arms on the table. "I have sent some of the Guard to see what may be done. Arran follows in the footsteps of many of his predecessors, and historically, his castle has been only rarely infiltrated with any level of success. It is difficult for us to do much on land in the mortal realms, and we must take care that any rescue attempt does not result in more losses. But we are working to determine if it is possible. Were she another man's wife, 'twould be easier. We have rescued others in the past. But Arran is an especial foe."

A thought suddenly occurred to Ceana, and she wondered how many people who were assumed to have drowned had, in truth, been selkies rescued and returned home. She wasn't sure whether to hope 'twas most of them or not. But that thought opened up another question that would be useful for Onora... *"Must get her and cloak both?"*

"Ideally, yes," Fionntan replied. "That is part of the trouble. Rescuing her when she is traveling outside Arran's castle would be easier than rescuing her from his home, but we would still need to venture into the fortress to retrieve her cloak. On the other hand, Lord Arran's castle is a little less secure when he is away without his wife, but he would most likely take her cloak with him on such occasions, both for his own use and to keep it from her reach."

He sighed. "If a good enough opportunity presented itself to easily and safely recover her, even if it meant leaving her cloak behind, we would take it, and your kin could use the adoption ceremony to reclaim her and give her a new cloak. We have done such things in the past, especially when a selkie's cloak is damaged beyond repair in the rescue attempt. But none of us like to leave a cloak in the hands of an enemy. He can continue to use it, and he might have some measure of control over her should they ever meet again. 'Tis hard to say about the latter."

"*I understand.*" Still, if selkies could be rescued without their cloaks, that meant good news for Onora's plan. *"Tell me when there is news of rescue plans so I can pray, please."* And, of course, so she could let Onora know.

"I will. I would keep you and your cousins updated in any case, since she is your kin." Fionntan shook himself a little. "And I will see to it that you have a writ of permission for the Halls of the Lost before you leave today. Do you have someone to go with and guide you so you do not become lost yourself?"

Ceana nodded. *"Mairearad."*

"Ah, you said that already, didn't you?" Fionntan thought a moment. "I doubt you will be able to go through all the Halls in one day. I will ensure that Mairearad knows that she may be released from her duties at the keep as often as she needs in order to accompany you. Or, if she does not feel she can spare the necessary time, then let me know and I will provide another guide or go with you myself."

"Thank you." Ceana didn't bother protesting that he need not come himself, only noted that Mairearad's prediction had been right. Instead, she picked up a piece of paper and a regular pen, then used the stylus and tablet to add, *"Should we start with your questions?"*

"I suppose so." Fionntan seemed almost reluctant—or perhaps that was just the lingering thoughtful sorrow from their conversation thus far. "To begin, there were a few points I would like to clarify regarding Atìrse's understanding of our shared history..."

Chapter 31

MAKING THE MOST OF TIME

There could be no doubt that Fionntan was distracted during their interview that afternoon. It wasn't that he wasn't *attentive*. On the contrary, he attended very well to everything she wrote and to anything she might need. But his heart certainly wasn't in his questions, most of which related to small details of things she'd said in the past rather than covering new material. In between questions, they trailed down long tangents, which mostly alternated between Fionntan asking Ceana about her memories from her homeland and telling her stories of his youth and favorite spots in Emain Ablach. It made for a pleasant afternoon, to be sure, but having to constantly draw the conversation back on track grew tiresome, and Ceana half-wondered if Fionntan really had more questions or if he simply wanted company. She suspected it to be the latter.

He did, however, remember to call for his seal and some wax when a maid came to bring them their mid-session snack. As soon as he had them in hand, he took a piece of the parchment and wrote out the promised writ of permission for Ceana to explore the Halls of the Lost. He then signed and sealed it and passed it to her with the wax still warm. "Here. If anyone tries to give you trouble, show them this and their quarrel will be with me instead."

Ceana took it, noting the promises written out just as Fionntan had made them earlier, and then set it aside so the seal could dry. "Thank you. I'll make sure I tell you what I learn."

He smiled. "Of course. On a related topic, has anyone told you of how the Halls of the Lost were created?" At Ceana's shake of her head, he launched into the tale: of how the caves had been found, of how they had once been intended for use as a refuge in case of invasion or as a hiding place for treasure, of how someone had thought of using them as a place of remembrance. Of how they had bargained with the Daoine Math for the enchantments that kept the place dry and preserved. How it had, indeed, been a place of refuge for the selkies, but of a different kind than intended …

Eventually, Aíbinn appeared to remind them that it was time they returned to the Northwaves home for dinner. Together, the three of them made their way down the stairs and out of the keep. As they reached the edge of the forested part of the path, Fionntan glanced at Aíbinn. "Well, what will it be today? Wilt thou walk with us, or dost thou feel that there are yet bushes thou hast not sufficiently terrorized?"

"Someday, there will be a truly horrible monster lurking along the path, and then thou wilt thank me for my vigilance," Aíbinn retorted. "But I do not believe 'twill be today. Unless thou thinkst otherwise?"

"I think thou shouldst not frighten Kenna with talk of monsters." Fionntan turned to Ceana. "What do you say?"

Ceana laughed and pulled tablet and stylus from her pocket. *"Why be scared? You and Aíbinn will protect me, if you fight enemies as well as you do each other."*

Aíbinn's grin grew, and she started down the path. "Perhaps I should rattle the bushes more, then, Fionntan. Scare up *two* monsters and let us see who defeats theirs the quicker."

Fionntan and Ceana followed, arm in arm, Fionntan rolling his eyes. "Thou knowst thou had an advantage against the other men the other day. Too many of them were fighting to impress someone else, and it made them careless."

"As if thou wert not also fighting for the same reason," Aíbinn scoffed lovingly. "Hypocrite!"

"I said not that there was no one I wished to impress," Fionntan replied, laughing. "Only that it did not make me careless."

The rest of the walk went mostly in that vein, with Aíbinn and

Fionntan teasing each other and Ceana chiming in where she could. When they arrived home, they found Sir Cianán already there, waiting with Mairearad and Uaine. Fionntan greeted Mairearad and Uaine in the usual manner, then held out his hand for Sir Cianán to grasp in the way of warriors. "Good evening to you. I understand from Mairearad that congratulations are in order?"

Sir Cianán bowed his head in confirmation. "Indeed. My pearl has made me the happiest man on the island, I do believe."

"I have no doubt of it." Fionntan released Sir Cianán's hand. "Mairearad is like a sister to me, as you well know, and the man who marries her is fortunate indeed. I wish you both all the happiness Dèanadair may grant."

"Thank you, your majesty," Sir Cianán replied. "And I hope that you will find some of that same happiness for yourself before too long."

Fionntan's brows rose a bit, but he only said, "We shall see," in a thoughtful sort of way.

With greetings out of the way, they set to dinner. Ceana had worried a little about how the addition of Sir Cianán would affect their usual dynamic, but she found she had no reason to fear. Sir Cianán was clearly on friendly terms with his king, and Aíbinn and Uaine kept the worst of both their teasing and their questions behind sealed lips. It was, in fact, such a pleasant evening that the sisters insisted Sir Cianán and Fionntan stay after dinner for card games. And when Fionntan brought up his desire to make another excursion to one of the lovely places of the island after the singing trip, Uaine suggested that Mairearad and Cianán be included. Everyone heartily agreed with that idea, and so the matter was settled.

At last, however, the evening came to an end. Ceana joined the sisters in seeing their guests to the door. As they were leaving, however, Fionntan addressed her. "Kenna, may I speak with you a moment?"

Ceana nodded, stepping out onto the porch and producing tablet and stylus. She took a moment to set the stylus in place, then handed both to Fionntan so he could more comfortably read them.

Fionntan cleared his throat. "You may have gathered as much this afternoon, but at the moment, I have little else to ask you about Atìrse in an official capacity. I expect that will change once I receive word from those investigating rescue possibilities, but I do not know when that will be. I do not wish to take up your time on false pretenses, as I did today."

"I understand," Ceana wrote back. Then, emboldened by the evening's merriment, she added, *"If you wish for my company anyway, you may ask for it."*

"May I?" Fionntan asked, his voice unexpectedly soft. "'Twould please me very much if you would continue to come."

He seemed so *concerned*. As if he really thought she'd abandon their meetings simply because he no longer had an official purpose for them. *"Would please me as well. We are friends, after all."*

"So we are," he replied, a note of almost giddy relief in his voice. "Thank you, Kenna. Three days hence, then? Or—no, you'll be at court dinner that night. Four days?"

Ceana nodded agreement, and he smiled, handing back the tablet. "Then I will look forward to seeing you then." With that, he bowed and walked off into the evening.

<hr />

The next morning's dawn brought another day of drizzling rain. But Ceana put on her cloak and boots and ventured out to the standing stones anyway. There, she hauled herself into her little nook and shivered as her seal-shape fell away, taking its warmth with it. She huddled into her cloak, trying to keep the stone's dampness from seeping into her. If not for the amount of information she had to tell Onora, she would have just sent a quick message from some secluded corner of the house, or possibly from her bed again.

But she had too much to say to risk that. So, she wrapped herself up as much as she could, shivering a little in the chill, and pressed the rune on her necklace. "Onora? Art thou—are you there?" She needed to keep in practice, after all; eventually she'd have to go home, and people would wonder if she suddenly started referring to her family as *thou*. Though maybe she could say she picked it up from her grandmother ...

In any case, no answer came. Oh well. She'd just have to leave a message. She settled back and recounted all that Fionntan had told her about the selkies' rescue plans, about whether or not the selkies could be rescued without their cloaks, about Lord Arran and how there had been others before him in his holding who mistreated the selkies the same way. She told Onora about the faery market as well, since she'd not had a chance to do so the last time they talked.

When she finished, she waited a little while, just in case Onora might come back, notice a message had been left, and return the call. But as the drizzle from above and the spray from the sea and the wet of the rock combined to steadily soak any exposed part of her gown and skin, she grew less and less convinced that she'd receive a response in a reasonable time. At last, she gave up and slipped into the sea.

The warmth of her seal-shape wrapped around her, now comfortable and familiar instead of strange. Not for the first time, she wondered what it would have been like to grow up with this experience as part of her normal life, rather than something that, though no longer unfamiliar, was still extraordinary. Did her selkie ancestor, whoever that had been, mourn that so many of his or her descendants never knew the sea as selkies were meant to? Had that ancestor rejoiced when Ceana found her way back to her heritage, even under false pretenses?

She took her time returning. Drizzle did little to affect the world beneath the waves, and Ceana was in no hurry to face the long, damp walk from the lake to the Northwaves home. So, rather than a direct route, she took a more meandering path so as to pass some of her favorite underwater sites.

She was a little more than halfway along her intended route when she felt a sudden chill and sensed her seal-shape starting to give way to human form: fins loosening to free arms and legs, fur and insulation fading, lungs aching as air was forced from them.

No! Ceana thrashed in the water, fighting her way upwards as her lower half wavered between a tail and fins and legs wrapped in layered skirts. What was happening? *Dèanadair, don't let me die here—*

The seal-shape took hold again just as Ceana reached the surface. She poked her head up and took deep gulps of precious air. What just *happened*? What went wrong? Had she somehow triggered a mid-water transformation? Or had she imagined the whole thing? She felt no different now than she had before the transformation, just a little colder and with the buzz of panic in her veins.

No, she couldn't have imagined it. It had felt too real in the moment to be her imagination. Unless she'd managed to fall asleep mid-swim and had a very strange dream? But no, that was ridiculous.

Maybe she'd bumped a jellyfish without noticing, and its poison had done something to her. Maybe it was just because her cloak was old, or maybe this was just something that happened now and then. She might have eaten something she shouldn't have, or...or anything, really.

After a few minutes passed without further incident, Ceana started swimming again, this time at a quicker pace and on a path that would take her straight back to the island. She needed to get back to shore quickly; that was for sure. Should she tell someone? The sisters? Fionntan? Ninian? One of them might know. Ninian had told her to come to him if anything odd happened, hadn't he?

But if she told someone, they might tell her not to leave the island. Then she'd not be able to talk properly with Onora— and she'd miss the singing trip with Fionntan. Of course, if this happened again *on* the singing trip ...

Who was to say it would happen again? For all she knew, she'd passed through a pocket of the oceanic equivalent of Tìr Soilleir, or some mischievous sea-pixie had enchanted her just long enough to laugh at her fear without doing her serious harm.

She'd wait and see if it happened a second time. If it did, she'd tell someone—but not before.

Despite her resolution, she felt very much relieved when she reached the shores of Emain Ablach and could pull herself out onto dry land. She kept her aquatic ventures after that short as well, making sure to take the most direct route out and back when she made her way out to the rocks again two days later and only briefly going in the water of the bolt-hole on the days in between. The experience didn't repeat, though there was one day on which the transformation came a little slower than usual, and Ceana maintained her hope that it had been just a single odd occurrence, not the start of a problem. And it wasn't as if *not* going in the water was difficult. She still had plenty to keep busy with, between helping Uaine and visiting Fionntan, either in Uaine's company or, as promised, on her own.

This latter visit was especially pleasant, she had to admit. She had been a little worried about spending a full afternoon with just Fionntan and without a particular plan. But the hours sped past in conversation broken here and there by games of draughts or tafl. At one point, they wandered onto the topic of selkie legends, and Ceana slipped in a question about whether or not any tales told of selkies shifting shapes while fully on land or water, rather than just at the moment of moving from one or the other, justifying her curiosity with by claiming that she'd heard such stories in Atìrse. But Fionntan just shook his head and replied that he knew of no such thing.

At another point, late in the afternoon, Fionntan asked, in an offhand sort of way, what Ceana had planned for her future before she received her cloak and found her way to the selkies. Ceana gave him the same story she'd told her cousins, of an intended betrothal that fell through and her uncertainty about what would happen now.

Fionntan shook his head when she finished. "Glad as I am that you found your way here, I pity the man who turned you down. He would have been fortunate indeed to have you by his side."

Ceana just shrugged, looking down. *"He is fortunate anyway,"* she wrote. *"Found out after that he already loved an old friend of his. They will be happy together."*

"I suppose they will," Fionntan replied. "And, in any case, I cannot be too sorry for him, for had he agreed to marry you, you never would have come here. And I hope that you will find happiness enough in Emain Ablach to make up for what might have been."

At that, Ceana flushed and had to take a hasty drink to hide her reddening face. Oh, if only he knew! But she could say none of the truth, so she just nodded and wrote, *"Thank you. Getting late—one more game before I must leave?"*

"Gladly." Fionntan picked up the draughts board from where he'd stowed it under their bench and began setting it up between them. Ceana turned, setting her tablet aside. She'd done her best to cast away all dreams of what might have been had Fionntan not refused her, of coming here as herself instead of under a false name, but Fionntan's questions threatened to make them resurface. Still, she had to resist. It was no good dwelling on impossible what-ifs. Better to make the most of her time here while she had it.

Chapter 32
RETURN TO THE HALLS

Two days later came the day she and Mairearad had set for visiting the Halls of the Lost. As planned, Ceana met Mairearad at the entrance, and they descended into the Halls together, into the torchlit dimness of the caverns. As they made their way down the stairs, the weight of what she had learned last time she came down here settled again on Ceana's heart, hanging heavy—but not as heavy as it had that first time. Not now that she had so many memories of kindness and friendship and love to remind her that, even when they knew something of her family's rank, the selkies laid no guilt upon her.

It was strange, doing something with *just* Mairearad. Usually, Uaine or Aíbinn would have been present as well; Ceana couldn't think of a single time she and Mairearad had been alone together. And now, as Mairearad led the way through the Halls, silent save for occasional instructions to turn or continue on, Ceana found herself wishing she'd asked one of the others to come. It wasn't that Mairearad ever made Ceana feel unwelcome—but Ceana couldn't help thinking now of how reserved Mairearad always seemed, how she still called Ceana *you* after so long. Perhaps that was just because Mairearad was a diplomat—but even so, it didn't make things more comfortable now.

They reached the Northwaves portion of the Halls. Mairearad stopped just a little inside the entrance. "Here we are. Why don't you look for anyone you recognize while I check on things? Make a noise if you have any questions. Does that suit you?"

Ceana nodded. Mairearad swept off down to the far end of the cavern and set about inspecting some of the portraits. Ceana, meanwhile, turned to look at the pictures nearest to her. Most were very old and so stylized that Ceana doubted she'd be able to identify their subjects. Nevertheless, she studied each one carefully, as she did the sculptures, which were more common at this end.

Slowly, she moved down the hall, going back and forth from picture to picture to stay in order as well as she could. She found what she sought about halfway down the room, what she guessed to be six or seven generations back from her and the Northwaves sisters. Or, at the very least, the woman in the painting was *certainly* about seven generations removed from Ceana and her sisters, according to the portraits in her father's halls and the family tree Ceana had memorized as a girl.

She cleared her throat, and Mairearad joined her in front of the painting. "Is this someone you know?"

Ceana nodded. *"Mey. Five-times-great grandmother."* She was also the namesake of one of Ceana's sisters, but of course she couldn't say that—not that it wasn't a common name; even now, many girls every year were named for Good Queen Mey; but she'd only admitted to two sisters, and she'd used Mey's name for neither of them.

Mairearad gazed solemnly at the frame. "Her real name was Mairead. I'm named for her, as you can guess. She was the eldest daughter of the Northwaves at the time, like I am, and was expected to inherit, and she was betrothed to the second son of another noble house that has since died out. She had a twin brother, younger by ten minutes, from whom my sisters and I are descended, and a sister, both of whom she loved very much."

Sighing, Mairearad went on, "According to all I've been told, her disappearance nearly destroyed the family. Her mother withdrew into mourning and never fully left it; her father fared little better. Her sister took to a wanderer's lifestyle to search for her and swore not to return to Emain Ablach until she died or could bring Mairead with her; her bones rest just there." She gestured to one of the rectangular seams that typically marked spots where a coffin laid within the walls. "As for her brother, he married a woman of the island and inherited in Mairead's place, but his grief grew and grew until he went mad with it and nearly ran house and fortune into the ground. Had it not been for the wisdom of his wife and son, I doubt the Northwaves family would still exist."

"*I am sorry,*" Ceana wrote, knowing as she wrote it that the words weren't enough. If only she could tell Mairearad all she knew about Good Queen Mey's life on land! If only she could tell *everyone* how one of Atìrse's greatest queens had been a selkie, not a human.

But recounting everything would give away all Ceana still couldn't reveal. Still, she could tell Mairearad a little, and that was better than nothing. "*She had two sons and a daughter and loved them very much. Her husband died when her oldest son was 10. He was too young to inherit; M ruled lands in his name for 1 year. She led so well, she was made ruler in own right until one of her children was deemed fit to take over. Every girl in our land learns about her, is told to be like her.*"

As Ceana had hoped, a faint smile flickered into being on Mairearad's face. "That is some comfort. 'Twould have been better had she not been taken from us, but I am glad Dèanadair brought about blessing through her and that she is still remembered with such love. I wonder, though, that she did not leave when her husband died. If it is her cloak that you wear, then 'twas not destroyed by her husband before his death, and she was able to pass it down. She could have taken her children and come home."

That was a strange thing. Or, perhaps, not so strange. Ceana considered what might have come about if the whole royal family had died and vanished in the space of a week or two, thought again of the family tree she'd learned and recalled how few people would have remained with a clear claim to the crown. Had Queen Mey left with her children, Atìrse would have been thrown into turmoil. And had she abandoned her children and left alone, things would have been nearly as bad.

Finally, Ceana wrote back, *"Maybe she thought she was needed. Maybe Dèanadair wanted her there and she knew it."*

"So it must have been." With another sad look at the portrait, Mairearad turned away. "Have you recognized anyone else so far?"

Ceana shook her head. *"Will keep looking."*

"Let me know who else you find." With that, Mairearad stepped away to continue her own inspection.

Though Ceana searched through the rest of the pictures, she found no one else she recognized with enough confidence to point them out to Mairearad. Outside her own line, she could only reliably recognize the living members of any given family, having not spent an extensive amount of time studying *their* ancestral portraits.

Having finished with the Northwaves family's section, Ceana and Mairearad moved on to the next cavern over, which was, thankfully, unoccupied. Ceana moved quickly all the same, skimming over the older portraits and spending most of her time inspecting the most recent generations. Mairearad remained by the door, ready with Ceana's writ of permission to forestall anyone who might happen by and object, and only came inside when Ceana found someone she recognized as the wife of one of Arran's knights. Mairearad wrote this down, and then returned to her post.

They repeated this process for seven more caverns before Mairearad declared it time to go. Ceana wasn't sure how Mairearad could know that, down here with no sunlight to speak of. But she was growing weary of staring at faces and trying to match them with people she knew, so she made no argument. Fionntan had certainly been right when he said she'd not be able to survey all the Halls in one day; she almost thought she'd be lucky to get through it all before she had to return to Atìrse. Still, she'd managed to identify at least one or two people per family, so it wasn't as if she'd been unsuccessful. Mairearad had written all of them down, and Ceana had made mental note of everyone so she could tell Onora.

Mairearad led the way back out of the Halls of the Lost, Ceana following close behind and trying to keep track of the paths they took. They made their way through the tunnel and surfaced in the lake. Outside, the sun had sunk far closer to the horizon than Ceana expected; they truly had been in the Halls for hours.

She and Mairearad set off across the lake towards the village and the path towards home. They were halfway across when Ceana felt the chill again, more noticeable than the last in these comparatively warmer waters, and sensed the loosening of the seal-shape around her.

No, no, no, no, no...please, Dèanadair, no! She tried to focus on maintaining her seal-shape, tried to calm her racing heart, hoping that everything would go back to normal before Mairearad could notice. But her panic grew anyway, and the more it grew, the faster her seal-shape fell away. She floundered in the water as her half-exposed skirts started to pull her downward.

Mairearad's voice sounded in her mind. *"Kenna! Kenna, hold on!"* A moment later, Mairearad swam up beneath Ceana, pushing her rapidly towards the surface, propelling them both with strong strokes of her tail.

Ceana's head broke the water, and she gulped down the air. She was all right; she could breathe—She felt her heart steady, felt the seal-shape wrap around her again as panic drained away.

"Better now?" Mairearad's voice came again, full of hope and fear. Ceana nodded, turning herself over and rolling off Mairearad's back so they could continue towards shore.

Mairearad stuck close to Ceana's side the rest of the way. Once they hauled themselves out, she began moving almost before she fully transformed, pulling Ceana into a sitting position and grasping her hands. "Oh, Dèanadair—Kenna, art thou alright?"

Ceana nodded, managing a smile. Mairearad seemed unconvinced, patting Ceana all over as if checking for broken bones, or maybe as if making sure all of her was still there. "What was that? Has this happened before?"

Oh, bother. She couldn't lie. Reluctantly, Ceana nodded again. She fumbled for her tablet and stylus, but Mairearad shook her head. "Don't bother with the tablet; just tell me, *please.*"

337

She really *was* worried. Ceana cleared her throat, and her voice came out in a croak. "I just stopped being a seal. It happened once before, five days ago. I thought it was nothing. Please don't worry."

Mairearad gave a short, mirthless laugh. "Don't worry? Ceana, thou might have died!" Apparently satisfied that Ceana remained in one piece, she went back to clasping Ceana's hands. "Canst thou walk?"

Ceana nodded, pulling free of Mairearad's grip and scrambling to her feet to prove it. "'M fine. Just shaken."

"Thou changed in the middle of the lake!" Mairearad stood as well. "We're going to Ninian's *now*; perhaps he'll know what happened."

She grasped Ceana's hand as if Ceana were a mere child and set off up the path, skirts swishing around her legs. Ceana hurried to keep up, tucking away stylus and tablet—they were moving far too fast for her to attempt to write out any protest. Silently, she sent up a prayer: *Please, Dèanadair, let Ninian say it's nothing serious...*

They reached Ninian's shop and found it empty save for Ninian behind the counter, measuring out dried leaves into jars. He looked up and nodded as they entered. "Well, Lady Mairearad, Lady Kenna, what brings you here tonight?"

"We need to speak to you," Mairearad replied, as if it weren't obvious. She sounded calmer, at least, though she still had yet to let go of Ceana's hand. "There's been...Something's happened. I'm worried there's something wrong with Kenna."

"Well, she looks hale enough from here. Come into the other room, the both of you, and I'll see what I can see." Ninian covered the bowl he'd been measuring the leaves from and led the way into the back room where he'd previously examined and treated Ceana. "Have a seat and tell me what's the trouble."

Ceana sat obediently, though Mairearad remained standing as she replied, "She just started transforming midway across the lake, even though we were both still in the water. She might have drowned if I hadn't noticed. She changed back as soon as I got her head above water, but if it happens again —" Mairearad stopped herself. "She said it's happened once before."

"Hmm." Ninian crossed the room and stared into Ceana's face. "Twice you've transformed while still in the water? Did you change fully either time?"

Ceana pulled out her tablet and stylus so she could reply. *"Only halfway first time. Changed back at surface. Changed more this time. Don't know why."*

"Where were you the first time?" Ninian began gently pressing his fingertips against her skin, first at the sides of her head and then moving down her neck. "Inside or outside Emain Ablach?"

"Outside," Ceana wrote back, wrinkling her nose. *"Thought maybe sea-pixie?"*

"Were you dazed or disoriented afterward either time?" Ninian waited for Ceana to shake her head, then continued, "'Twas no faery-spell that did it. Tell me, did you find out how far back in your family the selkie blood runs?"

"We just did today," Mairearad answered for Ceana. Save for the way she held her hands clasped behind her back, she seemed perfectly calm—but Ceana could see the tension in Mairearad's arms, and she knew that trick of hiding white-knuckled anxiety too well to be fooled by it. "There are seven generations of separation."

"Ah, there's your trouble, then, just as I feared." Ninian stepped back. "It's an old cloak, and its first wearer is long passed. The magic only lasts so long, and the older the cloak, the sooner it fails. 'Tis hard to say for sure, as I've read of this more than I've seen it myself, but I'd say you've another two months at best before the cloak fails altogether. I know you were planning to wait until after Kenna comes of age to properly adopt her, but ..."

"Of course, we won't wait so long now." Mairearad shook her head, shoulders back. "I'll start making arrangements this very night. Is there anything we can do in the meantime to make sure this doesn't happen again?"

"As I understand it, 'twon't become frequent for several weeks more. It worsens in response to fear—perhaps you've seen so yourself by now." He addressed this last comment to Ceana, and she nodded again. "Stay calm and make sure you've air to breathe when you notice it happening. Then you can keep it from going too far, at least at first. 'Twill be harder to prevent as time goes on, though, and eventually there'll be naught you can do save to ride it out."

"*Can do that,*" Ceana wrote. She'd have to start keeping close to the surface, though, just to be safe. "*Am supposed to go on singing trip next week. Can still go?*"

"No, you shouldn't," Mairearad said at once. "If you transform in the middle of the ocean ..."

But Ninian was stroking his chin thoughtfully, and after a moment he said, "If it's in the next week, I'd say you're safe enough. 'Tis still early enough that you may be able to make the full trip with no unwanted transformation. All the same, make sure there's one or two with you who know of your trouble and can help see you to the surface safely if aught goes wrong. I'll mix you up a tonic before you go that'll help as well. And you've this for comfort; I've only ever heard of the change happening the one way. You're not likely to turn seal on dry land."

That was some comfort. Not much, but some. At least she'd still be able to go with Fionntan. And she'd known the whole time that she'd need to leave eventually. This time limit was a little sooner than she'd expected, but not much. "*Thank you.*"

"'Tis my pleasure, lass." Ninian glanced from Ceana to Mairearad. "Any other troubles I can help you ladies with?" When both shook their heads, he turned. "Then I'll make you your tonic and have you on your way."

It didn't take Ninian long to mix up the tonic or to write the instructions—a dose every morning, or morning and evening if the situation worsened—and soon, Ceana and Mairearad were walking up the path towards the Northwaves home. Mairearad didn't clutch Ceana's hand this time, but she still stayed close at Ceana's side rather than a step or two ahead.

Only when they were outside the village, amid the trees, did Mairearad speak again. "How are you feeling? Are you ill at all?"

Ceana shook her head. She pulled out tablet and stylus, set it up, and handed it to Mairearad so she could reply, *"Am fine."* Inwardly, she gave thanks that the stylus didn't show the shakiness of her hands. *"Only frightened."*

"So was I. I wish you had told me about this the first time it happened." Mairearad shook her head with a tired sort of sigh. "As I told Ninian, there's no question of waiting on the adoption now, not when it could mean your becoming stranded in human-shape in the middle of the ocean. Two weeks is probably the earliest we can manage, allowing for the formalities of our rank, but perhaps I can ask Fionntan's permission to set some of those aside so long as they're observed at the second ceremony. If he agrees, you might have your own cloak before you go out with the singers."

So soon! Even two weeks was far too quick, especially if Onora wanted her to stay with the selkies for her own safety. If necessary, she *could* remain within the island's borders—at least it would reduce the risk of her cloak failing while she was far from land— but she couldn't actually accept the adoption.

Ceana realized with a start that Mairearad still waited for a response. She smoothed out the tablet, somewhat unnecessarily, and wrote, *"Don't need to rush. N said we have 2 months; I'll be fine for a few weeks. Maybe plan a month from now? Month and a half?"*

"But what reason is there to wait?" Mairearad asked, tension rising in her tone. She stopped walking, stepped off the path, and turned to face Ceana. "The longer we delay, the greater the risk to you. Our family has lost enough people; we can't...we can't lose you as well."

If only she'd said *anything* else. Ceana thought of the faces in the Halls of the Lost: of Queen Mey's true story, of the Northwaves sisters' father, of Lady Eilidh. How was she to put them through more pain? But she didn't have a choice. Even if they went through with the ceremony, Ceana would still have to leave eventually. She had to go back to her life in Atìrse.

Mairearad spoke again. "Please, Kenna, tell me why the delay. Have we treated you ill in some way?"

Ceana hastily shook her head. She smoothed the tablet a second time and wrote, *"No! You have all been very kind."*

"Then why?" Mairearad started to take a step towards Ceana, then stopped. Her hands tightened on Ceana's tablet.

What could she say? Ceana searched for a reasonable lie, but all she could come up with was a version of the truth. *"I miss my human family. Adoption feels like losing them."*

"Oh. Oh, I'm sorry, Kenna." Mairearad's shoulders drooped as if a new weight had just settled on them. "I understand that you were close with your Atìrsen family, closer than many who come here were to their human kin. We're not trying to replace them, truly; we only want to ensure you are safe and welcome here. Perhaps, once you're properly settled, we can ask Fionntan about bringing some of your family here as well, or we can find a way for you to communicate safely with them."

She paused. But Ceana could think of nothing to say, so she kept her stylus still. After a few moments, Mairearad went on, "I know, too, that Uaine and Aíbinn were ready to name you our sister the day they learned we were kin, and I would be glad to welcome you as such officially if you wish it. But if that feels too much like an invasion of what your Atìrsen family is to you, we will bring you in as our cousin. Neither will change how we treat you."

Again, she paused, but less as if she were waiting for a response and more as if she were trying to will more words out of her mouth. "And I apologize, too, for my informality earlier. I did not mean to put pressure upon you, but I was worried for you, and it simply slipped out."

Oh! This Ceana knew how to answer. *"Didn't mind. Was only surprised. You never said it before."*

Mairearad gave a slight smile. "I did not wish to overwhelm you. Besides, it is not my habit to push for greater closeness in any relationship if I do not know the other person desires it. You seemed not to mind when Uaine and Aíbinn say it to you, but I... as I said, I did not wish to pressure you. And I do not want you to think I am seeking to replace your other family—none of us are."

"*I know.*" For once, Ceana was grateful to be writing instead of speaking; she had a suspicion that she'd cry if she tried to say anything aloud. "*You aren't replacing them. Thou art my sister as much as they.*" The worst of it was, she knew as she wrote the words that they were true.

Mairearad stared at the tablet a long moment. She touched one of the words with a light finger, as if making sure she read it correctly, then raised her head. "And thou art mine, as much as Aíbinn and Uaine, even if I have known thee a shorter time." She stepped forward for real this time, pulling Ceana into a gentle embrace. "A month we will wait, if thou wish it. Thou canst make thy peace in that time, and we will see what can be done to make sure thy other family is not lost to thee. And then I will name thee my sister before the king and every ear in Emain Ablach willing to listen."

Ceana had no idea if her tablet was visible, but she wrote a reply anyway, even as she hugged Mairearad more tightly. "*One month is good.*" Smooth the wax. "*Don't want to lose old family, but glad I found family here.*" If only, *if only*, she could find a way to not have to leave them behind!

Chapter 33
SINGING TO THE LOST

In the week that followed, Ceana's cloak failed her only once more, and that only for a few moments. Remembering Ninian's instructions, she forced herself to keep calm and surfaced at once. Within moments of breathing proper air, she felt her seal-shape wrap back around her as snugly as before.

At last, the day came for the singing trip. Mairearad and Uaine walked with Ceana in the early morning light down to the shore where the group was to meet. A pack with supplies—food, basic medical materials, and a change of clothes—hung from Ceana's shoulders, under her cloak. Aíbinn had showed her the trick of getting it on and off without removing the cloak the night before, while Ceana prayed silently that she wouldn't notice the necklace, and she had made Ceana practice until she could do it easily. Then she'd warned Ceana not to get between a shipwreck and a cliff face again, hugged her, and laughingly wished her well, since she'd have to leave for her Guard shift before Ceana woke.

When they reached the lakeside, they found the rest of the group already gathering. Ceana spotted Fionntan with a trio of guards, Ealar among them, as well as one of the nobles and a few people she didn't recognize. Several of the group were still being seen off by friends or family.

Ceana and her cousins headed over to Fionntan. All three of them curtsied, and Fionntan made a slight bow in return. "Good morning. Are you ready to depart, Lady Kenna?"

Ceana nodded, grinning back. She'd prepared her tablet and

stylus as soon as she spotted Fionntan, so she wrote, *"Excited to go."*

Mairearad cleared her throat. "Your majesty, may I speak with you a moment?"

"Of course." Fionntan took a step away. "Excuse me."

He and Mairearad retreated a few feet to the side and proceeded to stare at the lake for some ten minutes, occasionally glancing over towards Ceana. Ceana sighed. It had to be the selkies' thought-speech again. She had a good guess of what Mairearad was telling Fionntan, but it would have been nice to *know*.

What if Fionntan refused to let her come when he learned about her troubles with the cloak? She wouldn't be able to stand it; she'd been looking forward to this for nearly two weeks. But she'd not be able to argue either. He was the king, after all, and there *was* a risk ...

But when Fionntan and Mairearad returned, Fionntan's expression was serious, but not outright grim, and he didn't look like he was preparing to be the bearer of bad news. And Mairearad seemed as composed as ever. Perhaps all would be well after all.

"Lady Kenna," Fionntan said, his voice low, "Mairearad told me about your current...problem, we'll say. She also told me you still wish to come on the trip."

Ceana nodded emphatically and flipped her tablet over. *"Ninian said safe."*

"She told me that as well," Fionntan replied. "Never fear; I will not force you to remain here. Still, stay close to me or Ealar. If anything should go wrong, we'll make sure you reach the surface again quickly. Agreed?"

Again, Ceana nodded. She'd have tried to swim by Fionntan anyway, since she knew virtually none of the others in the group. *"Thank you."*

"Of course." Fionntan glanced out over the group. "I believe all have arrived, so say your farewells and we'll be off."

Ceana turned to Mairearad and hugged her. Mairearad returned the embrace gently. "Be careful. We'll see thee tomorrow or the day after."

Uaine joined the hug before Ceana could let go. "Goodbye! Enjoy the trip and the singing, and tell us what thou thought when thou returnst."

The three broke apart, and Mairearad faced Fionntan again. "Look after our cousin, your majesty. She's in your hands for now."

Fionntan put a hand on Ceana's shoulder. "No harm will come to her under my watch, Mairearad. I promise you that. I will keep her as if she were of my own blood."

"I know. But I have to say it anyway." A soft smile broke across Mairearad's face. "And look after yourself as well."

"Of course. We'll all be back safe and sound in a day or two; don't worry." With that, Fionntan turned towards the lake. "Now, Lady Kenna, let's collect the others and be off before we spend all day saying goodbye."

They made their way down the shore to the water's edge, and the rest who were going broke away from their well-wishers and joined them. Fionntan gave a few instructions, and then, in twos and threes, the group entered the lake. Ceana stayed just behind Fionntan as he led the way down to the tunnel. There, the three members of the Guard entered first, with Fionntan just behind them, Ceana after him, and then the rest of the group. After passing through the tunnel so many times, even the tightest sections no longer held any terror for Ceana. Still, she was glad when at last they emerged into the grey half-light of the open ocean and the ordinary mortal realm.

That day was the longest Ceana had swum since she first came to Emain Ablach, and by midday, she couldn't help wondering how she'd managed so well those first several days on her own. Even though her seal-shape was far heartier and stronger than her human form, swimming all day was just as tiring as walking would have been. And, reflecting on that first journey, she realized that they indeed must have slowed their travel to allow for her injury, and that they certainly were *not* doing so now. By noon, she could feel the weariness in every part of her.

She worried, too, that the swift pace would make her cloak

more likely to give out. The whole time, she stayed alert for any chill, any hint that her seal-shape was giving way. Twice, she felt the warning signs—but each time, she nudged Fionntan, and he swam with her to the surface so she could breathe. He stayed with her there, a steady, comforting presence, until she signaled that all was well again. Then they dove once more to rejoin the rest of the group.

Fionntan talked much to her during the journey, and he included her in his conversations with others, providing a welcome distraction from her aching muscles and her worries about her cloak. Several in the group had been on singing trips before, as well, and they spoke of their stories and memories. One, like Ceana, had been raised on land and had found the selkies because of their singing—though he'd known what he was beforehand, having been told in whispers by his mother. He'd been a runaway at the time, fleeing his father, and the party that he met had a higher-than-usual number of Guards and former Guard in it. 'Twas providence, he said, for the singing party became a rescue party when he led them back up the shores to free his mother as well. His father had been no lord, only a soldier, and the selkies had little trouble subduing him, finding both captive and cloak, and returning to the sea by morning.

The shores of Atìrse came in view as a grey mass on the horizon as the sun drew near to the waters. By the time its edge dipped into the waves, Ceana could, when she surfaced, see the land clearly enough to recognize the port city of Torrsea, with its many rocky pillars just outside the harbor. The selkies made for these pillars and the rocks around them, reaching them just as the sun disappeared beneath the sea. Still, no one made any move to haul out until the last bits of pink and gold had disappeared from the western horizon.

Then, at last, the selkies began to pull themselves out onto the rocks, seal-shapes falling away into flowing cloaks. Fionntan hauled out on a flat-topped rock that rose some feet above the sea's surface, then reached down to help Ceana clamber out as well.

"Here we are." He held her steady as she arranged herself with her cloak wrapped around her against the cold sea-spray and her legs tucked up under her skirts. Then he settled next to her, so close their shoulders almost touched. "Comfortable?"

Ceana smiled at him, not wanting to risk getting her tablet out where it could easily fall into the waves. Would Fionntan mind if she spoke aloud in the human tongue? They weren't in Emain Ablach anymore, but they were among the selkies still. If only she'd thought to ask before they left...

Fionntan's voice interrupted her wondering. "Let me know if the night grows too chilly. Summer it may be, but out on the water like this, it can be cold all the same. The singing will begin once everyone is ready."

Ceana nodded and waited, watching the skies as the first stars appeared and listening as the others found seats amid the standing stones. A few minutes of silence followed once all were comfortable.

Then, at some silent signal, Ealar's voice rose in song, and the rest followed. Ceana turned her gaze from the skies as she listened. She recognized the tune well; she'd heard it through her window many a time while staying in her family's various coastal residences. But now she could understand the words of their song.

> "Oh, selkie lost, drawn from the sea,
> Stranded in the stones and towers,
> Let our salt song wind its way to thee,
> Free thy heart from mortals' powers.
>
> "Hear us singing;
> We've not forgot thee.
> Ever we'll welcome thee home again.
> We've not forgot thee,
> We call for thee always,
> That one day thou will be home again."

They sang to call their stolen kin home. To remind them that they weren't forgotten. Why hadn't she guessed by now? Ceana thought back to the days of listening to the selkies' songs through her window and wondering what they meant. All that time, they *had* been a call, but not in the way she thought. They'd called not to her people, but to their kin among the humans, hoping they would be heard, hoping to give hope to the lost.

Then the verse changed, and her breath caught at the words.

> "Come now, selkie-kin, down to the sea,
> Find your heritage no more denied.
> Into the waves; see how they greet thee;
> Ever they were meant as thine.
>
> "Hear us singing;
> We've not forgot thee.
> Ever we'll call thee to thy true home.
> We've not forgot thee;
> We pray for thee always,
> That one day thou'll find thy true home at last."

It *wasn't* just their stolen kin they called to. They called to the family they'd never met, those who could not understand the words of the song but might just catch the meaning. They called to those who'd never known half their home and half their heritage.

They'd called to her after all.

The dampness of sea-spray clung to Ceana's cheeks, and she wiped it away, only to discover that some of the salt water was from her tears. In the old days, she'd thought now and then of walking down to ask the singing selkies the reason for their songs. What might have happened if she had?

Fionntan's deep voice left the song, and he bent to whisper in her ear. "Lady Kenna, is something wrong? Why do you weep?"

Ceana shook her head, uselessly wiping away tears again. "I always wondered why you sing," she whispered, her voice breaking so much she wondered if Fionntan would understand what she said. "It sounded like you were calling to someone. I never knew ..."

"Thou never knew that we were calling thee home?" Fionntan

asked, his voice soft and gentle. She felt an arm around her shoulders, felt Fionntan pull her in so she could lean on him and he could wrap his cloak—his *cloak!*—around her. "None in thy circumstances do. Yet we sing anyway, for some understand without the words, and some still have someone who can tell them the meaning. Now, dost thou see why I wished thee to come?"

Ceana nodded, giving up on holding back the tears. "I see." She rested her head against his shoulder. "Wilt thou sing again?" She realized only after the words slipped out how she'd addressed him—how he'd addressed her. But somehow, she felt as if she couldn't have done otherwise.

"That *is* why we came," Fionntan replied, a hint of laughter in his voice. He wrapped his arm more snugly around her and raised his head and voice to join the singing once more as the melody and words shifted to a new song.

> "Come down to the waters, come away with me,
> Come to rolling waves and come to oceans deep,
> Leave the mortal moors; come find what is thy own.
> Come away and once more thou wilt be free."

Ceana sat in the selkie king's embrace and listened and wept. She wept for the past that made these songs necessary. She wept for the beauty of the selkies' hope. She wept for grief, for all that she had never known.

And still the selkies sang on around her, their songs echoing off the cliffs beneath the silver stars.

Despite Ceana's hopes and prayers, no selkie-blooded human or escaped selkie captives joined their party that night or the following morning when they set out, having spent the remainder of the night in a sea-cave a little way up the coast. Even so, her heart was too overwhelmed with beauty and wonder to sorrow overmuch, and she still prayed that Onora's efforts would go well, that one day soon the selkie captives would be freed.

The journey back was uneventful, with Ceana's cloak only threatening to fail once, and they reached Emain Ablach late in the evening. Most of the group, save Fionntan and his Guard, dispersed quickly once they arrived, hurrying back to homes and kin. Fionntan, however, turned to Ceana and, in a voice soft enough for only her to hear, asked, "Lady Kenna, may I walk thee back to thy home?"

Oh. Ceana's heart did something very strange that made her briefly forget how to breathe, let alone talk, write, or otherwise respond. He'd been formal with her most of that day, and she'd thought that his calling her *thou* last night had been merely a thing of circumstance. But then again, they had been in public all day, and he was formal with everyone, even the Northwaves sisters, when there were others listening. Now...now there were few except his Guard to hear, and it seemed he'd meant something more than a momentary kindness.

And now he was looking at her expectantly and a bit concernedly, waiting for her answer, while she stared back at him like an idiot. What had gotten into her? Her parents and tutors had taught her better than this! She gave herself a bit of a mental shake and then returned Fionntan's look with a smile and a nod.

"Good." He turned and offered her his arm, which she took. Then they set off up the path to the house, two of the Guards falling in just behind.

They said little on the walk, though that hardly surprised Ceana. She was still tired from a late night and little sleep, and she had no doubt Fionntan was just as weary. Besides, he'd carried much of the conversation on the swim back here, making sure the group included her as much as possible, and so he was probably short on things to talk about just now.

They reached the house and stopped on the doorstep. Fionntan faced Ceana. "Here thou art, home again, safe and sound as I promised. Thou canst tell thy cousins I kept my word."

Ceana pulled out her tablet and stylus, set stylus to tablet, and handed both to Fionntan. Then she wrote, *"Thou couldst come in to tell them thyself. They'd not mind."*

Fionntan gave a regretful smile, glancing again at the door. "I've no doubt they would welcome me in, and I would be glad to spend longer with thee and them. But there are matters I wish to check on before I sleep, so back to the keep I must go."

Oh well. *"Remember to rest. I'm sure thou art tired, and kings always need sleep."*

"I will, never fear," Fionntan laughed. "I have no doubt thou art weary as well. But if thou wilt come visit my keep again tomorrow, or perhaps the day after, I would be most pleased."

Ceana didn't even have to think twice before answering, *"Will come tomorrow, if no objection from cousins."*

"I will look forward to that, then." Fionntan handed back her tablet, and hesitated a moment. Then, to Ceana's utmost surprise, he bowed, took her hand, and kissed it. "Good night to thee, Kenna. I am glad thou came for the singing; I hope thou art as well." Then he stepped onto the path and set off with a final wave.

What had *that* been? Ceana stared after him for several long moments, clutching her tablet to her chest with one hand and letting the other hang in the air where Fionntan had left it. Absolutely *nothing* about that farewell made any sense with regard to anything she'd been taught about decorum and etiquette or what she'd seen of selkie culture.

Well, Fionntan *was* tired. And she'd not even been here two months; surely there were some nuances or customs she'd not yet picked up on. Shaking herself, she turned and let herself in the door. An immediate rush of footsteps came from above, and a moment later, Uaine and Aíbinn appeared on the stairs. Uaine reached Ceana first and threw her arms around her. "Thou art back! Art thou hungry? We told Dorie to set aside some dinner for thee; come and eat, and then thou canst tell us all about how thy first singing trip went."

"Aye, now that she's done standing on the doorstep, she can tell us everything." Aíbinn winked at Ceana and embraced her briefly.

"Come on, then."

More strange behavior! But a proper meal, or even the leftovers of a proper meal, sounded excellent. So, Ceana followed Uaine and Aíbinn down the hall and dismissed all the day's oddities from her mind. There'd be time enough to wonder about them later, after all. For now, she would enjoy a good meal and the company of her kin.

Chapter 34
A HEART TORN

The second singing party returned to Emain Ablach two days after Fionntan and Ceana's, bringing with them a rescue: a boy of fifteen years, large for his age, the son of an Atìrsen knight and a selkie lady. He'd stolen the cloak from his father's closet without knowing what it was, he'd told his rescuers, and he'd only discovered the truth when he accidentally fell into a lake while wearing it. He was first-generation selkie-kin, easy enough for Ninian's tests to identify without the lengthy wait Ceana had experienced, and his mother's family took him in eagerly. All this Ceana heard secondhand from Aíbinn and Fionntan—Fionntan because all rescues were reported to him, and Aíbinn because she had been present when messengers brought Fionntan the news.

Ceana couldn't help thinking that the boy was lucky. Nothing could prevent *him* from staying with his newfound family. As for herself, with the singing trip over, she had less and less to distract herself from the looming specter of her failing cloak and the need to return to Atìrse. Mairearad was already busy making arrangements for the adoption ceremony, and every evening she seemed to have a new question for Ceana about her preferences on this or that detail.

Mairearad's frequent questions did have one benefit: they provided an easy opening for Ceana to ask if the ceremony would mean she was bound to the water like full-blooded selkies were, unable to stray more than a day or two away. Mairearad shook her head at the question, replying, "Thou art still part human, so thou hast no need to fear. Thou wilt maintain the freedom of both land and sea."

"Aye," Aíbinn had added. "And thy human blood means one

of us three, perhaps all of us, would be free to go about on land in the mortal realm as you can. But so long as things continue as they are, only some of the Guard have much need of that, and that only lately."

What did that mean? Ceana gave Aíbinn an odd look, but Aíbinn just shook her head. "Never mind. Fionntan will have my head if he knows I've been speaking of such things." And no matter how Ceana asked, she'd say no more on that topic.

But with this revelation came a new temptation, a little voice in the back of Ceana's mind that said maybe she could delay just a *little* longer. Maybe she *could* go through with the ceremony, then go back home to Atìrse after. After all, Onora had told her to stay in Emain Ablach for safety's sake. She couldn't fault Ceana for following her instructions, could she? And everything would reset once she turned eighteen anyway.

Yet, no matter how Ceana entertained the idea, she knew it could never be more than that. The legal component of the adoption would remain, even if the magical component faded—Mairearad and Fionntan had confirmed that when she'd asked, framing it in terms of curiosity about half-selkies discovered at young ages. Unless she formally sought to be re-adopted by a different family, she'd be considered a lady of the Northwaves, selkie nobility, until the day she died.

That would cause trouble if the rest of Atìrse ever found out; it could be seen as her rejecting her human kin, and that would mean losing her rights and status as a member of the royal family. Besides that, while the royal family having non-human heritage would be seen as scandalous enough back in Atìrse, embracing her selkie side so explicitly while tension lingered between their peoples would almost guarantee trouble.

No, going through with the adoption would mean staying permanently in Emain Ablach. More importantly, it would mean living a lie the rest of her life and being cut off from most of her family. At best, she could be an agent of Onora's here, gathering information and swaying selkie opinions towards giving humankind a second chance once Onora rooted out the Atìrsen selkie hunters. At worst...well, so far away from home, she probably *could* fake her own death. But even remaining in Emain Ablach wasn't worth taking that step. Even if it was, it would mean rejecting her duties to Atìrse and to the selkies; she would do far more good for both by going home again.

So, really, she had no choice to stay in Emain Ablach—but still, she lingered, putting off the day when she would leave for the last time. The mere idea of saying goodbye to the Northwaves sisters made her heart ache. And so, too, did the idea of saying goodbye to Fionntan.

Fionntan! He occupied steadily more and more of her thoughts. In the two weeks since their return from the singing trip, she'd seen him almost every day, whether in the company of others or during visits on her own to the keep. Some days, they remained in the keep, filling pleasant hours with conversation and games. Other days saw them venturing out around the island as Fionntan showed Ceana all the places he loved best. On one pleasant afternoon, they returned to the Dawnwood Spring, just the two of them and a pair of guards who stayed an unobtrusive distance back.

On one afternoon, he met her and Mairearad in the Halls of the Lost and guided her through those memorialized in his family's section. When they came to the end, to the paintings of his parents and grandparents, they lingered for some time, as Fionntan shared with her one memory and another. As they finished and turned to go, he added, "They would have liked thee, I think, had only thou and they been able to meet. Alas that it could not be so."

Ceana didn't know how to respond to that, but she smiled and squeezed his arm comfortingly, and that seemed to be sufficient. As always, she ignored the part of herself that gave a little flutter whenever he called her *thou*. He had continued to do so whenever they were in private, and by now, it seemed the most natural thing in the world to respond in kind. Yet knowing that this man, the king of the selkies, with his rightful suspicion of the human race, saw her as so close a friend never failed to stir up feelings she couldn't entirely explain.

Yet, even to him, she had to lie, and the closer they became, the greater the weight of her falsehoods grew, even if their number didn't increase. Always, she kept as close to the truth as she could. Yet not being able to tell him all, knowing that she could only be such friends with him under the screen of a false identity, galled her. More than once, she fantasized about confessing everything to him and praying that Dèanadair would inspire his heart to mercy. Yet she didn't dare do so, for if he took the news poorly, it could ruin any hope of future reconciliation with the selkies, at least for a few generations.

If only the treaty meeting hadn't gone so horribly wrong. If only she'd thought to ask the *selkies* why there was only a treaty and not an alliance before proposing the latter. If only her people hadn't started abusing the selkies in the first place. Then she might have learned her heritage properly, might have come to Emain Ablach as her father's emissary and not in disguise, might not have to worry about leaving now. Perhaps the betrothal even would have gone through after all, or at least have come under more consideration...Though, of course, it wouldn't have. Not with Uaine and Fionntan's promise in place.

But none of those *what-ifs* were real, and so instead she continued to bite her tongue and wish things had been different.

"'Tis terribly hard not to tell anyone," she told Onora one afternoon, as she sat in the little cleft in the standing sea-stones, knees pulled up to her chest and cloak wrapped around her. "I won't; you know I won't—but I *wish* I could."

"I understand," came Onora's reply. "If you feel 'tis too difficult for you to stay there, you can come home. So far, there are no signs that Lord Arran has noticed my agents' activities, and so you may be safe enough here."

"I...maybe. Soon." There was another lie, albeit one of omission—Ceana had carefully refrained from mentioning her failing cloak to Onora. Onora would only worry, after all, or tell Ceana to come home *immediately*. "I don't wish to leave, though.

I don't want to say goodbye to Mairearad and Aíbinn and Uaine. Or Fionntan."

She realized her slip the moment it left her mouth, and she could almost see Onora's raised eyebrow. "His majesty is *just* Fionntan now?"

"I ..." Onora might have been a hundred miles away, but Ceana could still *feel* her stare, strongly enough that she had to fight the urge to fidget and look away. Though she'd told Onora that she continued to see Fionntan often, she'd glossed over just *how* friendly she'd become with him. "I told you, 'tis much less formal here, and he believes I'm a noblewoman. And 'twould be hard for *anyone* to talk to him and not be friends with him—he's kind and honorable and brave, and he cares so much for his people and tries so hard to be a good king—and he *is* a good king, he really is. And he *listens* even when I can't properly talk to him, and he's always so thoughtful ..."

"Enough!" Onora interrupted with an exasperated little laugh. "I understand. King Fionntan is a good man. Really, Ceana, with that little rant and with how often you've mentioned him before now, I'd nearly believe you were in love with him."

Ceana started to laugh as well, but the sound stuck in her throat as she considered just *how* many times she'd wished that the betrothal had gone through. How much she enjoyed spending time with Fionntan, how much she admired him—

Onora's voice took on a warning note. "Ceana? Is there something else you'd like to tell me?"

"I—" Despite her best efforts, Ceana couldn't quite keep her voice from breaking, couldn't keep her heart from speeding up. "I didn't know—"

"Ceana!"

The scolding exasperation in Onora's voice broke through Ceana's paralysis. "I didn't *realize* it was happening! I just...He's just...Onora, what do I *do*? I wasn't supposed to fall in love until *after* I was married, and now it's *him*, and I've done *everything* wrong. I'm going to end up just like Aunt Gaie, and I'll be miserable

359

my whole life and do no good for *anyone*—"

Onora muttered something, only half-audible, that might have been "Dèanadair, give me patience." Then she sighed and, in her best big-sister voice, replied, "Ceana, we've been over this. Most people *do* fall in love, or something close to it, before marriage, and very few of them turn out like Aunt Gaie. And King Fionntan is nothing at all like Uncle Callum, so at least you have good sense about the *type* of person you're in love with."

"But—but—" Ceana clung to the necklace, pinching the symbol as if pressing it hard enough could bring Onora *here*. "What do I *do*? I can't marry him!"

"Well, half the point of this whole affair *was* to fix the rift between us and the selkies. Once we start setting things right and we've had a year or two to demonstrate our good intentions, if you still care for him, we can see if perhaps he'll be more open to the idea of a marriage alliance. He may look more kindly on our subterfuge as well once he sees the results."

Oh, glorious hope! But it faded as soon as Ceana considered it a moment or two. "I don't think he *would* want a marriage alliance even if we were on friendly terms. The selkies don't *do* that sort of thing. I think they think it's too much like what we did to them."

"Well, does King Fionntan love you?" Onora asked, fully in her matter-of-fact problem-solving tone now. "A man in love may be more forgiving than he otherwise would be."

Did Fionntan love her? Ceana thought through their interactions over the past months. He was certainly kind to her. He looked for opportunities to spend time with her nearly as much as she did with him. He'd given her the magical stylus and tablet so she could more easily communicate, and he'd shared his special places with her. He called her *thou*, though they'd known each other only a short time.

But there was the matter of his promise to Uaine. And Ceana could certainly see him doing everything he'd done for her for Uaine as well, if her and Uaine's places were swapped. So, was how he treated her born of the romantic kind of love? Or was it simply the love of friendship?

"Ceana?" Onora prompted. "Are you still there?"

Ceana sighed, slumping. "I don't *know*! I don't know how to tell—and, anyway, he and Uaine promised ages ago to marry each other at a particular time."

"At a particular time when they both came of age? Or ..."

"When Fionntan turned three-and-thirty, if neither of them found someone else first. And he's just waiting until then; I'm almost sure of it. He thinks so well of her. Or he's holding back until Uaine is properly of age so he can ask her to do it sooner." Ceana held back a sniffle. "I can't come in between them. I *can't*."

Now it was Onora's turn to be silent so long that Ceana wondered if something had gone wrong with the mirror. But, at last, Onora said, in a carefully measured tone, "I would be careful how much weight I put on that kind of promise, but I suppose you're the one who's seen them with each other. Even so, Ceana, it's not as if everyone can only fall in love once. There are many men in Atìrse just as noble as King Fionntan is and just as worthy of your affections. Once you're away from the selkies, you may find that your feelings for him become less strong and that you can come to love someone else."

"I don't think I *can*," Ceana almost wailed. "Or if I do, I don't think I'd know it was happening any more than I did this time. And it still wouldn't mean something like this would." She let her head sink back against the stone. "Maybe I should give up on the idea of marriage and become a contemplative. If I dedicate the rest of my life to Dèanadair, I can't get in any more trouble."

There came another very long pause, and when Onora spoke again, she was clearly holding back laughter. "Ceana, I love you dearly, but you would be a *terrible* contemplative. If you're going to run away from marriage altogether, please, pick a different way to do it. But I don't think you should give up on the idea of getting married. I think you simply need to change how you look at it."

Ceana sniffled again. "Maybe." She knew, at least, that Onora was right on one point—she *wouldn't* make a particularly good contemplative. "It's just so *hard*. How is anyone supposed to survive romance?"

"Dèanadair's grace, mostly. And it does have its own rewards, once you get past the awkward stages." Onora sighed in a way that suggested she was shaking her head. "Do you want to talk more about this, or would you like to hear what I've learned here in Atìrse?"

"Tell me what you've found out." She didn't need talk more about this; she knew that much. She needed to think, or possibly she needed to stay on this rock the rest of her life ...

"Well," Onora began, "I told you that I've been looking into archives and records for anything pre-treaty?"

"You said so, yes." It had been Onora's other large project, shared between herself and Maimeó and those of Onora's people not investigating Lord Arran and his cohort. "You told me it was difficult because it was so long ago and so much was destroyed when the old gods were thrown out."

"Did I tell you that? I thought I'd kept that particular rant confined to Maimeó." Onora huffed. "I understand the impulse; I really do. They wanted to make sure anyone who was tempted back towards the old pagan ways would have as hard a time as possible following that temptation. But they could have been a *bit* more selective in what information they destroyed."

"You said that too." Several times, in fact, though Ceana refrained from pointing it out. "But you learned something anyway?"

"I did. One of my agents in Gormthall discovered a collection of journals and records brought there by a priest of the old gods when he fled Atìrse. He wrote about the practice of capturing selkies to attain freedom of the seas, and if it was half as bad as he makes it out be—Oh!" Onora's voice was thick with mingled fury and sorrow. "It makes me sick just thinking on it. His records say that the practice started to decline as the path of Dèanadair became more common, but it never really stopped. But when the records of the old religion were destroyed, so were the records of the selkie-hunting."

"Probably for the same reason, too," Ceana replied. "They wanted to make it difficult for anyone to keep doing it."

"Exactly. This priest writes about how people were discouraged from so much as *mentioning* the practice. It's no wonder all memory of it disappeared in a few generations."

No wonder indeed. And now two peoples suffered for that overzealous approach. After all..."That probably made it easier for the selkie hunters, in some ways. They must have their own records that they'd hidden, and no one even knew to suspect them of anything."

"Exactly. And the selkies were still so wary of us that they never spent long enough on land to tell us what was happening," Onora replied, her voice grim. "I don't know why the faeries didn't say something, especially after Thrice-Great Uncle Diarmad went and married one of them. Maimeó thinks that they assumed we knew about it and were turning a blind eye to the matter, and that's why we don't have a closer relationship with them. But she's still waiting on Thrice-Great Uncle Diarmad to reply to her letter and confirm."

"I've wondered the same thing. It would explain why they're so much friendlier with the selkies than with us." Maybe, once they settled everything with the selkies, if her heart still hurt as much as she thought it would, she could convince Queen Moireach to petition Thrice-Great Uncle Diarmad to allow Ceana to come to Tìr Soilleir as an additional representative of the royal family. She could try to convince the faery folk of the truth, try to build a better friendship with them, and stay far away from anything that could make her think of Fionntan.

Then she recalled that the Lady of Northwaves dwelt in Tìr Soilleir as well, and she thought of seeing the faery traders and messengers leave for Emain Ablach every so often. She'd never be able to stand being so close and yet so far away. Besides that, someone might recognize her and mention her presence in Tìr Soilleir to Fionntan, and then he'd find out everything...

She dismissed the idea again, a bit reluctantly. "What now, then?"

"I'm still waiting on word from my people in Lord Arran's holdings to find the right time to act," Onora replied. "They've identified most of the selkie-hunters, they think, and a fair number of the captured selkies. Your reports from the Halls of the Lost have been very helpful to their efforts."

"Good." Ceana still visited the Halls of the Lost every few days, usually with Mairearad, and sometimes also in the company of the families whose caverns she surveyed. Hearing their stories of loved ones lost made her more determined than ever to see the captives returned, whatever the cost. "Do you think it'll be soon?"

"I hope so. My agents there still think Arran and his people are planning something, and hopefully that will give us an opening." Onora paused. "Alasdair is calling me; I need to go. Send another message if you learn anything more, and I'll tell you once I have news of the captives or the rescue effort."

"I will." Ceana slid to the edge of the crevice. "I love you."

"I love you too. Be safe."

"I will." Ceana let go of the necklace and shook out her hand. Then she gathered her cloak around her, took a deep breath, and slipped into the sea. Her seal-shape was decidedly slower to gather around her these days than it had been when she first donned the cloak, but as always, she forced herself to stay calm—a racing heart only delayed the shift further. Once fully transformed, she struck out for Emain Ablach, setting an easy pace and being careful not to go too deep. Staying right at the surface had proved impractical; she couldn't swim easily so close to the waves. But if she dove down ten feet or so, she could move easily while still staying close enough to the air for comfort.

She reached the island at a point about a quarter of the way 'round from the entrance. As she made her way along its edge, however, she noticed something further down—a faint, dull glow, like that of the runes carved into the island rock. Yet Ceana remembered no runes in this particular section. After a moment's consideration, she surfaced for a deep breath, then dove down to inspect it.

Some twenty-five feet down, she found the source of the glow. There *were* runes here, but instead of being carved directly into the rock, it was set in a circle of wax-like material nearly the size of a dinner plate. Most of the strokes of the runes looked smooth, as if they'd been molded in the wax while it was still warm. However, one stroke was thinner and rougher than the rest, as if it had been made after the stuff cooled.

All the runes glowed with a faint light. On this side of Emain Ablach, in seal form, Ceana couldn't see color properly, but she thought it might have been red. She studied the runes, committing them to memory, then glanced around. There was another wax-like circle attached to the stone about ten feet away, though this one didn't glow, and she started towards it.

As she did, however, a figure—another selkie—shot down from above. The selkie slammed into her side, knocking her backwards into the rock and driving half the air from her lungs. She barely kept herself from gasping, instead trying to wiggle free. But the stranger threw itself into her again, forcing her against the rock.

What was happening? Why was she being attacked? Had whoever this was discovered her true identity?

A sudden chill drew her thoughts to a far more pressing problem. Her seal-shape was loosening again, preparing to give way. She needed to get to the surface *now*. She tried again to break away, but this time the seal slammed into her and pushed her downwards, then kept pushing. She stifled a scream as the waters around her darkened and she felt the seal-shape slipping away—as fins gave way to fingers, as tail became legs, as her hair floated free of her hood.

Her attacker drew back in confusion, and Ceana seized her chance. Flailing and kicking and paddling with all her might, she raced back to the surface. A few breaths of air—nothing. In the waters below, Ceana could see the selkie who'd attacked her swimming after her. She fought the rising panic in her chest, then breathed deep again as she felt her seal-shape reforming at last.

As soon as it fully returned, she shot off towards the entrance to Emain Ablach. She'd been nearly there when she saw the glow, and it took her only a few minutes to reach it. Another breath of air, a plunge, and she slipped into the tunnel—but her attacker still followed.

Yet, here, she had an advantage. She'd been this way so many times that she had no trouble making her way through the twists and turns of the tunnel, while the selkie behind her slowed frequently as if uncertain. And she was smaller than her pursuer, better able to navigate the tightest points of the passage. When she burst free of the tunnel into the blue-green of Emain Ablach, she had put quite a bit of distance between herself and the other.

Still, she wasted no time in making for shore. She needed to find the Guard; tell them what happened. Even if her assailant *had* figured out who she was and attacked her for it, if this person was the *only* one, if she could tell *her* side of the story first, she might be all right. She might be able to play off the accusations as a fiction her attacker had invented to justify what had transpired.

But in open waters, her larger and stronger assailant began to regain ground. He was snapping at her tail when she hauled out onto the beach, and he pulled himself from the waters mere moments after she did.

As soon as Ceana's seal-shape fell away into the cloak, she sprang to her feet and started to run. She'd gone two steps when a hand seized her hair and hood and yanked her back. Ceana screamed as she lost her footing in the soft sand and stumbled. Her attacker—a young man, she could now see, large and round-faced—whirled her round in a moment, pinning her arm painfully behind her back. "Stay out of my business," he growled, the human language rough in his mouth. "Stay out of it, y'hear?"

Ceana struggled against his grip and tried to kick him in the place her father's guards had taught her to aim for. But he shoved her to the ground and planted a knee on her midsection, looming over her so she could see only him and the sky. He was, a particularly unhelpful part of Ceana's mind observed, quite young—more a boy than a man. But he was a boy big enough to hurt her without any particular effort. "Say you'll stay out of it, girl." He raised a fist, then stopped, his gaze fixed on her face, his eyes narrowing. "Wait. I know you."

A shadow fell over them both, and before the boy could say another word, he was yanked off of Ceana. Ceana gasped for breath and scooted back, pushing herself half upright, then looked to see who her rescuers might be.

Fionntan stood there, a small company of the Guard just running up behind him. In one hand he grasped the back of the boy's shirt and cloak; in the other, he held one of the boy's wrists, his grip firm even as the boy strained.

Two of the Guard stepped forward, and he passed the boy off to them. "Hold him fast." Then he turned to Ceana. His brows rose in surprise and worry as he saw her. "Lady Kenna, are you hurt? Let me help you up."

He offered a hand, and Ceana took it gratefully. She offered him what she hoped was a reassuring smile, though she suspected it was too shaky to do much good.

Indeed, he looked unconvinced. In a voice low enough that no others would hear, he said, "I ask again, art thou all right?"

Ceana nodded and pulled out her tablet. Giving thanks yet again for the steadiness of the magical stylus, she wrote, *"He attacked me outside. Don't know why. Chased me in here. Think he confused me with someone else."*

Fionntan's face darkened. "Did he?" He turned to face the boy. "I recognize you. You're the latest arrival to the island, are you not? What reason did you have to attack a lady of Emain Ablach?"

The boy barked out a laugh. "Lady of your island?" he asked, careless in his use of the human language. "You know who she really is?"

"Lady Kenna is my subject and my friend." Fionntan stared the boy down, his voice rich with cold anger. "Whatever feud you think you had with her where you came from, you left it on the shores of Atìrse. Do you understand me?"

The boy just smirked until Fionntan stepped forward and

gave him a backhanded blow across the face. "I am king in Emain Ablach. As you are of the selkie people, I am *your* king. If you have a legitimate grievance against any in my kingdom, whatever their status, bring it to my Guard, and they and I will see that justice is done. But if you take matters into your own hands, or if you needlessly attack another, you will find yourself on the receiving end of that justice. *Do you understand me?*"

The boy, no longer smirking, nodded. All the fight seemed to have leaked out of him with Fionntan's blow, though his eyes still gleamed with anger.

Fionntan waved a hand at his Guard. "Release him." He looked again at the boy. "As you are new to my domain, I offer you this mercy, that you will not face the usual punishment for attacking a noble lady. But should you do so again, should you attack *any* of my people again, I will not be so generous. And if this is the behavior taught you by your fathers, I suggest you unlearn their lessons as quickly as possible."

The Guards holding the boy let go of him, and he stumbled forward. With a bow and a grimace, he showed his understanding, then rushed away.

Fionntan turned back to Ceana. "I am sorry you were attacked. 'Tis well that we reached the shore when we did. Do you desire an escort home?"

Ceana nodded, then hesitated. *"Wert thou going somewhere?"* she wrote.

"A brief expedition, but it can wait a little while." Over his shoulder, Fionntan called to his Guard: "We see the Lady Kenna home, then set out."

A chorus of agreement came in reply. Fionntan smiled and offered his arm. "See? There is no trouble. Now, come, and you shall be home safe in short order."

This was the trouble, Ceana reflected, taking his arm. How could she *not* have fallen for Fionntan when he was so kind? She probably should have refused the escort, should be doing *something* to make it easier for them both when she had to leave. But she'd answered with her heart instead of her head, as seemed to be more and more common when Fionntan was involved.

Still, it was a relief to have Fionntan and his Guard with her so she didn't feel the need to peer at every tree and bush they passed in case the boy who'd attacked her was lurking there. He'd *recognized* her, she was sure. Not while she was in seal-shape, but after. He knew her identity. He'd nearly revealed who she was. What would she do if he told others?

They reached the house all too soon and yet not soon enough. Fionntan bid her good day there, asked again if she was all right, and promised to see her the next day as they'd planned. Then he headed back down towards the lake.

Safely back in the house, with Uaine and her bright spirits for company, Ceana found it easier to calm herself. Yes, this situation had unfolded poorly. But it could have been worse, and surely she could find an answer somewhere. She would figure it out. All would be well.

Or so she thought—until a messenger arrived that evening, bearing a personal missive for her alone. She unfolded the thin paper, and her heart thudded as she read the message: *Keep your mouth shut and I'll keep mine closed. Tell anyone what you saw and I'll tell the king WHO I saw today.*

That meant what she'd seen outside was somehow important. But it also meant something else for certain: Ceana's remaining days in Emain Ablach, already numbered, were now very short indeed.

Chapter 35
Leaving Emain Ablach

With this new threat hanging over her head, Ceana knew she couldn't risk staying much longer on the island. Still, she stretched out her time a few days more. One day, to see Fionntan and enjoy a visit to the Dawnwood Spring and dinner with him and her cousins after, as they'd planned. She did her best to make sure that her last day with him would be full of good memories only, so they would both have some final hours of happiness to look back on. Yet it was hard to do so when she found herself constantly wondering if any happy memories would survive if and when Fionntan found out who she was.

A second day she stayed to carefully venture out to the place she'd seen the wax-like thing and the glowing runes, so she could confirm that yes, there were at least two more nearby, these ones not glowing and also lacking that last rough line. She passed along a description of them to Queen Moireach via Onora, but the old queen didn't know for sure what that particular combination of symbols meant. It sounded, she said, like a fire rune and a stone rune and another rune for beginnings or wakefulness, but conclusively identifying its purpose would take research and more letters to the faery folk.

A third day, Ceana stayed, for one last visit to the Halls of the Lost, for one last evening with her cousins. If they noticed that she seemed unusually solemn, they said nothing—but perhaps they talked a little more brightly, stayed a little closer to her, were more ready than usual to offer a hug or squeeze her hand or bump her shoulder in a companionable way. It was almost enough to bring Ceana to tears—how would they react when she left and never returned? Would they mourn? They had already lost many people, and now she'd be one gone, unless she could find a way to keep in touch with them without going back.

Then, on the fourth day, she put on the dress she'd worn when she first came to Emain Ablach and filled her pockets with the things she'd brought with her and a few other items she thought she'd need. She hesitated over the tablet Fionntan had given her; could she risk taking it back? Then again, could she risk leaving it? Eventually, she slipped it in her pocket as well; at least she'd have something to remember him by, should she wish to do so.

Then she made her way downstairs. Over the last few days, she'd made her plans, for she knew that she couldn't simply sneak out or even leave for the day and not come back. Not if she didn't want search parties scouring the waters for her for weeks. After all, if that happened, it was all too likely that they'd find her before she got back to Atìrse. No, she needed an excuse that would ensure no one would miss her for a few days. And as nerve-wracking as the boy's threat had been, it did give her an opportunity for just such a cover.

So, once she was ready to leave, she set her face in as distressed and panicked a look as she could manage and went in search of Uaine. She found her, as she'd expected, at the loom in the workroom.

After standing a few minutes in the doorway, Ceana cleared her throat to get Uaine's attention. "Uaine?"

Uaine looked up. "Kenna? What's wrong?"

At least she looked convincing. "There's something...I need to go."

"Go?" Uaine's brow furrowed, and she set the shuttle aside. "Go where?"

"Back to Atìrse. Just for a little while. I'll be back in time for the ceremony." Ceana clasped her hands together, focusing on not looking away or trying to hide her face from Uaine. Those would be sure signs of guilt. "It's...Dost thou remember the message I received the other day?"

"Of course." Uaine slid out from behind her loom and hurried over to Ceana. "Is that that this is about?"

"It is. The newest arrival, the boy who came with the last singing party...he had news of my family in Atìrse. About one of my sisters. She's pregnant, and she was doing poorly, and she's taken a turn for the worse ..." Praise Dèanadair, even thinking of Linnhe in such a state brought tears to Ceana's eyes. "People say she may not survive."

"Oh *no*." Uaine's face paled—no doubt she, too, was imagining one of her own sisters in the same condition. "Folk don't usually go back once they've come to Emain Ablach, but I'm sure this could be an exception, especially since thy family knows naught about thy heritage. Canst thou wait a day, though? I'm sure Aíbinn and one or two of her friends would go with thee. 'Tis dangerous to go alone."

"I've spent three days trying to decide what to do, and the news was old when I got it. Besides, 'tisn't far—just a day past where we went for the singing—and I'll attract less attention if I go alone." Ceana took Uaine's hands. "Thou understands, dost thou not?"

"Of course, I do," Uaine exclaimed, as if offended by the suggestion that she might not. "If thou must go, thou must. But *do* be careful, please. How soon wilt thou leave, then?"

"At once. I can't waste more time." Ceana pushed a smile. "I'll be back as soon as I can, truly."

"I know." Taking Ceana's arm, Uaine made for the door. "Come—thou should take provisions with thee, just in case. And if thy cloak fails before thy return, make for Torrsea, where thou and Fionntan went on the singing trip. A party goes there every two or three weeks, and they'll be able to help thee, or at least get a message to us."

"I'll remember that." Perhaps she could even use that to communicate with her cousins or set their thoughts at ease about why she *wasn't* coming back—though Onora would know better if such a thing were wise or not. Perhaps it would be safer to let everyone think she'd drowned, even if 'twould be sadder too.

Uaine worked quickly, putting together—with some help from the servants—a bag of food that would travel well, the rest of the tonic Ninian had mixed to help keep Ceana's cloak from failing, bandages, a small jar of general-purpose ointment, and a shawl that Ceana could either wear or use to wrap up her cloak once she'd reached Atìrse's shore. Ceana tried to protest that it would only be a short trip and all this was unnecessary, but Uaine would hear none of it.

Once all was packed and ready, Uaine walked Ceana to the front door and hugged her tight. "Be careful. I'll pray every day for thy safe return."

"Thank you." *I'll miss you*, she wished she could say—but that would give her away. If only she could have said goodbye to Aíbinn and Mairearad as well—if only she could have said goodbye to Fionntan! But it would have been far more difficult to convince any of them to let her go alone. "I'll take care."

"I know." Uaine sniffled, but when she pulled back, she had a brave smile on her face. "I'll help Mairearad with the last preparations so all will be ready for thy adoption when thou art back."

"I appreciate that." Of course, there'd be no ceremony. All Mairearad's planning, all the sisters' excitement—it would be all for nothing. But there was no way around that. She pulled a few folded pieces of paper from her pocket. "These are messages for Mairearad, Aíbinn, and Fionntan. Canst thou see that they get them—today, if thou can?" Each note contained her cover story and her apologies for leaving so suddenly, but more importantly, they told of the wax rune circles around the island and of how she'd been attacked while inspecting one of them. Hopefully Fionntan and his Guard would know what to do about the runes and the boy both.

Uaine took the letters and tucked them in her own pocket. "I'll pass them on. Mayhap I'll go to the keep around noon."

"Thank you," Ceana said again. Then she glanced at the sky. "I'd best go before the day grows too late."

"Oh, yes, of course." Uaine grabbed Ceana for one last quick hug, then stepped back. "Goodbye, then, until you get back."

"Goodbye until then." Pushing a smile, Ceana stepped out the door and out on the path away from the Northwaves house and the home she'd grown to love.

Though she'd walked this way many times before, Ceana still found herself looking around nervously as she trekked down the path and through the village to the shore. She half-expected someone to jump out at her, to suddenly reveal that they knew who she was and what she was doing. But no one did, and before long, she passed through the tunnel and entered the open ocean once more.

Thankfully, between the singing trip and her general knowledge of geography, she had no doubt as to which way to go, and she set out on a course that she *thought* would bring her to a town in the royal holdings in a few days' time. Technically, she could come ashore somewhere closer, but anywhere nearer than her intended destination would land her in territory controlled by Lord Arran or one of his compatriots. She didn't like to imagine what would happen if they caught her either as a selkie or as a princess traveling alone. If they caught her as both...well, that would be the worst thing of all.

She kept up a slow and steady pace through the morning and into the afternoon, stopping for only brief breaks when she felt the warning chill of her seal-shape threatening to fall away. After the first occurrence, Ceana noticed that each chill was preceded by a strange warmth at her throat, but why she couldn't tell. Another quirk of her failing cloak, she supposed, and so she prayed every few minutes that the magic would last until she could get home.

In the midafternoon, she spotted a drifting raft of wreckage, the remains of some ill-fated ship, floating in the waves nearby. She swam to it and attempted to pull herself out. It took her a few tries to do so without tipping back into the water, but she finally managed to get safely atop it.

Once afloat, she wriggled a bit more until she found what seemed like the least precarious position possible. Then she pulled bread and cheese and an apple from her bag to eat—better to take advantage of proper human food when she had the opportunity. She finished all three off in no time at all and tossed the apple core into the water. With her stomach full, she reached for her necklace and pressed the symbol, intending to let Onora know that she was on her way.

She'd barely spoken the first syllables of Onora's name when Onora's voice interrupted her. "Ceana? I've been trying to contact you for hours; where have you been? You need to come home *now*."

"Swimming. I left this morning. What's wrong?" Ceana couldn't remember ever hearing Onora sound so panicked. "Is everything all right?" Silently, she sent up a prayer that the story she'd given Uaine hadn't been half-true after all.

"Oh, thank Dèanadair. The problem isn't here; it's there. I just got word this morning from one of my agents. Lord Arran set sail with nearly all his ships, and he's headed towards the selkies. I don't know all his plan, but I know he intends to capture or kill all he can."

"*What*?" Ceana mentally calculated how many men that would be. Lord Arran had a larger fleet than anyone in Atìrse save the royal family. And if even a quarter of his people had access to selkie cloaks…That would be a formidable force.

Still, nearly every man in Emain Ablach and many of the women had trained in the Guard, and they were in their home territory—and they had other advantages besides that. "How did he find out where the island is?"

"His wife," came Onora's grim reply. "My agent says she's been holding out for years, as far as he can tell, but somehow, Arran broke her resolve and is forcing her to guide him there."

Oh no. Eilidh would be able to lead Arran straight to the selkies. Even so, it would be hard for a large company to get in through the tunnels without detection, and it would be comparatively easy for the Guard, once they realized enemies were present, to post themselves at the inner side of the tunnel and stop their foes one by one. In order to attack effectively, Lord Arran would have to find a way to drive the selkies out of Emain Ablach, and Ceana could think of little that could do that.

Little except the island itself waking up and remembering its history. Ceana recalled with terrifying clarity the rune-embossed seals she'd seen on the stone of the island's roots. "Is Maimeó there? I need to ask her a question."

"She's not here. Can it wait?"

"No. I just realized...the runes I told you about. Maimeó said they looked like fire and stone and wakefulness. The selkies live in the ruins of a firemount. What if Lord Arran is trying to make it erupt again?"

"He wouldn't—No." Fury filled Onora's voice. "He *would*. Wait one moment. Don't let go of the necklace." Ceana's ears suddenly filled with a dim buzzing sound, but she held on as instructed. A few minutes later, the buzzing stopped and Onora's voice returned. "Maimeó says it's possible, though it would take an incredible amount of magic to fully wake any firemount that's been quiet long enough for people to settle *inside* it. But if it erupts, that's as dangerous to Arran as it is to the selkies."

"Maybe he only wants to partially wake it—just enough to frighten them into evacuating straight into a trap." And with families and non-fighters to protect, the Guard would have a far harder time defending against their attackers. "Someone needs to warn the selkies."

"I have my own ships already on their way. Dèanadair willing, we'll reach Lord Arran before he reaches the selkies. But you need to get the rest of the way to Atìrse. What town were you aiming for?"

"Somewhere near Craigkeld," Ceana replied. "You're *days* south of Lord Arran, even with good winds. By the time you get anywhere near him, you'll be too late. Do you even know where you're going?"

"Teine-Falamh," Onora replied at once. "After she told her husband, Lady Eilidh told my agent as well. He's been in contact with her almost since he arrived in Lord Arran's castle. She's the one who let us know about his plan as well—Arran launched the ships separately, so we wouldn't have even noticed if not for her warning. And I've called in a few favors to get a faery wind-weaver's help. It'll be close, but we've a chance of reaching him before he finds the selkies. Now, forget Craigkeld. Make for Kenbreck instead. You'll probably be able to reach it by nightfall. Go to the Blue Flower Inn and speak to Moray, the innkeeper. Ask for Honor's cousin. He'll put you in touch with some of my agents, and they'll see you safely back to Athair and Màthair. I'll tell them to be ready for you."

Back to Athair and Màthair. Back home, where life would be safe and comparatively uncomplicated. Where any further dealings with the selkies would be the provenance of her parents and Onora, not her. Where she could mourn for all she'd found and lost and begin to forget the pain of losing.

But she thought again of the distances between Onora and Lord Arran and the selkies. Even with a wind-weaver's help, Onora would most likely reach Emain Ablach at the same time as Lord Arran or a little after. And in the intervening time, who knew how many selkies would die or be captured?

Ceana had come that far today, and she'd been moving slowly. If she hurried, she could get back to Emain Ablach before Lord Arran, with just enough time to warn Fionntan and the Guard—perhaps even enough time to evacuate Emain Ablach ahead of Lord Arran's arrival, or to break or remove the runes, or to do something.

It would mean extra strain on her cloak; she would have to pray it would last long enough to get her all the way there. And it would mean revealing her identity to everyone. But they would all have found out eventually, one way or another.

"I have to go back," she said, cutting Onora off in the midst of more instructions on what to do if something had happened to Moray. "Someone has to warn them, and I'm the only one who can."

"Don't you dare," Onora snapped. "Ceana, you can't put yourself in danger like that. As your sister—no. As the *crown princess*, I am ordering you to come home."

"I'm sorry, Onora. I love you." With that, Ceana let go of the necklace, tugged it from around her neck, and slid it in her pocket with the tablet. Then she took a deep breath, pulled her hood over her head, and slipped into the sea. She might be the closest one to Emain Ablach right now, but she still had a long swim ahead, and not much time to make it in.

Ceana quickly became grateful for the slow pace she'd set the rest of that day, grateful that she hadn't worn herself out. Even so, it was hard going, pushing herself as quickly as she could, knowing every minute could be the life or death of who knew how many selkies. She didn't dare stop, even on the occasions when her seal-shape threatened to fall away; the most she could do was break the surface and slow a little, just long enough to get in a few deep breaths.

She didn't know how long she could maintain this pace. She could only hope it would be long enough. Each time she surfaced, she peered towards the horizon, praying she'd see Emain Ablach in the distance, begging Dèanadair that she would arrive on time. And still she swam on as the sun drew ever nearer to the sea.

It was late afternoon when she heard the calls. Well, she felt them, more than heard them, at first. It was the opposite of the pressure she sensed when the selkies used their silent thought-speech around her: a sort of seeking tickle in her mind. A few minutes later, that developed into a faint call from several voices, all overlapping with each other: *"Lady Kenna! Lady Kenna, are you out there?"*

They were looking for her. Why were they looking for her? They sounded concerned, not accusatory, so it couldn't be that the boy had told her secret. And while the voices were still too faint for her to make out individuals clearly, one of them sounded suspiciously like Fionntan.

She adjusted her path to a back-and-forth arc, trying to gauge which direction the calls sounded loudest in. A few minutes of this led her to the guess that they were coming from the direction she'd originally been heading—not much of a surprise there, really. Another ten minutes and she spotted a few figures she thought were other selkies ahead in the water. They were spread out, each tracing a curving path at different levels that brought them periodically in contact with one another. As she drew nearer, she recognized both individuals and voices: Fionntan and a half-dozen of the men of the Guard.

She saw the moment one of them spotted her, saw the moment they all shifted their courses to head straight for her. In the same moment, she heard Fionntan's call. *"Lady Kenna! We feared we'd never find you."*

She couldn't reply, but she pushed herself to a little extra speed to close the distance. Just as she did, she felt the ripples in the water and saw a shadow fall over her from above. She looked up to see a ship passing above, its massive hulk blocking out the sun. Hastily, she dove deeper to try to avoid the vessel.

A chill ran through her, too strong for the depth to which she'd descended. *No.* Ceana sent up a silent, desperate prayer: *Please, not now. Any time but now.*

But she could already feel her seal-shape falling away, faster than it ever had before save when she actually hauled out on shore. If it released completely while she was in the water, would she be able to get it back? And, more importantly, if she changed back to human form so far down, would she be able to make it back to the surface?

She couldn't risk it. With a desperate, helpless look towards the other selkies, Ceana shot towards the surface as fast as she dared. If she could just get her mouth and nose above water, perhaps that would be enough to set her to rights without revealing her presence. Anyway, she had no guarantee that the people in these ships would even be *looking* for seals or selkies; they might just be fishing or trading vessels.

Ceana reached the surface just in time and gulped down air.

Her seal-shape reformed around her, but far more slowly than she liked. How much longer would it last? She prayed it would be long enough to return to Emain Ablach. If there were selkies here, she couldn't be far ...

When her lungs were full, she turned to dive again. But she'd only gone a few feet down when she felt a net of fine cords wrapping round her, catching her fins. She frantically tried to pull free, but all her thrashing only entangled herself further. As she struggled, she heard muffled shouts and voices from above.

Then the net began to move upward, taking her with it. Ceana gave a last, desperate attempt to get free before the net carried her out of the waves and water and her seal-shape vanished. That gave her a little slack in the net's cords, at least, but she was still too tangled to escape. The most she could do was twist around to see that the corners of the net were attached to pulleys on a long beam connected to something on the ship's deck. Men hauled on the pulley-ropes, drawing the net up and onto the deck. She twisted a little further, peering at the pennant on the mast.

It showed Lord Arran's colors, his wolfs-head standard. *No. No, Dèanadair, please, anyone but him.* She'd hoped she was further ahead of him than this. And besides that—if *he*, of all people, found out ...

Oh, this would not end well.

Chapter 36
INTENTIONS UNMASKED

The men manning the pulleys swung the net in over the ship and lowered her, none too gently, to the deck. They called to one another as they worked, though Ceana tried not to listen to what they were saying. What she couldn't help but hear was bad enough—predictions on who would "get" her, comparisons between herself and the last selkie they'd caught, and worse. Mixed in were orders to crewmates and a demand that someone go and tell "his lordship" of their catch.

It was strange to hear so much of the human language after so long amid the selkies. Strange to hear it from people in front of her instead of by a voice on the other side of a magic mirror. Strange to hear it spoken freely; strange to hear it in Atìrsen accents instead of selkie ones.

Now that she was on solid ground, she set to trying to untangle herself from the net without anyone noticing. She hadn't gotten far when Lord Arran loomed up over her, flanked by two of his knights. "Well, what have we caught?" He surveyed her with a cold, appraising look, then raised an eyebrow, a hint of surprise coloring his expression. "My, my, your highness. I hardly expected to find you here, in the middle of the wild seas, particularly not in such... attire."

Oh, bother! Well, if he'd recognized her, there was nothing for it but to try to turn the situation to her advantage. Ceana gave up on trying to free herself and instead pushed herself into a sitting position. "Nor did I expect to see you, Lord Arran. I will thank you to have your men release me from this net at once."

"Certainly." Lord Arran made an impatient gesture at two of the crewmen. "Remove the net from her highness, but be sure to keep hold of her."

Ceana waited impatiently while the crewmen pulled the net away. She stood the minute she was free of the ropes, pulling away when one of the men tried to grab her wrists. "Now, I insist that you turn this ship around and take me home at once. That is an order, Lord Arran."

"I'm afraid not, your highness," Lord Arran replied. "I sail on urgent business that will not be delayed. Business that may interest you, it seems. Tell me, where did you acquire that cloak that you wear?"

"It was given to me." Ceana tilted her chin. "Unlike you and your men, Lord Arran, I did not steal what rightfully belongs to another." She gave a significant glance around the ship, at the many men with seal-cloaks over their shoulders. Lord Arran, strangely, wore only an ordinary cloak, and Ceana prayed that Lady Eilidh or one of Onora's agents had stolen his wife's cloak back from him.

Lord Arran's other eyebrow joined the first one in arching towards his hairline. "Oh? And what promises did you make to acquire it, I wonder?"

Ceana flushed despite herself. "I made no promises. It was left behind by an ancestor and came to me, and I chose to make use of it. What business out here is so urgent that you cannot obey my commands?"

Whatever Lord Arran might have answered, it was forestalled by a sudden commotion off the left side of the bow. He turned towards the sound just as Ceana heard Fionntan's voice in her head: *"Lady Kenna, if you can, run!"*

Oh no. If he was trying to rescue her...She made a break for the rail, but two of Lord Arran's men lunged after her. One caught her hair and yanked her back, and she screamed before she could stop herself. The other caught her as she fell, pinning her arms to her sides with one arm.

She couldn't help a whimper of fear, even as she struggled against her captors. Lord Arran glanced over at her, then turned away again. Up at the bow, several men were jabbing downwards with long harpoons, while others hauled on the lines of another net-and-spar arrangement like the one Ceana had been caught in.

One of the harpooners suddenly vanished, yanked off the deck from below by his weapon. There came a splash as he hit the water. In that same moment, the men on the ropes gave a mighty heave. The net came up, two selkie Guards within, both yelling and scrabbling for their daggers. One got his blade free and slashed through the thin cords of the net. But the moment he dropped to the deck, three of Arran's men set upon him. The other tried to dive out and help, but his foot caught in the net, and he ended up dangling upside down. One of the crewmen grabbed his cloak and yanked it off, over his head.

However Fionntan had intended this rescue to go, Ceana didn't think this was it. None of her struggles seemed to loosen the grip of the men holding her, but she had a voice now—she could use it. "Go!" she yelled. "Leave me—run! Lord Arran is going to at—"

One of the men holding her clamped his hand over her mouth. She tried to bite him, but he'd pulled his sleeve over his palm, so she ended up with only a mouthful of cloth. Still, she prayed her warning had been enough.

A sudden thud to Ceana's right pulled her attention that way. The second in a pair of selkie Guards vaulted onto the deck, clearly having climbed up the side of the ship. Both of the pair dashed towards Ceana and the men holding her, but others of Arran's crew ran to intercept them.

At the bow, another of the harpoon-men was jerked forward, but instead of falling off, he planted his feet and yanked back, pulling the selkie at the other end partway onto the ship. Ceana recognized Nes as he scrambled to reorient himself, halfway over the rail. *No, no, no...*She thrashed harder and was rewarded with a cry of pain from one of those holding her. Then something flashed in her periphery, and she felt a cold blade pressing to her throat. Something warm trickled down her skin, and she froze.

In the space of another breath, Fionntan appeared, launching himself up from the side of the ship, grabbing a rope, and swinging onto the deck. Barehanded, he struck the man who'd pulled up Nes. The man fell back and lost his grip on the harpoon, letting Nes drop back into the sea. Then Fionntan drew his sword and dashed to the two by the net. He cut the dangling Guard free and disabled two of those who'd been mobbing the other Guard. Then he turned, spotted Ceana and the two Guards nearest her, and dashed down the deck.

Lord Arran waited until Fionntan was halfway down the deck. Then, in an almost conversational tone, he said over his shoulder to those holding Ceana, "Gentlemen, if any of these creatures come within ten feet of our position, slit our guest's throat."

Fionntan skidded to a stop, and the two Guards who'd been trying to reach Ceana stopped pressing forward, though they didn't stop fighting. Lord Arran nodded. "Much better. Now, king of the selkies, set down your sword and tell your men to do the same."

Fionntan didn't budge. "Release her first," he shot back, matching Arran's language. Switching to the selkie tongue, he called to Ceana, "Lady Kenna, are you all right? Have they hurt you badly?"

With the one man's hand still over her mouth, Ceana couldn't reply, but she met Fionntan's eyes and tried to silently beg him to forget her and go. He could still get away, she thought, if he and his men moved fast enough. Lord Arran wouldn't dare kill her, even if he threatened to—but, of course, Fionntan couldn't know that.

Lord Arran stepped between the two of them. "You have five men against twenty. Lay down your weapons and you will all live. Refuse and the lady you sought to rescue will have the pleasure of watching all of you die for her." He turned to look at Ceana and gestured for his man to remove his hand from her face and for the other to take away the knife from her throat. "Your highness, do you wish to see such a fate for these men?"

Over Lord Arran's shoulder, Ceana could see the words hit Fionntan like a battering ram. His sword dropped slightly as his face turned suddenly white, his eyes widening in desperation and fear and despair. No hatred—but the lack felt somehow worse than the presence of such an emotion would have been. "What did you call her?" he asked, his voice hollow and haunted.

Something like amusement played across Lord Arran's face. "What is this? Do you not even know who you were failing to rescue?"

"She is one of my people," Fionntan replied, but his voice, normally steady, wavered just a little. "Kenna, what does this pirate mean?"

Lord Arran turned back to Ceana. Oh, he was definitely laughing to himself now! "Well, your highness? What do I mean?"

Oh, botheration! Ceana shot a last, swift prayer to Dèanadair that somehow this situation would come out all right—or, barring that, that lightning would strike both her and Lord Arran. Nonetheless, she straightened up as much as she could and lifted her head high. "My name is not Kenna. I am Ceana, seventh daughter of King Seòras and Queen Isla, descended of Good Queen Mey, who was born as Mairead of the Northwaves family. I am a princess of Atìrse, and as such, Lord Arran, I command you to release every true selkie on this ship under pain of death." Her voice broke a little on the last words—as the youngest in her family, she'd rarely given real commands even before spending months with the selkies, and she had certainly never pronounced anything so serious. But she had spoken it, and she'd not looked away as she said it.

Fionntan, by the look on his face, seemed to be struggling to keep calm amid a thunderstorm of emotions. Lord Arran laughed aloud, but not in a kind way. "So you have it. Her highness is, I think, not of your people. Perhaps, then, you would prefer to continue fighting, since her death would undoubtedly be a blow to the hearts of your enemies? Princess or not, my earlier warning stands."

All the warring emotions cleared from Fionntan's face, leaving only bitter rage behind, and he gripped his sword a little tighter. "You would slay the daughter of your own king? You, a lord, would kill a woman of your country, a woman who should be under your protection, so callously?"

The words, so clearly meant as stinging darts, found a stone-skinned target in Lord Arran. "She seems to have thrown her lot in with your people. I have no compunction about killing a traitor, whatever her rank, to save the necks of my men."

For a moment longer, Fionntan held his sword ready, knuckles pale around the hilt. Then, he dropped his weapon with a clatter to the deck. "Pirate, slaver—these words are too kind to apply to you. The lowest of the sand-worms is nobler than you. At least they clean the seas of rotting things. *You* are a pestilence to your own people."

"Very poetic," Lord Arran replied, his voice dry as an empty streambed in high summer. Louder, he addressed his men: "Bind these, remove their cloaks and weapons, and take them below." He stepped forward and picked up Fionntan's sword himself. "You have chosen wisely, selkie king. Tomorrow, you will have the opportunity to do so again, with all your people in the balance. I suggest you not fail in your choosing."

Fionntan did not resist as his hands were tied behind him or as one of Lord Arran's men pulled away his cloak and removed his other weapons. But he stared at Lord Arran with fury as deep as the ocean in his gaze. "What mean you by this?"

"You shall see." Lord Arran turned away and walked over to face Ceana. "As for you, little princess, your boldness impresses me. You seem to have gained the trust of the selkies. Help me and I will not inform your father that you turned traitor over the summer." His eyes glittered as he added, "And if you are particularly helpful, perhaps I will teach you how to properly tame a selkie, as you seem to have an interest in them."

Oh! How dare he even *suggest*—Had Ceana the ability, she would have spat in Lord Arran's face. The proposal deserved no less. But she couldn't, so instead she looked him in the eye and said, "I would never lower myself so much that I need take lessons from *you*. But by all means, tell Athair what you have seen of me. I'll have plenty to tell him as well, like how you and your confederates have been flagrantly abusing our neighbors and breaking the treaty for generations. I know which he will deem the greater crime."

"My dear princess, I believe you misunderstand the situation." Lord Arran stepped back with a laugh. "If you refuse to cooperate, you will be telling no tales to King Seòras. And even should someone else try to carry word to him, I believe that man would find the king far too preoccupied with mourning his daughter's untimely death to give those claims much heed."

"What?" Ceana's voice quavered as the word burst from her. "But..."

"I do believe I've made my position very clear. Nor will I be blamed for it, whether or not I reveal what you have done. It is, after all, very easy for accidents to happen at sea." Lord Arran paused. "And, of course, in a time of mourning and confusion, with my people controlling the seas...an enterprising man such as myself could go very far indeed. There are many who believe Atìrse needs a leader willing to reach for more than simply *peace*."

He wouldn't. Surely he wouldn't. Yet she couldn't miss the implications of what he'd said. "So, you intend to wipe out the selkies and then take Atìrse's throne for yourself? Is that your plan?"

"I would hardly put it so crudely, but you are not incorrect. Of course, should you choose to cooperate with me, plans can be changed. I would hardly act against the kin of one of my allies." Arran turned and started to walk away. "Have the princess locked in one of the cabins, so she can rethink her decision in comfort."

Oh no. *Oh no.* Now it wasn't just the selkies at risk. Now it was her own people. Her family, certainly, but all of Atìrse—they didn't need a leader like Arran. Not a grasping man willing to destroy or enslave an entire race for his own satisfaction. She had to do something to stop him, but what? She had no leverage, no cards left to play...

No. Wait. She had *one* thing she could offer. She would have to hope it would be enough. "Wait! Lord Arran, wait!"

Arran stopped and faced her once more. "Have you changed your mind so quickly, your highness?"

"Not exactly." Ceana swallowed and forced the words up her throat. "You offered me a bargain, so I'll offer you one. You want power in Atìrse. So, let the selkies go, as I said. The ones on this ship, the ones back in Atìrse, all of them, including Lady Eilidh. Just let them disappear and return to Emain Ablach. Set aside your plans to attack them now or in the future. Then, once I have received confirmation that every still-living captured selkie or their descendants have returned home, and once you are through the expected period of mourning for your wife having gone with them, I will give you leave to ask my father for my hand. I will entertain no other suitors in that time. I will tell Athair that I consent to the marriage. You will have the ear of the throne and we would be third in line to inherit it, as so many of my sisters have wed outside of Atìrse—third in line, and Onora is childless. Surely that is a safer choice than the gamble of attacking the selkies and attempting a coup. It would certainly cost the lives of far fewer of your men."

She thought she had spoken well, and she felt a momentary glow of pride. But then Lord Arran threw back his head and laughed aloud. "Do not mistake me for a fool, your highness. Whether or not you consented, your father would never entertain such an idea. Even were you to convince him, your sisters would see that I was dead or exiled long before any wedding could take place. No, I will keep to my own plans, and it remains your choice as to whether or not you will aid me in them."

What else could she do? Ceana glanced at Fionntan, whose fury seemed to have faded into numb shock. He might have ideas, but if he was down in the hold, and she was in a cabin… "Fine. But you gave his majesty a choice as well, and you are sending him to the hold. Should he and I not have the same treatment, as he is of higher rank than either you or I?"

"If you insist, very well," Lord Arran sighed. He addressed his guards again. "Remove the princess's cloak and lock her in the hold with our other captives."

"Yes, m'lord," the men holding Ceana muttered. One yanked Ceana's cloak over her head, pulling several strands of her hair in the process. The other marched her towards the other selkies, who were being pulled down the stairs to the hold.

Ceana slumped and let herself be pushed along. This wasn't what she had planned when she made that comment to Lord Arran. But, then again, she wasn't exactly *surprised* by how he'd interpreted it. It wasn't as if anything else had gone to plan today.

She glanced at Fionntan again, but she could only see the back of his head and the hopeless slope of his shoulders. Would he even be willing to entertain whatever little help she could offer? Perhaps he would, for the sake of his people—but he just as likely might think that whatever aid she could give wasn't worth acknowledging someone who'd lied so many times to him.

So, she did the only thing she had left to do and began another exhausted, desperate prayer. *Dèanadair, we're in trouble now. Show us the Path You have made before our feet; show us the next steps You wish us to walk. Let tomorrow not be the day we walk the Final Path and enter Your realm, but let Lord Arran and the evildoers who follow him receive their just end, as You have promised all the wicked will. And please, oh please, let Fionntan and the selkies live long enough to hate me.*

Chapter 37
IMPRISONED

She continued her prayer all the way down into the hold, which was lined with barred cells on either side. Lord Arran's men shoved them into the cells: Ceana and Fionntan each with their own on one side, the four Guard split between two on the other side. The selkies were additionally each chained to the wall by one foot, and their hands remained bound. Ceana expected Arran's men to do the same to her, but instead they simply took her bag and forced her to turn out her pockets. They let her keep most of what she'd had in them, though they took her knife, scissors, needle, and—worst of all—her message necklace. Then they locked her cell and left her there. She caught doubtful glances from a few of them as they went. Perhaps they hadn't realized that serving Lord Arran would mean treason.

She should be able to do something with that. Convince them to help her instead of Lord Arran. That was what Onora would do. But Ceana wasn't Onora, and she didn't even know where to begin. Anyway, it wasn't as if any of Arran's men had hung around for her to talk to.

She sank to the floor of her cell, her back against the sloping wall. Across the way, she could see the Guard going back-to-back, untying one another's hands and rubbing their sore wrists. She recognized all four of them; they'd been in the rotation of those Fionntan trusted enough, or was close enough to, that he chose them to accompany him and Ceana when they went on outings outside the keep. She'd learned their names—Fáelán, Éibhir, Ardgal, Árni—and something of their stories. She knew they were, every one of them, willing to die for Fionntan and for the other selkies. Now they just might, if they didn't end up enslaved instead because of her.

Beside her, Fionntan twisted his arms about, his face set in concentration as he attempted to reach the knots binding his own wrists without anyone to help him. Ceana eyed the length of the chain binding him to the wall, then scooted over to the bars separating them. She opened her mouth to speak, but the words she wanted to say refused to come out. So, she took refuge in the habit she'd developed over the last months, pulling out her tablet and stylus and writing what her mouth couldn't say.

She slid tablet and stylus between the bars and towards Fionntan. But his attention remained fixed away from her. Pursing her lips, she made several quick, deep lines at the very edge of the tablet wax so the force of the stylus would push the whole thing closer to him. Still, he did not turn.

Ceana cleared her throat, nudging the tablet still closer. Now he glanced over and down, then looked away again. "You might as well use your own voice. We're not in Emain Ablach; it's not as if my vow applies."

Ceana flinched, half at the bitterness in his voice and half at how he called her—*you*, not *thou*. Not that she deserved to be called *thou* by him. Not when she'd lied to him so long. Not when it was her fault he and his men were captured. But knowing those things didn't make it hurt any less.

She swallowed, cleared her throat again. She had to force the words out, even as simple as they were. "I just...I could help with the ropes, since there's no one else. I think I can fit my hands through the bars."

For a moment, she thought he would refuse. Then, wordlessly, he slid over and turned, offering his hands to her. She reached through the bars and picked at the knot until the rope fell away.

Fionntan picked the rope up and moved away again, still without looking at her or the tablet. Ceana slumped again, resting her head on the corner formed by the wall and the bars. Across the way, she could hear the Guard quietly discussing options for escape, speculating on whether they'd be fed and if that could be an opportunity to jump their captors, debating how hard it would be to pry out the thick staples holding their chains to the wall.

Did they have any chance of escaping the fate Lord Arran had planned for them? She couldn't even call Onora for help anymore. At least Onora would know to be on guard, would know better when Lord Arran claimed he had nothing to do with Ceana's death. At least Onora might still catch Lord Arran in the act of attacking Emain Ablach or, at worst, on his way back from the attack. Yet even if she did, Ceana would be dead by then, and who knew how many selkies would be either killed or captured.

She should pray more, she knew. That was the proper response to desperate times. But she couldn't seem to get any further than *"Please, Dèanadair,"* repeated over and over, sometimes whispered under her breath and sometimes simply echoed in her thoughts.

It was hard to tell time in the hold, with no windows to show the changing light and the only illumination coming from a few lamps hanging on support beams. But Ceana thought an hour or two had passed when she finally managed to find her voice again. "I'm sorry. I really am. I never intended any of this. I know you might not believe me, but it's true. And I'm sorry that I've gotten you all into...all this."

The selkie Guardsmen glanced towards her, offered faint and hopeless smiles, but otherwise remained focused on their efforts to dig the chain staples from the wall. Fionntan remained still, head bowed, but after several long moments, he replied, "What were your intentions, then, your highness?"

His tone was distant and tight and oh, so tired. And though he did not seem to speak to wound, his address still cut. Ceana clutched the edges of her sleeves, wishing the pain were a physical one, something she could bandage and salve, rather than something inside her that would remain raw and bleeding. "I...I wanted to understand. I told thee—" She saw how Fionntan flinched at that, and hastily adjusted—"I told you that the offer of a marriage alliance was my idea —"

"So, when you failed to catch me the human way, you decided to come try to win me by another method?" *Now* Fionntan's tone was meant to cut, and cut it did, as keenly as his sword ever had. "You thought my heart would fail where my honor held fast?"

"Nothing like that!" Ceana wished Fionntan would turn around and look at her so he could *see* that she spoke the truth. Yet, at the same time, she wished he'd stay just as he was so she wouldn't have to see his gaze filled with the hatred he must feel for her. "I swear to you, it was nothing like that. I never even planned to see you again, except from a distance. If you hadn't found me—If I hadn't been kin to Mairearad, Aíbinn, and Uaine—I would have stayed away from you.

"But I didn't understand why you were so offended when my father offered the alliance. I was listening from outside, and I heard what you said. You called us slavers and kidnappers, and you talked about buying your forgetfulness. I didn't understand, and I wanted to understand, and since your people never linger long enough ashore to talk to them, the only way I could think of to find answers was to come to you."

"Yet you had an easy enough time finding a seal-cloak." Fionntan didn't snap, but he didn't need to. The weight of judgement in his voice was enough.

"Most of what I said about my cloak was true." Ceana sighed, thinking of Queen Moireach. Would she ever see her again? "It's been passed down since Queen Mey—Queen Mairead. Maimeó had it, but she thought it was a…a replica, I suppose you could say. Not a true seal-cloak, but something that looked like and worked like one. She had no idea it was real. She prayed for nearly an hour before she decided to let me use it."

"I see." Fionntan replied. Ceana, guessing by his tone that he wished to hear no more, kept her mouth shut. Again, time dragged on. Ceana occupied herself by working her tablet back across the floor until she could reach through the bars and grab it. Then she slowly smoothed the surface so not even the smallest ridge remained.

No guards came to check on them, though Ceana supposed there was no reason for them to do so. The only sign of life other than themselves was a ship's cat that meandered down the line of cells, occasionally stopping to sniff here or there. It paused by the occupied cells, staring at Ceana with bright yellow eyes. Ceana slowly blinked at it, as Onora had taught her, and held out a hand, inviting it closer. She could see the stub-tail that marked it as a Glassraghey cat, much like Onora's Càirdeil, and she wondered how Lord Arran had come by one. Glassraghey folk rarely gave away their cats; it had been a great honor when they gifted one to the Atìrsen royal family years ago. Perhaps this one had wandered on by accident, for Ceana couldn't imagine Lord Arran finding sufficient favor to merit one.

Whatever the cat's reasons for being there, it slid through the bars and let Ceana pet its head and ears for a few minutes. Then it ducked away and padded off again, leaving Ceana and the selkies alone once more.

At last, Fionntan spoke again. "If you came only for answers about why we refused an alliance, why did you stay so long? You learned those answers when I spoke to you in the Halls of the Lost. You could have left then."

"I could have." Ceana had wondered that herself on a few occasions. "But I wanted to learn more. I hurt you once because I thought I knew everything I needed to know when I truly knew nothing. I didn't want to do that again. I wanted to know how I could help you. And I wanted...I wanted *you* to understand as well. You seemed so shocked when I told you that we didn't know about what we'd done. I thought if I talked to you more, maybe...maybe you'd be more willing to give us a chance to set things right."

"Is that all you stayed for?" Fionntan's voice was quiet; his head had sunk forward until it almost rested on his crossed arms. Ceana had never seen him so despondent, but she could hardly blame him. "Only royal business?"

Ceana couldn't answer for a long moment as she searched not just for words, but for an answer. But, at last, she managed to reply,

"No. Not only royal business. I'd found family in Emain Ablach. I was starting to find friends. And I had found a land that was lovely and beautiful and felt as much like home as Atìrse did. I didn't want to say goodbye to any of the people or to the land so soon, especially since I didn't think I'd be able to come back."

She managed a weak little laugh and immediately wished she hadn't. "You'd probably laugh at me if you knew how many times I wished you hadn't turned me down simply so I wouldn't have had to leave. Then I could have learned all I learned and loved all the people and places I loved as myself and not as someone else. I guessed that you would hate me as soon as you found out who I was, and that it would make everything worse again, so I put off leaving as long as I could. It still wasn't long enough."

"No amount of time in Emain Ablach could ever be enough," Fionntan replied softly. No doubt he was thinking about how he, too, would probably never see his home again, though for very different reasons. And his plight was far worse. At least in Ceana's case, Emain Ablach would have still been there, wonderful and beautiful and filled with those she'd come to love. For Fionntan, it would be empty and broken, shattered by Lord Arran's attack.

The thought was too terrible to bear. Hoping to get away from it for a little while, Ceana asked, "Why were you looking for me earlier?"

"We caught our latest rescue trying to sabotage us and realized he was a spy." Fionntan didn't say *like you*, but Ceana wondered if he thought it all the same. "Arran or another of his ilk must finally have caught on to the fact that all our safeguards focus on finding those who have their cloaks through a false vow, not an inheritance. We relied too long on the fact that the slavers are loath to share their power with others once they have it. By then, Mairearad and Aíbinn had read what you sent them, and they feared that his message to you was meant as a trap."

His tone once more took on a bitter note. "Of course, it seems to have been a trap for the rest of us instead. What was in the message in reality? Was it what you said, or did he warn you that there was an attack coming?"

Ceana shook her head. "There was no message. Or...there was, but it wasn't about my family or the attack. I made that up so I could go back to Atìrse without anyone trying to follow me and getting hurt. He did send me a message a few days ago, the same day you caught him attacking me, but it was a threat—that he'd recognized me and would tell you all if I didn't keep away from him."

"Ah. He did try to say something about you, but I refused to listen." Fionntan paused, his head lowering a little more. "Perhaps I should have."

"I'm glad you didn't." Ceana fiddled with her stylus. "Did you read the note I sent you? Or did Mairearad tell you the other thing in what I sent her?"

"I didn't have time to read it before I learned you were missing," Fionntan replied, still not looking at her. "Mairearad mentioned something about strange runes."

"The boy—the spy—was putting them around the base of the island. They talked about fire, stone, and waking." With nothing else to do, Ceana slowly traced the runes as she remembered them in her tablet. "I think Arran may be trying to awaken the flamemount."

"He would be more likely to cause an earthquake than rouse the flames." Fionntan heaved a long, shuddering sigh. "If he does so, and he has the island surrounded ..."

He didn't finish the sentence. He didn't need to. Ceana already knew what it would mean, and she could tell from the Guards' expressions that they did as well. "I'm sorry," she whispered.

Fionntan made no answer. Once again, they sat in silence until the rustle of soft footsteps came from the stairway. Ceana sat up and looked towards the sound to see Lady Eilidh emerge into the hold, carrying a flickering lantern in one hand. With the other hand, she clutched a dark blue cloak around her neck. A pang of deeper sorrow rang through Ceana's heart. She *had* hoped that Onora's agent had been able to free Lady Eilidh, but it seemed Lord Arran had brought her along instead. How cruel of him to make her look upon the destruction of her own people, knowing she had allowed him to carry it out!

Lady Elidh made her way along the row of cells until she reached Fionntan's. There she spoke, her voice low and rough, as if she had to work for each word. "Your majesty?"

Slowly, Fionntan raised his head. "Lady Eilidh. Why have you come here?"

Lady Eilidh gave a little gasp and almost seemed to sway. Ceana wondered why—until she realized that Fionntan had spoken in the selkie language. How long had it been since Lady Eilidh heard the tongue of her own people?

Then Lady Eilidh dropped to her knees and bowed her head. "Your majesty, please—please, will you forgive me?"

"What do you ask me to forgive?" Fionntan asked, his words slow and measured.

Tears glittered at the corners of Lady Eilidh's eyes. "I—I betrayed you all. I told Arran of how to find Emain Ablach."

Gasps of shock came from some of the Guards, and one of them bit back an oath. A hint of fury flickered in Fionntan's eyes. "Why?"

"He promised me my cloak," Lady Eilidh whispered, her voice shaking. "He swore to me in Dèanadair's name that he would return it to me if I only told him where my home lay. I...I could not resist." Her hands, clutching the bars of Fionntan's cell, tightened. "I should have. For years I have held fast, no matter what he tried. But when he offered my cloak ..."

She seemed to choke on the words, shaking with suppressed sobs. After a few minutes, she went on, "I thought he would return it to me as soon as I told him, and I could come home at last, confess, and warn everyone before he arrived. But he will not give it to me until we reach the island."

"Snake," one of the Guard muttered. Ceana thought it was Fáelán. The others muttered their assent, yet still Fionntan said nothing, just looked at Lady Eilidh.

Lady Eilidh went on, voice still wavering. "I have...I have tried to make things right. I am always under the eye of Arran or his people, but where I can slow him, I have. And I tried to send for help. One of the faery folk came to me in the last months, an emissary from his mistress, and I told him what had happened. I think he may have followed me onto the ship. Yet, if he is able to bring help, I do not know if it will arrive in time."

Her tears fell at last, shining in the lantern light as they ran down her cheeks and splashed on the floorboards. "I know I cannot do enough to make up for my treachery. But I beg your forgiveness all the same."

Fionntan reached forward and placed one of his hands on hers. The anger in his gaze had died, leaving behind only pity and a deep weariness. "You were faced with a cruel choice, before which few could stand. You are forgiven. But should you see an opportunity to halt Arran's plans, whatever risk it might mean for you, take it."

"I will," Lady Eilidh gasped. Still, she wept, but a bit of hope now flickered on her face. "Thank you, your majesty."

She stood, picking up her lantern. "I do not know how much I can do. But if I can send you any help or relief before the dawn, I will do it." With that, she left again.

As soon as she was gone, Fionntan slumped again, head falling onto his crossed arms. He seemed even more exhausted than before. Ceana wished she could comfort him somehow, but she could think of nothing to say. And so the silence stretched on between them once more.

Eventually, Ceana's stomach began to make its emptiness known, and she dug in her pockets until she came up with the three apples she'd brought from the Northwaves home. She started to raise one of them to her mouth, then hesitated, glancing around at the others. They had nothing with them; Lord Arran's men had searched them much more thoroughly.

So, she crept to the front of her cell and called to the Guards until she had their attention. Once they turned towards her, she tossed two of the apples to them, one to each group. "I'm sorry I don't have more."

They just nodded in acceptance. "'Twill be enough," Ardgal replied quietly.

Ceana returned to her spot against the wall, watching as the Guards shared their apples between them. She glanced at the remaining one, then at Fionntan. With a sigh, she set it on his side of the bars and gave it a push so it rolled over to him. "You should eat something."

Fionntan roused himself enough to pick it up and look at it. "You need it more than I." Pain edged his voice now—physical pain, Ceana thought. "I've survived missing meals before, and I doubt they'll bring any of us food. It's always easier to break the will of someone who's hungry."

"Then you should have it," Ceana replied. His words, much to her relief, bolstered her confidence in her decision. "If Lord Arran has his way, I'm ..." She swallowed, forcing the words out. "I'm going to die tomorrow. Maybe if you're not completely starving, you'll have a better chance of resisting or even escaping."

For a moment, Fionntan's eyes actually flickered to her. Then he turned away again, eyed the apple, and, with more effort than she would have expected, broke it in half along the stem. He passed one half back to her. "We'll both eat."

They did so in silence. Ceana nibbled on the fruit, trying to make it last as long as she could, and she could tell Fionntan was doing the same. All too soon, though, the last bites were gone, and it seemed to have done little to satisfy her appetite.

She'd thought perhaps Fionntan would say something again, but he remained still. So, she finally cleared her throat. "I truly am sorry for everything—for offering an alliance when I didn't know what we'd done to you, for deceiving you for so long, for getting you into this, all of it. I know I don't deserve it, but could you ever forgive me?" Perhaps, if even Lady Eilidh could receive mercy ...

Fionntan still didn't reply. But after several long and silent moments, Ardgal roused himself enough to say, "We cannot speak for his majesty, but we forgive you, your highness. You were as courageous as any of us earlier."

Ceana offered him the best smile she could manage under the circumstances. "Thank you. I wish I could have done more."

Ardgal shrugged philosophically. "You tried. 'Tis the most any of us can do."

He and Ceana both glanced at Fionntan, but Fionntan said nothing. Ceana's heart fell as she realized how foolish her hope had been. Lady Eilidh had been a desperate prisoner who only wished to return home. But Ceana had lied to Fionntan over and over again, had chosen to deceive him for her own ends—and now, because of that deception, he was trapped in the hold of his enemy with the demise of himself and his people looming over him. Of course there could be no forgiveness for her.

More time went by, so much that Ceana began to wonder if Fionntan had fallen asleep where he sat. Then he stirred and tilted his head slightly to look at her out of the corner of one eye. "The marriage alliance truly was your idea?"

What did it matter now? But Ceana just nodded. "It was."

Fionntan seemed to gather himself, as if the words took great effort. "Why? Why make a change when you believed we had peace?"

"We tolerated each other, I thought. I wished for us to be able to help each other. I thought it was a shame our peoples weren't friends." But the words were sour on her tongue with the edge of untruth, and the sourness lingered after she'd spoken. So, after a moment, she added, "And I didn't know what else to do. I wanted to serve my people, like all my sisters did, but Athair and Màthair said they didn't need me to marry anyone and that I could wed who I wished. I didn't know how to even think about marriage without it being for the good of Atìrse and whatever land I married into. The alliance with your people seemed like the only option left."

"Hmm." There almost seemed to be a hint of fondness in Fionntan's tone, though it was overlayed with hurt. "I think I understand." He took a deep breath, slow as if even that small action as a struggle. "What did you intend to do after you left Emain Ablach?"

"Tell my family what I'd learned and try to do what I could to make things right between my people and yours." Ceana sighed, leaning her head against the wall. "After that, I don't know. It would have depended if the half my heart I left in your country ever came back to me." She shook herself, turning to look directly at Fionntan. "Were you hurt earlier? You don't sound well."

"I'm a selkie out of water and without my cloak," Fionntan replied. He sounded as if he were trying to take a wry tone but was too tired to pull it off. "Even a slow death is hardly pleasant. Arran and his ilk have ways to keep their captives alive a bit longer, but 'tis still painful. Why else do you think those who are captured go through with the sham of a marriage they're forced into?"

Ceana winced. "I'm sorry. Is there anything I can do?"

Fionntan shook his head. "Only if you can work miracles, your highness. By the time morning comes, I fear that's what we'll need."

Chapter 38
BATTLE AT EMAIN ABLACH

Soon after that, most of the selkies lay down or leaned back against the side of the ship, trying to sleep. Ceana did the same, but she managed only a fitful rest, filled with unpleasant dreams.

She woke some time later to a voice softly hissing her name and something that felt like a cat's paw batting her face. Ceana blinked awake to see a slender man standing over her. All the lamps save one had been put out, and the stranger's features and form were shadowy and indistinct in the darkness. As she drew breath to scream, he clapped a hand over her mouth. "Shh! Hush, highness. I mean thee no harm. I'm a friend to all of honor's kin."

Honor's kin? What—Oh! The words jogged a memory of Onora's instructions yesterday. She'd said to ask for Honor's cousin at the inn. This must be the same code. Ceana relaxed a little, remaining still, and the figure removed his hand from her mouth. "Good lass. I knew thou wert a clever one, even if thou art practically still a kitten. Now, listen closely. I've told my lady that thou and the others are held prisoner aboard here, as well as all of what our dishonorable host threatened yesterday. She's coming as quickly as the winds will allow, but I'm to do what I can for thee in the meantime. I can't smuggle all six of you out, alas, nor can I smuggle your cloaks to you—not with all this salt air about."

Ceana gave him a searching look that she knew was probably lost in the darkness. He went on, "Still, I've a few tricks left to me. Hold out thy hand."

Ceana did so obediently. The figure pressed what felt like a key into her palm. "That unlocks the chest in which the cloaks are kept. It's tucked just under the steps thou came down to get here from the deck. There's a false top to it with a few ordinary sea-cloaks, but thou willst be able to find what thou art after easily enough if thou dig a bit."

He next produced another slim, metal object, flatter than the key and about the length of Ceana's first finger. The sides were smooth except for a little knob in a groove along one of the narrow edges. "A sliding blade. Not long enough to use as a weapon, I'm afraid, but kept in thy hand at the right angle, it should do to free thy wrists if they bind thee again. Or, if thou'rt lucky enough to be left unbound, thou mayst be able to free someone else before anyone notices. It's been in my pockets long enough that it'll cut what thou needst it to cut the first time, every time. And, last but not least ..." He set a small vial next to the knife. "A bit of the potion these pirates use to make sure their captives don't die. Share it out among thy friends tomorrow morning. It should relieve their suffering and give them back a little of their strength. Divided among them all, 'twon't be a full dose, but 'twill be enough if thou'rt quick with the other tools I gave thee."

"Thank you," Ceana whispered. "But what am I to do with the rest? I'm trapped in this cell—did you happen to get its key?"

"If I had, we would be having a very different conversation right now, highness," the figure replied. "Thy best chance to act will likely be when they reach Emain Ablach and bring thee and the others up on deck. Our host has to give you all your opportunity to refuse him again, after all. Wait until everyone's attention is focused elsewhere, then move. I'll do my best to be on hand to help."

Ceana tucked the key and knife into one pocket and the vial into the other. "All right. I'll try to figure something out. But how will I know who you are so I know who to trust?"

"I imagine thou wilt recognize me." He rested a hand on her shoulder. "I'd best be off before anyone hears the two of us chattering. I'll see thee in the morning, I expect. In the meantime, rest well. Thou wilt need it."

Ceana yawned. "All right." She felt her eyes drifting closed, and almost before she knew it, she was sound asleep again. But this time, if she dreamed at all, they were peaceful dreams, and what else passed in the night, she knew not.

The next time Ceana woke, the lamps had been relit, and the selkies were awake, though none seemed happy about it. Árni, the youngest Guard member present, was trying to perform some semblance of his morning exercises, but his movements were punctuated with a repeating chorus of pained, barely-audible exclamations. On the other hand, Fáelán, one of the older Guard, lay as still as possible and appeared to be fully focused on taking one breath after another.

Fionntan remained sitting, but Ceana couldn't miss the way he curled forward, gripping his knees, no more than she could miss the pain in each breath he took. She crawled over to the bars between them and pulled the vial from her pocket. "Fi—Your majesty?" She stretched her hand as far towards him as she could. "Can you drink a little of this?"

He managed to turn a little to look at her. "What ...?"

The way he spoke, even that one word must have been a struggle. Ceana strained to extend her arm a little further. "Someone came last night. A friend of my family. He recognized me, and he brought this. He said it'll help. There's enough there for each of you to have a little."

Fionntan still eyed it uncertainly. Árni slumped, holding onto the bars that made up the door of his cell. "I'll try it. If it doesn't kill me, the rest of you know it's safe to have some."

Fionntan took a deep breath. "Very well. Do it. Give him the bottle."

Ceana nodded and moved to the front of the cell. She couldn't quite reach Árni, even when they both stretched forward as far as they could, so she waited a few minutes, carefully noting the boat's movement. Then, choosing her moment, she rolled the vial across the space between their cells. It bumped to a stop against his fingers. He grabbed it and held it up to eye level, judging the amount. Then he uncorked it and took a long sip.

Every open eye was fixed on Árni. He stayed still for a few minutes, just breathing. Then he corked the vial again and experimentally stretched, testing each limb. "It helps. The pain's less, and it's easier to breath."

"Wait another ten minutes," Ardgal said, his voice quiet. "Make sure."

They all waited, counting off the heartbeats. Árni continued to stretch, working through all the different exercises. At last, at six hundred heartbeats, Ardgal spoke again. "Well?"

"Still fine. I feel a little stronger than I did." Árni stretched his arms above his head. "The princess's friend is a good one."

Fionntan gave a decisive nod. "Each of you drink some. Whatever's left, I'll take."

Ceana expected someone to question him, but none did. They passed the bottle hand to hand, each drinking a little and then waiting ten minutes to hand it off. When a last mouthful remained, they rolled it back over to Fionntan, who caught it and drained it to the final drops.

In the minutes that followed, Ceana could see Fionntan visibly relaxing and could hear his breathing grow steadier and steadier. At last, when the ten minutes had passed, Fionntan straightened up. "Did this friend bring anything else?"

Ceana dug the knife and key from her pocket. "These. One moment." She pulled out her tablet again and wrote, in abbreviated form, what her midnight visitor had told her. Then she passed the tablet to Fionntan.

He read it, and this time she actually heard in her mind as he passed on the message to the others. They all nodded thoughtfully. As Fionntan finished, Ardgal asked, in the same thought-speech, *"So, we'll be nearly home when we're brought up. If even one of us gets off the ship with his cloak, he can bring help and warn those on the island of the attack."*

Ceana smoothed out the tablet and hastily wrote, *"Warn of more than attack. Don't forget the firemount runes."*

Fionntan passed this message to the others, then said, "So, whoever can get off the ship also must both warn Emain Ablach and find a way to prevent the rune-magic." He shut his eyes for a moment, thinking, then went on: *"Very well. Here's what we'll do..."*

⁂

Arran's men came for them about an hour later. Fionntan and his Guard made a show of weakness, moving stiffly and slowly and groaning as the crewmen forced them to their feet and tied their arms behind their backs, winding the ropes several times around. Another crewman ordered Ceana out of her cell and bound her as well, though he used only a single loop of rope for her wrists. Ceana kept her hand closed tightly around the little knife, waiting for an opportunity. Fionntan had told her to watch for a moment when no one was directly behind her and, ideally, when she had either a wall or the sea to her back. Not too soon, lest there be too many opportunities for someone to notice. Not too late, or she'd not have time to free anyone else.

As they made their way out of the hold and up to the deck, Ceana noted the chest beneath the hatchway stairs, just where she'd been told it would be. It looked too large and heavy for her to move, but she thought there would be space for her to open it while it was still under the steps. It didn't look as if others had moved it much.

They emerged onto the ship's deck, and Ceana had to squint in the bright morning sunshine. Other ships had joined them in the night, she saw, bringing the fleet's strength to seven ships. Teine-Falamh loomed out of the sea, its sides jagged and unforgiving, and Ceana prayed that Lord Arran would think Lady Eilidh had steered him wrong.

But when she glanced over her shoulder, she saw both Lord Arran and Lady Eilidh with the helmsman. Lady Eilidh stood with her head bowed, barely looking up enough to see where they were going, her shoulders slumped. Lord Arran stood next to her, his hand on her shoulder in what might have seemed like a loving gesture had his grip not been clearly tight enough to hurt. He surveyed the firemount, a bright hunger in his gaze. "Is this the place?"

Lady Eilidh nodded once. Lord Arran smiled. "Excellent. And I see that our prisoners have been produced as well." Leaving Lady Eilidh with the helmsman, he strode down to Ceana, the selkies, and the crewmen holding them. "Here we are. Home again, home again." He stopped and faced them. "I believe you've had ample time to think on your decisions. Have you reached a wiser conclusion yet?"

No one said a word. Ceana, having wedged herself at the back of the group, carefully slid the knife blade out of the handle and began to move it towards the rope around her wrists. The person who gave it to her had promised it would cut on the first try, but what exactly did that mean? How forceful did the cut have to be?

"No one?" Lord Arran gestured to Fionntan, and the crewmen pushed him forward. Fionntan stood with his shoulders stooped, slightly bent as if in pain, yet with his head up. "King of the selkies, I have heard of your quality from many a mouth. Surely an uncomfortable life is better than death. A few words from you would ensure that no more lives are lost than necessary."

For a moment, Fionntan remained silent, as if thinking on Arran's offer, or perhaps as if gathering strength for a reply. Ceana set the blade of the knife against her bindings, then pushed it forward. She felt the ropes loosen and caught them just before they could fall away entirely. Now she had to keep them in place and figure out how to cut the others free. If only she'd thought to leave one or two strands in place!

Fionntan's shoulders heaved with a deep, effortful breath. "Where there is life, there is hope. But to hand my people over to you would be to doom them to a living death—far better that they find their way down the Final Path to eternal life."

Lord Arran's expression pinched. "A noble sentiment. I wonder if your people share it." He gestured again to his crewmen. "Take him aside." As the men dragged Fionntan some yards off, Lord Arran faced the Guard. "Your king has decided to throw your lives and the lives of your kin away. Are there any among you who would prefer to survive? The one who helps me will maintain his freedom."

"We are the king's Guard, and we stand with our king," Ardgal replied, face set. "And so long as we are alive and our brethren are free, we will do what we must to keep them free."

The other Guard nodded their agreement. Árni stepped forward to stand by Ardgal and added, "We've vowed, all of us, to defend king and kin and home. We'll not break that vow for the promises of a slaver."

Lord Arran's face darkened. "I see." He gestured again to his crewmen, who roughly pulled the Guard aside. The Guard made only a cursory struggle, though they could have done more.

Now Lord Arran faced Ceana, but before he could say a word, Lady Eilidh spoke, her soft, rough voice barely audible. "Where is my freedom, my lord?"

Ceana turned, as did Lord Arran. Lady Eilidh stood at the base of the stairs from the rear deck, hands clenched at her sides, head now lifted. She looked as if she'd not slept in days. "Where is my freedom?" she repeated. "You promised me my cloak returned should I guide you here. We are here; where is my cloak?"

"Ah." Lord Arran gave a long-suffering sigh. "Must it be now?"

She nodded, taking a step towards the rail of the ship. Her motion must have held some meaning, for Lord Arran sighed again. "Very well." He turned to another of his crew. "Bring Lady Eilidh her cloak from my quarters."

The crewman saluted and hurried away. Lady Eilidh glanced towards Fionntan, glimmers of hope and regret in her gaze.

A moment later, the crewman returned with a bundled sealskin in his arms, which he handed to Lord Arran. Lord Arran, in turn, moved forward and held it out to Lady Eilidh. "As you insisted, here."

Lady Eilidh snatched it with a cry of relief, but the sound turned into a wail as the folds fell, revealing great rents and tears in the sealskin. She fell to her knees, clutching the tattered cloak to her chest. "You—I should have known you'd lie. You always lie."

Lord Arran regarded her impassively. "I may have failed to mention that the cloak had suffered some wear since you saw it last."

Suffered some wear! From what Ceana could see, though some of the damage may have been natural, the lower half was shredded nearly to ribbons in a way that looked disturbingly deliberate. But Lady Eilidh seemed too overcome to speak. She buried her face in her ruined cloak, shaking with silent sobs. As Lord Arran turned away, though, she looked up with an expression of such despairing rage as Ceana had never seen.

Lord Arran strode up and faced Ceana. "Your turn, your highness. Do you truly wish to die for these creatures? Are they worth your life? Are they worth your father's tears? Or will you aid me and live?"

Ceana clutched her little knife behind her and straightened her shoulders. "I've seen how you keep your promises. You might let me live today only to kill me or one of my sisters in a week. And even if that weren't so, even if I knew you'd keep your word in both the letter and the spirit of the vow, I would never help you destroy a whole people, especially not one we're at peace with. If my family must mourn, so be it, but they and I would rather they mourn me as one who died doing what is right than have me live as one who turned on her friends."

"Insufferably noble as your father, I see. I should have expected no less." Lord Arran turned away. "Very well. Men, take those four—" he gestured to the Guard members—"back to the hold. The selkie king and the princess will remain here to see what ruin they have enabled, but be certain to keep them separated. And you—" he pointed to two other crewmen—"activate the final runes."

No! Ceana hadn't had time to free any of the selkies yet; Arran couldn't take them away! But crewmen already moved to obey, some pulling the Guard towards the hold and the other two diving off the side. She had to find some way to delay them, or else go with them...but that would mean leaving Fionntan alone. Would that be better or worse?

She glanced around, searching for something that might help. There was the cat she'd seen last night, sidling up along the side of the ship near the selkies. Strange that it would be up here, but Ceana didn't have time to think about that. There were probably selkie patrols about, but if they hadn't already noticed the fleet, there'd be little Ceana could do to catch their attention. Lord Arran was already walking away, towards the prow of the ship.

But as she stood, torn, two things happened. The first was that, as Lord Arran passed near Lady Eilidh, she dropped her cloak and lunged up and forward. She drew Lord Arran's dagger from its sheath before he realized what had happened, and she slashed wildly at him. One blow landed on his arm, cutting through his shirt and producing a thin line of blood. He swore and grabbed for her arms.

At the same time, Fionntan seemed to have been somehow freed, for he turned and punched one of the crewmen holding him squarely in the jaw. The man toppled, and the other crewman jumped back and drew his sword. Just behind Fionntan, the cat darted away, towards the other selkies. Fionntan's voice shouted in Ceana's head: *"Go get the cloaks!"*

One of the men guarding Ceana was already running to help his companion against Fionntan, who'd grabbed the sword from the man he'd knocked unconscious. The other grasped Ceana's arm, but he wasn't looking at her. She'd never have a better chance. Ceana dropped the rope, swung her hand around, and stabbed the arm of the man holding her. He yelled in shock and let go, just as she'd hoped.

At once, she dashed down the stairs, scrambling to close the knife as she went. She could hear the man chasing after her for a few steps, but then voices called for him to let her go and help with the selkies. Ceana didn't stop to ask why Arran's crew would need help with four bound prisoners; she just gave thanks and shoved the knife back in her pocket.

She nearly slipped and fell as she whirled round the bottom of the steps, but she managed to keep her balance. She dropped to her knees in front of the chest and fumbled with the key. For a moment, it jammed, and her heart stuttered—had the man been wrong? Had she picked the wrong chest? Had she broken something? But then she wiggled it a little more and felt the key turn. The lock clicked open, and she threw up the lid. As she'd been told, there were a few weather-worn sea-cloaks on top, which she tossed aside. Then the false bottom, the same style as the false-bottom Ceana knew others in her family used, with a little bit of thread attached to one side to lift the thin piece of wood.

Beneath were the seal-cloaks, shining silvery-grey. Hers was on top. She flung it around her shoulders and almost immediately felt a little calmer. The other five were beneath it; she glanced through them quickly to make sure they were the right ones. Fionntan's, she recognized at once. The others, she felt less certain about, but they looked familiar. And, in any case, they were the only cloaks here.

She bundled all five into her arms and dashed back up the stairs, leaving the chest open. On deck, she found that Fionntan's Guard had been freed as well. Fáelán had managed to claim a sword from one of their captors, and Árni had a sea-axe. Éibhir and Ardgal had taken belaying pins from the railings, one for each hand, and were using them to devastating effect. Yet they were heavily outnumbered by Arran's crewmen, and Ceana could tell from the selkie's faces and their movements that the effects of the tonic were wearing off.

Where was Fionntan, though? Ceana searched the deck and spotted him and Lord Arran about halfway up the ship. Fionntan still had the sword he'd taken earlier, and he'd found a bit of cloth, a tarp perhaps, to wind around his arm and use as a makeshift shield. He fought with Lord Arran and another crewman and seemed to be holding his own for now, though blood trickled from wounds in several places. As Ceana watched, Lord Arran tried to slip away from the fight, only for Fionntan to cut off his escape, taking another cut from the crewman in the process. He, too, seemed to be lagging a bit, from both his injuries and the returning effects of having been cloakless and out of the water so long.

Ceana wanted to run straight to him and help him, but the Guard were closer. She adjusted her load of cloaks and dashed towards them, calling their names as she ran. Ardgal glanced her way, and he must have said something to his companions, for their movements shifted. In a complicated bit of motion that Ceana didn't quite comprehend, they allowed themselves to be pushed back, but somehow changed the direction so they were moving towards the place where the rail of the ship met the rear deck.

Ceana turned to meet them there, and they closed around her, still holding off the crewmen. "Be ready with those cloaks," Ardgal called over his shoulder to her. Then he clubbed one of Arran's men first in the gut and then over the back of the head and kicked him backwards. Both groups of fighters shifted, with Arran's men rushing to close the gap and Ardgal nudging Árni back by Ceana.

Ceana fumbled through the cloaks and produced the one that she thought was Árni's. He took it and tugged it over his head. Almost as soon as he did, he seemed to stand a little straighter. "Thanks, lady." Then, shoving his sea axe into his belt, he jumped up on the railing. He slid two steps along it, expertly matching the roll and sway of the ship, then grabbed the collar of one of Arran's men and yanked, allowing himself to fall backward at the same time.

Arran's man, caught off-guard, fell forward and tipped over the rail. Both hit the water with a splash. Ceana didn't see what became of them after that, for next Fáelán fell back beside her. He pulled his cloak from her arms before she could hand it to him and shrugged it on. "That's better." He waited a moment, watching those before them, then rushed back into the line, fighting just a bit more fiercely than before.

Éibhir was next; he dipped back just long enough for Ceana to hand him his cloak before returning to the fight. He managed to knock down another two men, then grabbed a third and, like Árni, leapt over the side of the ship.

Only Ardgal and Fionntan's cloaks were left. Ceana shifted Fionntan's cloak to hang over her shoulder and gathered Ardgal's so it would be ready as soon as there was a break in the fighting. With only him and Fáelán left, though, Ceana wondered how he would manage to pull back long enough to claim his cloak.

She glanced towards the bow of the ship. Fionntan was clearly slowing down, though he still kept his feet. Red covered his side, but at this distance, Ceana couldn't tell how much was his blood and how much was the blood of his enemies. With each stroke and step, Arran pushed him a little further back towards the rail. And unlike his Guard, who had taken their battles into the sea deliberately, Fionntan still had no seal-cloak.

A sudden *crack* rang out, and the ship shuddered. Ceana felt its timbers shift slightly beneath her feet. She didn't understand the movement, but Arran's men did, for a cry of alarm went up. Several dashed down the stairs to the hold, while others ran for the side and peered towards the waves. A call went up from several throats at once: "Seals in the water!" One of those who'd gone into the hold dashed back up, soaked head to toe, and yelled, "We're cracked—taking on water!"

"Finish these and take the fight to the sea," Lord Arran snapped, his words sharp and punctuated by the clash of his and Fionntan's blades. "Get to the other ships and protect them."

His men repeated the command up and down the ship. Crewmen stripped away from their battles, dashed to the sides, and dove in. As Ardgal and Fáelán flagged more and more, their movements growing steadily slower and less forceful, more of Arran's crewmen left those fighting them and dashed away to other tasks. Then, when only two remained, Ardgal and Fáelán pushed forward with a sudden surge of vigor. Caught by surprise, their foes dropped in a moment.

Ceana passed Ardgal his cloak. He pulled it on with a sigh of relief. "There. You'd best get clear of here, your highness. This ship will sink all the way any minute now."

"I still have King Fionntan's cloak." Ceana shifted it back into her arms. "I need to get it to him."

"I can take it, lady," Ardgal said. "Get safe."

Ceana still shook her head. "You're a warrior. Won't they need you—both of you? Go defend the island; I'll manage."

Ardgal bowed his head respectfully. "If you insist, I'll not gainsay a princess as bold as you." With that, he and Fáelán stowed their weapons and vaulted off the side.

Ceana took a deep breath and turned her attention towards the bow. Lord Arran had Fionntan backed up to the rail of the ship. How much longer could Fionntan hold out? *Dèanadair, let it be long enough.*

She ran, feet pounding the damp deck boards. Twice she nearly slipped; twice the shuddering of the ship nearly toppled her. But still she ran. Ahead, Fionntan blocked a slash; parried a thrust. He had next to no room to maneuver, but somehow he managed to prevent or evade most of Lord Arran's blows.

Then Lord Arran unleashed a particularly swift flurry of attacks. Fionntan parried each, but the force of the last sent him toppling backwards. As he fell, he dropped his sword and grabbed Lord Arran's arm. Arran tried to pull away, but Fionntan's weight carried him forwards, and both went over the rail.

No! Ceana strained for a little extra speed, but she had none to spare. She scrambled up and over the rail without a thought and dove after Fionntan. As her seal-shape slowly gathered round her, she lost her grip on Fionntan's cloak, and it stayed floating on the surface when she dove.

She could see Fionntan and Lord Arran some distance away, struggling against one another and against the water, each trying to keep his opponent down while surfacing often enough to breath himself. Lord Arran, like Fionntan, had lost his sword, but he'd drawn a second knife and slashed at Fionntan. Fionntan struck back barehanded, then caught Lord Arran's wrist and squeezed until Arran lost his grip on the dagger.

Ceana turned from the fight and doubled back for Fionntan's

cloak. She caught its edge in her mouth so she could pull it along, then looked to see what was happening. Lord Arran had gotten his hands around Fionntan's neck and squeezed as Fionntan's struggles grew weaker.

No time to waste. With several flips of her tail, Ceana shot towards the pair.

She barreled into Lord Arran's side, shoving him away. Air bubbled from his mouth as her attack knocked the breath from him, and with a parting kick, he swam for the surface.

Ceana let him go, spinning in the water and pushing Fionntan's cloak towards him. He fumbled weakly for it, and she continued to nudge it in the right directions until he could grasp it and pull it over his head. As it slid down, it wrapped round him in a familiar way, transforming him from man to seal.

Fionntan blinked dark eyes at her. Then he righted himself and darted for the surface. Ceana followed just behind. As their heads broke the water, Fionntan's voice slipped into Ceana's thoughts. *"Are you well, your highness?"*

Ceana nodded, but as she did, they heard a rumble from the direction of the island. Ceana spun, remembering—the runes! Lord Arran's men must have activated them when he ordered them to, and now the firemount was waking.

Fionntan's gaze darted between Lord Arran, now swimming towards one of the ships, and the island. Ceana could guess his thoughts. Lord Arran had to be stopped—killed, captured, anything as long as it meant he couldn't continue to terrorize the selkies. But if the magic continued, Emain Ablach could be destroyed.

How many of the selkies knew to look for the runes? Had any of them save Ceana seen them? Or had they been too focused on other things to investigate? The thought made up Ceana's mind for her. She nudged Fionntan and tilted her head meaningfully towards Arran. Then she tapped herself with one flipper and indicated the island. He must have understood her meaning, for he bowed his head slightly and said in her thoughts, *"Be careful."*

Then he dove and sped towards Lord Arran just beneath the water's surface. Ceana watched long enough to see him lock his teeth into Arran's leg and yank him under the waves.

Then the firemount rumbled again, and Ceana turned as well and darted towards it. She swam as fast as she could, weaving through selkies and not-selkies. She could see more selkies emerging from both Emain Ablach's main entrance and other bolt-holes further down, rushing to the defense of their home.

None of them gave her more than a glance and a mental call of *"Get to safety, lady!"* Good. Ceana continued to dive until she could see the glowing rune-circles. She reached the first and dug into the material with the claws of her front flippers, scratching and gouging until the runes ceased to glow.

She moved to the next and repeated the process, then the next and the next. She could hear the noises of battle from above, but she remained focused on what was before her. She had to trust and pray that the fighting would stay well away from her.

Yet there were so, so many sets of the runes, and she could feel her lungs aching more and more. Eventually, she could stand it no longer. She rushed back to the surface—but the moment she poked her head out, an arrow struck the water just beside her. She dove back beneath, then cautiously raised her head again. Two more arrows flew from Lord Arran's ships, nearly striking her.

Oh, why *now*? But she had no other choice. By darting up and ducking down, Ceana managed to get enough of a breath to tide her over a little longer. Then she swam back down and attacked the runes again. Still the firemount rumbled, and she could feel the rock shaking slightly and growing warmer. How much longer did she have?

By now, she had the destruction of the runes down to a few precise movements that cut through what seemed to be the critical marks. But even that took time, and she was only one person.

Worse still, the selkies, despite their initial ferocity, seemed to be losing the fight. Somehow, Lord Arran's men still aboard the ships could tell who to shoot at and who not to shoot, making it difficult for any of the selkies to get a decent breath. And with so many of Lord Arran's men in the water as well, the selkies couldn't get close enough to the ships to disable them.

But it would only be worse if the firemount wakened, even if only enough for an earthquake and not a full eruption. So, Ceana kept to her work, praying with each attack that Dèanadair would send one more miracle their way.

Then she felt her seal-shape begin to loosen.

No! Not now! Ceana glanced back towards the surface. The fighting was thick above her in this area; making it up there would be difficult. And she could see and hear Lord Arran's arrows striking the water and selkies alike every few seconds. The time it would take to safely surface and get enough air to return herself to equilibrium might be too much. And when she looked at the runes she had left...she was nearly all the way around the island again.

It wasn't as if she could come back. And she'd told Arran her decision earlier. If Dèanadair willed that she made good on her words, so be it.

Ceana rushed to the next set of runes. She couldn't mar the wax so easily when her claws couldn't decide if they were there or not, but soon it faded like the others had. She moved to the next, destroyed that one.

As she did, her seal-shape fully fell away, leaving her only human, her dress and cloak billowing around her in the water. Her head spun, but she still had air in her lungs and five sets of runes left. Ceana pulled the knife she'd been given from her pocket, opened it, and pulled herself along to the next runes. The knife made quicker work of the runes than her claws had; praise Dèanadair for that.

Another set of runes. Another few strokes. Her lungs could hold far less air now than they could in seal-shape, and she could already feel them burning. Three runes down. Spots appeared in front of her eyes, and blood rushed in her ears, but she stayed focused. Two more to go. Now grey clouded her vision, and it was all she could do not to gasp.

One left. She fumbled, nearly dropping the knife. Her hands

shook as she made the cuts. *Please, Dèanadair.*

She needed air.

She needed to finish.

She needed air.

She needed to save Emain Ablach.

She managed one last stroke before she could no longer hold onto the knife. She clung to the rock, watching the glow of the runes fade and the blackness creep in from the edges of her vision. She saw the last light go out of the runes, felt the firemount begin to settle.

And then the blackness overcame her, and she knew no more.

Chapter 39
AWAKENED

The first thing Ceana realized was that someone was holding her hand. The second was that she was no longer wet, let alone underwater. The third was that her whole body ached.

She let out a little groan, blinking as she came more awake. She lay in a narrow bed set right up against a wooden wall, covered in soft linen sheets. The bed seemed to be set in a little nook exactly its size, with curtains covering the opening. The worn blue dress she last remembered wearing had been replaced by a white nightgown, and her seal-cloak was nowhere to be seen.

Where was she? She lay still another moment, paying close attention to her surroundings. She probably wasn't dead, since she hurt so much. She could hear waves somewhere, and the air smelled salty. Near the sea, then. And now that she was watching for it, she thought she could detect the rolling motion of a ship under sail.

The question was, whose ship? Yet, as Ceana focused on the hand holding hers, she had a good guess. She knew her oldest sister's hand as well as she knew her own, and if Onora was here, everything would be all right. Even if this was Lord Arran's ship, not Onora's—but, no, the last Ceana had seen of Lord Arran had been Fionntan dragging him into the depths. So, most likely, she was safe.

She pulled her hand free of Onora's and tried to sit up. From the other side of the curtain, she heard Onora stirring. Then the curtain was pushed back, and Onora was *there*, looking down at Ceana with mingled worry and relief in her gaze. "Thank Dèanadair, you're awake. Here, let me help." She bent and lifted

Ceana enough that she could sit with her back against the wall of the nook. Then she stayed stooped to hug Ceana tight. "What were you *thinking*, running back into danger like that?"

Ceana managed a weak smile and tried to reply, but the sound caught in her throat. Her heartbeat sped up as her words turned into coughing. What had happened to her? Had she somehow lost her speech all over again? What if she could never talk again, even to her own family? The thought frightened her less than it once would have, but even so, she knew it would be harder to manage among humans than among the selkies. After all, the selkies were used to such troubles.

Onora released her and stood, keeping one hand on her shoulder. "Easy. Here, let me call the healers."

She went to the door, cracked it open, and said something to someone outside. A few minutes later, two figures entered. One Ceana recognized as Tasgeal, Onora's personal physician, a man so tall he had to stoop to get through the door. Behind him followed Ninian, the selkie healer, looking even shorter than he actually was next to Tasgeal's lanky frame.

Both men started to speak at once and then shot each other cool not-quite-glares. Again they tried, and Tasgeal managed to get his words out first. "I see her highness has woken?"

Ceana nodded, and Onora returned to her former seat on a stool set against the wall. "Just a few minutes ago. I helped her sit up, as you told me. She seems to be having some trouble speaking."

Tasgeal's long face pursed in a frown, but Ninian just nodded impatiently. "And no wonder, under the circumstances. I can help with that, just let me check the rest of her over first to make sure I'll not make things worse."

Tasgeal drew himself up. "Her highness is *my* patient —"

"She's mine more recently than yours, and I doubt you know the first thing about the effects of cloak failure," Ninian snapped back.

Ceana made an impatient noise, wishing for her tablet so she could just ask Ninian to do whatever he could do to help and be done with it. Onora must have been hearing similar conversations for some time, for she said in an exasperated tone, "Gentlemen, I believe I asked you to settle your differences and make your plans some days ago. As you have not, Tasgeal, you may first make sure of Ceana's condition, and then Ninian may do his checks and offer whatever help he can with my sister's voice."

Grumbling slightly, both physicians obeyed. Ceana submitted to Tasgeal checking her breathing and heartbeat, asking her to move various limbs, looking in her eyes and throat, and performing all the strange little motions and tasks that physicians seemed to find necessary. He took a step back as he finished. "Her highness seems to be in good health under the circumstances. I detect no signs of water remaining in her lungs, her breathing is regular, and aside from the difficulties with speech, she seems to have suffered no mental harm. As long as my colleague is able to do what he claims towards restoring her voice, she should make a full recovery quite soon."

"Don't insult medicine simply because you don't know it," Ninian grumbled. He moved forward and went through a similar litany of tests and checks as what Tasgeal just had. When he finished, he produced a small bottle from his pocket and handed it to Ceana. "Drink this slowly. It'll speed along your recovery from the shock. Careful, it'll burn a bit."

Ceana took the bottle. She saw Onora's lips purse in worry, but of course, Onora didn't know Ninian the way she did. She uncorked the bottle and drank it in long sips. It tasted like herbed water, not at all like medicine, and she wondered about Ninian's warning. But as the last of it hit her throat, she felt it—a stinging as if she'd eaten too much ginger all at once. The intensity grew rapidly until she wondered if her throat was on fire, and she doubled over coughing.

Onora leapt to her feet and to Ceana's side in an instant, rubbing her back. "Ceana, are you all right?"

Ceana gasped for breath, but she could already feel the burn subsiding again. As it faded, she croaked, "I'm fine." Her voice came out scratchy, but still her own. Thank Dèanadair. "Is Fi—Are his majesty and the Guard all right? Is Emain Ablach safe?"

"All is well," Onora assured her, hand coming to rest on Ceana's shoulder. "Don't worry. I'll tell you all shortly, once Tasgeal and Ninian assure me 'tis safe to do so."

"Why wouldn't it be safe?" Ceana demanded, looking around at the three gathered there.

"You've been unconscious for almost three days, your highness," Tasgeal replied promptly. "We only wish to be certain that you are not too weak to handle the excitement."

"Three days?" Ceana echoed. "But—how?"

Tasgeal reluctantly looked to Ninian, who shook his head. "You nearly drowned, lass, and there's the shock of your cloak giving up the ghost for good while you were still transformed. Either of those alone would be enough for concern. Between the two of them, for a long while, we couldn't tell if you'd wake up at all."

"Oh." Ceana felt as if that ought to frighten her, but all she could manage to feel was a ripple of sorrow for the fact that her cloak —Mey's cloak—was now as dead as its original wearer. She had known it was dying, of course, but as long as some magic remained in it, she might have had *some* chance of seeing her cousins again. Now her time among the selkies had truly ended. But if that were so, she hoped the cloak had at least remained otherwise undamaged so Mairearad, Aíbinn, and Uaine could lay it and Mey to rest properly in the Halls of the Lost.

"Both Tasgeal and Ninian have been working hard to ensure you would wake again," Onora added, her voice soft and weary. "And the rest of us have been praying." She shook her head and seemed to steady herself. "And now Dèanadair has seen fit to answer that prayer along with the rest, but we wish to take no chances. So, gentlemen, will you finish your examination?"

Tasgeal and Ninian obeyed, asking Ceana several more questions—thankfully, they didn't seem to see the need to each ask her separately—and checking a few more things. Once they were done, Tasgeal said, "As I said earlier, her highness seems in good health. No harm should come from telling her what has passed."

"Aye, the worry would do far more damage than the telling would," Ninian agreed. "Let her know all, and if others wish to come in to help, allow them." He directed his next comment to Ceana. "And if you care to take a turn about the deck or simply get some fresh air, there should be no harm in that either. Just see that you've someone on hand to help steady you."

Tasgeal gave Ninian a dubious look. "I believe her highness would be better served with more rest. She should remain in bed or, if she must go outside, be carried, least until we reach Atìrse."

Ninian snorted. "Carry on that way and you'll kill the lass with care. She'll heal far better if she moves about a bit and gets some fresh air."

"Fresh air, certainly." Tasgeal glanced around the small cabin with resignation. "And I suppose that in these conditions, venturing out is the best way to get it. But she must do so cautiously."

Onora sighed and held up a hand. "Thank you both for lending your expertise. I believe that will be all for now, unless you have any further instructions?" She paused, but both men shook their heads. "Good. We will act according to what Ceana feels comfortable attempting, though we will be careful not to push too hard. You are dismissed."

Both men bowed their way out of the room. Once they were gone, Onora shut the door. "Goodness. I've never met a pair of professionals so determined to snipe at each other." She crossed the room in six strides and hugged Ceana once more. "I am so very glad you're all right. I've missed you."

"I've missed you too." Ceana returned the hug, burying her face in Onora's shoulder. "But what *happened*? The last I remember was trying to destroy the runes—I think I scratched out all of them?"

"You did. The selkies checked multiple times over. But I'm getting ahead of myself." Onora straightened up from the hug just as a knock came on the door. "Oh, what now?"

She went to the door and opened it, and then let out a relieved sigh. "Oh, 'tis you. Someone told you Ceana is awake, then?"

"Ninian did, and he said she was well enough for visitors. May we come in?"

Was that *Mairearad's* voice? What was Mairearad doing *here*? On *Onora's* ship? And...looking for Ceana? Did she somehow not hate Ceana after all?

That question was rapidly followed by the realization that Mairearad had sounded *friendly* towards Onora—not just diplomatically so, but genuinely. Ceana glanced down at her covers, debating the merits of pretending to have fallen back asleep in the last five seconds. If both Onora *and* Mairearad decided to scold her for recklessness and running off at the same time, she might not survive that much sisterly exasperation.

But before she could make a decision, Onora opened the door, and Mairearad entered, with Uaine and Aíbinn just behind. Mairearad crossed the room swiftly, started to reach for Ceana, then pulled back and dropped into a curtsey. "I am glad to see your highness awake at last. I began to wonder ..."

Well, no scolding seemed imminent. Ceana offered Mairearad a cautious smile. "I'm sorry. And I'm sorry for lying to all three of you so long. The longer it went on, the more I wanted to tell you the truth, but I was afraid of what might happen—what you might think. I didn't want to lose you any sooner than I had to."

"I understand." A hint of wry smile crossed Mairearad's face. "Just as I now understand why all my efforts to move up the adoption were met with such resistance."

Ceana couldn't help a sheepish laugh. "That was one of the hardest parts of all, having to put you all off and not properly explain why. I did truly think of you as my kin—I still do, if you will allow me to."

"Only if thou wilt allow us the same privilege." Mairearad stepped forward, eager as if she'd been only just holding herself back, and drew Ceana into an embrace. "Thou art still our cousin, whatever else may lie between us."

Ceana hugged Mairearad back as tightly as she could. "Oh, thank you. You all aren't angry with me, then?"

"I am not." Mairearad drew back, keeping her hands on Ceana's shoulders. "Or, if I am, 'tis because thou worried us all by vanishing without warning and only saying goodbye to Uaine and then, when thou wert nearly home safe, thou turned around and swam as fast as thou could back into danger. What wert thou thinking?"

"What were you thinking indeed?" Onora cut in. "You set out without giving *me* enough warning to send someone to find you—I could have had a ship at your halfway point so you'd not be traveling so far alone. Then, you not only went straight back *towards* Arran and his men, you took away any ability I had to contact you and make sure you were all right."

Under two such disapproving glares, Ceana couldn't help but wilt. "I'm—I'm sorry. I was trying to keep everyone safe. When I left the island, I didn't want to tell anyone in Atìrse about where Emain Ablach was, and I didn't want anyone from Emain Ablach to come with me or come looking for me because that might have put them in danger. And then I was afraid that if I *didn't* go back, no one would have any warning that Lord Arran was coming."

"She was right about that," Aíbinn said, her voice gruff. She still hovered at the door, arms crossed, not looking at Ceana. "Even though we found the real spy, he didn't know *when* the attack would take place. If Nes hadn't run into her and Arran and then gotten away, we would have been almost completely unprepared."

Ceana perked up. "Nes is all right?"

Aíbinn nodded. "He took a few minor wounds in the battle, but he's fine. He reached the island the night before the attack and told the rest of us what had happened to thee, Fionntan, and the other Guard and about Arran's plans. Thanks to thee, and thanks to his warning, we were ready for Arran when he arrived. And since he took so long trying to get someone else to turn traitor, we had time to cripple a few of his ships as the battle began."

"What did you do to the ships?" Ceana asked, leaning forward a little as she recalled the sudden crack and the feeling of the deck shifting beneath her feet.

"Put a few large cracks in the hulls." Aíbinn's expression turned fierce and proud for a moment. "We can't afford to do it often. The material we use, we get from the faery folk, and the price on it is too high to trade for often when there's more practical things to be had. But we keep enough on hand for a few ships, and we used all we had."

Ceana nodded slowly. "And after that?"

"After that, we were mostly facing Arran's men in the water, and even with both of us in seal-shape, we have the advantage." Aíbinn sobered a little. "Still, it's a good thing the crown princess and her ships showed up when they did. Arran's men were shooting at us every time we tried to come up for a breath, and we couldn't get anyone on his ships to deal with the archers. The new ships drew some of the attention off us, especially once they started boarding Arran's vessels. Now that all's over, there are a fair number wounded, but not many casualties except among Arran's people."

"What happened to Arran? And F—King Fionntan?" Ceana asked. "The last I saw of them, they were fighting."

"Fionntan's fine," Uaine offered, the first time she'd spoken since entering the room. "He was wounded, but he's recovering well, and none of his injuries were very serious."

Thank Dèanadair for that. "And Arran?"

"Drowned." Onora's tone made it clear that further discussion on that element of the battle was out of the question. "We're working out what will come of that now."

Ceana just managed to catch herself before she could say *"Oh, good."* Whatever Lord Arran's character, it probably wasn't right for a princess to express relief at the death of one of her subjects. "Will Lady Eilidh be able to go home, then? Is she all right?"

"She's fine. As to what will happen to her, well, that's part of what we're working out." Onora glanced towards Mairearad. "Nothing will be decided until we reach my castle. Athair and Màthair are to meet us there. Lord Arran's actions have broken the treaty—by any understanding of it—in such a major way that a new treaty needs to be written. Deciding on what that entails will take time, though I've already started some informal discussion on the topic."

"We intend that whatever the nature of the treaty, it must be more explicit about what it's forbidding," Mairearad added. "Given what thou told us and what we have learned since, from Onora and others, 'tis clear that obscurity isn't the shield thy ancestors thought it would be, no more than isolation has protected us to the degree our ancestors believed it would. And if a new agreement is to be reached, we hope to make it such that it benefits each of our people more than the old one did."

Well, that was good. A better treaty wasn't an alliance, but it was closer. And given how well Onora and Mairearad seemed to be getting along, and given that there were selkies willingly aboard Onora's ship, perhaps a true alliance wasn't yet out of the question. "If I can help with any of it, I want to. Unless my being there would make things worse."

"You'll have your chance," Onora assured her. "But not today. You need to rest, and we should leave you alone to do that. Would you prefer to stay in here or move outside?"

"In here for now." Ceana glanced towards Uaine and Aíbinn. She hadn't missed that neither of them had responded to what she'd said to Mairearad, nor could she ignore the way they were hanging back—so unlike when she'd first come to Emain Ablach and they'd been quick to welcome her. "Uaine, Aíbinn, will you stay with me a minute? Long enough to talk a little more?"

Both hesitated. Uaine nodded. "I'll stay."

Aíbinn's lips pinched. "I should go. I'm still technically on duty. I'll talk later."

She slipped out the door before anyone could protest. Onora and Mairearad made their way out a few minutes later, after admonishing Ceana to actually rest and Uaine to make sure she did so.

Ceana patted the edge of her bed. "Wilt thou come sit with me?"

Again, Uaine seemed to debate a moment. Then she slowly

came and sat down. "If you're going to apologize to me again, you don't need to."

"I want to, though. Thou —" Ceana stopped herself and started again. "You treated me as a friend and sister, and I'm sorry that I wasn't honest with you." Ceana fiddled with the edge of the sheet. "I suppose you *are* angry with me."

"I'm...I'm not angry anymore." Uaine stared at the wall across the cabin, which was painted with a mural of the stars and constellations. "I was when Fionntan and the Guard first told me about who you are. Then the three of us—Mairearad and Aíbinn and I—talked to your sister, and she told us everything she could about why you'd come to the island and how you'd come there and what you were doing. But...it still hurts. I called you my sister and my friend, and now I know one of those can't be true, and I don't know if the other ever was."

"We can't be sisters, but we're cousins still," Ceana offered, though she could hear how flimsy the offer sounded. "And I'd like to be friends again."

"Were we ever friends?" Uaine asked, shoulders tensed. "I didn't even know your real name until two days ago."

"I ..." Ceana searched for the right words, staring at the covers as if they held the answers she needed. "I thought of you as a friend. I still do. And even when I couldn't tell you the whole truth, I told you as much of it as I could, and I hated that I couldn't tell you everything. I'll understand if you don't think that counts, though."

Uaine's gaze dropped to the floor now, and her hands squeezed the edge of the mattress. "I...I want it to count. But I don't know."

"Then can we start again?" Ceana hadn't intended her voice to come out with such a desperate edge, but she couldn't help it. "Now that there aren't any more lies between us?"

Uaine considered this for a moment, then nodded. "I think I'd like that." She turned to face Ceana. "Should we re-introduce ourselves?"

"If you'd like. I'll go first." Ceana straightened up. "I am Ceana, seventh princess of Atìrse, and cousin to the Northwaves of Emain

Ablach."

"I am Uaine of Northwaves, third of that house," Uaine replied. "I'm glad to meet thee in truth, Ceana."

"So am I." Ceana sent up a silent prayer of thanks to Dèanadair. There remained the matter of Aíbinn and Fionntan to deal with, as well as whatever fallout came from Arran's plan and her deception and everything else. But she hadn't fully lost Mairearad or Uaine, and there was no war, and that was reason enough for praise.

Chapter 40
ALLIANCE

Ceana spent the rest of that day resting, mostly staying inside the cabin, alternating between sleeping and talking with whoever happened to be there. Onora, Mairearad, and Uaine took turns staying with her—as they, along with Aíbinn, had the last three days, Ceana learned. Once, Lady Eilidh visited along with Mairearad and Uaine. She said little, but her face had clearly remembered how to smile again.

Several times, Ceana woke to find Onora's cat lying on top of her, purring. She couldn't help rolling her eyes at the creature's presence—could Onora go *nowhere* without bringing Càirdeil along? But he was a welcome bit of home, so she merely stroked his head and ears until he roused himself and wandered off.

By the next day, Ceana's headache had receded, and the rest of her body no longer hurt so much either. So, supported by Uaine, she ventured out of the cabin and onto the deck.

Outside, the ship was a bustle of activity, though those who noticed her still nodded or bowed as she passed. Six other ships sailed along behind this one, three of which Ceana recognized as vessels belonging to the royal family, and three of which she guessed were formerly of Lord Arran's fleet. Onora had informed her the day before that these ships were, for the moment, considered property of the royal family as well, and that they were being used to help transport the surviving members of Lord Arran's crews back to Atìrse to await trial.

Ceana and Uaine made several circuits of the deck, walking slowly. Onora and Mairearad were nowhere to be seen, though Ceana heard their muffled voices coming from one of the cabins now and then, along with those of Alasdair and a few others. Once, she heard Fionntan's voice from there as well. After that, she glanced hopefully at the door from time to time, but he never emerged. Perhaps, though, that was just as well—Ceana wasn't even sure what she'd say to him if she did see him, beyond "I'm glad you're alive," and, once again, "I'm sorry for lying to you."

Sooner than she'd expected, though, she grew weary again, and so Uaine guided her over to a crate where she could rest and watch the waves. After a few minutes of sitting with her, Uaine excused herself again and hurried off, promising to send someone else over in case Ceana needed help.

Ceana waited, staring into the water. She could see selkies swimming alongside the ship, easily keeping up with it, and she wondered how many of them she knew. She waved down to them, though none seemed to notice, and noted that one of the rowboats had been lowered so it hung upside-down beside the ship, skimming along the sea's surface. A ladder hung just above the rowboat, leading up to the deck. So, Onora must have wanted to make sure any selkies who wanted to come aboard could easily do so.

She wondered when someone else would come over and who Uaine would send. Probably one of the few servants Onora had brought along—that would be the most logical option. But instead, a few minutes later, she spotted Aíbinn approaching.

Aíbinn stopped a foot or so away, arms crossed, looking as if she might just walk away again. "Uaine sent me over. She said thou needed help."

"Ninian and Tasgeal say I'm not allowed to be left alone." Ceana offered Aíbinn a tentative smile. "I'm fine, though, really."

"No, they're probably right. Thou didst almost die." Aíbinn spoke as if she were half trying to convince herself, shifting her weight from one foot to the other.

Ceana patted the crate beside her. "In that case, come and sit with me?"

Aíbinn hesitated a moment, then did so, though she remained

tense and kept her arms close so she'd not so much as brush against Ceana. They sat there in silence a few minutes. Then Ceana said, "I understand if thou art still angry with me. Art thou?"

"Not with thee." Aíbinn shook her head slowly. "'Tis...'tis complicated. But thou hast apologized enough. Thou needst not do so again to me."

Ceana couldn't help a hollow laugh. "Sometimes I still feel as if I'll be apologizing the rest of my life. But if thou art not angry with me, why dost thou act as if thou art? I wish to make things right, if I can."

The corners of Aíbinn's lips twitched. "Of course, thou dost. That's what this whole business started with, as I've heard it." She grew solemn again, staring out at the waves. "'Tis nothing thou needst worry about."

Ceana considered this, fingers worrying at a crack in the crate's edge. "I'd still like to know. Thou art my kin still, and I want to help thee."

"There's not much thou can do," Aíbinn replied. But after a few more minutes, she went on, "I don't hold it against thee that thou hid thy identity. And I know thou meant only good. If thou meant ill, thou would have acted sooner. I gave thee opportunity enough."

Oh. *Oh.* Now the pieces clicked into place. "Thou art angry with thyself, then?"

Aíbinn drummed her fingers against the side of the crate. "I'm meant to guard Fionntan and all the people of Emain Ablach. Instead, I welcomed a spy of sorts into our midst. I showed thee all I could of the island. I encouraged Fionntan to spend time with thee and thee to spend time with him, even alone. If thou wert a real spy, like the one we caught the other day, I would have unwittingly allowed—even encouraged—whatever evil you might have done."

Ceana carefully put a hand on Aíbinn's shoulder. When Aíbinn didn't pull away, she replied, "If my spying can be forgiven, thou canst be as well. And thou wert not the only one who could have seen it."

"No, but I should have." Aíbinn shook herself, though not quite so hard as to dislodge Ceana's hand. "I know others will forgive me for it, especially since most folk will hear that thou nearly died destroying the runes before they hear of thy true name. But 'tis harder for me to stop thinking on all the clues I should have seen, and I don't wish to take out how I feel about myself on thee. So, I thought it best to stay away."

Ceana reached a little further to give Aíbinn a one-armed shoulder hug. "Please don't. If thou should snap at me because thou art hurting, I forgive thee in advance. But I've been dreading having to say goodbye to thee for weeks now. I don't want to lose thee just as I've found out I might not have to bid thee farewell forever after all. If thou shouldst need space sometimes, 'tis all right, but not all the time, please."

Aíbinn reached up and squeezed Ceana's hand. "I suppose that's fair. I don't wish to say goodbye to thee forever any more than thou dost. I'll do my best, but I need thy patience at first, please."

"I can do that." Ceana leaned over to rest her head on Aíbinn's shoulder. "I'll be patient as long as I need to be."

<hr>

The ships reached Onora's castle in Atìrse that evening. Only then did Ceana see Fionntan. He emerged from the water with his people—evidentially, he'd slipped off the ship while Ceana wasn't looking, unless she'd only imagined his voice in the cabin. He acknowledged her with only the briefest of bows before they all made their way up to the castle.

At the castle, Onora gave orders to the castle guard that the great main gates were not to be shut until a new treaty had been agreed upon with the selkies. Ceana caught the murmur of approval from many of the selkies who'd come along, and she noted that they seemed far less on edge as they continued into the castle and keep proper.

Old Queen Moireach greeted the party in the Great Hall, first embracing Onora and Ceana and then turning to Fionntan. "On behalf of my family, your majesty, be welcome to our home. We are, all of us, glad to have a chance of setting right all the wrong that has been done to your people over the years."

"So your granddaughter has told me," Fionntan replied, bowing slightly to Queen Moireach, as was proper for one royal visiting another. "I thank you for your welcome, and I hope that good will come of our meeting."

"I have no doubt that it will," Queen Moireach replied, and then summoned servants to show Fionntan and his party to their accommodations. Then she turned to Ceana and embraced her again. "Welcome back, my dear girl."

Ceana leaned into her grandmother's embrace, drinking in the warmth of her arms and the scent of tea and rosewater that hung about her. "I've missed thee."

"And I thee." Queen Moireach chuckled. "I see that the selkies have thee talking like they do now. Careful, or the whole kingdom shall think thee as strange as they think me."

Ceana wrinkled her nose playfully. "I think that would be a compliment."

"Perhaps so." Queen Moireach rearranged herself so she had just one arm around Ceana's shoulders. "Come. Onora and Alasdair will see to things from here. I have ordered that tea be waiting in my chambers, and I wish to hear from thy own mouth what has befallen thee, not just settle for thy sister's summary."

"Of course, Maimeó." Ceana followed her grandmother towards the stairs. "But dost thou not wish to meet our cousins?"

"The cousins will wait." Queen Moireach let go of Ceana so she could balance herself with one hand on the wall of the staircase and use her cane with the other. "Now is time for the two of us alone."

So, they made their way up to Queen Moireach's apartments at the very top of the keep. There they found waiting a pot of hot tea, with scones and cream and jam to go with it, and for a little while, there was no conversation, just food and drink and pleasant silence. Then, Queen Moireach made Ceana tell her all that had happened since the last time they'd spoken—nearly two weeks ago now, for Ceana had gone out to the rocks for longer conversations only rarely in that time, and Queen Moireach had been otherwise occupied during the last two of those conversations.

She listened patiently, occasionally asking for clarification on a particular detail. At last, Ceana finished both her tale and her cup of tea. Queen Moireach refilled the cup without being asked. "So, now that thou art home again and thy secrets are known to the selkies, what dost thou intend to do?"

"I don't know." Ceana wrapped her hands around her cup. "I want to help with the new treaty. I want to find a way to stay in contact with Mairearad, Aíbinn, and Uaine. And when that's over, I suppose I have to figure out who to marry." The reminder settled like a stone in her stomach. "Unless thou've heard that Athair and Màthair have thought of someone?"

"Nay; remember, thou told them that thou might find a potential husband here, as thou may recall." Queen Moireach set down her own cup. "Thou need not rush into marriage, in any case. Thou hast much time yet ahead of you to find the right man."

"*If* I can find him." Ceana slumped. "So far, I've been an absolute fool and fallen in love with the one person who's already turned me down, and I don't know what to do. I don't want to marry someone else, but I can't marry him."

"Hmm." Queen Moireach picked up another scone and spread jam over it. "Did I ever tell thee how I met my husband, thy grandfather?"

Ceana nodded. "Thy parents were trying to find thee a husband quickly because thy brothers had died, and they and thou set princes who visited challenges to see if they were worthy of thee, because thou wert going to be queen."

"That is the story, but not the full story," Queen Moireach replied. "I met my love while visiting our Uncle Diarmad when I was still quite young, and I spent most of my visits after that at least partially in his company. As I grew older, I found myself in love with him, but though he was human, he was under a curse, and we both believed he could never leave Tìr Soilleir. The last summer I spent there, we attempted to break his curse, but then I was called home, and I knew not whether or not we had succeeded until he appeared at the castle gates. After that, between the two of us, we saw to it that he succeeded every challenge my parents or I could set."

"Thou...*thou* married for love?" Ceana hastily set down her cup so she wouldn't drop it. "Why didst thou never tell any of us?"

"Oh, some of thy sisters know, and thy parents are well aware, but 'twould be unwise to have it known far and wide that I had met thy grandfather in the faery lands, full-human though he was." Queen Moireach fixed Ceana with a look. "But the important matter for thee is that he was my choice, though I was only a little older than thou, and that I had my choice even when I thought 'twould have been impossible."

Ceana made a face. "But what if he hadn't come? What if the curse hadn't been broken and thou couldn't have married him?"

"Then Dèanadair would have let my love for him cool, and He would have shown me the one He wished me to wed instead." Queen Moireach reached out and put a hand over Ceana's. "As He will do for thee, if 'tis necessary—but do not give up hope so soon. Much is changing these days; thou knowst this already. Wait a little while and see what comes."

<hr />

King Seòras and Queen Isla arrived late the next day, having ridden as fast as they could from the royal city with the necessary retinue. They greeted Onora and Queen Moireach, then embraced Ceana with a fervor that confirmed what Ceana suspected: that Onora had already told them at least some of what had transpired.

Once Ceana had finished assuring them that she was all right, they turned to the selkies. King Seòras stepped forward and, to the shock of all, made a partial bow. "King Fionntan, welcome. My queen and I were outraged to learn of what your people have suffered all these years, of the atrocities committed under our very noses. I promise you that we will do everything in our power to set right these wrongs."

Fionntan actually smiled and extended his hand. "King Seòras, Queen Isla, my people and I thank you for your welcome. I have been informed from multiple sources that the true plight of my people was far less well-known in your country than we believed. No doubt some of the fault for that lies with us; we should have spoken sooner about what was happening, rather than making assumptions and isolating ourselves."

"And we should have been more vigilant to see what our people were doing and asked more questions of why you drew away when we should have been strengthening the bonds of peace. No more!" King Seòras clasped Fionntan's wrist, and the two shook hands.

A few more greetings followed before all retreated to the Great Hall for dinner. After the meal, Ceana and Onora once again explained all that had befallen Ceana in the past months, though Ceana carefully downplayed the effects of her cloak wearing out in the last weeks of her stay. She was also careful not to mention any of her feelings towards Fionntan, only that she had considered him a friend in Emain Ablach and that he seemed a good and honorable king.

The negotiations for the new treaty began the next day and extended for nearly a week after. Onora kept her promise and made sure that Ceana was included in as many of the meetings as possible, even when her presence wasn't strictly necessary. True, there were some aspects she could help with. She was periodically called upon to provide a human's perspective on selkie culture, or to help assemble lists of families or individuals who might have been involved in stealing selkies based on what she'd seen in the Halls of the Lost. Very occasionally, when this or that Atìrsen nobleman expressed doubt on some point, she was able to speak up and put her support behind the selkies.

Yet life at the castle still had to go on as well. And as the focus of the treaty meetings turned from figuring out what had happened and what needed to be done to discussing the minutia of how that change could be accomplished, Ceana found herself involved less and less in the arrangements. Instead, she spent much of her time on Onora's behalf, seeing to the running of the castle and making sure their human and selkie guests were at ease and properly entertained.

While Ceana wished she could have still been included in the treaty discussions, she had to admit, there was some relief in being outside of them as well. After all, Fionntan was in every meeting, but he remained only stiffly polite with her and rarely spoke to her at all outside of what the conversation and propriety demanded.

Ceana told herself that it was all right, that it was better this way—that it should be easier to get over Fionntan when he clearly disliked her now. But that was easier said than done when even the way in which he approached the treaty reminded her of the kindness and noble spirit he'd shown her when they were still in Emain Ablach. Even when she only saw him outside the meetings, each stiff *your highness* and diplomatic brush-off made Ceana's heart a little sorer. After a day or two, she took to avoiding him as much as he avoided her.

Yet, she couldn't *always* avoid him.

When Uaine invited Ceana to the ceremony to return Lady Eilidh to the Northwaves family, Ceana was happy to accept. Why would she not wish to celebrate such a joyous occasion with them? They were her family, after all. And in any case, she was curious; even after all her time in Emain Ablach, she'd never seen such a ceremony.

But when she reached the shore the next morning, the first thing she saw was Fionntan standing at the edge of the water, barefoot amid the surf and staring out to sea. In that moment, she nearly turned around and walked straight back to the castle.

That would have been rude, however, so instead she made her way over to the small group of other guests. At Lady Eilidh's request, the ceremony was to be small and private, so there were only a few others present: Lord Muir and his wife, a few of the Guard, and, of course, Lady Eilidh herself and the Northwaves sisters. No other humans had been invited, though Ceana spotted a few curious fishermen watching from their boats out amid the waves.

Ceana had arrived last, and a few minutes afterward, Fionntan turned around to face those assembled. "Let Lady Eilidh of Northwaves and the sisters of the Northwaves house come forth."

They did so, walking forward to stand with Fionntan amid the surf. Their feet were bare like his, Ceana noted, and she wondered if that was part of the ceremony. Perhaps she could ask Uaine later.

The group arranged themselves with Mairearad, Aíbinn, and Uaine facing Lady Eilidh, Fionntan between them. Fionntan turned to the sisters. "Who speaks for you?"

"I speak for my sisters," Mairearad replied, stately as ever. Behind her, Uaine let out an eager squeak and then hastily composed herself, grinning at Lady Eilidh.

A flicker of a smile flashed on Fionntan's face. "Do you welcome Lady Eilidh of Northwaves into your home and acknowledge her as your kin?"

Mairearad spoke as if she'd practiced the words, though her tone was warm. "On behalf of my sisters, my mother, and my whole family, before all assembled here and in the sight of Dèanadair, I name Lady Eilidh of Northwaves as my kin. I welcome her as my aunt, lost and found again, and by blood and bond I call her my own."

A few tears glittered in Lady Eilidh's eyes as Fionntan turned to her. "Lady Eilidh of Northwaves, do you accept the name and welcome you have been given?"

"I accept it." Lady Eilidh's voice was rough and barely audible, yet Ceana could hear barely restrained eagerness in it. "I accept as kin those I lost before I could meet them, and I accept the name they give me. Let me be theirs and them mine, by blood and bond and Dèanadair's blessing."

"Then in Dèanadair's name and by the authority He has placed upon me, I declare it to be so." Fionntan placed a hand on Lady Eilidh's shoulder and one on Mairearad's. "Let it be known to all that Lady Eilidh of Northwaves has returned to her rightful home and that she has been accepted by her kin, and let that which was stolen from her be restored."

He removed his hands and stepped back. Mairearad pulled Lady Eilidh to her, and Aíbinn and Uaine darted forward so all three embraced their aunt at once. Then, Aíbinn and Uaine pulled back, and Mairearad put arm and cloak around Lady Eilidh, and they walked into the sea until they disappeared beneath the waves.

Ceana held her breath, watching the spot where they'd vanished. She'd read of the ceremonies in the books Fionntan had lent her, but it always seemed so much more formal there. Was that really all? Had it worked?

Then she saw two seal-heads emerge some distance away, surfacing for air. Now that she'd seen them once, she could track them as they turned and swam back to the shore. A few minutes later, they emerged from the surf and reappeared in human form, now with a pristine seal-cloak hanging from Lady Eilidh's shoulders.

With tears running down her face, Lady Eilidh stumbled towards Mairearad and embraced her once again. Ceana felt, as she had many times before, the pressure of the selkies' thought-speech passing her by.

The other selkies moved forward in a rush to offer their congratulations. Ceana hung back, waiting until all others had their turn before she approached. She addressed Lady Eilidh, "I'm glad you're able to go home at last. I wish I'd known sooner so you wouldn't have had to wait so long."

"Dèanadair knew His timing, your highness," Lady Eilidh replied, and now her voice was clear and sweet and strong. "You were always kind to me, even before you knew, and I thank you for it."

Ceana could think of nothing more to say that didn't sound like more self-blame, so instead she asked, "Will you return to Emain Ablach then? I know Athair said something about your having a choice."

"He offered me charge of Arran's lands, should I wish to stay, yes." Lady Eilidh put an arm around Uaine, the nearest of the Northwaves sisters, and pulled her close. "But Emain Ablach is my home, and I have been away too long. I wish to see no more of these shores."

"I don't blame you." Ceana shook her head. "Emain Ablach is beautiful, and I'm sure you miss it. I do, and I only spent a little time there."

"Thou couldst come back sometime," Uaine suggested, wiggling a little until she could stand up straight without leaving her aunt's embrace. "Thou art kin still, remember, and we have space aplenty."

Ceana wished she could have felt joy at the invitation, but she only felt the lack of a cloak around her shoulders. "I'd have to have a cloak again to do that, and we already know you can't adopt me officially."

"No one would *truly* have to know." Uaine wrinkled her nose, then grinned playfully. "And I know of another way thou couldst gain a cloak of thine own."

What was *that* supposed to mean? But before Ceana could ask, another selkie walked up to speak to Lady Eilidh. So, after a few minutes, Ceana started back up the shore.

She didn't notice Fionntan until he spoke from just beside her. "Are you returning to the castle, your highness?"

Ceana shied away instinctively, then forced herself back to a more composed state. Schooling her expression into a polite smile, she nodded. "I am, your majesty."

Fionntan offered his arm. He'd put his boots back on, Ceana noted. "May I escort you there?"

"You may." Ceana took his arm, trying not to think of all the times he'd walked her from the shore or the keep to her home in Emain Ablach.

They walked some distance in silence, taking the longer and less steep route rather than the cliffside path. After a while, Fionntan spoke. "How are you doing these days? Are you still feeling all right after what happened to you and your cloak?"

"I'm fine." Ceana gave a little shrug. "I still get tired a little more quickly than I used to, but Ninian says that will go away in time."

"I'm glad to hear as much. I was worried when you remained unconscious for so long."

If he was so worried, he might have come to see her! But Ceana squashed the thought ruthlessly. "Thank you. I appreciate your concern."

He nodded as if not quite sure what to say next. After a few more minutes of walking, he spoke again. "I'm sure King Seòras has told you that we've nearly finished drawing up the documents for the alliance. After today, all that will remain is to sign them."

"Alliance?" Ceana gave Fionntan a sharp glance. "The last I heard, you were drawing up a new treaty. Not a full alliance."

"Such was the original intention, but when the main point of the agreement is to ensure cooperation between your people and mine in punishing those who broke the old treaty and restoring the captives to their home, 'tis foolish to consider it anything but an alliance. And both your parents and I agree that, so long as they keep their word, more than that may come of it."

"I—I'm glad to hear it." Ceana could hardly get the words out. Not only would there be no war, not only would things be set right, but the alliance she'd originally hoped for would happen after all.

"I thought you would be." The slightest smile appeared on Fionntan's face. "'Twould seem you were right all those weeks ago. The time *was* right for something to change between our peoples, if only I could have seen it."

Ceana flushed and dropped her gaze at the memory of that first meeting. "I was terribly foolish in how I went about it, though. I'm sorry for how thoughtless my suggestion then was. And I'm sorry, truly sorry, for my lies afterward."

"Do not apologize for what you said and did when I came to your home to renew a treaty that had long since outlasted its usefulness." Fionntan stopped and turned so he faced her. "You were the first person in generations to ask why things were the way they were between our peoples, and you were the first to try to make a change for the better. That you, in ignorance, made choices that seemed foolish to those who knew the larger picture is no fault of yours. You *acted*, and I admire that. I admire you for it."

"You —" Ceana raised her head again, looking into Fionntan's face: solemn and proud, but with a warmth in his eyes she'd not seen—not directed at her, at least—since leaving Emain Ablach. "I thought you hated me."

"Hated you?" Fionntan echoed. "Princess Ceana, I could never hate thee."

Thee. He called her *thee.* The word stabbed, needle-sharp, into her heart. "Please—*please.* Don't call me that unless...unless you mean it. I don't think I could bear it."

"I mean it," Fionntan replied, his voice soft. "But if thou—if you will not allow it, I will not."

"I...You...On the ship ..." Despite her best efforts, despite all her diplomatic training, Ceana couldn't quite seem to put a proper sentence together. "I thought ..."

"I was angry on the ship, yes." Fionntan nodded slowly. "And for that, I beg your forgiveness. On my knees, if I must."

He started to kneel, but Ceana grabbed his arms to stop him. "Don't. You were right to be angry. You thought I'd been lying to you about everything for months."

"I had a right to anger, but it was not a right I should have exercised." Fionntan straightened his shoulders, met her eyes. "I knew even then that you had told the truth far more than you had lied. After our conversation in the Halls of the Lost, I sent my Guard to visit Atìrse's shores, and when they returned, they confirmed that what you had told me seemed true. That your people knew so little of mine; that your father and your family were far more honorable than I had believed. And so, I should have thought less of the name you bore and more of who you had proved yourself to be in that moment and every moment I have known you. You may have worn a false name, even a false history, but you never lied about the things that mattered." He paused. "Do you know why I chose to pursue an alliance, not merely a treaty, between our peoples?"

"Because it was the best way to make sure everyone would cooperate?" Ceana asked. "Because it would help both your people and mine?"

"Well—yes." Fionntan's brow furrowed. "Those were reasons. But not the reasons I referred to. I pursued an alliance because of who I knew you to be, because I knew evil folk could not have raised a woman such as you. Because a princess I thought was my enemy turned back when she was halfway home, rushing into peril in the hope that she could save my people from hers and then, when that failed, offered up everything she had to prevent doom from falling upon me and mine. *That* is why I pursue this alliance."

Ceana's head swam. She would have reached out for something to steady herself, but the only option nearby was Fionntan. "Then why did you avoid me so long?" At least her voice came out steady! "I thought all this time that you despised me."

"There were...other things I had to work out. Other questions I had to answer before I could trust myself to speak with you." Fionntan cleared his throat. "But I have thought much, and sought the counsel of those I know to be wise, and I now know something else that is true: that thou art among the bravest and noblest women I have ever met, and there are not words enough in the selkie and human tongues combined to express how much I admire and love thee."

He loved her. *Loved* her. Had she heard him say so, truly? Ceana felt she ought to say something tender and noble and heartfelt back, but instead what came out of her mouth was, "But what about Uaine?"

"Uaine?" Fionntan echoed. "What of her?"

"She...I thought...she and you ..." Ceana licked her lips, forcing herself to think through her words properly and not give in to the part of her heart that wanted to cry and dance and throw herself into Fionntan's arms all at once. "She told me of your agreement."

"The agreement that stood between us was a failsafe should I, as I feared, reach three-and-thirty and find no woman I could love as a man should love his wife." Fionntan took Ceana's hands and squeezed them gently. "She and her sisters know of my feelings—they knew of them before I did, in fact—and have given their blessing most emphatically"

"Oh," was all Ceana could manage to say. "Then you and she... aren't in love?"

For a moment, Fionntan just stared at her in disbelief. "Thou thought...Princess Ceana, I have spent the last *month* trying my utmost to court thee!" He raised his hands in exasperation and paced a short circle before returning to face her once again. "Didst thou truly believe me in love with thy cousin the whole time?"

"Well ..." Ceana felt her face grow warm as she searched for a minimally-embarrassing way to say that yes, she had, and her confidence in that fact had caused her no end of grief.

Fionntan broke out in an exasperated laugh. "Well, as showing thee all my private hideaways in Emain Ablach, giving thee gifts, and spending every moment I could spare with thee was not enough, may I try another way to convince thee of my true intentions?"

Ceana nodded once. "You may."

She should have expected what he did next—but somehow, she still found herself surprised when he bent, pulled her close, and kissed her. "There," he said, when he had finished. "Dost thou understand now?"

"Yes." Her voice came out in a breathless whisper. "I understand thee very well at last."

"Good." He straightened. "Then, once all is settled with the alliance, may I ask thy father for thy hand?"

"Of course." Ceana cleared her throat, managing to get her voice back to normal. "I suppose 'twill be a marriage alliance after all."

"Not a marriage alliance," Fionntan corrected. "I will not have thee as my wife because thou thinkst thou must wed me to ensure goodwill between our peoples. Whether thou say yea or nay to me,

I will keep the agreement I have made with thy father, thy family, and thy land. But I would have thee as my queen because I love thee, and I hope thou lovest me. Dost thou love me, Ceana?"

"I have loved thee since thou found me in the Halls of the Lost. Perhaps even before. And I will love thee 'til the day I die." And with those words, Ceana reached up to draw Fionntan's face towards herself, and now it was she who kissed him first.

But their kiss was cut short by someone clearing their throat from down the path. Ceana and Fionntan pulled away from each other and turned to see the Northwaves sisters and Lady Eilidh standing there. From the front of the group, Aíbinn regarded the two of them with a smirk and a raised eyebrow. "Not to interrupt, but others need to use the path as well. Besides, I think I saw guards at the top of the cliff looking for Ceana, and I don't think you wish them to catch you kissing."

Ceana flushed and ducked her head, but Fionntan only laughed. "Alas, thou art right." He offered his arm once more to Ceana. "And in any case, we have business yet to finish before my happiness can be complete. Shall we go find thy father, my princess?"

Well, if Fionntan wasn't embarrassed...Ceana took his arm. "We shall." And so, arm in arm, with her cousins behind them, they made their way up the path.

Epilogue:
Vows to Keep

Ceana married her selkie king a year later, gowned in blue, on the cliffs overlooking the sea near Onora's castle. There had been debate over that; selkie tradition demanded that the couple and officiant stand in the surf where the waves met the shore, while human tradition called for a Tùr-Faire. Eventually, they had compromised on the cliffs.

At first, neither she nor Fionntan had wanted to wait so long. Long engagements were rare among the selkies, and Ceana wanted to waste no more time than necessary. But King Seòras and Queen Isla had insisted on the delay, just in case. If Ceana's marriage was not to be part of the alliance, they'd said, 'twould be better to allow time for the alliance to mature before any wedding took place. Neither Ceana nor Fionntan could argue with that logic, especially not Fionntan. After all, he might trust Ceana's family now, but there was no telling how the new agreement would go over with either nation.

Yet, by Dèanadair's blessing, rather than faltering, the alliance flourished. King Seòras and Queen Isla put out a proclamation the day after the new treaty was signed: all those who had broken the old treaty by stealing away a selkie spouse would face execution, unless they came forward, confessed their crimes, and returned the stolen seal-cloaks to their rightful owners. These still forfeited land, titles, and wealth and were exiled from Atìrse, but they kept their lives.

A few took the merciful option. But for the rest, King Seòras and Queen Isla wasted no time in sending investigators and, where necessary, troops to seek out anyone who might have earned that punishment. Each investigator was accompanied by one or two selkies skilled in identifying others of their kind, and with their combined efforts, they found many seal-folk who had been thought lost or dead for years—or, where the selkies themselves could not be found, descendants were often identified. The investigators made no distinction between rich and poor, noble or peasant, in their search—nor did the executioners, once the guilty were identified.

Whether or not the perpetrators chose mercy, any lands, titles, or wealth they might have owned passed to their spouse or, if none lived, their descendants—assuming these didn't choose to return to Emain Ablach. In such cases, the inheritance continued down the line, or if no proper heir could be found, the holdings reverted to become property of the Crown.

Some of the nobles grumbled at the idea of selkies in the ruling classes of Atìrse, unsurprisingly. Yet they shut their mouths quickly once Ceana revealed the truth about Queen Mey. It helped, too, that only a few selkies chose to remain in Atìrse. Most went back to Emain Ablach, and every letter that Uaine, Aíbinn, and Mairearad wrote to Ceana mentioned at least two or three homecoming celebrations and told of pictures being removed from the Halls of the Lost as those they portrayed were found again.

And with the new alliance working so well, other nations began to take notice. King Seòras and Queen Isla seized upon each nation's questions as an opportunity to press their neighbors to search among their own people for any captured selkies so they, too, might be returned home. Far fewer were found in those places than had been in Atìrse, but every selkie saved was cause for rejoicing.

At last, the day of the wedding arrived. That afternoon, Ceana stood before the priest, hand in hand with Fionntan. One blessing of the delay had been that it gave her sisters time to travel, and so they, along with her cousins, stood behind her—all but Mirren, who had found married life more exciting than expected and couldn't leave Glassraghey.

Ceana wished her final sister could have been there. Yet even that was not enough to dampen her joy as the priest spoke of love and duty and the way in which the bonds of marriage, be they between human and human, selkie and selkie, or human and selkie, reflected Dèanadair's vows to His people.

Then came the part Ceana had been waiting for. The priest turned first to Fionntan, speaking the words that the selkies had taught to him, the words of the old ceremony that they had preserved. "King Fionntan of Emain Ablach, do you take this woman as your own, to love and cherish, as two souls sharing one body, one breath, and one blood?"

"By Dèanadair's grace and blessing, I do," Fionntan replied, not looking away from Ceana's face. He squeezed her hands as he went on, "I name her as my bride and queen, and all that is mine becomes hers. My soul shall cleave to hers 'til one or both shall take the Final Path, and by breath and bond I call her my own."

She would *not* cry. Ceana focused on that determination as the priest turned now to her. She would not cry, and she would speak her own vow without tripping over her tongue. Oh, but the waiting was so close to over!

The priest addressed her. "Princess Ceana, seventh daughter of Atìrse, do you take this man as your own, to love and cherish, as two souls sharing one body, one breath, and one blood?"

"By Dèanadair's grace and blessing, I do." So far, so good! Fionntan's hands were warm in hers. She could hear one of her sisters, or perhaps Uaine, quietly weeping behind her. "I name him as my husband and my king, and all that is mine I give to him. My soul will cleave to his until he or I shall take the Final Path, and by my breath and my bond I call him my own."

The priest looked around and raised his hands. "Do you assembled witness this union, the vows that these two have made to each other?"

A chorus of assent came from those gathered. The priest lowered his hands again. "Then in Dèanadair's name and by the authority He has granted me, may it be so. I declare these two man and wife, forever united in the sight of Dèanadair and equal in standing before him, so long as they both shall live. Let them now seal their union in the way they think best."

Fionntan didn't hesitate a moment before drawing Ceana close. Before she could even think to raise hand or veil to shield them from view, he bent and kissed her. All thoughts of the crowd vanished from Ceana's mind, and she wrapped her arms around his shoulders so she could better answer in kind. *Now* she felt dampness upon her cheeks, but the tears could flow all they liked. Fionntan was hers, and she was his, and nothing could change that anymore.

They broke apart at last and faced the crowd. All assembled let out a cheer. Then, Fionntan took Ceana's arm to escort her back to the castle, where the festivities would take place.

They only made it to the castle courtyard before they were mobbed with well-wishers. King Seòras and Queen Isla came first of all, embracing first Ceana and Fionntan. King Seòras, when he released Ceana, put his hands on her shoulders and nodded towards Fionntan. "You have chosen wisely, daughter of mine. I am happy for you."

Then he and Queen Isla moved off to the side to field their share of congratulations. Onora and Alasdair were just behind them, and now it was Onora's turn to pull Ceana into a hug. "'Tis hard to believe that you're married at last. I told you that having your choice wouldn't be so bad." Then, releasing Ceana, she faced Fionntan. "Take care of her, or I'll come get her from you. Remember, I know how to find your island."

Fionntan put an arm around Ceana's shoulders and pulled her into his side. "I'll guard her with all my life and heart, sister. Thou hast no need to fear."

Onora studied him a moment, then nodded. "I know." Then she moved on to make way for the next sister, and the next and the next.

Queen Moireach followed after all the sisters had their turns. She, too, embraced both Fionntan and Ceana. "I am happy for both of you. You two remind me of myself and my own love when we were both young. Watch for my letters, now, and keep a room in your keep ready for me. I still have friends among the faery folk, and I'm still not so old that I can't travel by a faery path."

The thought of seeing her grandmother again—of showing her Emain Ablach in person—made Ceana's heart soar even higher. "We'll be ready. In the meantime, I'll miss thee."

"And I thee." Queen Moireach gave Ceana a last kiss on the cheek, and then she, too, moved off.

After Queen Moireach came a succession of Atìrsen and selkie nobles, each bowing and offering their congratulations and well-wishes. In the midst of these were Mairearad with Sir Cianán, now her husband and the Lord of Northwaves, and Aíbinn and Uaine behind her. Ceana's cousins hugged first Fionntan, then her, while Cianán clasped hands with Fionntan and bowed to Ceana.

Mairearad smiled as she let go of Ceana, keeping a hand on her shoulder and placing the other on Fionntan's arm. "You two had best not abandon our dinners simply because you're married now."

"We'd not dream of it," Fionntan assured her. "After all, you're doubly family now."

"So we are!" Uaine laughed, and hugged Ceana a second time. "I'll visit thee every day, or however often thou shouldst like, once thou art home."

"I'll look forward to it. I've missed thy company." Ceana looked to Aíbinn. "And I'm sure I'll see plenty of thee—or not, now that thy time in the Guard is almost up?"

Aíbinn shrugged carelessly. "I may serve another term still. I'm in no rush to leave, not when everything is just becoming exciting. Anyway, thou wilt need traveling companions if thou plans to visit thine own sisters as often as thou claim, and 'tis more efficient if one of those companions is thy guard as well."

"I'll keep that in mind," Ceana laughed. "I'll see you all soon."

Then they, too, moved off, and a steady stream of others followed. At last, however, bells within the keep rang to signal that the banquet was ready, and she and Fionntan were able to escape.

Onora's cooks had outdone themselves with the food that night. All of Ceana's favorites were in evidence, and despite the significance of the occasion, there wasn't a peacock in sight. The fact that neither she nor Fionntan had any intention of letting go of each other's hands slowed her only a little. Even so, when the musicians stood up and the floor was cleared for the first dance, she had no trouble springing up or following Fionntan down to open the dancing. As he spun her round, he leaned in and kissed her again, brief and light. "The next night we dance, we shall be back in Emain Ablach, in our own Great Hall. What thinkst thou of that?"

"I think that to dance with thee is lovely wherever we are," Ceana laughed, following Fionntan's steps without even thinking about it. In the past year, she and Fionntan had danced together in nearly every coastal holding in Atìrse, for he visited as often as possible, both to attend to matters of the alliance and to see her. "And I look forward to being able to dance with thee there without having to keep silent."

"As do I—home will be all the sweeter for having your voice in it," Fionntan replied. "And perhaps someday soon, thou wilt be able to speak thy birth tongue freely as well—thou and all others on the island who were born in the human lands."

Ceana gazed hopefully into his face. "Thy vow still stands, though, does it not?"

"For now." Fionntan drew her closer, as close as the dance would allow. "Yet even the severest vow may be set aside when it ceases to be needful, and the cause for that one is quickly waning, for the human lands hold more friends than foes these days, and Emain Ablach's queen is also Atìrse's daughter."

"So I am, and so Dèanadair has worked the miracle thou hoped for." Ceana gave Fionntan a mischievous smile. "Yet even before then, we shall be able to speak all day long if we should choose. Art thou sure thou won't run out of things to say?"

"I doubt it." Fionntan's smile widened, just a little, as he brought her into a spin. "If all else fails, I can list all the ways I love thee, and thou canst do the same for me."

Ceana couldn't help laughing at that. "We would need a very long dance indeed to do that."

"Then I suppose we'll have to dance several songs together," he replied, and then he leaned down to kiss her again.

The dancing went on late into the night, but Ceana and Fionntan didn't linger to see the end of it. As the moon rose and the night drew on towards midnight, they said their last goodbyes, and Ceana embraced her parents and sisters one more time. Then they made their way down to the shore. Ceana looked out at the sea and huddled into Fionntan's side. "Art thou sure 'twill work?"

"This is an old, old magic, as old as our two peoples. It has never failed before, and tonight will not be the first." Fionntan wrapped his cloak around her, holding her tight to his side. "Come, 'tis time we were away."

He walked forward into the waves, and she walked with him, matching step to step, holding tight to his arm. As they reached the edge of the shallows, he bent and kissed her once more, long and slow. "Have no fears, my love."

They dove together. Ceana felt Fionntan's arm pull away from her, and for a moment she panicked. Then came the familiar sensation of a seal-shape wrapping around her, warm and safe. Fionntan's voice slipped into her thoughts as he came up beside her, nuzzling her. *"See, I told thee all would be well."*

"So thou didst," Ceana replied in the same fashion, and then almost laughed in delight as she realized what she'd done. She nuzzled Fionntan back, and together they swam further out into the waves, darting and diving and nudging into each other every so often.

Eventually, the lights of a ship came in sight, just as Onora had promised. She knew the ceremony required that they leave by midnight, but she'd insisted that Ceana not spend her wedding night traveling—something neither Ceana nor Fionntan had argued with. In the light of many lanterns, Ceana could see the symbols of the royal family and the crown princess painted on the stern and bow of the ship and flying from the masts in the form of pennants.

A wood-and-wicker platform hung from the side of the ship,

secured by thick ropes. Ceana and Fionntan hauled out onto this. Their seal-shapes fell away, and once more Ceana felt the weight of a seal-cloak around her shoulders, falling around her in silvery-grey folds that shone in the lantern glow. She pulled it close to herself, rubbing her cheek against its softness.

"I had nearly forgotten how fair thou look in a proper cloak," Fionntan said, his voice soft. It took Ceana a moment to realize he'd spoke in the selkie tongue. "And now thou hast one that will not fail thee, no more than my love for thee will fail."

Ceana started to reply, then paused, focusing until what she sought sprang to her lips. "Or mine for thee, so long as we both live."

Fionntan startled, looking down at her, and a smile curved across his face as he pulled her close to himself. "Long I have waited to hear thee speak my own tongue. Now I know 'twas worth the wait."

"And thou shalt hear it every day." Ceana nestled against his chest, watching the lights reflected in the rippling waves. Far in the distance, she could hear the selkies singing, their voices raised in a hymn of praise to the One who brought the lost home again. Aboard the ship would be refreshing drinks and a warm bed, but all of that could wait. For now, there was her and Fionntan and the ocean, and all the future ahead of them. And with the two of them together, what a future it would be!

ACKNOWLEDGEMENTS

Just as Ceana couldn't have completed (or even started) her adventure without help from friends and family, so *Song of the Selkies* wouldn't exist without the support I received from others. The full list of people who deserve thanks is too long to include here, but I want to express special gratitude to the following people:

Wyn Estelle Owens, who brainstormed everything from plot-hole solutions to potential sequels with me, who got excited over every snippet I sent her, and whose fangirling over Fionntan is a continual delight.

My beta readers, Rachel, Meghan, Emmarayn, Grace, Jenn, and Laura, who took on 140,000-odd words of rough draft and a short turnaround time without complaint. Their suggestions and critiques were essential to making *Song of the Selkies* what it is.

Kendra E. Ardnek, whose Arista Challenges inspire and motivate me year after year. It's hard to believe this is the second-to-last time I'll get to participate in one.

My parents, who never fail to encourage me in my writing and publishing and who are consistently patient with me when I have to run away and write for long hours or when my brain is full of nothing but selkies and stress.

And finally, my Great Author, who set my path before me and guides me every step of the way. May He use my words to draw others into His way.

About the Author

Sarah Pennington has been writing stories since before she actually knew how to write, and she has no intention of stopping anytime soon. She is perpetually in the middle of writing at least one or two novels, most of which are in the fantasy and fairy tale retelling genres. When she isn't writing, she enjoys knitting, photography, and trying to conquer her massive to-be-read list.

Sarah can be found online at sarahpenningtonauthor.com. She also maintains two blogs: Light and Shadows (tpssarahlightshadows.wordpress.com) and Dreams and Dragons (dreams-dragons.blogspot.com).

OTHER STOLEN SONGS STORIES

WHEN ON LAND
Kendra E. Ardnek

On their sixteenth year, every mermaid visits the Sea Witch to view the omen that will direct her steps in the years to come. But when Lona's shows her a castle on land, does she dare brave her father's wrath and follow it?

MY FAIR MERMAID
Sarah Beran

The Little Mermaid meets Pygmalion

LOCKS OF GOLD AND ETERNITY
Abigail Falanga

A flipped retelling of The Little Mermaid combined with an underwater reimagining of Rapunzel, set in an epic world of oceanic beauty and peril.

A LITTLE PERSUADED
Kendra E. Ardnek

Seven years ago, the mermaid Enna loved a human prince, but fate was against them. Now Kelantis is in danger and her journey to save it has brought the prince back into her life.

Made in United States
Cleveland, OH
22 May 2025